He who has an ear,
let him hear.

Overcomer

He who has an ear,
let him hear.

Overcomer

kristen wisen

credo
house publishers

Overcomer: He who has an ear, let him hear.

Copyright © 2009 by Kristen Wisen

Published in the United States by Credo House Publishers,
a division of Credo Communications, LLC, Grand Rapids, Michigan.
www.credocommunications.net

ISBN: 978-0-9787620-3-2

Scripture is taken from the NEW AMERICAN STANDARD BIBLE®.
Copyright © The Lockman Foundation 1960, 1962, 1963, 1968, 1971,
1972, 1973, 1975, 1977, 1995. Used by permission.

Lyrics for "Surrendered Hearts" on pages 360–361, copyright © 2007 by Steve Busch.
Used by permission of Burningbusch Productions.

Editor: Diane Noble
Assistant Editor: Shelly Beach
Proofreader: Elizabeth Banks
Cover Design: Grey Matter Group
Interior Design: Sharon VanLoozenoord

10 9 8 7 6 5 4 3 2 1

Printed in the United States of America

To David
and my precious children:
Calvin and Mary,
Katherine, Marinela, Alexandra,
Nicole and Christopher
Thank you for loving me
and providing me with countless
characters and storylines.
God has greatly blessed me
through each one of you
and to Him I give all the glory.

"So remember what you have received
and heard; and keep it, and repent.
Therefore if you do not wake up,
I will come like a thief,
and you will not know
at what hour I will come to you."

REVELATION 3:3

Part one

Present Day

"At that time many will fall away
and will betray one another
and hate one another. . . .
But the one who endures to the end,
he will be saved."

MATTHEW 24:10, 13

one

September

*S*teady now.

Calm down.

Slow your breathing.

You can do it.

It was taking every ounce of self-control, but Tara could feel her chest relaxing and her breath becoming steadier. Occasionally, she cringed with the volume of each inhale and exhale, but she kept reminding herself that everything sounded loud when surrounded with silence. She could even hear her heart pounding. A drop of sweat broke from her hairline and rolled down the side of her face, stopping near her ear. She lifted her shoulder to stop the droplet, and the salty sphere was quickly absorbed into her tee shirt.

The voices outside the barn moved closer, and she held her breath again. The sounds of footsteps seemed as loud as thunder in the silence of the night. A couple more moist drops rolled down her cheek, but this time they were from her eyes. At the thought of Noah, his dark, sober eyes and wavy hair, his half smile and suppressed chuckle, his selfless sacrifice, Tara's chest immediately began to ache. A lump swelled in her throat and she choked back a whimper.

How did I get here? Why am I still alive?

The voices outside began to fade. A car door clicked closed, followed by a second, then an engine started and the car shifted into gear. Slowly the wheels began to roll on the loose gravel.

Incredibly slowly.

Headlights flashed through the loose wooden slats of the barn, and Tara squinted against its glare. She breathed easier as the car headed down the dirt road back to the highway.

But she knew the car—and those that pursued her—could return at any time.

She peered through a knothole, watching as the glow of taillights disappeared. A low, flat layer of clouds blocked the moon's light and the darkness lay like a thick blanket across the countryside. She had followed Noah's directions to the barn, traveling only at night, running for hours at a time to cover as much distance as possible, and now all she could do was wait. Terror had seized her when the car pulled up just minutes earlier, and her heart still thumped hard against her ribs. If she had been spotted, she would have been shot. As the sound of the tires faded to silence, Tara shook her head in wonder. Once again, she was alone. And safe.

By now her eyes had adjusted to the dark, and she studied the tractor next to her. It was large, and felt rusted and old. Tara stood and stretched her legs. She wiped her arm across her forehead, trying to stay the flow of perspiration. She grasped a metal rod on the tractor for balance. She was tired and hadn't eaten all day. Through the barn she heard the crack of a branch and it made her jump. Tara thought they had left, but perhaps she had been fooled. She crouched again to look out the knothole, but saw nothing. She held her breath and waited but saw no movement. After a few minutes, she steadied herself, stood again, turned and leaned against the barn's wall. She looked across the space littered with farming equipment, then toward the door she had entered through. It was open. A man stood in the doorway, his arms outstretched, hands resting on either doorpost. Tara gasped, realizing he was looking at her. There was nowhere to run.

"Tara?"

Tara bit her lip. She put her hands over her mouth and chose not to answer. Her ears were playing tricks on her.

"Tara? That is you over there, isn't it?"

"Noah?"

"Yeah, it's me."

At the sound of his voice, relief flooded over Tara's whole body. She had not quite let herself accept that she would never see Noah again, but deep in her heart she had feared the worst. Now he stood in the door and without any thought, Tara began to run to him.

"I thought you would never make it!"

"It's me, Tara. You have nothing to be afraid of."

Tara suddenly stopped and forced herself to think. How could it be Noah? Then again, stranger things had happened in the last twenty-four hours alone. She studied his silhouette in the doorway and her fears dissipated. Yes, it was Noah! It had to be. She'd know him anywhere. She quickly moved again, cutting the distance between the two of them in no time. Without hesitation, she flung her arms around his neck and squeezed him hard as she began to weep.

"Don't cry," he whispered. She felt him wrap his arms around her and for a brief moment all was right with the world. She struggled to speak, but after a few seconds she broke the silence.

"I thought you were . . ."

"Oh, come on. You should know by now it's going to take more than a couple of policemen to do me in."

Tara pulled away, squinting as she tried to make out his face. Oh, how she loved his voice! And his ability to downplay a crisis . . .

"A couple? It was more like an army, if I remember correctly!"

"Whatever. I've got more lives than a cat, but I'm starting to get low on my count, thanks to you!"

Tara squeezed him again and smiled.

"Stop joking! Did you just get here?"

"Yeah. We can talk later, but for now we need to keep moving."

"This isn't the meeting place?"

Noah took Tara's hand and led her further into the barn.

"Be careful—there's a lot of equipment in here. Don't cut yourself."

He pointed to something with his left hand, his right firmly grasping her own. There was so much she wanted to say, so much she needed to know. She decided to just follow directions and keep her questions to herself, though they were adding up quickly in her mind. Noah led her back to the corner where she had originally been hiding. He bent down and started to gently run his hands across the floor. She heard him wince, and she bit her lip, assuming a splinter had found its way into his finger. The sound of his hand sweeping back and forth across the floor continued a few more times until the creak of a rusted hinge broke the silence.

"Here it is. I knew there was a ring to pull here somewhere."

Noah grunted a few times until Tara realized she was standing on the trap door, and quickly apologizing, moved to the side. He lifted the door and carefully laid it on the floor, revealing a black hole.

"You go in first. I'll lift the door back into place once I'm in."

Tara tried to take a deep breath and move toward the opening, but all she could muster was a whimper. She put her hands to her face and began to sob. It wasn't like her to struggle with emotion, but she found she'd reached her breaking point. She heard Noah take a step toward her and felt his warm arms wrap around her again.

"I know this is a lot to take in," he whispered gently in her ear. "I'm not going to leave you, and the hard part is over. Getting here was a big deal, and I am so proud of you. This tunnel leads to safety. Soon you'll feel much better."

Tara stood in his embrace and let his words soak in. He had never lied to her before. In fact he was the most honest man she knew. And what was the big deal about a black hole? Hadn't she gone through worse to get here? After a moment, Tara decided she could do this, and she pulled away from Noah and looked down at the dark opening in the floor. Before she even asked, he answered her question.

"Charlie left us a flashlight. It should be on the floor by the bottom of the ladder."

Tara felt around the circumference of the opening. Eventually her fingers rested on the rounded wooden end of a ladder. She sat and put her feet into the hole, reaching with her toes until she felt a rung on the ladder. Noah put his hand on her back to steady her as she carefully lowered herself into the tunnel. Climbing down, an even greater darkness enveloped her.

And I thought the barn was dark. I'm not sure I can do this.

In a few moments her feet touched solid ground, and she let out a sigh of relief. She could hear Noah replace the door and then start down the steps. She quickly bent down and felt around for a flashlight. Just as Charlie had promised, the flashlight was at the base of the ladder. Tara decided that no matter who he was, this Charlie guy was getting a big hug when she met him.

Noah was nearing the ground when Tara clicked on the flashlight. The light was a welcome sight for seriously sore eyes. Tara turned the beam toward the ladder so Noah could see what he was doing as he took the final three rungs with ease. She felt a tickle on her neck and without thinking swatted at something that was working its way toward her shoulder. She shivered and mussed her hair with her free hand, hoping any other unwelcome pests would fall away. Her hair felt damp, either from perspiration or even worse, lack of shampoo and water. This was no time to worry about cleanliness, she told herself as she glanced down at her filthy tee shirt. She lifted her head and watched as Noah turned around and flashed that familiar crooked grin at her.

"Nice to see you again." He reached for the flashlight. "Do you want to lead?"

"Uh, no, thanks," Tara stammered, as she handed the flashlight to Noah, hoping he wouldn't notice her hair.

Noah touched her shoulder. "Are you feeling any better?"

"Yeah, thanks," she replied. *Now that I'm with you.*

Noah pointed the flashlight up the hole they had just descended. It was about twenty feet to the top and Tara could see the wooden trap door back in place. Noah turned and scanned the tunnel with the light. There was only one direction to walk, and the ceiling was low, forcing Noah to duck as he walked. Though she was considerably shorter, Tara still felt cramped.

As she followed Noah closely, Tara's thoughts continued to reel with the details of the past few weeks. Colors flashed before her mind's eye—the yellow police tape across her front door, the gray sky hanging over the fields of dying brown corn stalks, the orange glow from the bonfire on the street, the body of little Isaiah covered with a crisp white sheet. She shivered in the dampness of the tunnel and reached for the hem of Noah's shirt. Holding it made her feel connected, safe.

Occasionally they would pass a familiar strong odor in the tunnel, but Tara couldn't place the smell. Tree roots? Sewage? Then she remembered where the memory came from. As a child she would go camping with her parents. Fresh pinewood had a distinct smell, strangely like vomit more than anything else. She twisted the end of Noah's shirt tighter around her finger and covered her mouth and nose with her free hand.

Oh, dear God, how did it come to this? Did You really try to warn me? How could I have been so blind?

A thought came to Tara, and she suddenly glanced behind her into the darkness. Her heart was pounding again, and the sweat was starting to return. What if they were being followed? Was that a light she saw or . . . no, it was nothing. She looked back at Noah and decided it was too frightening to look behind her again. What could she do if she saw a light? She was already moving as fast as she could, and there was only one way to go. Trust was a new concept for her, but for now she would have to trust Noah. And God. Especially God.

The tunnel had been dug through layers of soil, rock, and large tree roots that protruded into the tunneled-out area, tearing at Tara's arms. The beam from Noah's flashlight was pointed ahead of them, so she didn't always see the dangerous limbs. Twice she tripped on roots and loose stones, stumbling into Noah's back. The first time he stopped and asked if she was all right, then he kept on moving and she did her best to keep pace.

The only sounds Tara could hear was the heavy breathing coming from her guide as well as from her own mouth. She was amazed at the work that had gone into digging the tunnel and wondered if anyone else had used it out of desperation or if she was the only one so completely unprepared for this crisis. As her mind wandered in multiple directions, she finally told her thoughts to shut up and started to pray. This wasn't about her anyways—it was about Him.

About an hour into the tunnel, Noah stopped, sat down, and leaned against the wall. Normally a dirty rest stop would not have been appealing, but considering her current state, Tara didn't think twice and sat next to him. She needed the break. Noah turned off the flashlight.

"I don't know how much battery time we've got, so if you don't mind . . . we need to conserve."

"Sure, just don't leave without me."

"I'm not going anywhere." She felt him reach and find her hand. She choked back a tear, not from fear but out of the sheer relief of the touch of his hand.

After a moment of silence, as the two caught their breath, Tara spoke.

"So who is Charlie exactly? I know his name but not many details."

Tara could hear a soft chuckle and imagined a grin on his face.

"Where do I begin?" Noah started. "I've known Charlie for about five years now. He's the one who brought me to the fellowship. I met him at a picnic—he was working for a caterer at that time, and we struck up a conversation while folding up tables and chairs. He's an amazing follower—one of those fearless, "I'm-going-to-die-when-God-is-good-and-ready-for-me-to-die" kind of guys."

"What do you mean?"

"It took him about five minutes to ask me if I knew Jesus at that picnic. Here we are, in broad daylight, people everywhere, and in full voice he was like, 'Hey, do you know Jesus?'"

"What did you do?"

"Well, back then, I looked around, lowered my voice and asked him if he was crazy! He looked back at me and laughed. He said, 'You've got to be kidding me! Do you really think anyone around here cares what I say? They've all heard it from me before and will most likely hear it again!' And you know what? I'm pretty sure he witnessed to them until he became a runner."

Tara swatted at another tickle on her ear. "A runner? What's that?"

"Oh, sorry. That's someone who runs the tunnels from the compound to the real world. There are about ten of them all together. They can get news or supplies, but mostly just help newbies arrive."

"I must be a newbie."

"Sorry again. We have developed our own vocabulary and, yeah, you are a newbie."

"So, you're a runner."

"Everything is changing so quickly, I don't know how much longer we'll need runners."

"But after you get me to the compound, will you have to go back out?"

Noah sat quiet for a moment and Tara waited for his answer. She felt him fumble with the flashlight and then it turned on. She looked at his tired face.

"Do you trust me?"

"Of course I do."

"Then stand up and look at me."

Tara stood and faced Noah. The flashlight was pointing down, but in the glow of the light she could still see his face. It was smudged with dirt, and she couldn't help but smile at him.

"Close your eyes."

"Come on, Noah," she protested. Why was he stalling?

"Just close them."

She closed her eyes. Her heart skipped a beat as she felt his hand brush her shoulder. Confused, she opened them again, and dangling from his fingers was one of the biggest spiders she had ever seen, the kind with the fuzzy legs. She stifled a shriek as Noah smiled at her.

"I was hoping to step on this before you saw it."

"There're more of those, aren't there?"

"Probably, but if we keep moving we should be fine."

After doing a spin so that Noah could see if there were anymore, Tara checked him, not sure she could actually pull one off him if there was one. Thankfully, there were none. She shivered at the thought that it was one of those hairy monsters she had swatted away twice before without knowing.

"You never answered my question," Tara said, as they started walking again.

"Which one?"

"Are you going back after you get me to the compound?"

"Since I haven't recovered the supplies stored at my house, I have at least one more trip."

"But the Day of Destruction has changed everything, Noah."

He said nothing but continued through the tunnel. Tara knew what this meant. A few days earlier he had attempted to retrieve those supplies, and she thought he had been captured. They knew where he lived and no doubt, they knew what he wanted from there. But Tara knew him well enough. When Noah had his mind set on something, it was nearly impossible to change it.

Tara mustered all the courage she could find and looked behind her once more. Still darkness.

Were they truly going to be safe? Was there anywhere that was safe anymore?

And did safety matter if the man she loved chose not to stay with her?

Tara made up her mind. She had proven she was as stubborn as Noah. She had to convince him to stay. It was their only chance to be together.

two

September

Mayor Wayne Durbin sat at his desk, deep in thought. He glanced down at his watch and then gazed out his window. 2:27 p.m. The bus would be leaving in half an hour. He turned from the window and looked at the framed picture of his dog sitting on his desk. He picked it up, his reflection in the glass catching his eye. He reached up and ran his finger over the black numbers on his forehead. He hardly even noticed them anymore when he looked in the mirror. It made no sense to him why some people were such fanatics that they couldn't take the mark.

There was a quick tap on his half-open door, and his secretary entered with a rolled up newspaper under her arm and a hot cup of coffee in her hand. Wayne put the picture back on his desk and reached for the coffee.

"Good morning, sir," Linda said, dropping the paper on his desk.

"What's so good about it?" Wayne grumbled as he sipped his coffee.

"Now, come on, Wayne. Are you going to have another one of those days?" She dropped her chin and peered at him above her glasses.

"I guess I'm just worn out," he said, looking out his office window.

Linda made a quick tour of the room, straightening the pillows on his couch, throwing scraps of paper in the garbage, preparing his office for another day. It was her usual routine, but instead of exiting as quickly as she'd entered, Durbin heard her sit down in the chair opposite his desk. She cleared her throat and spoke.

"Wayne, I know this is taking a toll on you, but you have no choice. Everything you have done is for the good of Creston. You know that when this is over, all the promises that were made to you will be acted on. In no time our farms will have their research funding." She paused. "Do you remember how easily the businesses switched over to the One World Denomination system?"

Durbin took a deep breath and sighed. He knew she was right. "It was amazingly flawless. The systems arrived one day and were up and running the next. I never heard one complaint from any owner."

"It's technology. People are drawn to anything that makes their lives easier."

"Well, it's a great system. I don't even carry magogs anymore. The chip in my hand is all I need. Speaking of that, have you finished my travel arrangements for the end of the month?"

"Yes. It's still hard to believe you can travel to Europe without a passport."

Durbin took another sip of coffee. "I will never understand why some still won't accept change when it's truly for their personal benefit. A chip in your hand and a mark on your head are all you need for complete access to a whole new world. And while they refuse to get with the program, the rest of us sit and suffer." Wayne pushed away from his desk and stood. He walked over to the window and looked out at the bus parked in front of city hall.

"Wayne, don't get worked up again. Religious fanatics have always slowed the process of progress. But soon they'll be gone and you'll get the funding the FWP has promised you. I heard they might accept ninety percent participation."

"Never. It's all or nothing and I think the Federation of World Powers is tired of waiting on towns like mine. It doesn't matter how many meetings I've held, some just can't get past taking the mark." He turned and looked at Linda, who was now standing with his empty coffee cup in her hand. "Why he had to choose that number, I'll never understand, but we're living in strange times."

"Well, this was quite an undertaking, wouldn't you say?" Linda started toward the door. "And we're only a town of thirty thousand. Imagine Chicago or New York City. There's no way they are all marked yet."

"Money is already flowing into Chicago. I heard that two weeks ago. If they can get it done faster than us, there must be something wrong with the way we're going about this."

"Wayne," Linda spoke with a sternness that Durbin wasn't used to hearing from his fifty-something-year-old secretary. "You chose a far more humane way to handle this. Don't ever second-guess yourself. You know what they did in Chicago."

He turned back to the window, back to the empty bus. There were still a few things that bothered him, but leadership never came without its costs.

"Roger will be here in a moment for you to sign the transfer papers." Durbin heard the door close and was glad to be alone again.

He looked at his watch again. 2:41.

Why does this still bother me?

But he knew the answer. Today was harder than usual, and there was a reason for that.

Another knock on the door, and Roger came in with a clipboard and a pen. Durbin knew all he needed was a signature, but this one was killing him. He took the board and sat at his desk. He scanned down the short list. Thomas was number three out of nine names.

"So, Roger, let me ask you a question." Durbin put down the pen, prolonging the agony of the moment. Roger looked confused, since Wayne had never been overly friendly with the transport driver from the training facility. "You've been at the facility from day one. Do you think Governor Slate made a good choice with our system?"

"Um, what do you mean?" Roger shuffled back and forth, shifting the weight of his enormous body from side to side. Durbin wondered where Slate found the monsters he called guards.

"The training program. How long is the average stay down there?"

Roger stopped moving and his eyes narrowed. "Most people never left, sir, but you know that. What's your point?"

"But some took the mark after attending classes, didn't they?"

"A small percentage. I wouldn't say the program was overly successful in convincing people to change their minds about him."

"You mean about . . . ?"

"Yeah. Most just couldn't get past who it is requiring them to wear a mark." Roger leaned over and looked at the clipboard.

Wayne Durbin picked up the pen and signed at the bottom of the cover page. "Here you go."

Roger took the clipboard and left without another word. Durbin swiveled in his chair back to the window. He knew the leader of the Federation of World Powers was shocking at first, and in his first life he was an unbalanced tyrant. But he had changed. He was stable now. And powerful. And generous . . . though not overly patient.

Look at how he has brought peace to the world, Durbin reminded himself. He controlled the Arab nations, brought Israel into submission (not an easy task by any means), and ensured oil trade for the world. Language was no longer a barrier because supernaturally he had unified speech.

Supernatural.

That was the best word to describe him. After all, what other word could one use to describe a man who was raised from the dead?

Durbin watched as the police ushered the nonmarkers into the bus. A small group of people gathered on the sidewalk opposite where the bus was parked. Durbin remembered when people used to plead with the prisoners to mark up. Now they came to mock. These people had plenty of time to comply. He had no choice but to ship them off.

It was for the good of his community. The quicker he cleaned house, the quicker aid would arrive. His eyes rested on the last man to climb on the bus. He touched his hand to his chest. He felt a dull pain, but Durbin suppressed the emotion of the moment. He had a job to do for the good of his town, and he was going to do it. They'd elected him to do it. What choice did he have?

Three o'clock on the dot. The bus pulled out of Creston with perhaps the final prisoners headed to training camp. Durbin returned to his desk and dropped his head in his hands. He knew he just about had them all. He would go to Memorial Park later and check his counts. The thought of hearing the phrase, "You've got them all!" put a smile on his face. Maybe today would be the day, and then the floodgates would open and Creston could finally start to make a name for itself. Research money, new wells, high-tech milking stations—the sky truly was the limit.

And they would have one visionary to thank. The man the world once knew as Alexander Magorum. The leader the world now recognized as Adolph Hitler.

Thomas Larson sat alone in his seat on the bus. There were only four guards plus a driver, but considering the guards were the ones with the guns and the passengers' hands were handcuffed, Thomas was pretty sure the guards weren't worried about the ride. Sitting across the aisle from him was a man he had recognized from church. He had seen him in the cafeteria at the jail, but the prisoners had no contact with each other until now. Thomas suspected this man was in the same predicament as himself, and when he was brought to the holding room to wait for the bus to arrive, he spotted him again and his suspicions were confirmed.

"I recognize you from church." Thomas waited for a response.

The man turned from the window. His face was worn and tired. His eyes were dry but heavy.

"Yeah, I saw you there, too. You have a family, right?"

"My name is Thomas, and my wife is Robin. I have two daughters, too."

"Were they caught?"

Thomas looked into the man's eyes and saw true concern. "Yeah. I think the three of them are still together, but who knows? There's a part of me that hopes to see them at the facility and another part that can't bear the thought of seeing them at all. The hardest part is not knowing where they are or what is happening to them."

The man nodded, and then he leaned a bit toward Thomas and lowered his voice. "They haven't found my family."

Thomas looked ahead at the two guards who were sitting in the front seats. They were deep in a conversation with the driver, so Thomas looked behind him. One guard in the back was looking out the window and the other was engaging a prisoner in conversation.

"How did they catch you?" Thomas asked under his breath.

"We'd been hiding in an abandoned shack up on Cranyers Lake. We were running out of food, so I headed back to town to try to see what I could find. I was caught by the statue in Memorial Park."

Thomas shook his head. "How many in your family?"

"My wife, her parents, and three kids. I'm just praying that the Lord provides for them. They have no idea what has happened to me, but I told them if I wasn't back in two days that I'd see them in heaven."

Thomas watched as the all too familiar tears welled up in his new friend's eyes, and he nodded in agreement. "I never imagined this would happen. Not here, not in America. Then again, it's not like I wasn't warned."

Thomas heard movement from behind him, and he turned his head away and looked back out the window. Footsteps stopped in the aisle beside him.

"Found a new friend, Larson? I'll bet the two of you have a lot in common."

The guards were antagonistic to the nonmarked prisoners, and Thomas knew better than to engage this man, so he dropped his eyes to the floor.

"Look at me when I talk to you!"

Thomas turned but not before the butt of the guard's shotgun hit him on his shoulder, knocking him against the window. The sound of his head hitting the glass silenced the passengers. The two guards up front stopped talking and stood to see what was going on.

"No more talking. Got it?"

Thomas nodded and put his hand to his head. An egg was already forming and his temples were pounding. How in the world would this nightmare end? Thomas heard the guard walk toward the front of the bus. He glanced up and saw the guard join the two in the front, and he breathed a sigh of relief.

It wouldn't be long before the bus arrived at the training facility. Thomas closed his eyes and opened his heart before his Creator.

Father, this is so unbelievable, I really can't put my arms around it. Where are my girls? Will I ever hear their little voices again? Is Robin with them? Lord, I can't bear this alone. I have to give this to You. There is nothing I can do. My life is over, but I am here because of You. I willingly lay down my life, but I need to know that You've got my family in the palm of Your hand.

As he opened his eyes, the ache in his heart matched the one in his head and he returned his gaze out the window. The Indiana countryside passed quickly, and the speed only made his head pound more. He closed his eyes again.

I'm sorry for my fear. I know You love them, Lord, I just can't believe how hard this is. I am so broken and so worried. Take my fear, Lord. Let me be a light, even in these last days of my life. I love You, Lord.

When he stopped praying, Thomas looked back over to his new friend. His head was bowed toward the floor and Thomas couldn't tell if he was praying or sleeping. A large teardrop fell from his chin and Thomas followed the path to a puddle on the floor. He knew exactly what his friend was going through. He felt his own heart heave and a tear escaped his eye, rolling down his cheek. He didn't swipe at it for fear that movement would draw attention and ridicule. It fell onto his shoulder and created a path for others to follow.

Thomas knew deep down in his heart he would never see Robin or his daughters again.

At least not here on earth.

Part two

Seventeen Months Earlier

"Therefore when you see the
abomination of desolation which was spoken
of through Daniel the prophet,
standing in the holy place,
then those who are in Judea
must flee."

MATTHEW 24:15, 16

three

April

Thomas leaned back and put his arm around his wife. A little movement was all he needed to return his focus to the preacher. He'd have to remember to get more sleep next week because it can be embarrassing to doze off in church.

"I liken religion to a village full of blind people," Reverend Dale Blackmore continued, standing behind his large, wooden pulpit. "One day a man leading an elephant came to their village. As they heard the elephant coming, one villager said, 'There must be a storm on the way—I hear thunder.' Another villager said, 'No, there is an earthquake—can you feel the ground shake?' When the elephant arrived in the village, the man leading it gathered the people around it and told them it was an elephant and to touch it. Some touched its ear and decided an elephant is like a rough, hairy curtain. Others touched its large trunk and concluded that an elephant is made up of long, snakelike appendages. Still others touched the large, hard toenails of the elephant and decided elephants are hard like rocks."

The reverend paused and stepped from behind his pulpit, leaving his left hand still resting on the side trim.

"Why do I share this story with you? Because it is a beautiful illustration of what religion is. God has revealed Himself to all peoples and cultures in many ways but we are like the blind villagers. We can only know God in the small context of our own experience. An elephant is much bigger than a toenail or an ear. So, too, God is much bigger than just Muhammad, Buddha, or Jesus. Just as an ear, a toenail, and a trunk are all aspects of an elephant, so are the various religions of the world."

He returned to his pulpit. "One day we will see the big picture, but for now we are limited. Therefore, we will join with believers all over the world, celebrating what God has revealed specifically to us, knowing He has chosen many different ways for many different peoples. Isn't our God something else?" He raised his open arms, directing a response from his congregation.

"Amens" and a generous applause spread throughout the sanctuary that morning at Creston Bible Church. As the congregation stood to leave, Thomas leaned over to his wife and asked what was for lunch.

"After a message like that, all you can think of is food? Perhaps you might want to nap first." Robin gave him that look that let him know he hadn't fooled anyone.

"You should know me by now," he said with a smile. "But for lunch—I was thinking about all those Hindus in India, which made me hungry for your curried chicken."

She gave him a smirk and bent over to retrieve her purse from the floor. She stood as Thomas waited for a response.

"I'll go get Christie and Sarah, if you pull up the car. And sorry, there's no curried chicken today."

Thomas frowned. "So what should I look forward to?"

"Tacos, burgers, or pizza—it just depends which one you want to pick up for lunch."

Robin flashed the same smile that made Thomas fall in love with her eleven years earlier. As he walked to the parking lot, he thought how her green eyes tend to sparkle when she is truly happy. He was glad the girls had her eyes. Thomas pulled the car around and stopped where his family was standing on the sidewalk just outside the church. When they got in the car, the girls, eight and six, started chattering about their classes at the same time.

"Whoa! Slow down . . . one at a time."

His heart warmed to the sound of his daughters retelling Bible stories with excitement and wonder. It was so freeing to be able to come to church and know that his children were learning from the Scriptures in the light of tolerance. Christie's teacher was actually a Muslim on loan from the mosque on State Street. She came every year to talk to the third graders about Islam. It was part of the multi-religion training third graders went through before their confession of understanding.

"Daddy? Today in class the teacher said that Jesus was a prophet like Muhammad. Is that true, because I thought Jesus was God?"

"Well, of course He was God, honey," Thomas answered. "I think the Muslims believe He was just a good teacher, but we know He was God . . . I mean, *is* God. But that's fine if they think He was a good teacher because they can learn a lot from His teaching."

"Do they need to trust that Jesus died for their sins to go to heaven?"

"We've talked about this before, Christie. We believe in Jesus because we believe the Bible is a letter from God to us. But God has written other letters instructing other things to other people. We don't need to worry about them, we just need to be sure we believe in Jesus."

Thomas glanced over at Robin, feeling a bit guilty at his answer. This was not exactly how either of them was raised, but it was the easiest way to teach tolerance to their children.

And the safest.

Robin smiled at Thomas and raised her eyebrows as if to say he had done a good job. Thomas pulled into the local taco stand and parked. Robin went inside to order, while he stayed with the girls. As they sang their Sunday school songs in the backseat, Thomas reasoned through his guilt. Life had changed since he was a child. Intolerance, even toward another religion, was punishable by fines and even jail time, so in the interest of his children's safety, he had no choice but to sugarcoat all religion. As long as his children knew Jesus, he knew their eternity was secure. He was not so sure about the others, but then again, who was he to claim to have a corner on truth?

Tara Warners sat across from Noah Greer at the café around the corner from their place of employment, Smith and Brumsby. She noticed his hand casually grasped his soft drink, but his eyes were fixed on hers as she told him about the elephant analogy she had heard at church.

"I really thought it was ingenious! It gives such a practical illustration of how little we know about God!"

Now that Tara was again attending church, she chose to share things with Noah, as if she had been there her whole life. She was amazed that in the two weeks since they met, they already knew that the other was a believer. Most conversations didn't get around to religion that quickly. She hadn't told him, however, that since she graduated high school she had avoided church like the plague. She didn't think that would impress him. She was back in church now, and that was all that mattered.

"Well, I have to admit, that's an interesting take on religion." Noah didn't seem overly enthusiastic, as he lifted the straw of his soda to his lips.

"Don't you agree with it?" She wondered what she had said wrong.

"Well, that illustration would work if Jesus hadn't claimed to be God. If He had just been a good teacher or a prophet, then other religions could possibly fit together with Christianity. The problem is,

Jesus wasn't just a great teacher. He is God. So what He says bears more weight than other so-called prophets and teachers."

Noah picked up his burger and took another bite.

"But morality is really just morality," Tara continued. "And religion in general promotes good living and strong morals. That sounds like a god-thing to me."

"But Tara, Jesus made claims that you have to deal with. He said nobody comes to God the Father, except through Him. That means, unless you go through Jesus, there is no access to God."

Tara glanced around the café, concerned their conversation would be offensive to other patrons.

"But don't you think God could reveal Himself to different cultures in different ways?"

"Then Jesus was a liar. He said He is the only way."

Tara didn't like the tone of his response. She put her fork down beside her salad and shifted in her seat. She leaned over her plate and purposely lowered her voice.

"So, as my pastor says, you believe you have a corner on the truth."

Noah lowered his voice, too. "Jesus said 'I am the Way, the Truth, and the Life.' You've either got to take Him at His Word or walk away, Tara. As a matter of fact, before Pilate, He said He came to testify to the Truth." He picked up a fry and dipped it in ketchup. "Truth has always been up for grabs and today, when life has become so man centered and subjective, truth is hard to find." He popped the fry in his mouth.

Tara was starting to get annoyed at his judgmental attitude.

"I won't go so far as to say that truth is relative. I believe the Bible is truth."

"Then how can you sit there and tell me there are other ways to God and that He is too big for us to really know or understand?"

"But the law clearly states . . ." Tara began.

Noah quickly interrupted. "Which law?"

"Our law."

"As in American law?"

Tara had just about had enough. What began as a nice lunch with a friend was now somewhat adversarial.

"It is illegal to be intolerant of other religions, and if God has set this government over us we should comply. And furthermore, if God is love, shouldn't we . . ."

Noah interrupted again, his voice returning to its original volume. "I don't know what church you've been going to, but if they do not stand solely on the Word, you've got real problems." His dark eyes bored into hers, but Tara refused to break the stare. "Yes, we should submit to our government, but there is a higher authority, and that's God. We know God through His Word and we have an obligation as believers to preach the gospel—it's called . . . the Great . . . Commission."

Noah pulled back as if he knew he had gone too far, but it was too late as far as Tara was concerned. This guy was way too opinionated for her.

"I'm sorry, Tara. I shouldn't have attacked your church. It's just that we are living in such a volatile time. Who would have thought that our freedom of speech would be so easily taken away? The temperament in America, the freakish weather patterns and all the changing alliances overseas—it's like we're seeing prophecy come true right before our eyes."

She was tired of arguing and didn't want any more of her salad. She pushed the plate away from her and wiped her mouth with her napkin.

"Well, considering we could be raptured at any moment, I'll accept your apology now, since by the time I get to heaven I'll probably forget all about this conversation."

She didn't really mean it as a joke. Tara dropped the napkin on her half-eaten salad and stood to leave.

"Does your church teach you to look for the signs for Christ's return?" Noah asked as Tara reached for her purse on the floor. She stood and put a hand on her hip.

"What signs? When He can come back at any time, what do you think you should look for?"

Doesn't his church teach him anything?

"Well, there're several things, actually . . ."

It was Tara's turn to interrupt. She shook her head and put her hand up to stop him. "I really don't have time for this. I've got to get back to work."

Tara had pulled a ten-dollar bill from her wallet and dropped it on the table. "I'll see you around."

Noah picked up the ten and started to hand it back, but she flashed a warning to him with her deep blue eyes that ended the debate.

Tara fumed all the way back to Smith and Brumsby. Two weeks into her friendship with Noah and this is the kind of conversation she gets! She was just trying to encourage a fellow Christian, which, in fact, was rather bold of her considering the restraints on evangelism these days. Tara had made the decision to look for Christian companionship but it just might not work out with Noah. He was nice and all—she didn't mind the dark, wavy hair and his crooked, half smile. Those things were kind of endearing. But his know-it-all accusations about her church's beliefs? His kind of Christianity was one of the reasons she quit attending church ten years ago. No, she didn't need that kind of religion. She would look inside her own church for a more tolerant man. One who was more accepting and less narrow-minded. With a man like Noah, someone could get herself arrested. And who wanted to be fined for being a Jesus freak?

The following day Tara received an inner-office mail envelope from Noah Greer. She held it, turned it over in her hand, and considered throwing it away. After about thirty seconds of consideration, she lifted the self-adhesive flap and looked inside. A ten-dollar bill with a Post-it attached lay at the bottom of the envelope. She reached inside and pulled it out.

The Post-it read:

"EVEN AN IDIOT CAN AFFORD
TO PAY FOR LUNCH
AND SHOULD BE EXPECTED TO.
I WOULD LOVE A SECOND TRY
TO SHED MY IDIOT STATUS.
WHAT DO YOU THINK?
CELL—649-1137"

"I think not," Tara said aloud and threw the Post-it in the garbage.

Charlie West picked up the phone. He had told Noah he would call if he could pick him up for the fellowship meeting. He dialed Noah's cell number and waited for the voice mail to click in. Noah never answered his own phone. Half a ring later Noah was on the other end.

"Hello?"

Charlie was surprised to hear a real voice.

"Hello to you. What's up? You expecting a call from the president?"

"Oh, Charlie. I just . . . well . . . my caller ID isn't working and well . . ."

"Okay, buddy, calm down! You can tell me all about it on the way to the meeting. Do you still want to go together?"

"Yeah, come get me at seven."

Charlie flipped his phone closed and squinted his eyes in thought. He knew Noah pretty well and a distracted Noah meant one thing—a woman. Later, as he pulled into the driveway, Charlie began to chuckle at all the one-liners he had prepared for Noah, but he changed his mind when he looked at Noah's face.

"Thanks for the ride," started Noah when he got in the car.

"You're welcome—it's on my way," answered Charlie. "So what's going on? You look down."

"Reality is sinking in, I guess."

"What do you mean?"

Charlie pulled out of Noah's driveway and headed toward town.

"I had lunch with a Christian girl today—I think I've mentioned her . . . Tara?"

"Really, a Christian? Are you sure?" Charlie tried to lighten the atmosphere.

"I don't know if I am more mad at myself for confronting her or just discouraged that Christianity is so watered down that faith really means nothing anymore."

"What happened?"

"We got into a discussion on tolerance and other religions today at lunch, and I basically went off that Jesus claimed exclusivity."

"So, what's wrong with that?"

"I was just harsh. I pushed too hard, and when I lost my cool, I questioned what kind of church she attended. It's just that it's so hard to find anyone who really values the Word anymore. What are they teaching out there anyway?"

"Figurative speech and symbolism—you know that."

Charlie smiled, thinking he'd get one back from Noah, but no such luck.

"Seriously, by the end of the conversation she made a flippant remark about being raptured soon, so she might as well be forgiving. I tried to recoup and talk prophecy with her, but it was too late. She basically walked out on me. I sent her a note with my cell number. That's why I was so weird on the phone."

"You mean that's why you answered."

"Yeah."

"Well, put a smile on, little buckaroo—you're not alone in this world!"

It always made Noah smile when Charlie did his John Wayne impersonation, and this was no exception.

"What do you mean?"

"Maybe you were too harsh. Flowers and an apology go a long way. As for being discouraged about the state of the church, join the club. The decline in America is way past the title of apostate or backslidden. We are just out-and-out heretical. Once a church strays from the authority and sufficiency of the Word, they can symbolize their way into believing anything, everything, and nothing at all." Charlie hit his turn signal and began to slow into the left turn lane. "The rare believer holds to the Word at face value. I remember a pastor of a huge, growing church telling his congregation that the church has surpassed God's standards set in the Scriptures in many places, therefore it was no longer authoritative. As if we were better or more evolved than those the Scriptures were written for. He also said it made him want to vomit when people referred to the Bible as a handbook for life. I was shocked back then when people fell for that. Today, that's commonplace." He completed his turn and continued down the road.

"What can we do about it? I get so overwhelmed."

"I don't think we can stop it, Noah. Matthew 24 tells us as lawlessness increases, most people's love will grow cold. It literally uses the word "most." I don't think Jesus was exaggerating."

"I thank God every day for the fellowship."

"Yeah, me too. I think this group is going to play an important role in the near future. I just sense the Spirit preparing our hearts for a very difficult time. You asked what we can do? We can continue to prepare for the time of great tribulation. The compound is almost ready, and I don't think it's happening one moment too soon. So many will be confused, and we have to provide them a way out."

Noah sighed and looked out the window as Charlie pulled up to the home of the fellowship leader, Dave Conover. Charlie always looked forward to his time with Dave, a godly man who loved the Word and held to its truth. Charlie heard that his wife died unexpectedly, and a few years after that he started the fellowship, using his own money to purchase a large farm in the middle of almost nowhere in Indiana. After the purchase he had found a large cavernous space under the farmhouse that allegedly was carved out during the mid-1800s to house runaway slaves on the Underground Railroad on their way to Jeffersonville. He, with the help of the fellowship, had expanded that space into a multiroomed compound, running water and all, able to house about two hundred people for an extended period of time.

"Dave said an inspector was nosing around the farm last week, checking around the barns and the garage."

"Really? Did he find anything?"

"Nope. Every time he thought the inspector might find the stairs to the compound or some of the storage areas in the barns, he would get a call on his cell or ask a question, and move away from where he was looking. He said that only God could have interceded, because half of the doors that were supposed to stay locked were open and completely accessible."

Noah and Charlie got out of the car and walked toward the house.

"I could hardly believe it when Dave told us last week that it's done," said Noah. "How long have we been building out the space?"

"It's been five years now—we started a couple of years before I met you. The space is finished, and most of the access tunnels are done. The one that surfaces down south near Spencer is giving us some trouble. Dave could use some help this weekend, if you're free. I have a catering job and can't make it."

"Doesn't seem like I'll have social plans any time soon, so why not?"

Noah's shoulders slumped again. Charlie patted him on the back and pushed him toward the door.

"These meetings always have an uplifting effect. I heard someone was bringing a guitar tonight."

"Great. Are you trying to depress me? You know I can't sing."

Noah flashed his crooked smile at Charlie and walked through the open door.

What a head case, Charlie thought as he followed. Dave met Charlie at the door and reached out to shake his hand.

"Things are heating up, Char," he said.

"Yeah, this Magorum is a scary dude."

"We're keeping a close eye on him, but I don't like where this is headed. He's got too much support without any discernable history. I was hoping you could pull together some background information on him."

"I got it covered."

"Thanks. Is Noah all right?"

"Woman trouble."

"Yeah. Any idea on this one's religious bend? I'm not sure this is the best time to be pursuing a relationship."

Charlie looked across the room at Noah. The last girl that caught Noah's eye ended up being a pretty outspoken atheist. "I think this one might actually be a Christian."

"We'd better get started. I'll talk with Noah later."

The front door closed and the light from the bay window caused shadows to fall on the yard. A man in a short black jacket stepped out from behind a large oak tree, just feet from the front door where Dave and Charlie had been talking. He wore a black baseball cap and a pair of jeans, with well-worn tennis shoes, gray with dirt. The men hadn't noticed him in the shadows, but he'd heard every word they'd said. From where he stood, he could see clearly into the living room where the fellowship had begun with a time of singing. He smiled to himself.

They were right about several things. Historically speaking, Noah's choice in women was poor. This was also not a great time to start a relationship and Magorum was frightening. More frightening than either of them could possibly imagine. But they wouldn't have to imagine for long.

He stayed for another fifteen minutes, and when he had heard enough, he turned and disappeared into the blackness of the night.

four

May

Wayne Durbin leaned back in his desk chair and crossed his feet at the ankles on the top of his desk. With the phone cradled under his ear, he was able to flip through the Worley file while talking with his lawyer.

"I'm telling you, Frank, it was the best thing that ever happened to me," he said, closing the file. "I knew he had no case against me—I didn't leak his unpaid taxes. I didn't even know about his bad checks until it was on the ten o'clock news just like the rest of Creston. I'd love to say I ran a flawless campaign, but it was his own stupidity that lost the election last year. The fact he tried to accuse me of slander when he knew he hadn't paid taxes in years just proves it."

"Well, you can sleep easy tonight, my friend," Frank said. "The case is gone, and so is ex-mayor Sheffield. He'll have about four years to think about what he did and then he'll probably be paroled."

"Four years, huh? Doesn't seem that long."

"Not for someone who's trying to change a town, that's for sure. That time will fly by for you. Look how quickly your first year in office has flown."

"No kidding." Wayne slapped the file closed and reached with his right hand to open a drawer in his desk. He dropped the file in and pushed it shut.

"So what's on your agenda today?" the lawyer asked the mayor.

"Oh, I've got to run. Thomas Larson is on his way over and I think I have an offer he can't refuse."

"Good luck with that one. Your offers with him never seem to work. Well, Mayor Durbin, I'll send you my bill."

"I'm sure you will."

Wayne took his feet down and leaned over his desk to hang up the phone. There was a soft knock at his door, and his secretary stuck her head in.

"Thomas is waiting in the conference room, Wayne."

"Thanks, Linda."

He got up and grabbed his suit coat that was lying on the chair next to his desk. He slid his arms into the jacket and glanced in the decorative mirror his wife had hung by the door. She had told him to always take a look before he left, to make sure there were no crumbs on his face and that his tie was straight.

Behind every good man . . .

His five-foot-seven frame filled the suit nicely. Another suggestion of his wife. She had said, "If you win, we'll need a tailor." He might be small, but he definitely looked the part.

He walked through the outer office and stopped at Linda's desk.

"Send my wife a dozen roses and put on the card, 'You were right.'"

Linda gave him a quizzical look, but he didn't have time to explain. He walked down the hall to the conference room and found his old friend sitting at the table, a travel mug of coffee in his hand as usual, looking out the window. It was the beginning of May, and Indiana was greening up nicely. There was a massive tulip tree growing right outside on the front lawn of the city hall. The yellow blooms were still a month away from opening, but the buds were already forming on the branches. A sign that summer was right around the corner.

"Well, it's no use beating around the bush. It's been a year, Thomas," he said as his friend's gaze turned from the window. He walked across to where Thomas now stood, hand outstretched. He took Thomas's hand in both of his and shook it warmly.

"Good to see you, too, Wayne. Up for some small talk?" Thomas grinned and returned to his coffee, as both of the men sat across from each other at the table.

"I never was one for small talk, but I am a person who never forgets a detail. You said for me to ask you again in a year, so I'm asking, will you officially join the team?"

"You know your team is full, Wayne. You don't need me."

"City planning is right up your alley, and it wouldn't take much for me to shift Corey to another role. I think Hal Smith is retiring soon, and that makes an opening that I can play with. People love when they get moved around a bit—keeps it fresh."

"Who are you fooling, Wayne? No one likes to be shifted around. It amazes me how quickly you've learned to spin your decisions."

"Ouch! Was that meant to hurt?" Wayne laughed nervously, not sure if his friend was teasing or serious.

"I'm sorry. I just don't like the whole political scene."

"That's what I'm here for. I can front run the politics. I just need you behind me, overseeing the city growth. Come on, what do you make at your firm? I'll match it and give you a ten percent raise!"

"It's not the money, Wayne. It's more the time. My girls are in school now, and between family and church, I don't have time for much else."

"Church? You're putting church before me? You've got to be kidding! That church you go to is big enough to survive without you. I need a better excuse than church."

"You just don't get it, Wayne. Church is not a club I belong to or an obligation I have. It's family. Yeah, I know the church is growing, but there are people there I love like my own brothers and sisters. They keep me accountable to be the person God would have me be. I can't walk away from them."

Wayne was well aware of Thomas's religious convictions. During the campaign, he often referred to Thomas as his spiritual advisor because he constantly urged him to stay on the high road. His advice was always solid and moral, and with him around Wayne consistently made better decisions. Thomas had been a friend, not an employee, and Wayne wanted that to change.

Wayne shifted in his chair and leaned forward on the table. "Well, I'm going to shift gears here a second and see if I can throw some bait in your path. My vision is farming renovation. I believe we can put our little Creston on the map by upgrading our facilities. We have prime land and the perfect environment to breed cattle. I heard the other day over at the Wilson farm, they've been experimenting at their breeding facility. Wilson said he was close to breakthrough innovations in immunity milk production. Milk that fights disease! It's calcium rich and boosts immune levels, especially among senior citizens."

"What's the point?" Thomas gave Wayne an interested stare, as he leaned forward in his seat.

"The point is, with funding and improvements, our Creston farmers could produce something the world really needs! I just need to come up with the funds. That's why I need you. With your connections in agriculture—I know you've served on the Agricultural and Farmland Protection Board for the state of Indiana for five years now—surely you know people in Washington who can lobby for aid for research?"

Thomas tossed his head with a chuckle and sat back in his chair. "I don't know what you think the committee is, but it's not anywhere near as connected as you hope it is! There are five of us, and the biggest decision we made last year was to have farmers clearly mark their fence lines in red so the assessor could identify the county easements in comparison to the owned land, which was in yellow. It was really a thrilling day."

"Oh, I think you can dig a little deeper than that, Thomas. Come on, in that little Blackberry of yours you have to have names of people who know people who can help little ol' Creston!"

Wayne grinned. He knew he was begging for help, but he really wanted Thomas to join the team. "The trouble with Creston is that no one has dreamed big in years—in decades, maybe even in centuries. Well, I'm here now and I'm going to make a name for us. We're going to use our resources and our experience to capitalize on our strengths. I need you on the team, Thomas. There's no two ways about it."

Thomas shook his head.

"I hear you, but it's just not the right time. You know I'll always be around for you. I don't need an official capacity. I will do this for you . . ." Thomas stood and reached to shake Wayne's hand. "I'll wade my way through my contacts and see if anything pops out at me. If it does, I'll make a call. Will that make you happy?"

Wayne stood and returned the gesture by again grasping Thomas's hand with both of his.

"I won't be happy until we're working side by side and Creston gets the funding it needs to become great!"

Mayor Durbin watched Thomas get into his jeep. From the window in his office, he could see the good people of Creston milling down the streets and talking on the sidewalks. This was his kingdom, small as it may be, and he was determined to make it the best kingdom in Indiana.

He returned to his desk and opened his *Internet* browser. It was time to see what was going on in the world. He had time for a quick surf and then back to calls. The red bannered headline on the CNN news page caught his eye—TEMPLE MOUNT CONSTRUCTION COMPLETE IN JUNE. He shook his head in disbelief. The territorial battle was finally over.

Who would have ever thought the Israelis would share the mount with the Arabs or visa versa? Alexander Magorum is too good to be true. I need to keep my eye on him. Who knows? I could learn something useful.

"Miss Orion?"

The red light on her telephone flashed, and Alexander Magorum's voice came over the speaker.

"Yes, sir?"

"Would you call the staff and set up a meeting for this afternoon?"

"Consider it done, sir."

"And for next week, cancel any appointments. I will be touring the new temple and then spending time with Prime Minister Rabin and his wife at their Haifa villa. I am leaving Sunday afternoon."

"Sir, is your security arranged?"

"I don't know, Miss Orion. Have you called my chief of security yet?"

"Of course, sir, I will handle the arrangements."

"Thank you."

It took approximately twelve minutes for Elise Orion to contact PM Rabin's secretary of state, receive fax and e-mail confirmations of the schedule in Israel, arrange a security detail with Agent Vasiliev, confirm departure times, arrival times, and flight times, call Klara to instruct what to pack, schedule a late Saturday afternoon manicure/pedicure for herself so that she would be presentable (because of course, she would be going also), cancel all prior appointments, and order a four course dinner for Alexander Magorum and his entourage so that they wouldn't be hungry when they arrived in Jerusalem. She even remembered to order his favorite Swiss chocolates for the airplane. At thirty-two, some questioned that she was mature enough to handle this job, but she had consistently proven them wrong.

Elise reached up, pulled at her blonde bangs and swept them down on her forehead, tucking them behind her ear, her natural waves controlled in a short bob. Maybe someday she'd allow a little more length, but for now, this was more manageable.

"Have I told you lately how good you really are?" she said aloud.

The sound of books falling, a glass breaking, and the low rumble of her employer's voice snapped her from her self-adulation, and she jumped. Immediately she stood and went to his office door. When her hand touched the knob, she stopped. She leaned in and gently placed her ear near the door.

If someone walks in now, this will be hard to explain.

But Elise had learned the hard way that noise in that office did not always mean her assistance was needed. She hadn't perfected her discernment in this area yet, but she was getting better at it. She closed her eyes and listened. She couldn't make out words but there were definitely two voices.

Speaker phone, no doubt.

She waited, and the voices quieted. Then the distinct smell of cinnamon wafted from beneath the door. She opened her eyes and smiled.

"You chose wisely," she quietly said as she lifted her hand from the doorknob. By the time she returned to her desk, Magorum's phone light was out. Things should return to normal now. Elise opened the file drawer to her right and pulled out a calendar. She opened it up to May and made a small red *x* on the current date, then glanced up at the month as a whole.

More x's than last month. Considerably more. I wonder why?

Elise returned the calendar to its file and shut the drawer. Her gaze lingered on Alexander Magorum's door for a few moments, her mind deep in thought. One day she would find out exactly what made him tick, and when she did, she would help him avoid these outbursts. It was part of her job to make him the best man he could be. That was her goal. That was her commitment. That was her calling. Therefore keeping track of his mood swings was necessary for her to understand the man as a whole.

And Elise Orion never stopped short of complete success.

five

Tara Warners picked up her Bible from the coffee table where she had placed it after church the previous Sunday. It was Saturday night, and she was worn out from a long week. She carried the book into the kitchen and set it on the counter near the garbage can. She flipped through the pages and pulled out a month's worth of bulletins. Her mind wandered again to Noah Greer. She had avoided him all week and hadn't heard anything else since his inner-office mail delivery. After throwing away his note, she decided she would seek out Christian friends through her church, but for some reason her mind returned to that man. Her irritation was fading, and deep down she felt a little silly purposefully avoiding him over such a small disagreement.

When she dropped the old bulletins in the garbage, an insert fell from one and landed on the floor. She reached down and picked it up. Her eyes scanned the bold print at the top of the page. It was titled "Total Reach":

Are you single and tired of being alone? Do you watch the married people pass you by and wonder if you'll ever fit in? Well, look no more. We are a group of single adults, committed to Christ, not looking for love but looking to REACH out on His behalf. We are TOTALly committed to Him and want to REACH into our community and embrace the local community on His behalf. We want to share the love of Christ with the Muslims, Mormons, and Hindus in our town—they will grow for knowing us and we will be enriched for knowing them. Join us every third Saturday night of the month as we gather to REACH. It's a TOTAL experience you'll never forget.

Tara walked over to her calendar hanging on the fridge. She took a pen from her junk drawer and wrote on the third Saturday "Total Reach." She was a bit disappointed it would be two weeks before the meeting, but at least she was following through with her plan to look for single Christian friends. Then when her mind wandered toward Noah, she would remind herself she was looking elsewhere. Tara set her Bible next to her purse and headed off to bed.

Sunday morning came quickly, and Tara threw on a pair of khaki capris and a blue tee shirt with ruffled edges, the one that accented her eyes. She topped it off with a white cardigan, in case it was chilly outside. It wasn't overly fancy, but it looked nicer than jeans and a tee shirt. She tossed her damp hair with a little gel, which held the curls in place, grabbed a Pop-Tart and a glass of milk, and headed out the door. Church started at ten and, as usual, parking was a nightmare.

She found her seat with a few minutes to spare, so she read through her bulletin. As the music on the stage began to call the congregation to worship, she felt a tap on her shoulder.

"Is that seat next to you taken?"

She glanced up. Noah stood in the aisle, looking down at her. Surprised at seeing him, her heart jumped a bit, but she hid it well. She grabbed her Bible and purse and scooted over a seat so that Noah was on the aisle.

"Thanks. That's a pretty color on you."

Tara nodded, trying to act cool, and Noah smiled that crooked little smile of his, as if he had won round one. Unfortunately, Tara was no longer in the mood to sing, but the music swelled and the service began, despite her distracted state. Noah seemed to know most of the songs and he sang wholeheartedly. Occasionally, he listened with his eyes closed. Tara sang for the first few songs and when Noah was quiet, she stayed quiet, too. She worried that he would notice that singing wasn't necessarily a strength of hers. Plus, she didn't want him to think she was overly happy that he had surprised her.

But by the time the sermon began, Tara had decided that she was glad he was there. He could hear for himself that her church was not some liberal, Bible-straying disaster, but truly a house of worship, filled with genuine Christians. Sometimes seeing is believing. She smiled to herself and settled in for the message.

Noah took a deep breath and opened his Bible to the passage being read. He had taken the bold step of coming to her church, but he knew the day was far from over.

"For the grace of God has appeared, bringing salvation to all men, instructing us to deny ungodliness and worldly desires and to live sensibly, righteously and godly in the present age, looking for the blessed hope and the appearing of the glory of our great God and Savior, Christ Jesus, who gave Himself for us to redeem us from every lawless deed, and to purify for Himself a people for his own possession, zealous for good works."

Noah's ears perked up. Dave Conover had taught this passage to the fellowship recently, and the notes from the study were fresh in his mind. He had stressed the call for believers to deny their natural desires and develop godly ones. He said the motivation was the return of Christ, and the sacrifice Christ made was to purchase us and make us like Him. He added that believers are called to look for Christ's return and reviewed the signs listed in Matthew 24 that Christ Himself gave. It was pretty straightforward, Noah remembered as he followed along in his Bible.

Reverend Blackmore had a different take on the passage, however. He stressed that God had brought salvation to all men and that culturally God had revealed Himself through various prophets and religions. All paths went to God, who used various belief systems to purify man. The ultimate sign of a God-led man was his zealousness for good works. Then he showed a video of the good works done in the world through various religious efforts. "Ultimately," he said, "good works evidence a true relationship with God, no matter what belief system you hold." This roused the congregation to a brief applause.

When they quieted down, Blackmore finished his message. "Our Lord and Savior could return at any moment. When He returns, will He find you zealously serving? Or will He find you selfishly living to please yourself?"

Blackmore walked off the stage, leaving the congregation to ponder their actions.

The worship leader closed the service, saying, "Join with me as you consider your call to serve Christ." Then he began singing, "Reach out and touch . . . somebody's hand . . . make this world a better place . . . if you can."

Noah sat stunned in his seat. He glanced at his watch and marveled at how much damage a pastor could do in fifteen minutes. Suddenly, he realized Tara was standing, waiting for him to let her into the aisle. He regrouped, remembered why he came, stood and faced her.

"So, do you have lunch plans?" Noah blurted. *What a jerk. I should have started with small talk first.*

"What are you doing here, Noah?"

"Well, I didn't get a chance to see you this week, and knew I'd find you here, so . . . I . . . "

The response died, and he just looked at her, hoping she would bail him out.

She didn't.

Noah cleared his throat. "So I decided . . . since I accused your church of poor teaching, I should come and hear for myself."

As soon as he said it, he wished he could have taken it back. He'd set her up for the next question, as if he'd wanted her to ask . . .

"So, what did you think?"

Noah tried to tread carefully. This wasn't the place to pick a fight. "I think I need some lunch." He flashed the smile again, hoping it would buy him some time. "Care to join me?"

Tara squinted her eyes and pursed her lips as she seemed to consider his offer.

"Fine. We'll go to Annie's Café just down Washington here. Follow me."

As Tara worked her way to the door, Noah shrugged his shoulders and followed. *At least she didn't say no . . .*

When they got to the door, Reverend Blackmore was shaking the congregants' hands as they left. Tara introduced Noah, and he made a quick compliment on what a big church the reverend had in his care, hoping to get away before anything deeper was discussed. The pastor let go of Noah's hand and reached for the man behind him, so Noah breathed a sigh of relief and continued on out the door. They made their way down to Annie's and engaged in small talk for half an hour while they waited to get a table. Before long, they sat in a booth by the window, a Caesar salad in front of Tara and a bacon double cheeseburger in front of Noah.

"So, here we are again," started Noah, "a second lunch date." He took a huge bite out of his burger and wiped his mouth with his napkin.

"Who said anything about a 'date'?"

"Well, I meant lunch 'meeting.' Don't be so quick to read into my words, or I'm afraid this lunch may end poorly, too." He raised his eyebrows. Would she laugh?

Tara wiped her mouth with her napkin but Noah was sure he saw a twinkle in her eye.

"So, what did you think about the service?"

"Before we get into that, I need to know if I've been forgiven for last Monday."

"I doubt I would be sitting here if you weren't forgiven, so let's just move on."

Tara took another bite of her salad.

"It's just that I felt like you were avoiding me all week, and I didn't know if . . ."

"It's fine. I was just busy. So, again, about church?"

"Well, where do I start?" Noah carefully chose his words and his tone so as not to put Tara on the defensive, though she was already there with his opening question. "I agree with Reverend Blackmore that God has brought salvation to all men." She smiled and nodded. "But that's where the agreement ends. I don't believe that all men are saved."

Tara put down her fork, and Noah watched as the smile faded from her lips.

"So you think that Buddhists are going to hell."

"Yes."

"As well as Muslims."

"Yes."

"So, only Christians go to heaven."

"Yeah, Tara. Hear me out on this. You understand what the Bible teaches about the sacrifice Christ made because of our sin, right?"

She nodded, sipping her Diet Coke.

"Okay, we'll start with sin as our foundation. Sin completely nullifies our good works. Most other religions are based on winning favor with good works, but we do good works out of gratitude, not to win favor. That favor has already been bought by Christ."

"I'm with you." The tilt of her head indicated her interest was piqued.

"So to say that anyone who was zealous for good works, no matter which system they follow, pleases God—you have to believe that the Bible isn't accurate. Romans 8 says that because of our sin nature, anyone controlled by it cannot please God. You also have to believe that Jesus wasn't being truthful when He said that no one can get to the Father unless they go through Him." Noah tried to keep his voice calm and not aggressive, but he couldn't help but think he was putting her on the defensive.

"It's not that Jesus was lying. That is the truth for Christians. And for Buddhists, they have their own truth system."

"But if Jesus' blood is not necessary to appease God's wrath on sin, then why in the world would He choose to die? Why would He even offer Himself when other methods of religion work just as well? I really think believing that all religions lead to God minimizes the cross as well as Christ Himself."

Tara sat quietly for a while, and Noah prayed that she would understand what he was trying to say. He ate a couple more bites to give her time to process her thoughts.

"Isn't it arrogant to think we are the only ones who really know God, when most other religions are far more committed than many Christians? What's the harm in thinking your good deeds earn His favor?"

"Tara, it's misleading. They need the truth." Noah wiped his mouth again and leaned forward, his elbows resting on the table. "We know truth because we know the Creator. His view on any subject is always truth, and our source is the Bible. Why God would give me the gift of salvation when my sin has earned me the same fate as the rest of the world is a mystery to me, but I am so grateful and humbled that I'll do whatever He wants me to do. Since we have the truth, don't you think it's loving to share it with others?"

Tara sighed and leaned back in her seat, her shoulders slumping a bit.

"So, in general, you weren't impressed with my church?"

"I am sure there are great things going on there and good people attend. I just worry about a church that doesn't hold to the supreme authority of Scripture and one which places idol worship on the same platform as Christ."

"Idol worship?"

Noah sensed a turn by the alarm in her voice. He knew the conversation was heading south, and he tried to apply the brakes and explain himself.

"Most other religions worship idols or personalities. Saying other religions bring you to God in the same way Jesus does places those religions on the stage with Christ. You do know what the Ten Commandments say about that?"

Tara paused, and her eyes flared. "Questions like this are unloving and judgmental."

"Like what?"

"Like 'You do know what the Ten Commandments say about that?' Of course I know and in the religion I have chosen, I don't worship idols. But you need to quit trying to apply Christianity to everyone else! Don't you get it?"

"No, Tara. I don't get it, but I also don't want to argue about it either. I'm sorry if I sounded unloving. You asked my opinion on the message, and I tried to point out my concerns, comparing what your pastor said with scripture. Within Christianity, I am allowed to do that, aren't I?"

Tara wiped her mouth and stood. Noah sighed. He'd seen her do this before. Once again he ended a lunch "meeting" on a bad note.

"This is useless, Noah. We just don't look at Christianity the same way. I don't see the need for continuing this type of banter. It certainly doesn't make my day any better, and I can't imagine you are enjoying yourself either. I think we're done for today." Noah picked up the bill and followed Tara to the door. He paid, and they headed back toward the church where they had left their cars. Noah looked at Tara as she walked beside him and wondered if she was mad or just indifferent at this point.

"Thanks for lunch," she said.

"No problem, Tara. Do you think we could have lunch next week sometime if I promise not to talk about church or religion?" He looked at Tara, who fumbled with an answer, clearly uninterested in another lunch.

"I've got a busy week—some . . . um . . . deadlines on some projects . . . um . . . that are overdue . . . and . . . oh, dear!"

Tara's Bible slipped from her hand and fell onto the sidewalk. The pages fell open and the bulletin flew out. All the extra inserts began to blow along the sidewalk and into the street. Noah responded quickly and stepped on a couple of sheets. As he bent over to pick up the runaway paper, he heard Tara yell.

"Noah!"

He first looked over at Tara, who was focused on something beyond him and then instinctively turned his head to his right just in time to see the grill of a black Dodge Ram pickup coming directly at him. There wasn't much time to react, but then he felt a hard shove on his shoulder, and he lurched back toward the sidewalk. The push was strong enough to save his life, and Noah watched as the driver of the truck swerved to the left, missing Noah by a few feet. He hit his brakes and looked back. Noah was lying on the sidewalk, papers in his hand, unharmed but a bit stunned.

"Are you all right?" Tara ran to Noah, bent down and reached for him as he rolled over, sitting on the sidewalk. Without thinking, he handed her papers back to her and she asked, "Do you want to sit a bit?"

Noah blinked a few times and cleared his mind. His heart was racing, but he knew he wasn't hurt.

"No, I'm all right. He didn't hit me, but who pushed me out of the way?"

"What are you talking about? No one was near you."

Noah thought for a moment and replayed the scene over in his mind. "When you yelled, I didn't have time to react. Someone shoved me."

Tara put her hand on his arm and gave it a squeeze. It was the first time she'd ever showed any affection to him, and Noah appreciated the gesture.

"Noah, no one was near you. I saw the whole thing."

By this time some bystanders were gathering around to see what all the commotion was about, and the truck pulled away. Noah knew someone had pushed him. He could still feel exactly where the hand had been on his shoulder. Tara helped him up, and as Noah scanned the crowd, he pointed at people and asked them, "Did you push me? Did you? Did you see anyone near me?" One by one they shook their heads and eventually walked away as the real excitement was over.

"Noah, I think you are just shook up. No one pushed you. You just jumped away quickly when I called to you."

"No, Tara. I'm not kidding. Someone pushed me."

"Then it must have been your guardian angel," Tara said with a smile.

Noah thought for a moment. He knew he hadn't imagined it, but an angel . . . ?

"Are you sure you're all right?" Tara put her hand on his shoulder and patted it tenderly.

Noah glanced at his knees, which were starting to sting pretty badly, completely aware that once again she was touching him. "Yeah, I'm fine, but, man, these pants have seen better days."

Noah walked Tara to her car, his knees aching with each step. "So, one final question," he said as he opened the door. "Do you think risking my life to save your bulletin earned me a lunch this week?" If he couldn't guilt her into another date, this might be the end.

She turned to him, resting her hands on top of the opened door. "You are relentless, aren't you?"

"That didn't answer the question."

"You know you've trapped me. What choice do I have?" Her eyes sparkled and Noah knew he had won. "Fine. Lunch on Thursday. That will give me enough time to come up with an excuse to cancel."

"You're welcome," Noah said, with a half smile. "For the bulletin."

Tara returned the smile and got in her car. Noah closed the door for her. He stepped back as she pulled out of her parking space. He noticed that there was a blood stain on both knees, and he gingerly walked to his car. Sitting in the driver's seat, he said a prayer before he turned his car on.

"Father, thank You for sparing my life today. I don't know who pushed me, so I'm giving You the credit. I also don't know what to do about Tara, Lord. There's something about her that I am drawn to, but I don't even know if she truly knows You. Please soften her heart to Your Word and use me to show her the truth."

Noah pulled out of his parking space and headed back home. He would clean up his knees and maybe catch a baseball game on TV. There was a meeting at Dave Conover's house at seven, and he would try to get some practical advice from Dave after the meeting was over.

Across the street, the man in the black baseball cap was leaning against a tree, watching. Today he wore a tee shirt and jeans, but the hat kept the sun off his face.

That was certainly a close call. This guy's going to be a lot more work than originally expected.

He stood to leave and something caught his eye in the air above the church. There was definite movement, like a swirl of dead leaves caught in a wind burst, except without the leaves. There was no sound and no wind, but he definitely saw a swirl. The invisible force moved from its roost on the roof of the church and lighted on the ground in front of the man with the black cap. The spirit materialized just enough to reveal an impish face, with a large forehead and deep set eyes. Its mouth was but a slash between its cheeks, with poorly spaced teeth set in the gap.

"What are you doing here?" it snarled.

"Nice to see you, too. You're looking good."

"You've never been here before—who are you following, and do I need to let my master know about him?"

"So you're going to act like you had nothing to do with that little scene over there?" Black Cap nodded with his head toward the site of the near miss incident.

"I have no idea what you are talking about."

"Lies only make you uglier. But you've chosen your doom, so you may as well look like your master. Enjoy the freedom you have now because it's quickly coming to an end."

"Talk. Talk. Talk. That's all you guys do. We rule this earth and we have prepared for any attempt to usurp our throne!"

"Prepare all you want. You couldn't stop Him the first time, and your little preparations will be futile the second time. You know Who rules and you know Who wins. It's just a matter of time."

"You have sung that song for thousands of years. It bores me! I enjoy watching the fruit of my labor. Do you like my little church? They make me so proud! They are ripe for the future—I've done my job in preparing them. Your team seems to be losing steam every day. You must be here because you've lost another church. Yet the battle rages on and you continue to lose. It must be frustrating."

Black Cap smiled. "Like the humans say, ignorance is bliss. Don't say I didn't warn you, but it's not like you can switch over. Your destiny is set and your time is short. You can do nothing without God's permission so enjoy the freedom He has allowed you. We both know the end so quit wasting my time."

With that, Black Cap grinned, knowing his adversary wouldn't argue his point. The imp's eyes flashed and his temper flared. Black

Cap watched as the imp flew down the sidewalk, wreaking havoc with anyone in his path. He knocked the ice cream cone out of the hand of a small child, who proceeded to throw a temper tantrum. He bit a dog in the leg, causing him to growl and lunge at an elderly couple passing by. He knocked a wheel off of a skateboard, sending the teenager sprawling on the sidewalk. And he removed the "s" from the sign outside of the gas station that read "Come to Shell for your hot coffee!"

Then he returned to his roost. One last sneer and the imp smiled at his handiwork. Black Cap shook his head in wonder.

Why He has such patience I'll never understand.

Setting his mind on the task at hand, he turned and disappeared, leaving the scowling demon to his domain.

six

June

Elise Orion sat quietly next to her employer, a pad of paper in front of her and pen in hand. The trip had been a whirlwind up to this point, from the flight over to the tour of the temple. But now, she could catch her breath. They all could. Magorum had kept her close at hand, and while she manually took notes, she also recorded every conversation per his request.

Prime Minister Rabin sat across from Magorum on the patio of his Haifa villa overlooking a clear blue swimming pool, the warm June sun graciously deflected by the large floral umbrella that shaded the table. Beside him, wearing sunglasses and a white cardigan, was his wife, Devorah. Elise sat opposite her, enjoying the warmth on her bare arms. Three of Israel's security detail joined them as well as Agent Vasiliev, all taking great pains to keep just enough distance to maintain the appearance of a quiet, intimate lunch between friends. Rabin's Russian was nearly flawless, which made the conversation flow much smoother.

"There are times I look at the mount and shake my head in disbelief," Rabin said, lifting his china teacup to his lips. He took a sip and continued. "Someday you must share your secret with me." He smiled.

"Befriending the Palestinians is not a secret, it is just a matter of knowing how to communicate with them." Magorum met eyes with Elise and nodded toward his cup. She reached across the table and re-filled his tea, adding two lumps of sugar and a drop of cream. "It was unrealistic for them to believe Israel would cease to exist. Once they accepted that fact, then negotiations became effective. And may I say it again, your temple is truly splendid."

Rabin leaned toward Magorum. "I still fear the Syrians. They may have a good relationship with you, but I have no confidence they have accepted your terms."

"They are an emotional people but I know how to work with them," Magorum replied. "Historically speaking, your surrounding neighbors have all been difficult people. But now that they have the right leadership in place, we are all desiring the same result—a peace-ful coexistence."

Elise fully believed everything Magorum said. She smiled as she jotted down Rabin's ongoing concerns.

"I do believe you are generalizing volatile personalities," Rabin cautioned. "My people have not been successful with communica-tions and relations with Syria, let alone Iran and Lebanon or even Turkey for that matter. Even our relationship with you is a new expe-rience for us. History has taught us to rely on no one."

Elise could sense a tension in the conversation and did not raise her eyes to look at the faces of the conversing men. She glanced at Rabin's wife, but though she was listening attentively, her face re-mained expressionless.

"Oh, Prime Minister! You offend me!" His voice was not angry but amused. "Have I not delivered every promise I made to you? Ev-ery time you look at your beautiful new temple, you should think of my faithfulness and goodness to your country. If your intelligence overhears some rumbling from time to time around you, that's just your neighbors voices, not their strength, being exercised. My aides labor day and night, maintaining good communication with your neighbors. We keep them happy and we keep you . . . safe."

Magorum paused. Elise loved how he could always hold the attention of his audience in his hand. She suppressed another smile.

"What do you think about a Russian Diplomacy Headquarters in Jerusalem?" Elise glanced up from her notes. This request was not expected. She looked over at Rabin, who raised an eyebrow.

"You have an office in Tel Aviv. What would one in Jerusalem accomplish?" Elise sensed speculation in his voice.

"It's just a thought. Jerusalem has so much . . . history."

"As long as the other embassies are located in Tel Aviv, Russia's place is among them."

Magorum took a slow sip of his tea and set the cup back on the table. "Of course, this is true. I know I am speaking from my heart, not my head. Jerusalem has always been of great interest to me. Someday I will find the time to enjoy it in a manner that will suit my curiosity. Perhaps then I will have the opportunity for a second home there."

Devorah stood and all eyes turned to her.

"I must see to the details of tonight's dinner." She extended her hand to Magorum. "Alexander, we will serve at seven, if that suits your schedule."

Magorum stood and took her hand, and Rabin and Elise followed suit.

"Thank you, Devorah. I am looking forward to it."

"Elise, you may enjoy a swim in the pool, if you like." Devorah looked kindly at her.

"Oh, thank you. It is very inviting." Elise glanced at the pool and knew that she would never feel the coolness of the water on her warm arms. This was not a vacation. As a matter of fact, she wasn't even sure what that word actually meant. There was always work to do, and at the bare minimum, she needed to start to transcribe her notes and tapes before the day got away from her.

Elise examined her arms as she picked up her pad of paper from the table. A slight pink hue was appearing, and she smiled.

Sunburn? Now, there's a new sensation. Perhaps I could work outside on my computer and get another hour in the sun.

The thought passed and she returned to her work. Magorum and Rabin headed back into the house. She took a deep breath and smiled.

"Never a dull moment, that's for sure," she said to Agent Vasiliev under her breath as she walked past him into the villa. She tossed him a smile but got none in return. He turned and followed her inside. Elise knew he would not let Magorum out of his sight on this trip, except for sleep.

A home in Jerusalem? What was he thinking?

She climbed the stairs to her suite, updating her to-do list in her head.

Thomas hung up the telephone and walked back into the family room from his kitchen.

"Durbin again?" Robin asked with a frown.

"You know he always calls when I take a day off. It's like a part of his routine—shower, coffee, newspaper, find out if Thomas is home and then call him. Why are you frowning?" Thomas sat down next to her on the couch, a little too close apparently because she gave him a shove.

"He just drives me crazy, that's all," she answered, pulling the sports section from her newspaper and handing it to him. "He knows you won't work for him, but he never lets up."

"He didn't ask today."

"Really? Why not?"

"I haven't come up with any contacts to help him with his fundraising. He continues to meet with the farmers and gather their wish list, but I don't know where he's going to find the funding." Thomas opened the sports section and glanced down the baseball standings column. "He just wanted to shoot the breeze today, that's all."

"I don't trust him as far as I can throw him. He's a politician first, and don't you forget it."

Thomas turned his head from the paper and met eyes with Robin. "So tell me, how do you really feel about him?" Robin was never one to hide her feelings. Thomas knew it was a strength and a weakness both at the same time.

Robin looked at her watch. "Mom and dad will be here in an hour. I'd better make sure the girls have all their stuff packed."

"I thought you did that last night."

"All the essentials, but now we need to make sure their baby dolls and teddy bears are in their backpacks. A week at grandma and grandpa's is a long time to be without Snugglin's."

As he glanced through the sports section, Robin stood. But then a surprise kiss on his cheek made him lift his eyes to meet hers.

"Thanks for taking the day off to be with me."

Thomas grabbed her by the arm as she turned to leave and pulled his wife onto his lap. He reached around her and kissed her like he meant it. When they both came up for air, Thomas smiled and said, "Your welcome." He set her back on her feet and sent up a quiet prayer of thanksgiving. *Thanks again, Lord. She was a great gift from You. I really love her.*

As Robin walked out of the room, Thomas could hear the scampering of little feet in the upstairs hallway. Every summer Christie and Sarah spent a week with Robin's parents. It was a nice break for Robin who went straight from teaching fourth grade right into Vacation Bible School at church, swimming lessons, and a birthday party for Christie. By the end of June, she really needed a week off.

Thomas stood up from the couch and walked back into the kitchen. Spotting his Bible by the cookie jar, he laid the newspaper on the counter and walked over to it. Flipping open the front cover he pulled out last Sunday's bulletin and opened it. Robin came bustling into the kitchen, two backpacks in one hand and one teddy bear in the other.

"Are we planning on going to that picnic Sunday afternoon at church?" he asked as she dropped the packs on the counter and walked over to her desk.

"Which picnic?" Robin pulled the girls' coloring books from her bottom desk drawer.

"The one with the Mormons. You know, it's one of the summer mixer events."

Robin stood, coloring books in hand, and wrinkled her nose.

"We went to the first one with Holy Spirit Chapel. Do you really want to do this one, too?"

Thomas breathed a sigh of relief. "I was hoping you'd say that."

"Are we terrible people if we don't go?"

"It's a big church—there are plenty of people who will be there. I have nothing against the Mormons, but I'm just tired. And we have that cookout on Saturday night with my department from work. We may even need to sleep in on Sunday . . . ?" He raised his voice in a questioning manner.

"Works for me. Now, help me find Snugglin's. He was just in here for breakfast."

Soon the girls and their bags were safely packed into their grand-parents' car, and Thomas and Robin decided to head to downtown Creston for lunch. As they pulled out of the drive, the radio news-cast was describing the fallout from an earthquake in Japan. Robin turned down the volume and said, "I'm just not interested in bad news today. My vacation has just begun, and I'm going to enjoy it."

Thomas pulled out his iPod from the center console of the car and handed it to Robin.

"The plug is in the glove compartment."

Robin plugged it in to the lighter, and soon they were listening to their favorite Kenny Chesney CD.

"So Durbin thinks Magorum is going to unite the world into a one world government."

"Durbin also thinks Creston is going to become the next Indianapolis."

"He watches Magorum like a hawk. Ever since Israel aligned with Russia, things have been pretty quiet in the Middle East. He credits Magorum." Thomas hit his turn signal and slowed the car.

"Did I just read that their temple is up and running now? That was fast."

"I think Israel wanted that for a long time, and once they got the right to build, they ran with it before anyone would change their minds." He completed the turn on to Washington Street.

"Do you think any of this has prophetic implications?" Robin reached over and took Thomas's right hand in her own.

"I don't know. Have you asked your dad about it?"

"He's so busy with his own church and all, I rarely even talk to him."

"Didn't he think that the temple would be rebuilt before Jesus returned?"

"Yeah, that's why I'm asking you what you think."

"Well, there are so many end-of-the-world fanatics out there right now, I don't want to jump on that bandwagon. We have enough problems here in America. We really can't solve the problems of the world, too. We tried for decades to bring peace to the Middle East, yet Russia did it so easily. Maybe this means we should have kept our nose out of their business a long time ago." Thomas pulled into the parking lot at Annie's Café. "Is this all right?"

"Sure—they should be serving lunch by now."

Thomas put the car in park and looked at Robin as he unbuckled his seat belt. "As for 'prophetic implications,' I have to be honest with you. That stuff is way over my head. I just trust that Blackmore will let us know what we have to know and leave the rest in God's hands. Ultimately, I'm called to love you and provide for you and the kids. That takes up most of my time."

"That and golf." She smiled.

"Golf inspires me to love you more."

Robin opened her door and got out of the car. As Thomas unbuckled his seat belt, she ducked back in and looked at him. "That one was pretty lame."

"I tried." He got out of the car and the two of them walked toward the café. "I'm not a pastor. I don't really understand a lot of the Bible. I get the basics, but I guess I just don't really read it that much to know it better. I wish I had more time to read."

Thomas felt Robin reach for his hand. She patted it and said, "That's okay, Thomas. You have so much on your plate. You do the best you can."

They entered the restaurant and settled in to a booth by the window. Thomas pushed aside his feelings of inadequacy. He really was a good husband and father, and that was enough.

Now, what looks good for lunch . . .

Charlie West sat across the kitchen table from Dave Conover and Noah Greer. In front of each of them was Charlie's summary report on the life and times of Alexander Magorum. Charlie had diligently worked for a few months on this dossier and was anxious to share his findings. He hoped they would come to the same conclusions as he.

"To date, he is closely aligned with China and Germany." Charlie worked his way through his notes with the other men scribbling in the margins of their own copies. "There are rumors that Magorum is working on a larger alliance that would include the EU, as well as simplifying the monetary system through Europe to Asia. Photos and articles were easy to come by—not a day has gone by where he hasn't been quoted or mentioned in the news."

Charlie slid a file of newspaper clippings and *Internet* articles across the table. Dave reached for the folder, opened the cover and started flipping through the clips as Charlie continued. He was pretty sure that his thoroughness was impressive to say the least.

"Of course his most visible and recent accomplishment was securing the Temple Mount for Israel to rebuild the temple on. Details from the negotiation process were sketchy and vague at best. But as we all well know, the temple is up and running, all thanks to Magorum."

Charlie watched as Dave pulled out a few pictures of the new temple and handed them to Noah. He knew that Dave had often talked of traveling to Israel.

"Any plans on seeing it firsthand?"

Dave shook his head. "Don't I wish. I just can't pull myself away from the compound. We are in the basic supply phase, but I worry a bit that we didn't allot enough storage space."

"You can always store supplies in the garage, Dave," said Charlie.

"I just don't want to give any indication that there is a community beneath the ground. If we eventually have to use the garage, boxes of food and toilet paper will be suspicious." Dave sighed and reached for his drink. "Enough about this—back to the matter at hand. What about Magorum's childhood? What did you find?"

"I couldn't find out much about it, but here goes. He was born in Russia to middle-class parents, Fedyenka and Galina Magorum." Charlie slid his finger down the page as he listed the facts. "They passed away sometime in his youth and Alexander was sent to a boarding school with the money left for him. There were no aunts or uncles, no siblings and not even an observant neighbor who could give insight into his childhood years. He entered boarding school at age thirteen. His grades were on record and he was an above-average student. But again, there were no roommates . . . no teachers . . . and no coaches to testify to his time in boarding school."

Noah scratched his head. "It's all too strange that such a high profile politician has such an empty history page."

Charlie knew that Noah was wondering the same things he had, and he nodded in agreement. "Then, he emerged onto the political scene at twenty-five, when he was hired to work as a research assistant to Yuri Babkov, a Russian ambassador to Germany. From there he worked his way through the ambassador system, spending a majority of his time in Arab nations. Go figure. By the time he was forty-seven, Magorum was the chairman of the Liberal Democratic Party of Russia and set his sights on the presidential election three years later. One exhausting campaign, and his three *P*'s platform—Peace, Prosperity, and Principles," he counted them on his fingers, "earned him the presidency."

Dave flipped through the *Internet* articles and paper clippings. "Could you find any negative press?"

"Everything I found was pretty positive. I will admit, the ease at which Magorum maneuvered peace in war-ridden relationships is a mystery to most. The media as well as the pundits scratch their heads at his success rate. As for negative press, there was the occasional comment on his height. At five-foot-seven, he seems a rather average build for a man who speaks with such authority."

"Whoa, I didn't realize he was shorter than me," said Noah. "He looks a lot taller in the pictures."

"Bottom line," Charlie continued, "Alexander Magorum has his sights set pretty high—a lot higher than just ruling Russia. He talks of world peace more often than a blonde at a beauty pageant, but his words have force behind them—the force of a world power and the force of a proven track record. He is definitely a character to keep an eye on. He could very well be the one Daniel the prophet called the abomination of desolation—the Antichrist."

The three men sat in silence for a moment and contemplated the consequences of that statement. Charlie was pleased with his research, but the possibility of Magorum actually being the one Daniel prophesied about and Christ warned about left a knot in his stomach.

"Well I, for one, am glad the compound is finished." Noah broke the silence. "Now we just have to wait and figure out how we're going to fill it."

Dave fiddled with his Coke can and Charlie knew he was in decision-making mode. He had seen Dave like this many times before.

"I don't know if the community is ready for us to cry "Great Tribulation" yet. But I do think it's time for us to talk with our families and friends. Magorum may be the Antichrist and he may not be. But we need to plant the seeds in case we find ourselves in the dead center of the final week of Daniel."

Charlie nodded in agreement. "Wars overseas, terrorist attacks here on American soil, miserable weather—did you hear about the earthquake in Japan? Over a thousand are considered dead. And now the temple is rebuilt. I know some of the natural disasters have been increasing over the past hundred years, but they seem relentless of late. I also know that every generation has cried "tribulation" and has been wrong up until now. I don't want to read into current events and fit the Bible into their context. But when current events fulfill biblical prophecies . . . " He shook his head. "I just don't want to be wrong."

"I understand how you feel, Charlie," Dave said. "I think the planning we've made can be passed from us to the next generation if necessary. Despite the decay of the church here in America, which is a major red flag to me, I have to keep reminding myself that America doesn't necessarily play an active role in the end times."

Noah sat forward and leaned on his elbows. "What do you mean? I thought the persecution by the Antichrist affected the whole world. Isn't that why we're preparing for the great tribulation?"

"You're absolutely right, Noah," answered Dave, pushing the Coke can away from him. "Revelation 12 says the whole world will worship him and in 13, everyone will be required to take his mark. These are global descriptions. What I meant is that America is not a major power in prophetic Scripture—no power from the West is mentioned. All too often I think we try to center the focus of God here in America, when His focus for that time is actually on the Middle East."

"Are you saying that the prophetic passages in the Bible are only referring to Israel then?"

"No, Noah," Charlie chimed in. "That is a big mistake that many make. When the disciples asked Jesus what to look for in regard to His return, Jesus didn't say, 'Don't worry, you won't be here, but anyone in Israel who follows Me after the rapture, this is what they should look for . . .' He just came out and answered their question. He described weather disturbances, wars, famine, false teachers. Then He pointed to the Antichrist desecrating the temple, martyrdom, and a great and horrible time of tribulation. Finally, He told them to look for the sign in the heavens—the natural lights going out. Then Jesus will return with His angels to gather His children."

"As we discussed again at our last fellowship meeting," Dave continued, "these events which Jesus described perfectly coincide with the seals of Revelation. Same order, all the way up to the sun, moon, and stars falling from the sky."

"I got into a discussion with a guy at work that just went off on me about the church still being here through the last seven years," said Noah. "The thought of going through any type of persecution was just ludicrous to him."

"Christ Himself said we would enter this time in confusion, so it doesn't surprise me," said Dave. "Hey, not to change the subject, but what ever happened to that girl from work you were seeing? Have you talked with her about this?"

"Tara?" Charlie thought he saw Noah blush when he said her name. "Well, after I had a near death experience with her, she's actually become my friend."

"Near death? What are you talking about?" Dave stood and walked over to the freezer. He took out a half gallon of Reese's Peanut Butter Cup ice cream and shut the door. He grabbed three spoons and brought it all back to the table.

Picking up a spoon, Noah continued. "Once again we ended a lunch with an argument, but I almost got hit by a car while we were walking back to the parking lot, so she agreed to another lunch. Since then, I've been careful not to be judgmental of her church and it ends up, we really enjoy being together . . . as friends."

"And you're sure she's a Christian?" Charlie gave Noah a questioning look. He knew it was a fair question, considering Noah's track record.

"Yeah, I think she is. She's just never had good teaching. But she understands the basics. For now, that's enough."

"Have you talked end times with her?" Dave asked, digging in for another bite of ice cream.

"Not yet—there's no way she's ready for that. I touched on it once and she looked at me like I was from outer space."

"Well, you may have to get there sooner than later," said Charlie, setting his spoon on the table.

After the three men had their fill of ice cream, they spent some time in prayer for the fellowship, then Charlie and Noah left for home. As Charlie pulled out of Dave's driveway, he sent up his own prayer of thanksgiving for his friends and their commitment to the Word.

"And above all else, Father," he prayed aloud, as he pulled onto the street, "please find us faithfully following Your Word and looking for Your return. Give us a boldness to share the truth with our friends, and give them ears to hear and hearts to understand."

And he knew exactly where he would start. This weekend he would be working a party for an old high school friend. He was a Christian and had a family already. Charlie determined to set up a time where he could share his convictions about the Lord's return and ask his friend if he was prepared to protect his family.

And Lord, please prepare Thomas's heart for our conversation. He's a good man in a dead church. But he fears You, and I believe with some good, solid urging, he will return to Your Word and respond to it. In Your precious Son's name I pray, Amen.

seven

June

Thomas savored the last bit of pie. *A second piece would definitely be doable, but would it be wise?* He shook his head and put the fork down on the plate. *Maybe tomorrow.*

"Another piece of pie, Charlie?"

Robin stood and carried her dessert plate as well as Thomas' to the sink.

"My heart says yes, but my head says no. Thanks, though. Fresh strawberry pie with real whipped cream . . . Robin, why didn't you marry me?"

"Thomas asked first."

Thomas jerked in his chair and looked over his shoulder at his wife who was still at the sink behind him. "Because I asked first? Is that the only reason you married me?"

"That and the fact you had a lot more money than Charlie." Thomas saw his wife wink at Charlie as she put her plate in the dishwasher.

"Don't feel bad, Thomas," Charlie teased. "She's a bit old for me anyway."

"Neither of you are making me feel better," Thomas laughed as he stood and picked up his coffee cup. "You were such a squirrelly freshman, Charlie. You were pretty lucky to have such nice seniors in your Spanish class."

"Lucky? If I recall, it was Spanish II and neither of you would have passed if I hadn't worked with both of you. Anyway, I think just knowing me keeps the two of you young!"

Thomas led Charlie into the family room. He sat on the couch next to Robin and Charlie grabbed an armchair with an ottoman. It had been months since Charlie had been over, and Thomas was looking forward to catching up. They just didn't see each other as often as they would like, but when they were together it was like old times.

"By the way," Thomas leaned back and crossed his legs, "the food was great the other night."

"Yeah, Chef Fredo sure knows how to put on a great barbeque."

"Fredo? Like Alfredo?" Robin smiled.

"Yeah. Short for Frederic. He's French."

"How much do you work with him?" Robin reached for Thomas's hand and he naturally gave it to her.

"During the summer, I'm with him almost every weekend. Fridays and Saturdays. With weddings and graduation parties, we keep pretty busy."

"What do you do during the week? Are you still doing Websites?"

"On and off. I have a couple of corporate accounts that I update on a regular basis, and I do some work for a few individuals. It's not very consistent, but the catering pays the bills."

"Okay, so . . . are you dating anyone?" Thomas squeezed Robin's hand when she asked and she turned to him. "Come on, honey, I waited until after dinner to ask. You've got to admit, that's pretty good for me."

"Where are the girls?" Charlie winked and Thomas knew he was changing the subject.

"They're at their grandparents until Thursday. And they're doing fine. But enough about them—back to the matter at hand. A girlfriend?"

"Well, I'm kind of glad you brought that up," Charlie started.

Robin let go of Thomas's hand and raised her arms above her head. "I knew it! We don't hear from you for half a year and there's a woman in your life."

"Now don't go jumping to conclusions. Actually, I'm too busy for a girlfriend right now."

Thomas shook his head and squinted his eyes. "A little bit of Web design and catering doesn't fill a whole week. What do you mean?" It always seemed like Charlie had an excuse to put off relationships.

"What I mean is that right now is not the time for me to even be looking for a girlfriend." Charlie took his feet off of the ottoman and leaned forward, and rested his elbows on his knees. Thomas could see the seriousness in his face, and he wondered if perhaps Charlie was ill.

"This may sound crazy to you, but I wanted to come over tonight because I have an agenda. I wanted to talk with you two about the return of Jesus."

Thomas released his breath and said, "Thank goodness—I thought you were going to say you were sick. Now what is this about Jesus?"

"Well, I know you both are Christians and I feel an obligation to tell you what I have been doing for the past couple of years." Thomas furrowed his eyebrows, not sure where this was leading. "I have been involved with a fellowship of men who study eschatology . . ."

"Essca-what?" interrupted Robin.

"Eschatology," he answered. "It's just a fancy term for end times. We've not only been studying the Bible, but we have been studying current events. Between the increase in world famine and weather catastrophes a lot of people are saying it's the end of the world. But I think there's an even better reason." Charlie paused a moment, rubbing the back of his neck with his hand. "The Russian president is a man of interest."

"What do you mean?"

"He single-handedly negotiated with the Arabs to give the Jews back the Temple Mount. He stepped in when America could no longer protect Israel and has ushered in a peace they have never before experienced. He negotiates with the surrounding Arab nations with no restrictions and is rumored to be working on a one world currency."

"So he's a great politician," said Thomas, still a bit confused. "What does this have to do with Jesus? I'm just not following you."

"I think Alexander Magorum might be the Antichrist. I think we may be heading into a time of great persecution here in the world."

Thomas was still trying to figure out what Charlie's agenda was, when Robin piped in. "Well, then we're out of here. What are you so worried about?"

"What do you mean?" asked Charlie.

"I mean that we'll be raptured before the Antichrist comes into power, so is that what you are trying to tell us? The rapture is going to happen soon? What do you want us to do about it?"

"Robin, the reason I am here is to warn you."

"Warn us? Of what?" asked Thomas, looking from Robin to Charlie and then back to his wife.

"I know that this may sound radical to you, but I believe the Bible teaches that we'll still be here when the Antichrist begins persecuting the church."

"You mean the Jews," corrected Robin.

"No, I mean the church." Thomas noted a force behind Charlie's words.

"Are you one of those people who don't believe in a rapture?" Robin continued. Thomas knew she was much better studied on this topic than he.

Charlie took a deep breath and leaned back in his chair. "I believe in a rapture, and like you, I believe it comes before God's wrath on the world is poured out. I just place that event in a different place on the prophetic timeline than you."

"But Charlie"—

"Hear me out, Robin. Give me just a few minutes. Daniel 9 gives us the timeline for the last seven years of history. Most agree on this point. The seventieth week of Daniel will begin with a covenant that Israel signs with the Antichrist, though at that point they don't know his real identity. Halfway through the seven years, he desecrates the temple and demands the worship of the world. You know what I am talking about, right?"

"Yeah, we're with you," answered Thomas.

"When the disciples come to Jesus and ask Him what to look for before He returns, like a sign or a signal, He starts to tell them that things on the earth are going to get bad—wars, famine, false christs trying to lead men astray. Then He says—this is in Matthew 24—He says that when the Antichrist which Daniel prophesied about desecrates the temple, believers need to go into hiding, because the Antichrist is going to bring upon the world a tribulation like it has never seen before."

Thomas listened intently, but he noticed that Robin was starting to fidget.

"Jesus even says that the Antichrist's rule will be cut short so that the elect would be saved or else all of them would be killed. Then, the sign to look for before He returns is the natural lights in the sky going out and then He'll return for His children."

"Can I talk now?" Thomas didn't like the curtness in Robin's tone. He flashed her a look, but she didn't back down. "That's a nice little story, but I am afraid you have a lot of your details screwed up. You know my father is a minister and he even wrote a booklet on this for my church when I was growing up."

Thomas watched Charlie receive this information. He wasn't sure what was going on in Charlie's mind, but he decided to just let Robin handle this one, since she at least knew what she was talking about.

"The first thing you are missing is the fact that the church is gone for this time. You'll agree that the book of Revelation describes the last days?" Thomas watched Charlie nod in agreement, as Robin continued. "Well, early in the book, like around chapter four, the Lord calls John up into heaven to give him the vision to write down. This is actually symbolic of the church being called up into heaven before the beginning of the end times."

Thomas could hear the teacher coming out in Robin. The sarcasm was subsiding, and since Charlie wasn't interrupting, she continued to instruct.

"So, that is the first proof that we are gone. Secondly, 1 Thessalonians 5:9 clearly states that we are not going to be put through the wrath of God. Another proof that we are gone. Thirdly, Matthew was not written to the church—the church didn't even show up on the scene until Pentecost. It was written to Israel and is instructions to the Jews as a nation. So you can clearly see that once we are taken, the last days begin."

Thomas felt her ease back a bit in the couch. They sat in silence for a moment and then Charlie leaned forward again.

"I know this is an emotional issue. The thought of being here through a persecution that will make the Holocaust pale by comparison is obviously not a pleasant one. I also know that the first time I heard this, I didn't like it either. But I am asking that you just consider the possibility. If you read the seals in Revelation, they line up with Christ's teaching perfectly. All the way up to the lights in the heavens going out. Then, between the sixth and seventh seal there is a whole chapter break. I am just asking that you read it and tell me what you see in that chapter."

"You're just wrong, Charlie. The end times has nothing to do with the church. We're gone. We're not here. It's for the Jews." Robin set her jaw, crossed her legs, and folded her arms across her chest, as if that was the end of the discussion. Thomas knew that posture and it wasn't good. He decided then to reenter the conversation.

"When you began all this, you said you wanted to share with us what you have been doing. Did you mean studying? Is that what you have been doing for the past couple of years?"

"Yes, there has been a lot of studying. This is not a whim. But I also have been preparing."

Thomas tilted his head to one side and reached up with his hand to rub his forehead. "What do you mean, preparing?"

"This fellowship that I am involved with believes that Jesus instructed His children to hide when the persecution begins. We have been preparing a hiding place outside of town. An underground bunker of sorts. It will house about two hundred people, and I want you to know, there's room for both of you and the girls, if you want to come."

"When? Like now?" Thomas wasn't sure what Charlie was suggesting.

"No, not now, but possibly soon. I don't know . . . a year, ten years, six months . . . we're just waiting for the Antichrist to reveal his true identity in the temple and then we're off to hide. But those of us in the fellowship want our friends and family to start mentally preparing themselves."

Thomas could sense the tension rising as Robin unclenched her jaw and jumped back in. "You know we are more conservative in our views on end times than Reverend Blackmore, but this is ridiculous. The mere thought that God would make us go through His wrath is outrageous."

"It's not His wrath. Not in the beginning." Charlie leaned toward Robin and seemed to focus his words on her. "The natural disasters seen in the seals are just an increase in what is already commonplace. His wrath begins with the supernatural sign in the heavens and then there is no mistaking that God's wrath is come. Fire from heaven, one hundred pound hailstones, water to blood—we're not destined for that, but we are here while Satan makes his final attempt to rid the world of believers and Jews."

"So you're telling me that God is going to allow Satan to put my daughters through intense persecution? Is that what you are saying?"

Thomas could feel the heat of Robin's temper pulsing from her body next to him on the couch. He needed to put an end to this.

"Listen, Charlie, I believe you are sincere about this, and bottom line, we're all believers here in this room. No matter what happens, we'll all end up in heaven, so let's not lose sight of that fact." He threw a smile in Robin's direction that was not well received. "Believers can have disagreements on theology and still be friends. So let's just calm down here and agree to disagree. Personally, I am not very well versed in end times theology, so I feel a bit in the dark."

"I don't mean to upset you, Robin. I'm sure your father is a good man, I am just asking you to look at the Scriptures again. Look at it in the same way you would study the book of James or read the Psalms. Take it for what it says at face value."

"I do that already." Thomas knew Robin was not cooling down, but before he could try to change the subject, Charlie continued.

"Good, good. And I know we are all believers, but if I am right," Thomas felt the intensity as Charlie stared him in the eyes, "you have a family to protect, Thomas. I need you to look at this for yourself. I am praying that the Holy Spirit would"—

"I've heard enough!" Robin stood and looked at Thomas, who was still on the couch. "Thomas, he can't talk down to me like that." She turned to Charlie. "We've been friends for years, Charlie, but tonight you pushed me too far."

Thomas watched as Robin stormed out of the room. He heard her footsteps march down the hall and then up the stairs, most likely to their bedroom. He looked back at Charlie, sitting with a sober look still on his face. Charlie spoke first.

"I didn't mean to upset her. I'm sorry." They both stood.

"She'll calm down. She has a soft place in her heart for you, Charlie. You know that. But she does get emotional about this, probably because of her dad and his teaching."

"I really love both of you, so humor me, Thomas. Read the Scriptures. You know where to find me. At least for now you do."

Charlie shook Thomas's hand and then walked alone to the front door. Thomas heard the door open and close. He headed upstairs and found Robin fuming in the bathroom, as she took her contacts out.

"Can you believe that? We invite him over. We feed him. And he starts this radical, I-know-the-Bible-better-than-you conversation about us and the girls being slaughtered by the Antichrist. You have got to be kidding me!" Her hands flew in the air as she spoke, making Thomas take a step back so as not to get hit.

"He's gone, you can calm down now."

"And Thomas, you just sat there. You didn't defend me or my father."

"I said I didn't know much about it."

Robin turned to him, eyes flashing. "How long is that going to be your excuse? When will you start to learn for yourself? Do I have to teach you everything?"

"Why would I bother learning it when you obviously have it figured out for both of us?" He had been patient with her long enough.

"What does that mean?"

"I couldn't get a word in edgewise tonight because you were going to get your point across with or without me."

"I had no choice. You were mute."

Thomas watched as she stared at her own reflection. "Why did you turn this on me? Be mad at Charlie, but why me?"

She looked down into the sink. "Because you are supposed to defend and protect me. I felt like I was being attacked and you just sat there."

"You have a twisted version of what happened tonight." He turned and walked out of the bathroom. Thomas grabbed his pillow from his side of the bed and headed back downstairs. He grabbed a blanket from the chest in the corner of the family room and made his bed for the night on the couch. She could stew in her own juice for a while. He didn't need her attitude or her warmth tonight.

Thomas grabbed the remote control and turned on the television. At the same time he heard his bedroom door upstairs slam. All hope of returning upstairs was extinguished with one fell swoop. This was the same old same old. How many nights had he spent on the couch in the last month? Three or four? He loved his wife dearly, but sometimes she was just completely irrational. There was no reasoning with her. Though he'd rather be upstairs next to her in his own bed, he knew with the sound of that slam that his night would finish out on the couch. He reached up for the lamp on the table behind the couch and noticed Robin's Bible sitting there.

What would it hurt to look at those passages? What were they? Matthew twenty-something? The seals in Revelation?

Thomas decided his growing headache wouldn't get better with additional stress, so he turned off the light, and a few minutes later, the television. Hopefully by the morning Robin would calm down. Then he heard the upstairs door open and steps in the hallway. Thomas smiled and knew that she was coming to apologize. He sat up and pumped his fists in victory. *No couch tonight—no sir-ee!*

Instead of footsteps down the stairs however, he heard a thump, like something falling to the ground from the second floor. He turned on the lamp over his head and saw his shoes and some clothes lying in the hallway. That answered that question. He wouldn't be seeing his wife in the morning. He now had his clothes for work and the argument would continue for another day.

eight

February

It took several months for Noah to finally attempt to discuss the return of Christ with Tara. He was pleased with the progression of their friendship and though the fellowship was still committed to sharing their concerns with loved ones, Noah just couldn't bring himself to throw a wrench into their growing friendship. But time was passing and the signs were not fading. Noah decided he couldn't wait any longer.

They had gone out for dinner and a movie, but the movie had been a bust and they left early. He suggested they stop by a small coffee shop and she readily agreed. He was becoming more and more comfortable with their friendship, though he still didn't discuss spiritual things too often. This was going to be a difficult conversation because he knew he would have to go into specifics and that's where they always went separate ways. He had held this off long enough but knew as they sat at a small table in the corner that it was time to broach the subject.

"Do you remember last April when we first met, and it didn't go so well?" started Noah.

"I try not to, but yeah," Tara said with a smile, as she sipped her mocha latte.

"It's hard to believe we had such a rough start. I really enjoy your friendship, Tara."

"I do, too." Tara's eyes fluttered a bit and he noticed the color rise in her cheeks.

"There's something I want to talk with you about. Actually, it's more like something I'm involved with that I would like you to know about."

"O . . . kay . . ." Tara sounded apprehensive.

"I have been a part of a fellowship for a couple of years. It's a group of Christian men and we meet every month to study the Word."

"Like a Bible study group?"

"Kind of, but it's a lot deeper than that."

"So, why do you want me to know about this?"

"Well, back at our rough start, you made a joke about forgiving me before the rapture happened. That really struck a chord with me."

"I don't even remember that—maybe I should have apologized for my sarcasm. But come on, Noah, that was almost a year ago. We weren't even friends then. And if I remember correctly, it still took us three or four months before that even happened." She smiled and Noah quickly responded.

"No, that's not why I am bringing it up. You see, the fellowship is based on our beliefs of Christ's return."

"You all meet together because you believe in the rapture?"

"We believe that the rapture is something we are to look for, based on some very specific signs Christ gave."

"What do you mean?"

The door was open and Noah began to share his beliefs on Christ's return. He laid out for her the Scripture concerning Christ's return, starting with Daniel and working his way to Revelation. He was encouraged, even a bit excited that she sat listening so intently, even smiling at his points. He hadn't brought his Bible, but was able to explain how Christ's warnings and the seals of Revelation lined up perfectly, placing His return right before God's wrath, but after a great persecution of the church and Israel.

"So," he concluded, "what do you think?"

"Oh, it's fascinating! I can really tell you're passionate about this! Does this fellowship only study end times?" Noah was pleased she was still smiling. He breathed easier and felt his fears fading away. Maybe their relationship was mature enough now to talk about spiritual things.

"Um, no, but lately that topic has taken most of our time. We are suspicious of the Russian President Magorum and are concerned about his enlarging power base."

"What do you mean 'concerned'? Do you think he's the Antichrist?"

"I wouldn't quite go that far . . . yet . . . but he's worth watching." Noah paused a moment and decided to ask her the big question. "What does your church say about what's going on in the world?"

Noah prepared himself for the standard answer—"We don't talk about it" or "We're not going to be here" but he was surprised at what came out of Tara's mouth.

"We actually just did a series on end times."

"Really? What was the main point?"

"Reverend Blackmore talked about the spirit of antichrist in America, as well as in the world, and how the tolerance movement is opening doors for us to be understood. Historically speaking, Christians have had such a bad reputation from the Crusades to the slaughter of the indigenous peoples in South America. The new tolerance movement is quieting the radicals and allowing the true message of the gospel to be enjoyed by believers around the world."

"And this has to do with end times because . . ." Noah knew he should watch his tone.

"Because, in order to usher in the return of Christ, we need to spread the gospel to all the world. The new tolerance movement allows our message to be heard in a nonthreatening manner. Soon the gospel will be heard throughout the world and Jesus will return!" Tara exclaimed boldly, and Noah sensed her confidence.

At that point, he chose not to argue. This was the first real theological discussion they'd had in a long time and he didn't want to turn her away. Charlie had told him to simply plant seeds. The fellowship knew their message would not be understood until it was nearly too late, but for now all they could do was let those around them know what they believe.

The conversation turned from beliefs to politics and eventually rested on favorite movies. As Noah walked to the car, reality began to settle in on him. He really liked Tara but they fundamentally viewed their Christian walk differently. He was grateful the relationship had simply stayed a friendship, but felt it was necessary to keep it there. It wasn't fair for him to lead her on and lately he sensed a growing attraction between the two of them. They were just ending a nice evening together and now was as good a time as any to address the situation.

"Thanks for the bad movie," Tara joked as she stood by the passenger side of Noah's car.

Noah reached for the car door to let her in and she touched his hand.

"I really had a nice time."

She smiled and Noah suddenly started debating with himself why he wanted to stay just friends. Tara leaned in and gently kissed him, an action which ended the debate in his head and erased all logic and reason.

"Uh, well . . . I wasn't expecting that."

"We've only been going out on and off for nine months. I hope that wasn't being too forward."

"Yeah, but you barely tolerated me for the first four—remember? We can hardly count those months." Her eyes sparkled and

Noah knew she got the joke. "It's just that, well, we see things a lot differently."

"Like what? We both love the Lord and we both need Christian companionship. Who cares that we don't see eye to eye on everything. I'm willing to listen to you and all you need to do is occasionally put up with my view on things!"

"Tara, you're forgetting how intolerant I can be!"

"Oh, Noah, why can't you just lighten up? You do like me, don't you?"

"Of course, but . . ."

"Then no 'buts.' I've been waiting for months for you to hold my hand and I'm done waiting!"

"So this is how it's going to be? You want something and you just go for it?"

"I'm sorry. I didn't hear you complain, did I?"

"It's just that . . ."

Another kiss. This one lasted a bit longer. Noah pulled away and gave her that crooked smile that admitted defeat, then added one final condition.

"If we're going to actually start dating, then we're also going to study together."

"Study?"

"Yeah, end times. Because the sermon series you described didn't quite hit the mark, and this is really important to me."

"Deal. Now, take me home."

"Now she gets bossy."

Noah opened the door and Tara got in the car. As he headed around to the driver's side, an uncomfortable thought hit him. He didn't do that great a job explaining himself to Tara. And now he's moving the relationship to a new level with a girl who is not very like-minded with him. Explaining all of this to Dave was going to be difficult, but not quite as difficult as explaining it to Charlie. He shook his head. Accountability is really a bummer, he thought as he climbed into the driver's seat and shut the door.

Noah put the key in the ignition, started the car, checked the rearview mirror then backed out of his parking space. He heard the screech of tires and saw the look on Tara's face an instant before he felt the impact.

A silver Suburban, making its way to the exit, hit the car full force on his door. Tara's head must have hit the passenger window because Noah heard it shatter. He was thrown toward Tara on his right, then back to his left, his own head hitting the window, too. The driver's door ended up right where Noah had been sitting. His seat belt tore at the shoulder, allowing his body to be thrown across the front seat again, where he landed just short of Tara's lap.

An eerie silence settled over them. Noah tried to figure out what had just happened. His head was pounding and his vision blurred for a moment.

Where are my air bags? With an impact like that they should have gone off.

He tried to look outside the car to see if there was movement in the Suburban, but couldn't turn his head enough to see the vehicle. He searched for his rearview mirror, but it was twisted and pointing downward. Noah looked over at Tara, and his heart dropped. Her head was bleeding. He tried to reach her, to at least touch her arm to comfort her, but his arm was paralyzed.

Within minutes, the flashing lights of the emergency vehicles filled the dark parking lot. A fireman knocked on the windshield and yelled through the window, "You two all right in there?"

"Yeah, I think so." Noah watched Tara reach up and touched her forehead. There was blood on her fingertips.

"Stay put and we'll get this door open in a minute."

Noah fought a wave of nausea. "Are you okay?" he finally managed to say. His voice was hoarse.

"I think so, but once you get off my leg, I'll know more."

Noah realized he was still practically on her lap, but the collapsed door restricted both from moving. It felt like an eternity, but it probably had only been a few minutes when the firemen pried the door open. The first EMT quickly moved to Tara's side and held her in place so she wouldn't fall out of the car. Noah watched him cut off her seat belt and then pull her from the car. They told Noah to sit still and he saw them put her on a stretcher. Then it was his turn.

Noah was pretty sure he could walk but the EMTs weren't going to take any chances. Two of them pulled and for a moment Noah felt some pain in his shoulder. But that soon vanished as they strapped him on his own stretcher and began to roll him to the ambulance. A police officer stopped Noah's stretcher and asked for a minute with him.

"Are you the driver of the car?"

"Yes, sir."

"Can you remember what happened?"

"I looked and didn't see anyone coming, started to back out and the next thing I know, I'm on the passenger side of the car. I must have missed it in the shadows."

"How did you cut your seat belt off?"

"How did I what?"

"Your shoulder strap was cut. Did you have a knife?"

"No, I . . . I don't have a knife."

The officer looked at the EMT.

"I'll follow and get a statement at the hospital. He's still a bit confused."

"Sir?" stammered Noah. "Is the other driver all right?"

"Who?"

"The driver of the car that hit me?"

"There's no other car, sir. We were hoping you'd remember something about that, because with your damage, there had to have been a lot of damage to their car. It's amazing you're alive, to be honest with you."

"There's got to be skid marks—I heard the tires screech."

The officer glanced behind him and then back at Noah. "No skid marks."

"What about Tara? She was in the car with me."

"She's fine. Just a cut on her head. A few stitches will fix her up."

They loaded Noah into the ambulance and headed off for the hospital. He must have hit his head harder than he thought because he was starting to drift off to sleep. He breathed a silent prayer and thanked the Lord for protecting them and sparing their lives.

As the ambulance pulled out of the parking lot, Black Cap leaned against a tree. He folded up his version of a Swiss army knife, similar in size but far sharper, and dropped it in his back pocket.

There's something about being with that girl that is not healthy for Noah. It's like he lets his guard down.

Black Cap glanced over his shoulder and noticed the swirling wind above the wrecked automobile. A man with a tow truck was loading it onto a trailer, but he didn't notice anything unusual. Black Cap scowled and headed for the hospital. It was a cold night and no matter how much time he logged in on this assignment, the cold always got to him. As he faded into the night, he said a prayer of his own in a language only understandable by the Receiver.

nine

March

Elise was exactly where she should be. At work, on time, prepared for another day of service. In fact, she was exactly where she should be in life, too. Working for an up and coming, dynamic world leader, overseeing his professional schedule as well as his personal schedule, making him dependant on her without him even knowing. One day he would understand how important she was to him.

She reached for her to-do list and checked off the first three items. Glancing at her watch, she knew today was a big day. Magorum had been rather anxious and specific about the details of this day and she had followed each and every one of his wishes to a *T*.

Elise Orion had her suspicions about Magorum for years. She wasn't exactly sure how he would do it, but she knew one day he would one day rule the world. She recognized this bandwagon and had made a concerted effort to jump on it. She made herself indispensable to him, thus insuring her ride to the top. And now she stood at the threshold of world domination, behind Alexander, of course, and could taste the power as if it were a . . .

"Miss Orion?"

The buzz of her intercom roused her back to the matter at hand.

"Yes, sir?"

"Could you come in for a moment?"

"Yes, sir. Right away, sir!"

Elise grabbed her note pad and a pen and walked to his door. She knocked twice and waited for his response. Through the door she heard the familiar grunt and she entered. Alexander Magorum sat at his desk, curtains open behind him, fresh air pouring through the open windows, with nothing laying on his desk but a single sheet of paper in front of him. The faint smell of cinnamon filled the room and she could tell the candles on the coffee table had been burning recently.

"Is everything in order for tomorrow?"

"Yes, sir. The final approval from the legal department was sent over this morning. I have made copies of the Currency Act so that each member will receive a copy once they sign the original."

"Excellent. The Federation of World Powers cannot be stopped—do you realize that, Elise?"

Elise loved it when Magorum used her first name. He rarely did it—usually only when he was excited and wanted her to join in his excitement.

"Yes, sir. It is all very exciting. The leaders from Germany and China arrived last evening and the rest will arrive this morning. We are on schedule for the two o'clock meeting. Most will be in the conference room by one thirty, as you requested."

Magorum turned in his chair and looked out the window. Elise stood quietly, admiring a genius at work.

"The Currency Act is only the beginning. Other nations will be lining up to join when they realize the benefits of the FWP. Stability. Insurance. Trade. Travel. Employment. I provide it all. But I must not lose sight of the goal. I must never lose sight of the goal. While they thank me and say they love me, they can also turn on me, and I cannot allow that to happen. We are close but I cannot hide forever. Yes, I will stick to the plan but I will not conceal my face forever. They will have to learn to trust me again and when I provide stability and prosperity for them, they will forget and I will accomplish my goal."

Elise was a bit confused by his rant, and cleared her throat so that he would remember she was in the room. He turned and his eyes met hers. They were black as coal and almost completely dilated. His face was pale and he looked right through her.

"Do you believe in me, Miss Orion?"

"Of course I do, sir."

"Would you follow me no matter what I did?"

"To the death, sir."

"No matter where I went?"

"Absolutely." She kept her voice calm, though her heart began to race.

"No matter where I came from?"

"Sir?"

"No matter what I looked like?"

"Sir, I don't understand . . ."

"No matter what I had done in my past?"

"You're scaring me, sir!"

Alexander Magorum had slowly stood up and with his eyes glazed over, he walked toward Elise. Sweat dripped from his forehead and the color was still drained from his face. With each question he got closer to her. Carefully she backed up. She was finally standing with her back to the office door and he was within inches of her face. His eyes flashed and in an instant, he had her in his trance.

Elise did not know what was happening to her, but she felt herself being pulled into his eyes. Deep, dark holes. It was as if she was falling into a tunnel or a well, for quickly the office disappeared and all she could see was darkness. Cool, damp darkness. She could feel the wind in her hair and she wanted to reach out with her arms to try and break the fall, but she was paralyzed. Far in the distance she could see a light. As her body sped toward the light, a heat started to surround her. The tunnel was coming into focus and it looked to her as if the black walls were melting. She was beginning to become uncomfortable from the heat and she had to turn her eyes from the light, for the brightness was blinding.

The heat was nearly unbearable and she heard a thud. She realized she was no longer falling but she was on her back, lying on a burning bed of fire. She could feel the skin on her legs start to peel from the intense heat, but she still could not move her arms. Her hair disappeared in a cloud of smoke and the smell of burnt hair filled her nostrils. She looked to her side. Maggots and worms spilled from her exposed shoulders onto the fiery floor. They gnawed on her flesh and crawled on top of each other to feast some more. By now she could hear screaming and she realized it was coming from her own mouth. She shut her eyes tightly to try to moisten them, but to no avail. The pain was excruciating and she could no longer reason herself into observing the scene. She simply wanted to die. Survival was not even an option. She wanted death and she wanted it now.

She opened her eyes and immediately the pain was gone. She knew instinctively that she was not burning but standing in Magorum's office, staring into his pale face. He took a step back from her. She felt her knees relax and raised her hand to her damp forehead.

In a quiet voice, he spoke.

"I've been there, Elise."

She continued to stare at his expressionless face.

"That used to be my home. It was hell. There's no other way to describe it because that's exactly what it was. Hell."

"But . . . how . . . why . . . ?" She felt the tears begin to stream down her face. Could what he showed her—what he was saying—be true?

"Don't believe it when you hear that God is love. He isn't." Magorum's voice rose with intensity but not volume. "He's sadistic. He likes to watch humanity suffer. On earth and in hell. He sits by and does nothing. He sent me to hell and wants to send me back, but I am not going back. Not ever."

Elise held her hands to her heart, trying to stop the pounding in her chest. She was struggling to process exactly what Magorum was telling her, but then she remembered the last question he had asked her. She mustered up her courage to speak.

"Who are you?"

Magorum's expressionless face turned into a smile. Apparently she asked the right question. His reply was quiet and soft again, as if he was trying to calm her with his tone.

"I am the one who will save the world from God." He reached out to her hands which were still clutching at her heart, and wrapped warm fingers around them. "He has destined us for hell. I will give us life. He causes famine. I will cause feast. I have been given a second chance and I will not lose this time."

Elise still didn't understand. His words made no sense.

"But . . . who are you?"

Magorum lifted her quivering chin with his right hand. He stared again into her eyes, and for a moment she feared another fall, but she looked nonetheless. He was standing closer than he ever had before and his voice was now barely over a whisper.

"I am the savior of the world. I'm sorry I had to show you, but most will not understand when they see me for what I really am. Don't forget what you have seen today. That's where you are headed if I lose. We're in this together and because I love you, I will save you."

"Who . . . are . . . you?" She asked one final time.

"You don't need to be afraid, Elise. The world will follow. I've been promised power, authority, and dominion. I am taking you with me, Elise. You and the rest of the world."

He stepped back from her and returned to his desk. He sat and picked up the lone paper on his desk. Then he looked up at her and spoke.

"Now, we need to get ready for this afternoon. You need to go back to your desk and compose yourself. Someday you'll thank me for keeping you so close."

Elise left Magorum's office and felt numb. She sat in her chair and looked at her arms and legs. All intact, though quivering uncontrollably. She took a deep breath, shook her head and tried to clear her thoughts. She had a lot to do this afternoon, but the vision she was just given would not leave.

It had rocked her world, but now that she knew she was safe, her mind started to process the experience. Who else knows about this? Why was she chosen to see this? Had he really been in hell? How could he control her mind?

Her body relaxed and her breathing steadied. What she felt wasn't terror, at least not anymore. But what was she feeling? Could she put it into words? Only one seemed to fit so she claimed it.

This must be what power feels like.

She looked at his office door. A faint trail of smoke ascended from beneath the closed door. She wasn't alarmed, for the faint smell of incense often flowed from his office. She closed her eyes and another shiver ran up her spine. At the same time she experienced fear and excitement. She had always felt there was more to him than just ruling Russia. She had been given a gift today and her suspicions were now confirmed.

Magorum would rule the world. Sooner than later.

And she was by his side.

"Who are you, Alexander Magorum?" she whispered under her breath.

When Thomas pulled into the garage and opened the door of his car, the smell of lasagna filled his head. He reached up and pushed the remote button to close the garage door. He grabbed his briefcase from the passenger's seat and got out of the car. He could feel his stomach rumble and he remembered all he had eaten today was a granola bar for breakfast that morning.

Christie was the first to see him. She ran toward him and jumped in his arms. Soon Sarah was sitting on his foot, her legs and arms wrapped around his leg. He stiff-legged it into the kitchen where he found Robin tossing a salad.

"My life is really good, did you know that?"

Thomas shuffled over to Robin and gave her a kiss.

"Are you hungry?"

"Starving. The smell of lasagna hit me in the garage and my stomach started to holler for food. How long 'til we eat?"

The girls giggled and loosened their grip on their father. Thomas set Christie down and kissed her on the top of her head.

"Fifteen minutes. Here—have a breadstick." Robin tossed Thomas a warm garlic breadstick from a basket in front of her. "I got a new student today."

"Really? In March?" Thomas took a bite and walked to the fridge to grab a Coke.

"Yeah, it's a transfer situation. Darling little boy. His name is Isaiah Hamilton. His mother is from India and he has the most beautiful big brown eyes and light brown skin."

"Where did he come from?" Thomas took his Coke and sat at the counter as Robin added the finishing touches to the salad.

"From Shelton, Michigan. They've been here only a week or so."

"Smith and Brumsby has an office in Shelton. I was there once for a regional meeting. Nice place. At least they won't have culture shock, moving from Michigan to Indiana."

"They seem like nice people. We might see them in church, actually."

"Why? You didn't invite them, did you?"

"Of course I didn't invite them, Thomas. But I did get into a strange conversation with Isaiah. I wrote down the name of our church and sent it home with him." Robin picked up the salad and nodded toward the family room. "Get the girls and I'll get dinner on the table."

Thomas rounded up the girls from the family room and helped them put their toys away quickly. Then he sent them to the bathroom to wash their hands and minutes later all four Larsons were sitting at the dinner table, heads bowed in prayer.

"Bless mommy and daddy and grandpa and grandma and Christie and the *lazza* we are about to eat. Amen." Sarah's smile was as wide as her face when her daddy raised his head.

"Thank you, sweetie. That was perfect."

Thomas put a breadstick on both girls' plates and served up the vegetables, as Robin dished out the lasagna. Soon the girls were describing their day and in great detail telling every conversation they'd had since breakfast. At one point, in between stories, Robin looked at Thomas and said, "No one ever said having daughters was a quiet job."

Soon the girls finished their food and took their plates to the sink.

"May I be excused, daddy?" Christie stood next to her father, arm around his shoulder, big green eyes looking into his own.

"Of course you may," he answered.

"How about me?" asked Sarah from the other side.

"How about me what?" Robin asked.

"How about me being *scused*, too?"

"May . . . I . . ." Robin gave her a clue.

"Daddy, may I be *scused*, too?"

Thomas kissed her on the forehead and said, "Nicely done, honey. Yes, you may." As she ran from the kitchen, he called out to her, "Don't trash your bedroom. It's almost time for bed."

Thomas turned to Robin. "Peace and quiet."

She nodded. "Tell me about your day."

"First, finish your story. Tell me about your strange conversation with this new boy. I'm not happy you invited him to church." It's not that he didn't trust her, but with laws that prohibit proselytizing, Christians had to be extra careful.

Thomas waited as Robin wiped her mouth with her napkin and took another quick drink of water.

"It's not that big of a deal, Thomas. Because he's new, I kept a close eye on him most of the day, putting him with kids with similar interests. He told me he was a Pacers fan and I hooked him up with Alex Starkwell. He's a fanatic. They seemed fine."

She took another drink of water and handed the breadbasket back to Thomas.

"At the end of the day, he came to me and asked me if I were a Christian."

"Really?" He shook his head. "The innocence of children."

"I am sure he doesn't know that school is not the place for religious talk, but I told him I was. Then he asked me to pray for his cousin. He said her name was Emma and she was hiding with her parents. When I asked why she was hiding he said that a bad man was after her. He said she writes letters to him that scare him. It was really strange. The look on his face was true fear."

"So then you invited him to church?"

"No, I put my arm around him and said I would pray. I also said that if she was with her parents, I was sure she would be safe. I asked him if his parents knew that Emma was hiding and he said yes. He said his parents think that Emma is in a cult and that's why they are hiding. Anyway, it was frightening enough for him to tell me on his first day of school about it."

"Is this something that the school should be notified about?"

"I don't know. It was just so strange. When he left, he turned to me and said that Emma said the man was after him, too. I mentioned in the office to keep an eye out for any one wandering around here that shouldn't be here, but I don't know what else I should do. I could ask if I could see one of her letters, because that might help explain what is going on."

"So exactly how did you get to writing down the name of our church? I hope that doesn't come back to bite you."

"It'll be fine. It's not like I was witnessing to him. He simply said his family was looking for a church and I didn't even say the name out loud. I wrote a note to his mother, explaining he had asked me, so I was sending this note per his request. That should cover my motives. Don't worry—I remember what happened to Sue. I wouldn't risk my job to invite a student to church."

Thomas stood and carried his plate over to the sink. "I hate that we have to be so careful. But the government has made sure that we keep our mouths shut. I just want you to be careful, that's all." He rinsed his plate and put it in the dishwasher. He was tired and would probably watch a little television and then go to bed early. Things were busy at work and it was catching up with him.

"Do you need help in here?" he asked, halfheartedly.

"Go get your paper—this won't take me long."

As Thomas put his feet up on the ottoman and opened the paper, he could hear the girls laughing upstairs and his wife humming in the kitchen. When he first married Robin, they would have never dreamed that inviting someone to church would be illegal, but for all intents and purposes that's exactly what was happening in America. Even casual conversation about beliefs was frowned upon. It was best to just embrace diversity and worry about yourself. Thomas and Robin worked hard to protect their daughters by teaching them to be loving and accepting of everyone, while carefully explaining that they need to have Jesus in their lives. So far there was no law against proselytizing your own children, but who knew what the future would hold?

Robin is smart. I'm sure she was careful how she handled this boy. I'm too tired to worry about it tonight anyway.

Thomas took a deep breath and felt a heaviness settle over his eyes. In no time he was sound asleep, newspaper still in his hands.

ten

March

March fifteen started like any other day. Noah arrived at work by seven thirty. He had been trying to make up for the week he missed after the hit and run. His arm was still sore but he wasn't wearing a sling any longer. The morning flew by and before he knew it, his cell phone rang. Typically he didn't answer his cell at work, but when he picked it up to look at the caller ID, he glanced at the clock which read 12:13. Lunch time. The ID was still broken, so he flipped the phone open and said, "Hello."

"Hi, Noah."

He immediately recognized Charlie's voice.

"What's up?"

"Do you have access to a TV at work?"

"There's one in the cafeteria. Why?"

"I'll bet CNN has a live feed on the *Internet,* too. Something's going on in Jerusalem and I think you had better turn it on. Dave called me a few minutes ago and he said to call you. There's a press conference and it's been delayed a bit. But Magorum is involved and he's got the leaders of the FWP with him. They're moving the press conference from the outside of the temple in Jerusalem to the inside. Oh . . .

wait . . . it's coming back on. I'll call you when it's over, but get to a screen."

With that, Charlie hung up. Noah pulled up his *Internet* and typed in the address for CNN. There was a live feed and it took a few seconds to download. In the center of the screen was a close-up of Magorum behind a microphone. Noah could tell there were people standing behind him, but he couldn't tell who they were. He clicked on the volume and turned it up.

". . . North Korea no longer threatens the world with nuclear development. I have persuaded them to turn their focus from aggression toward peace. I have shown them the benefits of contributing to a cause, rather than threatening the cause. Israel enjoys freedom like they never have before. The children no longer carry gas masks to school in their lunch boxes. They live without threat of Arab aggression. Why is that? Because I have protected them.

"Don't get me wrong. I respect the Arab people. They are a culture with great leadership and vision. They will be great allies to me in the days ahead. The world CAN live at peace! The world WILL live in peace!"

Noah could hear cheering in the background and Magorum waited for the crowd to quiet down.

"Today, my fellow members of the Federation of World Powers have joined me in making a financial alliance. We will distribute to each government leader as well as the news agencies our formal agreement to consolidate our monetary system. As of yesterday, our ten nations have begun the process of unifying our currency, which brings with it benefits to our people. And we invite the rest of the world to follow suit. My dear friends believe this is what I called this meeting for. However, there is more."

With a smile on his face, he continued.

"I was once a man who failed his people. I made promises that I could not keep. In the end it cost me my life. I haven't made those mistakes this time around. I haven't turned the world against me. I have systematically proven that my vision is pure and my motives are true."

"Oh, no," Noah said under his breath. His chest tightened and he felt his heart begin to race.

"Many don't receive a second chance, but through my master's graciousness, I have been given a second chance. I have seen the Enemy first hand and now I know with whom to make alliances. I will not make the same mistakes again!"

"Whoa!" Noah exclaimed, half in disbelief and half in anticipation of what would come next.

"Today, I will hide no longer. What I am about to reveal is not meant to turn you away but to explain why my efforts to unify the world have been successful. I am not the man you think I am. I am greater than Alexander Magorum could ever be, for I have a power that soars beyond human capacity. I once dreamed of a superhuman race that could defeat death itself. Today, I will prove to the world once again that I am a man of my word!"

Magorum took a step back from the microphone and stood still before the audience. The camera pulled back to show his whole body. Behind him, the leaders of the FWP looked on with as much interest as the rest of the room. Magorum raised his hands out from his sides until they were parallel with the ground, palms up, forming the shape of a cross. He dropped his head backwards and began to tremble. Noah could hear a collective gasp from the audience.

There was a sudden commotion behind the camera, though the lens stayed on Magorum. Noah could hear the sound of water running or wind blowing, and women were shrieking. The room was plunged into darkness and Magorum stood alone in a spotlight. The cameraman obviously struggled to keep his camera steady and Noah wondered if there had been an earthquake. The men on stage behind Magorum were suddenly engulfed in a swirling wind that blew through their hair and almost knocked them over. They steadied themselves by putting a hand on their neighbor's shoulders.

The wind pulled away from them and began to twirl around the feet of Magorum. He did not move. It slowly worked its way up his body, swirling around him until he was lost in a blur of air.

Magorum let out a cry that could barely be heard over the wind through the microphone. Then the wind lowered itself until it only swirled around his feet. It was over. There was a loud noise, as if a door had been slammed shut and the *Internet* view from the cameraman went in and out as he apparently tried to refocus on the action.

Initially Noah thought he recognized the man standing where Magorum had been standing. Again the camera went out of focus and then focused again, as if the cameraman couldn't believe what he was looking at. But standing in front of the camera, where Alexander Magorum once stood, was a totally different man. One who had been dead for years. Adolph Hitler looked straight into the camera and said, "Yes, that's right. No need to adjust your televisions. It is truly as you see!"

There was a collective gasp in the office when his voice was heard. Noah could feel his heart pound and he grabbed his cell.

"I am Adolph Hitler, back from the dead! I told the world I could defeat death and today I am living proof of that very fact! Please do not be afraid—I have come to bring peace on earth!"

Hitler turned and addressed the men behind him. He said something that Noah couldn't make out, but by the looks on the men's faces, it probably wasn't good.

He turned back to the microphone. "This is not a trick. I am alive! Cameramen you will want to get a close-up of this."

The camera once again zoomed in closer to his face as he turned his head sideways and lifted the hair behind his right ear. A scar about the size of a quarter could be seen, however faintly. Noah knew it was the scar from Hitler's suicide bullet. Noah took a deep breath, as he felt his heart continue to race in his chest.

"I have been to the depths of hell and I know Who put me there. He is my enemy and He is yours, too. He intends to send all of you there. I have risen from the dead to bring this message to you.

"Now is the time to unite. We must if we are to defeat this Hebrew God! I have proven to you that I can lead the world to peace. You cannot deny this! I disguised myself so that you would readily follow and now that you trust me, it is time for you to know who you are truly following.

"Today I stand before you, in this Hebrew God's place of worship, to give you a choice. Follow me and live. Or follow Him and die! I am your only chance for salvation. I alone have the power to save you! I have power beyond your wildest imagination! And I will join with you to use this power against a God who thinks He has the final word.

"He has prepared a home of torment for all of you. The isolation is unbearable! The pain! The loss! The sorrow and regret! I cannot possibly describe how horrific hell is! What kind of God destines man to that kind of suffering? He wants man to worship Him but He only offers an eternity of torment and pain. I have been there. I have not only seen it but I have felt it. I have lived through it and was saved from it. I was pulled from the depths and offered a plan to save mankind. The very power which raised me from the dead is available to you. My lord and master is Lucifer, and through me he is offering you salvation from this destiny."

Hitler paused. He looked around the room. In general the audience was quiet but Noah could detect a slight murmuring.

"You do not believe me? Then I will show you. Prime Minister Szabo, please join me in a demonstration!"

The camera backed away from Hitler again and Szabo walked toward Hitler and was met with an embrace. He raised his right hand in the traditional "Heil Hitler" salute. Noah's stomach turned.

A curtain hung behind the men on stage. Hitler stood next to Szabo and they turned to look at it. Noah knew what it was. It separated them from the Holy of Holies, where the priests had placed a new ark of the covenant. In history past, God's presence rested on the mercy seat which was in between two angels on the top of the ark. Noah had studied that as a high school student in his Sunday school class.

By now four other employees had gathered around Noah's computer screen and were drawn in to the announcement.

"What's going on?" one asked.

"Just watch," stammered Noah, not wanting to miss a detail.

"Is that . . . is this a joke?" another exclaimed, as she pointed at Hitler.

"Shhhh," demanded Noah. "I'll tell you when this is done . . ."

Szabo faced the curtain. He opened his arms and said, "Oh, father, now is the time to show your strength! Send fire from heaven and reveal to us your might!"

The cameraman struggled to capture the scene. A pillar of fire appeared to be shooting from the ceiling down to the floor in front of the curtain. Quickly the curtain caught on fire and disintegrated. Then the fire retreated through the roof, as best Noah could tell. There, exposed in front of the whole world was the ark of the covenant.

There was more dialogue but the microphones didn't pick it up. Hitler and Szabo lifted their hands and pointed their fingertips at the ark. Their backs were to the cameraman, and apparently they didn't have other angles so it was hard to see on TV. Streams of fire flew from their hands at the same time. The fire sped past the other leaders, who scattered to the ground to avoid being hit. The fire hit the ark and began to melt the golden angels. Its heat melted them down in a matter of seconds and then the fire stopped. There was movement but Noah couldn't make out what was happening until Hitler and Szabo turned and revealed a twelve-foot statue of Hitler himself. Somehow the gold had formed itself into an idol.

Noah put his hand to his mouth. Nausea was overwhelming him. The others at his cubicle were still wondering out loud if this was a hoax, but he knew the truth. Adolph Hitler turned back to the camera. He walked over to the microphone and stood triumphantly, as if he had just won a battle. Noah's throat tightened as he began to process all he was seeing. It wasn't nausea. Instead hatred was welling up inside of him—an emotion he had never felt so strongly before.

"Thank you for your help, my friend. Make no mistake—my power comes from Lucifer himself, the Morning Star that fell from heaven and will now save us from the Hebrew God's plan to destroy us all!

"Today I call on the world to take a stand. If you are with me, you will join forces with the greatest alliance in the history of the world. Together we will defeat this God, but if you stand with Him, we will be forced to remove you from our midst. There is no room on this earth for intolerant, insolent, Jew-loving enemies of the FWP. We will rid the world of our Enemy's people. When we do that, we will have complete reign and His plan to destroy us will be defeated! Our only hope is to kill them all.

"So decide. If you stand with me, you will do two simple things. First, you will place my number on your forehead. Six hundred sixty-six—the number of months I spent in torment before Lucifer rescued me. Six hundred and sixty-six reasons I will fight this battle to my death. I will never go back there.

"Second, you will build an idol for your home and your town squares to remind you of whom you worship. This idol can be constructed with whatever you have in your homes, but it must bear my image, my face. That is how everyone will know you are worshiping a new leader.

"These two simple things will show your alliance and will afford all the benefits the Federation can offer—full banking privileges, unrestricted travel, higher education and investment opportunities. If you are found without a mark or an idol all will know that you are an enemy of the Federation of World Powers and there is only one fate for you. Death.

"How will I enforce this, you ask? Let me give you a demonstration. Prime Minister Rabin, come join me a moment."

"Don't do it," Noah spoke to the screen as Rabin cautiously approached Hitler.

"Are you a member of the FWP?"

"No, my country is not."

"Will you take my mark?"

Rabin leaned in and answered Hitler. Noah couldn't make out what he had said to Hitler but it had an effect.

"Say it for all the world to hear," Hitler said, as he shoved Rabin toward the microphone.

"I will not take your mark."

Once again there was movement off camera and a loud scream was heard. It was more of a screech. Rabin and Hitler looked at the ceiling. Suddenly the creature that made the noise appeared on the screen. He had wings and was hunched over, complete with arms and legs and glowing orange eyes. He had no clothes on, but didn't appear to be a human. He looked more like a hairless gray monkey. The noise he made was not a painful screech but one of laughter. He was grinning at Rabin and was suspended in the air at eye level with him.

His shape began to change and he turned from an animal-like form into a spear. The end of the spear was glowing red, as if it were a branding iron. In one swift movement, the demon thrust its tip through the heart of Prime Minister Rabin. Rabin grabbed hold of the spear and fell to his knees. In a moment's time, the spear pulled itself through to the other side of Rabin and the demon reappeared as Rabin fell dead to the floor. Then it flew off screen and there was a moment of silence.

And then chaos broke loose. The cameraman tried to get a shot of the roof and the room. Apparently hundreds, maybe even thousands of the demons flew into the room from a hole in the ceiling. They swirled around and through the crowd and between the screams of the audience and the shrieks of the demons, the noise coming from the screen was indescribable. So loud, in fact, that Noah went to turn it down but someone stopped him.

After a few minutes of mayhem, the demons left and Hitler was left on stage next to Rabin's dead body. The other members of the FWP had left the stage area, but Noah didn't know where they had gone. Hitler was looking down at the body and wiping his brow with a handkerchief. He looked up at the camera and continued.

"He belongs to a nation which is not part of the FWP. My power still reaches him. I am speaking now to all world leaders. Sign on with me in the next forty-eight hours, or I will ask my aides to persuade you. No mark means alliance with the Enemy. I will give the rest of the world two months from today to comply."

A smile spread across his face.

"If you join me, you will have a life of freedom and supply. Everything you ever wanted. There will be food for all, jobs for all, and peace on earth. As soon as we rid the world of our enemy, we will live in peace. In sixty days, we will know exactly who that enemy is."

With that final statement, the camera was turned off and temporarily the screen went black. Noah stared at the screen and then looked up at his coworkers.

"What in the world was that? Was that live?" one asked.

"My friend called and said there was a big announcement, so I turned it on and you pretty much saw what I saw . . ."

CNN had thrown in a commercial break as they tried to regroup and reconnect with their reporters in Israel. Noah's coworkers all headed back to their desks to call friends and surf the net for more information. Noah reached for his phone just as it rang. He flipped it open, knowing it would be Charlie.

"Did you see it?"

"This is incredible, Charlie. I mean unbelievable. I don't even know . . ."

"I talked to Dave and we're all heading over there after work. Are you in?"

"I just can't believe this is happening."

"Believe it, Noah. I've got to make a few calls but I'll pick you up at six—okay?"

"Yeah, great. Thanks."

Noah flipped his phone closed and looked around his office. He didn't know how long he could stay at this job but he did a quick inventory in his head of those he had talked to and those he had missed. Then it hit him—Tara. Did she see it? Does she have a clue about what is about to happen? Noah picked up his work phone and dialed her extension.

"This is Tara Warners' phone. I'm either on another line or not at my desk at the moment. Please leave a detailed message and I will return your call as soon as I can. Have a great day!"

After the beep, Noah started, "Tara, I need to speak with you. Call me at my desk when you have a moment. It's urgent. Bye."

After he hung up his phone, he remembered that Tara was at her mother's for a long weekend. He left the same message on her cell and prayed she would get it soon.

The noise level in the office was rising, as the employees pulled up the announcement and watched it over and over. CNN, MSNBC, FOXNEWS and all the network stations were interviewing their onsite reporters. Word was, for all intents and purposes, this was a real event. There were no tricks and no actors—the eyewitnesses vividly described the demons, the murder of Rabin, and the supernatural appearance of Hitler. Some even reported when he left the building that the crowd inside the temple bowed and cried out "Long live Hitler!" out of fear they would be killed.

Noah sat at his desk, wondering what to do next. His mind was reeling with the consequences of what he had just witnessed. He had prepared for this as best he could, but never really imagined it would happen the way it did. On live TV, Adolph Hitler just desecrated the temple in Jerusalem and demanded the worship of the world, exactly how Daniel predicted the abomination of desolation would.

Unbelievable.

Then the second wave hit him. The tribulation that would start two months from today, if they really had two months, would be the most incredible persecution the world had ever seen. And it was going to be swift and thorough. Everything he had worked for, his house, his savings account, his portfolio—all of it was worthless now. Now, he just had to survive.

And convince Tara to survive with him.

Wayne Durbin looked up from his desk. Thomas Larson was bounding in the door like a man on a mission.

"You've obviously seen it," he started.

Durbin pointed to the phone on his ear and held up one finger. It would only take a minute more to finish the call.

"Completely verified. You're sure about that? Yep, thanks."

Durbin hung up the phone and told Thomas to take a seat.

"What in the world is going on?" Thomas sat on the edge of his chair.

"The official word from Washington is that this is the real deal."

"It's really Hitler? Come on, is this a joke? And the number 666—who does he think he is? Doesn't he realize that would be offensive to Christians?"

"If it's really Hitler, who knows what he's thinking."

"If it's really Hitler, we had better drop a bomb on his head and do it quick! He's already killed the Prime Minister of Israel in front of the whole world!"

"I hear you, but have you forgotten he had some help? I don't know what they were, but those little imp things seem to be at his beck and call."

"Well, this is absolutely unbelievable. I mean really—I can't—I won't believe it. It's ridiculous. I can't believe we're even talking about it."

"You saw it with your own eyes, Thomas. But calm down a minute and think this through with me. As Magorum, he accomplished incredible things. The humanitarian aid alone to Africa has saved millions of lives. Look at his peace initiatives. Even this unified currency act—the benefits of joining the FWP are unlimited."

"What are you saying? He's a changed man? We should follow him? I can't believe you would even"—

"Quit focusing on the man and look at his actions. Obviously he had to hide his identity or no one would have ever elected him in the first place. But he's had twenty years of peaceful and successful service in Europe and the Middle East, and his actions prove he's not the same man anymore!"

Thomas took to his feet. "What are you talking about? He wants everyone to tattoo a number on their bodies and build idols to worship him. That sounds like the same man to me!"

"So he's a little power hungry. He has come through with every promise he's made, so why shouldn't we trust him?"

"Rabin sure didn't get a good deal."

"They had a past—and in front of the whole world Rabin turned on him. Considering everything Mag . . . I mean Hitler, has done for Israel, what kind of man would oppose him on international television? That man was a spineless loser anyway. You watch—Israel will be the first to sign up because they can see a good thing from a mile off."

"And what are we going to do? This guy was our enemy. Back in World War II he tried to get Mexico and Canada to turn against us. We're not going to sit by and let him get away with this? He slaughtered millions, you haven't forgotten that?"

To Durbin, this all made perfect sense. He couldn't figure out why Thomas was so worked up.

"We were prepared to sign the FWP treaty next month and I'll bet we move up the date. By tomorrow, our leaders will have their mark and their idols in place. Listen, this is much more than a man with a past we're dealing with. He's got quite a convincing army and as best as I can assess the situation, all we have to do is align with him and we get all the benefits in the world. It's really not that hard of a decision."

Durbin watched Thomas take a step back from his desk. "I can't believe you are taking this in stride. Wayne, wake up and smell the coffee! This man is insane. I can't believe we're even talking about him like this is real."

"We need this alliance, Thomas. This could be a huge break for Creston. There are unlimited research funds just waiting to be tapped and I for one want to be one of the first to apply for them!" Durbin leaned back in his chair and put a little more distance between himself and Thomas.

"Do you only see dollar signs here? Are you really missing the big picture?"

"You're the one who's missing the big picture. This alliance is our ticket to prosperity in this country. It's not just Creston—it's the whole country. We're not going to have a choice, Thomas, so you may as well just get used to it."

"It seems to me we all have a choice. I just can't believe you would choose so quickly to jump on board with a dictator who's proven to be the worst killer in the history of mankind."

"He's proven to be a peacemaker. You of all people should know how to forgive past sins and give someone a second chance."

"Don't try to turn this on me. I'm telling you right now, Wayne. I am not taking that number and there won't be any idol in my house!"

"Oh, come on, Thomas. You're making a bigger deal out of this than it needs to be. Go home and sleep on it. See what Washington says about it tomorrow. It's not worth getting this upset over nothing."

Durbin stood and extended his hand to Thomas. He took it without looking Durbin in the eye, then turned and left.

Wayne Durbin watched from his window as Thomas got in his car and pulled out of the parking lot. It concerned him that his friend reacted so violently and he decided he had better work on a statement for his own people. First he would put another call in to Governor Slate and then he would meet with his staff. It was going to be a late night. It was probably a good thing now that Thomas didn't work for him.

His intercom buzzed and the voice of his secretary said, "Mayor, I have your wife on line one. Do you want to speak to her?"

Durbin sighed and shook his head. "Sure. Put her through."

eleven

The ride to Dave's house flew by while Noah shared with Charlie the reactions of those around him when Hitler was revealed. By the time they got to Dave's, there were already several cars in his driveway and more parked on the street. It looked like all seventeen of the fellowship members were present, and when Noah walked through the front door the buzz of discussion was deafening. Noah met eyes with Dave and he motioned with his hand for Noah and Charlie to join him in the kitchen.

"How're you two doing?" Dave asked as he handed both of them a soft drink.

"Shocked," answered Charlie. "That's all I can say. It's shocking . . . shocking."

"One hundred ninety-nine . . . two hundred! His last two 'shockings' pushed the total to two hundred since he picked me up," teased Noah. "I think it's safe to say, Charlie's in shock."

Dave patted Charlie on the shoulder and they joined the rest of the fellowship in the living room. Noah sat down and waited for Dave to get things going.

"I have very mixed emotions tonight," he began as he stood before the fellowship. "I don't know if we should be rejoicing or mourning.

I am somewhat in awe of the fact that we have been called to experience this time. There is a lot of emotion flowing through this room, through the church, and through the world in general. So my goal is not to go long tonight. Those of you with families need to be home with them. I'll try to be brief and to the point."

Noah could hear his pulse beat in his ears and tried to mentally coerce his anxious heart to settle down. He was sure he wasn't alone, as the whole room seemed to hang on Dave's every word.

"Before we get to our plans, I want to share with you some possible responses by believers to what we have witnessed today. Some will completely discount the reality of the situation until it's too late. They will say it was a Hollywood-style stunt and they will do nothing to prepare for the coming persecution."

Dave walked over to his fireplace and threw another log on the burning fire. "Others will say that Israel may be in for a bad time, but we in America are too far removed. And still others will refuse to believe this is the beginning of the end. They will be confused why the rapture hasn't happened and they may turn from their faith. I'm not even talking about the world, yet. But you must understand this— today the death warrant of the church was just presented to the world and in two months it will be signed and served. We have two months and then we disappear."

Still silence. The burden of understanding and responsibility fell upon the shoulders of the seventeen men in the room. Noah thought of his mother and his sister. Would they listen to him now? Would they come? His eyes fell to the floor as he envisioned that conversation and he hoped with all his heart they would hear him out. Dave's voice pulled him away from his thoughts.

"We need an accurate list of occupants and final supplies. I don't know if ordering more MREs is a good idea now because that might draw attention to us, but a few of us can hit the military supply stores in larger outlying cities and buy their stock, if there is any left. We have a hefty supply already, but after the demonic display in the temple, we may have more than two hundred of us hiding."

"I'll take the names for the occupancy list," volunteered Todd Lothamer, who was sitting to Noah's left. "When do you want people to move in?"

"I think we can start the move one month from today. The compound needs to be accessed by the tunnel system so be sure to give good directions and most of you should accompany the residents. We have to limit the above ground activity to avoid suspicion. We will also need to assign men to run the tunnels for supplies and security. Some of you are in better shape than others, and that may be your role. I also would like to have a meeting with any of the wives who are coming. Though most of them have been in the compound already, I think another look, I guess a more realistic look at this point couldn't hurt."

Noah listened as the married men finalized a time for their wives to go to the compound. He wondered if Tara had tried to call him during the meeting. He still hadn't talked with her yet and he pulled his cell out of his back pocket and looked for messages. Nothing. This was starting to worry him.

"What do we do with our houses . . . our cars?" asked one of the married men.

"They're not much good to us anymore," answered Charlie. "And they're not going to be worth much money either. What do you think, Dave? Do we just shut off the utilities and lock it up?"

"Well, anything that we could use at the compound should be brought over. Larger items will be easier to bring in through the stairs underneath the farmhouse, but we don't want to draw attention. Perhaps we could do some unpacking at night, in the dark, because our other option is to park at our tunnel entrances and no one is going to want to carry a couch through a tunnel." The group chuckled nervously at that one. "As for selling our goods to get cash, that will soon be useless. Once the new currency system is up and running, our dollars will be obsolete. And we won't be able to exchange them without the mark. Unless we work a deal where someone with a mark exchanges our cash, I doubt we'll be able to do it at all. And that doesn't seem too safe to me. The plan is to have our supplies complete and not need to purchase anything else. So I guess now is the time to sell and buy."

A thought came to Noah. "What about medicine? What if someone gets sick or comes with an existing condition?"

"Good question, Noah. Make sure the people who you bring get a couple years worth of their prescriptions. We have a good supply of over the counter meds already, and Andy's wife is going to run the infirmary, but individual daily meds will be up to each person. If or when we run out, we'll just have to hope the Lord comes quickly."

It wasn't meant to be a joke but for the second time that evening most of the men smiled.

"It's just shocking. I mean, imagine that," said Charlie, shaking his head as if in disbelief. "He's coming soon. This is so amazing. I mean . . . He really is. He's coming. Exactly like He said He would. This is all just . . . well . . ."

"We know, Charlie, it's shocking," answered Noah. Then the men did laugh.

Dave was still standing by the fireplace. He walked over to an empty chair next to Noah and sat down. As the men quieted again, all eyes stayed on Dave.

"I've got to tell you, I'm still back on the house question. Most of you have been with us for a couple of years now and you know that as a group we have committed to living debt-free lives for this very reason. For some of us, that was easy. For others, I've watched you hone your lifestyles down to the bare minimum to get rid of your debt. At this point, I don't like disappearing without clear accounts, so once our storage areas are full, any left over money should go to paying off your debt."

One of the men on Noah's left broke in. "Come on, Dave. Do you really think our debt is an issue now? We're three and a half years from the end of the world!"

Dave reached up and rubbed his forehead, as if he was still processing information. "I just think we need to be above reproach. We can't do anything to tarnish the name of Christ, so as best we can, we need to leave with a clean slate. If you owe on your house, the day you leave, take your mortgage papers, anything you have regarding the house and give it to the bank that holds your loan. Sign it over to them and go. Same with your car. You're not going to need it."

"Will that look suspicious? I thought we don't want to draw attention to ourselves when we leave."

Dave looked at Noah. "There's enough craziness going on in the world right now, I doubt anyone will put a tail on you. Just tell them you can't make any more payments, so you're giving them the house. As to drawing attention to ourselves," he turned back to the rest of the men, "we have to be careful now. Those who you have shared your beliefs with, go to them and see if they will come—family, friends— but be wary of strangers. Christ said in Matthew 24 that people are going to turn on each other pretty quickly here, and for the good of those we are hiding with, we have to be careful."

"That's a good point," said Charlie from across the room. "As obvious as we see this turn of events, there is still going to be a lot of denial out there. Be careful what you share and don't take anyone to the compound until they commit to staying. We know this group is trustworthy so let's keep it at that."

Dave added, "Our preparations are good, but even more important than our plans right now is the necessity to share Jesus with anyone and everyone we meet. Tell them that this is a prophesied, all out attack that won't end well for them if they take the mark. Our time is short and we have to be discerning. This doesn't change our message, though and right now more than ever it needs to be shared.

But the time is quickly running out. Once a mark is taken, there is no turning back."

For the first time that day, Noah began to feel uneasy. Oh, he had run the gamut of emotions during the day: anxious, nervous, shocked, angry, but not uneasy. What he was feeling was not unprepared, but uneasy. There was something unsettling about the tone of the conversation, and though he knew the persecution was going to be unbelievable, he had never thought that someone from within could possibly betray them.

Dave stood and walked into the kitchen, returning with a stack of papers in his hand. Noah jumped up, took them from Dave, and handed them out to the other men.

"Here's a list of supplies that we still need. It also has all our phone numbers on it so that we can be reached, as well as e-mail addresses. Strange that in a few months, they'll be obsolete. I'm going to try to prepay a couple of years on the phone service we get out at the farm, so that possibly we could get *Internet* for a while but I am worried about being traced. We'll have to think that through and make a decision later." He stopped a moment and glanced around the room. "I think we should talk to the Lord before I send you all out of here. Char, would you mind?"

Dave moved to the center of the room and got on his knees. Noah stood and the rest of the men followed suit and gathered around Dave, also on their knees. This was a tradition of the fellowship to end their nights in this position before the Lord. Noah made his way around the group and knelt by Charlie, resting a hand on his shoulder.

"Gracious Father, I don't even know how to enter Your presence tonight but on my knees. In humility, I praise You for our salvation and for Your Word. Without Your Son, we would all be lost. Lord, it is with a heavy heart that we come to You, knowing that the days are short before our faith will become sight. We are sober, not out of fear, but out of concern for what is about to befall the world, our town, and the church in general. Please use Your faithful servants in this hour of testing to spare the lives of Your children. Please open the ears and give understanding to our families and friends. Please stretch our supplies and give us enough room at the compound. Keep our tunnels open and our location a secret. We lay all our concerns at Your throne and worship You as the Author and Finisher of our faith. We love You, Lord, and we ask that You send Jesus quickly for Your children. It is in His precious name we pray, Father, Amen."

One by one the men left, and rather quietly, Noah thought to himself. When the time came for him to go, he shook Dave's hand and followed Charlie to the car.

"I'll talk to you tomorrow night," Dave called to Charlie from his open doorway.

Charlie stopped at his car door and looked back at the house. "It's going to go fast, Dave. I'm going to quit my job tomorrow. I think we have one or two catering events in the next two weeks that he may need me to work at, but then I will be done."

As Charlie spoke, Noah shook his head. He hadn't even thought about what to do with work. All he could think about was talking to Tara. He checked his cell again and was relieved to see her call back number in his recent calls. He would call her when he got home.

Noah and Charlie sat quietly in the car on the way home. Noah didn't even realize how quiet it was until Charlie spoke as he pulled into Noah's driveway.

"Mind racing?"

"No kidding," answered Noah. "There's a part of me that doubts things will get bad here. Is it possible that Christ was only telling the Jews to hide who were in Jerusalem during this time? I mean, come on . . . realistically, can Satan really pull something like this off in a worldwide setting?"

Charlie put the car in park, as Noah waited for an answer. "Jesus did say to go hide and He was addressing the disciples in Jerusalem.

But remember, Noah, He also said the whole world would see and be amazed at the appearing of this risen leader. He also said the Antichrist would demand the worship of the world, which is what we saw today, and He said that if He doesn't cut this time short, none of the elect would survive. It's a global event. Satan knows his time is short and he's not going to sit around and wait for man to respond. He's sending his legions to do his bidding. Nope, Jesus wasn't just talking to the Jews. He was warning us. Right here, right now."

"I just know my family is going to think I'm nuts."

"Even after what happened today?"

"I'm hoping seeing Hitler was a wake-up call."

"How can it not be? Honestly, I'm scared to death we're going to try to put two thousand people in a space for two hundred!"

Noah smiled and put a hand on Charlie's shoulder. "Don't worry—if that really happens, God will provide. I've got to call Tara." He opened the door and added, "Pray for me."

"I'll call you tomorrow."

Noah hurried into his house, hoping to finally connect with Tara. He flipped on the front hall light and hung his coat on the hook by the door. He would check his phone messages and then call her. Walking down the hallway he heard a noise behind him and turned. There was movement at the front door, then a knock. He glanced at his watch. It was nine fifteen. Thinking it was most likely Charlie, he walked back to the door and looked out the window. A man about Noah's height stood at the door, wearing a black jacket, jeans, and a baseball cap on his head that cast a shadow over his face. Noah cautiously opened the door.

"Can I help you?"

"Hi, Noah." The man raised his head a bit and extended his hand. Now Noah had a clear shot at his face, but still didn't recognize him. Surprised that this man knew his name, he hesitated before taking his hand.

"Do I know you?" Noah asked, trying to place the face.

The man locked eyes with Noah, and he couldn't turn away. His deep blue eyes fastened on to his own and Noah tried to pull his hand away, but the grip was too strong. Then he spoke.

"I know you, Noah. I have been with you for a long time."

Noah wanted to respond, but his voice wouldn't come.

"I have a message for you from Yahweh."

Noah's chest tightened. For some reason, he knew this man wasn't kidding around. Everything in Noah told him to listen and remember whatever came next. Unable to move his gaze, Noah watched as the blue hue in the man's eyes started to lighten, as if there were a deep glow behind his stare.

"The days have begun where great persecution has come upon the earth. Lines have been drawn and you have a choice. If you take the mark of the Antichrist, then you will spend eternity separated from Elohim. If you remain faithful, your reward in heaven will be great. Do you understand me?"

Noah nodded, still unable to form words. The glow in the messenger's eyes continued to pull Noah's eyes toward him.

"Yahweh knows your plans, Noah, and they are good. Be careful whom you trust, for brother will now turn against brother and friend against friend. Yahweh is with you."

The glow behind his eyes began to fade and the magnetic draw to this man released its hold on Noah. When Noah realized he could speak again, he swallowed hard and forced himself to talk.

"You're an angel."

The man smiled, raised his eyebrows and tilted his head as if to confirm his suspicions, but only spoke one word. Then he turned and walked away from Noah's front door. A few seconds later, the light from the porch no longer reached his form and the man disappeared into the night.

Noah walked back into the house and closed the door. He turned the lock and then leaned his back against the door. His breathing was steady and his heart was remarkably calm. He knew he had to call Tara, but he couldn't bring himself to move. He feared that the sound of his shoes on the hardwood floors would drown out the echo of the man's voice in his ears.

And he wanted to remember what he was told.

The word was a charge, a command, an instruction. The word was a call.

Noah closed his eyes and listened to the sound of the man's voice in his head one more time. He remembered the coolness of the night on his face. He saw the glow in his eyes. He heard the voice he would never forget. And then the word. Just one word.

Overcome.

Tara had taken a few days off of work to visit her mother who lived about an hour away in a suburb of Indianapolis. Her mother was recovering from a minor surgical procedure and though she protested, Tara wanted to be there to help her recover. She was able to move around easily and that morning, they had gone for a late breakfast at a small diner just a few blocks from her mother's home. After breakfast, they window shopped a bit and then headed back home so that her mother could rest.

"I think I'll lay down for a while, if that's okay with you," Sondra Warners told her daughter. "Some of my friends are going to stop by later for dessert."

Tara followed her mother into the house and dropped her keys into her purse as they walked into the kitchen.

"Sure, Mom. I need to check my e-mail and maybe get a little reading done."

"It's two thirty now. Don't let me sleep past four or I'll never get to sleep tonight." Her mother kissed Tara on the forehead and left the room. Tara heard her bedroom door close and she powered up her laptop and logged in. Her mailbox was full of junk mail, as usual, plus a couple of personal notes. But what caught her eye was an urgent message from Creston Bible Church. She clicked on the title and read the message.

"In light of the international events which transpired earlier today, Reverend Blackmore has agreed to hold a meeting tonight at the church. He cannot possibly handle all the phone calls that are coming into the church today, but feel free to e-mail him your questions. He will try his best to answer them tonight. We will meet at 8 p.m. in the sanctuary."

Tara went into the living room and picked up the remote. Her heart fluttered a bit as she imagined what could have possibly warranted an e-mail like that. Over the past few years terrorist activity had increased in America, with major bombs going off in New York, LA, and Dallas. America was still recovering from the loss of life and its sense of security. But the e-mail said "international events", which gave Tara a little relief, but not much. She quickly flipped through the stations until she found a news channel. She sat on the couch and turned the volume low so that it wouldn't wake her mother. The female news anchor read the script with two pictures in a small screen to the right of her head. One was a man Tara recognized but couldn't remember of which nation he was the president and the other was Adolph Hitler.

". . . waiting for statements from several government officials, but every eyewitness so far is verifying the authenticity of the event. In response to the announcement today, the Federation of World Powers posted this statement on their Web site: 'We completely and unanimously stand behind the statements made by Adolph Hitler today, and urge the nations of the world to unite with us to bring peace and prosperity to the world. This is not a time for divisiveness; this is a time for unity. The One World Denomination system is designed to do as promised—to make trade simpler, to make travel easier, and to provide stability to regions of the world which need our help. Joining us is not an option—it is a privilege that should not be taken for granted. We have given our full allegiance to Adolph Hitler and urge the leaders of the world to comply with his request within forty-eight hours. Once the leaders respond, their citizens, we believe, will follow suit.'"

The anchor paused a moment as the camera pulled back from its focus on her alone, revealing several others sitting at the anchor desk. She then continued as if on cue.

"We're going to break for a moment and when we return we will analyze the international response to the resurrection of Adolph Hitler and the specifics of his demands. Also, we will try to get the latest information coming out of Jerusalem and hear Israel's response to the death of Avi Rabin."

Tara furrowed her brow as she listened to the reports, station after station, which talked about Adolph Hitler, like he was alive and well. Finally, she found a channel which played the announcement in its entirety and suddenly everything came into focus. When she looked at her watch again, it was four fifteen and she jumped from the couch and went into her mother's room.

"Mom? It's after four."

Tara gently sat at the edge of her mother's bed and stroked her forehead. Her mother opened her eyes and yawned.

"Wow, I was really gone," she said.

"Mom, something has happened. You need to see this."

Her mother sat up. "What? What's wrong?"

"Don't be frightened, Mom, but something unbelievable has happened and you need to see this."

Tara turned on the television in her mother's bedroom and flipped on CNN. In the background, a muted version of the transformation of Magorum into Hitler was being played as the men on the screen analyzed the action.

"What is this?" Sondra asked her daughter.

Tara could feel her heart begin to race. She wasn't even sure she could accurately describe what she had just seen. "Alexander Magorum, the Russian president, had an announcement today about a new currency the FWP is putting in place. In the middle of the announcement, he did kind of a magic thing and turned himself into Adolph Hitler."

"What? What do you mean?"

"It's hard to explain, Mom, but just watch a bit. There," Tara pointed at the screen, "did you see that? There was some wind and people were screaming and then suddenly it was Hitler, or maybe a man who looks like Hitler, standing there. The news stations are saying it's really Magorum and not a body double, according to the eye witnesses at the announcement."

"What does he want? How does he explain this?"

"He claims that he is back from the dead and is going to lead the world into a time of peace and prosperity, that he is a new man and has a power behind him to unite the world. But Mom, he said that the God of the Jews is the enemy. He wants everyone to show their allegiance to him by marking their foreheads and building idols that look like him in their homes."

"Is he crazy? Who is going to do that?"

"Mom, he killed the president of Israel on live television."

"What? What do you mean? How?"

Again, Tara struggled with her description. "This demonlike thing came from the ceiling and turned into a spear and pierced him through. He's really dead, Mom."

Sondra Warners threw back the covers and swung her legs off the side of the bed. Tara stood as her mother walked around the bed and out the door.

"Where are you going, Mom?"

"I need a glass of water." She went to the kitchen sink and turned on the faucet. She took a glass from the cabinet over the dishwasher, filled it, drank it all, and turned back around to face her daughter.

"What does he want on the forehead?"

"Three sixes."

Sondra set down her glass in the sink and headed into the living room, where Tara had left the television on. "This has to be a joke. Who would actually follow Adolph Hitler? How can a man raise himself from the dead?"

"Mom, he wants all world leaders to be marked within the next forty-eight hours or he threatened to send demons to kill them. Then he wants the rest of the world to follow suit within two months."

"What is our president saying?" Sondra sat on the couch and Tara sat next to her.

"He hasn't made a formal statement yet, but Press Secretary Crevell says he will give us his statement as soon as he issues one. He also said that there is absolute mayhem in Israel right now."

"No kidding. The greatest murderer of the Jews has just returned from the dead. And he is the one who holds their peace in his hands, if I remember correctly. Didn't he get the Temple Mount back for them? This is all so strange."

"Yeah, he did. He acquired the rights from the Arabs for the Jews to build there." Tara turned her eyes from the television and looked at her mother. "Mom, could Hitler be the Antichrist?"

"No, because we won't be here when the Antichrist is revealed, but this could definitely be a precursor to his arrival."

"But I thought the Antichrist desecrates the temple and demands the worship of the world. That's what Hitler did today."

"It can't be him, Tara. Why would God leave us here for this? No, it must be a sign that Jesus is definitely coming soon."

"Noah and I have been studying the Scripture and he said something like this would happen."

Tara's mom reached for her hands and she willingly gave them to her. Her mother then patted them gently and said, "Tara, you know what the Bible says. We are not here during the final seven years, because we will not have to go through the wrath of God. Hold to what you know is true, dear. I don't care what Noah thinks, he's wrong because God won't let this happen until He takes us to heaven."

"But Mom, what about the 666? Isn't that a sign?"

"That's just a trick to scare people. Everyone knows the prophetic implications of that number and whoever this character is, he is trying to rile everyone up. He has to be insane to think Americans will mark their foreheads and build idols, let alone the rest of the world. I wouldn't be surprised if he hasn't already been arrested for killing Rabin."

"Mom, he hasn't been arrested. People are frightened by what they saw. And the FWP came out with a statement in full support of Hitler."

Tara sat quietly and turned up the volume on the television. Within an hour, her mother heard everything Tara had explained to her. The two sat watching as the sun set outside and the room darkened. Finally Tara stood.

"Mom, there is a meeting at my church tonight. My pastor is going to answer questions about this whole thing. I got an e-mail this afternoon. I think I'm going to drive back for it. Will you be all right if I go?"

"Sure, dear, but you'll miss my friends," her mother replied, tilting her head as if to ask her to change her mind. Tara really didn't want to miss this meeting, so she waited and hoped her mom wouldn't lay on a guilt trip. "Oh, well, fine then. Drive safely and let me know what he says." She reached again for Tara's hands, and Tara thought her mother's fingers were chilly. "If I don't see you before the rapture, I'll see you in heaven." There was a peace in her mother's eyes and Tara knew her mother wasn't joking.

She threw her arms around her mother's neck and hugged her tightly. "Oh, Mom, do you really think that might happen?"

Returning the hug, her mother answered, "Yes, the rapture is right around the corner. Don't be afraid, but be excited. God's Word is true and He loves His children. He's coming for us soon."

Tara gathered her clothes and gave her mother one last hug before leaving the house. A part of her wanted to pack her mother up, too, and take her along, but she knew that was overreacting. The thought of the rapture was so exciting that Tara left her mother's house with a smile on her face and hope in her heart. She tried to call Noah on his cell but it went straight to his voice mail. She called his home phone with the same results. After the beep, Tara left her message. "Hi, Noah. I see on my phone that you've been trying to call me. I am heading back to Creston tonight. There's a meeting at eight at my church. I really can't believe this is happening—it's so exciting! I will call you in the morning, okay? Bye."

She flipped her phone shut and took a deep breath. What a crazy day, she thought to herself as she merged onto the highway.

The rapture could happen at any moment, I'm leaving my mother at her house, I can't get ahold of Noah, and I'm running late for the meeting. What could happen next?

Then a thought occurred to her and Tara looked up at the clear, starry sky.

Didn't Noah say something about the stars and Jesus' return?

With one eye on the sky and one on the road, she increased her speed and prayed that the highway patrolmen had other things on their minds tonight.

twelve

March

Noah lay in his bed until the clock read 6:03. He had been awake for an hour and finally decided it was time to give up on sleep and get showered. Before he went to bed he had made a list of everyone he needed to talk with and added to it periodically through the night. He would start with a seven o'clock call to his mother and then plan to knock on Tara's door by eight. Technically she was still on vacation and he would call in and take the day off. Though tax season was in full bloom, he could get away for a day without too much trouble, and he would be quitting soon anyway.

The incredible transformation of Magorum was still the talk of the news shows and overnight the president and vice president, as well as congress, came out with statements in support of joining the FWP and marking up. Noah shook his head in disbelief as he poured himself a cup of coffee and watched CNN in his kitchen.

He glanced down at his watch. 6:37. He knew this was going to be a long day. Then he heard the sound of a car pulling into his driveway and the engine shut off. He made his way down his front hall to the door, glancing out the window in the living room. Tara got out of her car and headed up the sidewalk to his front door. They reached it at the same time and before she could knock, he had it open.

"Good morning! I didn't know you could get up before ten on vacation." Noah stepped back as Tara stepped into his foyer.

"Ten. Yeah right. I'm just glad you're up and going." She unzipped her jacket and took it off, handing it to Noah. As he hung it in the front hall closet he said, "Come on, I've got coffee in the kitchen."

"Noah, is this really happening?" She grabbed his arm and he stopped and turned to look at her. Her eyes were bloodshot and she had dark circles under them. She looked exhausted and Noah took both of her hands in his.

"Did you sleep last night?"

"Barely. You?"

"The same. You just look so tired. And yes, this is really happening."

Despite her upbeat message on his answering machine, Tara's eyes now communicated fear and Noah pulled her to himself and wrapped his arms around her. She returned the embrace and they stood quietly in the hallway, just outside of the kitchen. Noah could hear CNN's anchor droning on, the word "Hitler" interspersed throughout his commentary. The moment was surreal.

Noah pulled away and led Tara into the kitchen. She sat at the table as he poured her a cup of coffee.

"What did they say at your church last night?" He handed the cup to her and went to the fridge for creamer.

"It's good black," she said. "There were a lot of people there and a whole lot more confusion. No matter what Reverend Blackmore said, people would call out more questions or comments and it wasn't very organized."

"Did he tell your congregation not to take Hitler's mark?"

"Yes, he did say that."

Noah breathed out a sigh of relief. "That's really important, Tara. I'm glad he said that."

"He said the church leaders needed more time to figure out just exactly what to do. Most of them feel that things in Israel are going to get pretty bad, but they all agree it is just a matter of time—maybe even just days—before Jesus' return."

Noah reached up and scratched his head. He wanted to be careful with his words and his tone. "Why do they think that?"

"Well, Reverend Blackmore said that he had always been taught, and truly believed himself, that Christians would not be around to see what we saw yesterday, but since yesterday seems to be the fulfillment of Daniel's prophecy, we must be at the half way point of the tribulation. He is still confident that we aren't going to go through the wrath of God so the rapture is probably going to be a midtrib rapture. Since Hitler put a date on the time to get a mark and an idol in your home—May fifteen—then we're going to be gone by then."

Noah thought Tara's tired eyes searched for agreement, but he couldn't agree with something he knew wasn't true.

"He is right about the wrath of God. We looked at that together. Do you remember?" Tara nodded and Noah carefully continued.

"But before God's wrath comes, Tara, the Antichrist is going to bring a terrible persecution upon the world. I think that starts on the fifteenth. And I'm pretty sure we're still here for that. Christ told his disciples to hide when the Antichrist begins this persecution, and I think that's what we should do."

"In your bunker?" Noah didn't detect sarcasm. She was sincere.

"Yes, I prefer to call it a compound, but yeah, in my bunker."

Tara stood and walked to the window above the kitchen sink. As she looked out across his backyard, Noah wondered what she was thinking so he asked.

"This is just all so unbelievable," she started. "I have a million questions running through my mind. What about my job? My mother? My church?" She turned from the window and looked at Noah. "How much room is there in the compound? How long will we be down there? What do I bring? Is it really going to get bad here? It may not be a big deal here in Creston."

"I understand how you feel, Tara. I hope it isn't a big deal here, but Satan has a very short timeline to kill believers before the return of Christ. I doubt he's just going to focus on the Middle East and leave whole continents alone. Christ said to hide and I think we have to obey."

Tara walked back to the table and picked up her empty cup. "I just don't know that I have the same kind of faith you do, Noah. It just seems so drastic to just up and disappear. And there are so many good people here. What about them?" She went back to the sink and rinsed out the cup.

"We can only do so much, Tara. But everyone has a couple of months here to figure something out. To wake up and be overcomers."

As if on cue, the phone rang. Noah got up from the kitchen table and answered it.

"Hey, it's Charlie. Did you ever get ahold of Tara?"

"She's here right now. Can I call you back?"

"I'm having lunch with a friend from high school but I'll touch base with you this afternoon. One quick question?"

"Go ahead." Noah watched as Tara walked out of the kitchen.

"When are you quitting your job?"

"I haven't decided yet but I want to liquidate as much cash as I can for supplies right now and I was thinking of trying to sell my house for, say, half price for extra cash. Listen, I've got to go. We'll talk later, okay?"

"All right."

Noah hung up the phone and went into the hall. Tara had put her coat on and was waiting by the door.

"Are you going to be all right?" He reached up and tucked one of her curls behind her ear.

"Yeah, I really think I need to sleep. I am going back to my mom's and I'll be home on Sunday. Let's have dinner Sunday night."

"Call me when you get back into town." Noah leaned forward and awkwardly gave her a kiss on the cheek. That made her smile, the first one he had seen all morning.

"The timing really stinks, doesn't it?" She paused, still smiling. "A part of me just wants to run off and hide with you, but another part doesn't believe this is really happening."

"I know. But I'm here and I'm going to help you through this. You're not alone. I know this is frightening, but God hasn't abandoned us, He'll help us through this."

Tara's tired eyes asked for a kiss, a real one, and Noah obliged.

As he shut the door of his house, Noah agreed with Tara.

The timing really did stink.

Every question was answered in one fell swoop. Every detail fell into place. In one whirling, swirling motion, that merely took but a few seconds, her whole life changed.

And for the better.

Elise had been in the temple when her boss became the first man ever resurrected from the dead to lead the world in unity and peace. He had made sure she was near the front of the crowd. Women around her fainted and men fell to their knees. But Elise just stood and watched. As he exited the temple, he stopped and locked his eyes on hers. She could feel her heart race and her knees weaken, but not from fear. There was a power in the room flowing from this man like she had never felt before. She returned his stare and curled up the corners of her mouth. He nodded and moved on. And it was at that moment she understood.

She knew he was meant for something more. She knew he had a drive and passion from a deep, hidden source. The vision he shared with her had been his past, and now she understood that a man who had been to hell and back had the motivation to accomplish the goal set before him. He had no intention of returning there.

Elise sat on a bench in the lobby of her hotel the morning after the announcement. A limo was scheduled to pick her up and take her to the airport at 6 a.m. A growing contingency of press and cameras were gathering outside the hotel. Elise could hear the muffled sounds of reporters lobbying for good positions outside the hotel doors. Extra security had been brought in to handle the mayhem. She wasn't even sure if her boss had stayed at the same hotel last night, but apparently the press thought he had. She glanced across the lobby. A man with a concierge tag was talking with Agent Vasiliev at the front desk. Vasiliev was in his travel clothes, complete with a belted black trench coat and a matching wool felt hat. Elise thought the hat accentuated his square jawline and made him look a lot meaner than he probably was. They didn't speak much, but maybe someday . . .

One other guest was sitting on the other side of the lobby and he stood and started to walk over to her. She glanced back toward Vasiliev, who showed no concern that she was being approached by a stranger. The man was rather handsome, in casual dress, and didn't cause any alarms to go off in her mind so she returned his gentle smile with one of her own. He was definitely coming over to talk with her.

"Miss Orion?"

"Yes?"

"May I sit?"

"Certainly." She nodded to the space beside her, curious that he knew her name.

"May I get straight to the point? I know who you are and I must give you a warning." His eyes were troubled, and Elise began to feel uncomfortable. "Adolph Hitler has begun a war against Elohim and there are only two sides in this battle. Today you must choose which side you are on, one leads to life and the other leads to death."

Elise looked back behind her, over to the front desk where the concierge and Vasiliev continued their deep discussion, apparently unaware of her predicament.

"What do you mean?" she asked cautiously, yet politely.

"Elohim will not be defeated by this man. But sides are being drawn. If you take Hitler's mark you will align with Satan and spend eternity in hell, separated from Elohim."

"I . . . I don't understand," she began.

"Yes, you do. If you take the mark of Hitler, you side with Satan and your fate is secured. Don't take it, Miss Orion. I am a messenger from Elohim and you are facing a life and death decision."

"I am afraid you are delusional, sir. Herr Hitler is here to save the world."

The man stood. Elise felt a wave of relief at the thought of him leaving, but he had one final warning.

"Your eternity hangs in the balance, Elise. He knows your heart. It's not too late to follow Him, but once you're marked, it's over. Consider yourself warned."

He turned to walk away and Elise looked back over at Vasiliev. He was now approaching her with the concierge. She widened her eyes and tilted her head toward the man, but Vasiliev held his cold stare. She looked back at the man, but he was gone. She quickly scanned the lobby and he was nowhere in sight.

She stood and addressed Vasiliev.

"Did you see that? Where were you?"

"What are you talking about?"

"That man who was just here."

"What man? There was no one here with you."

"Agent Vasiliev, I expect you to be more alert. When I am being harassed, the least you could do is help me out."

Vasiliev didn't appear to appreciate being reprimanded and he set his jaw without answering her charge. The concierge held out an envelope to Elise and spoke.

"This is for you." He handed her the envelope and seemed to wait for her to read it.

She took it, saw her name handwritten on the front, and pulled the note out. She knew his handwriting and her heart fluttered a bit. She had been quickly ushered back to the hotel last night and wasn't sure what he had done, because there were no interviews or follow-up comments after his spectacular announcement.

Our flight has been delayed for the moment. Go with Vasiliev and he will explain what to do next.

She stared at the note a moment and pursed her lips in thought. It was a good thing she knew his scribble. She wondered why Hitler had taken the time to write her a note, when she was used to communicating with Agent Vasiliev, and he could have directly instructed her.

She lifted her eyes from the note and met Vasiliev's cold stare.

"Let's go," she said to him, slinging her attaché over her shoulder and extending the handle on her wheeled suitcase. *I wonder why he doesn't like me?*

The concierge took the bag from her. "Allow me." He slid the handle back into the case and picked up her bag.

She followed Vasiliev across the lobby and behind the front desk. They went through a series of doors and hallways without speaking a word. The longer they walked, the more curious she became, but she held her tongue and followed. After several minutes of hallways and silence, they arrived at their destination. Elise looked behind her and realized the concierge, as well as her suitcase, had disappeared at some point on the walk. She was a bit surprised she hadn't noticed sooner.

The hallway was poorly lit. They were in a service area, perhaps where deliveries were inventoried or where the hotel staff would take breaks. Agent Vasiliev knocked on the door and a voice from inside permitted entry. When the door opened, several security agents and staff members were standing around the perimeter of the room, with a few sitting on a worn-out couch. In one corner, there were two technicians, sitting at a table with tools of their trade spread out before them. Vasiliev finally spoke.

"Herr Hitler has instructed his staff to be marked this morning before we head back to Russia. It is important that we are united in his cause, and he will not be seen with unmarked staff members. Get in line."

Elise looked around the room and realized she was standing at the end of a tattooing line. Triple sixes were being applied indelibly on the foreheads of each person with remarkable speed and ease. With so much information to absorb from the night before, she had hardly thought about Hitler's instruction to wear his number. Now she had perhaps half an hour to consider it. However, it wasn't as if she really had a choice in the matter. Her thoughts went from irritation to complacency. On one hand, marking a woman's face was not a flippant decision one should have to make on a moment's notice. On the other hand, she had always believed that true leaders led by example, so why wouldn't he expect his staff to mark up on day one.

Seven minutes later Elise was resolved to receive her mark. Now she had approximately twenty-three minutes to decide how big, what color, and the appropriate placement of the mark. Thirteen minutes later, with those decisions made, she had ten minutes left to decide how to handle Vasiliev's unacceptable behavior. She may not be the Premiere of Russia, but she was his personal assistant and that fact alone demanded certain protections. How many demented religious fanatics would be allowed to approach her before one goes too far? She would discuss this directly with Hitler.

As she approached the technician's table, she tossed a resolute glare over at Agent Vasiliev. He returned the look but there was something about that handsome square jaw that made Elise reconsider what approach she would take. Still engaged in a stare, she gave him a half smile and batted her eyes a bit. She quickly turned her head, thinking it was better not to wait for a response from him.

"Don't worry, nobody's getting any marks on their foreheads. Give me a little credit." Thomas shook his head at the mere suggestion.

He sat across from Charlie at the local diner and watched as he took a bite out of his cheeseburger and reached for his Coke.

"It's not that I don't trust you. I just want to make sure you understand how serious this is."

"Well, you're not the first one to tell me that today. Before we were even up this morning there was a guy knocking on my front door. A perfect stranger telling me not to take the mark. You guys start early, don't you?" Thankfully, Thomas had answered the door, or he could only imagine what Robin would have said to him.

"He wasn't one of us, Thomas. And you hit the nail on the head when you called him perfect. That was an angel you met this morning."

"An angel? What in the world are you talking about?" Thomas dipped his onion ring in ketchup and took another bite.

"Most everyone I've talked to today has received the same message you did. Revelation tells us that God will send angels to tell the world not to take the mark of the beast or else you'll . . ."

". . . spend eternity separated from God." Thomas shook his head in agreement. "Yep, that was his message. And I'm supposed to believe he was an angel. How do you know all this?"

"I've tried to tell you, I've studied this for quite a while."

"Apparently you've read stuff I didn't even know was in there."

"Thomas," Charlie leaned in on his elbows, "two months from now all hell is going to break loose in the world. Things may seem pretty peaceful now—take my mark and live in peace. That's his message. But taking Hitler's mark is aligning with Satan. If you don't take his mark, you'll die. That's it—no two ways about it. You've got Robin and the girls to think about now. You won't be able to provide for them without a mark, so you'd better make plans right now for the changes you're going to experience in a few months." He leaned back in the booth. "My offer is still open. Come and hide with me. We've got food and shelter, but I would think that after yesterday the reservations are filling up."

Thomas's head started to pound again. It began last night and he thought he had it under control this morning. But when his father-in-law called, it started again as a dull ache at the base of his skull, then moved behind his eyes when Robin found out he was meeting Charlie for lunch. Now it was full-fledged throbbing, one step short of a migraine. He rested his head in his hands, his fingers pressing on his temples to relieve the pressure.

"I need time to process everything. I've got Robin's dad telling me not to do anything rash, like quit my job and disappear, and I've got you telling me to do exactly that."

"What does he think is happening?"

"He says one of two things is going on—either the rapture is right around the corner or this Hitler look-alike is trying to scare the world into submission by trying to make it appear like he's fulfilling prophecy. He did say not to worry about the mark or idol thing, that no one is going to really care here in America. And he said that he thinks this Hitler character is pretty insane to think the world will bow to him."

"Well, the world already is bowing to him. He has an army of demons to ensure that."

"Yeah, I think the demons are one of the facets in this that her dad can't explain."

"There's not a lot of time to think, Thomas. Personally, I wouldn't rely too much on your ability to think this one through. I would pull out my Bible and see what God says about it."

"I started to do that after you met with us but I've just been so busy . . ."

"Thomas, this isn't a mere coincidence. Life is going to change quickly here. Everything is in place for American banking to switch over to the One World Denomination system. As soon as that happens, without the mark you won't be able to access your money. Cash out now. Buy supplies, and come and hide. You don't have other options."

"I met with Durbin after the announcement. He thinks Hitler is the answer to the problems of the world. It's like he never took a World History class. How could anyone pledge allegiance to Hitler? It's absolutely outrageous!"

Charlie wiped his mouth on his napkin and dropped it on his plate. "The world has been overcome by a deluding spirit, and those without the Holy Spirit can't make sense out of it. But we can see clearly and we know this is the beginning of the end. Thomas, you've got to make a decision here."

"I know. Give me a few days. I've got to convince Robin that we need to act."

"Two months is not a long time."

"I know. Where exactly is this compound?"

"It's not far from town, but that really doesn't matter right now. What matters is that you have faith in what God says is going to happen and act on it."

Lunch was over and it was time to head back home. Thomas started his car after he watched Charlie pull out of the parking lot. The radio played a song Thomas probably knew but at this point he couldn't stand the noise. The pounding of the drums only magnified the pounding in his temples and he turned the radio off. He pulled out onto the street and headed home.

He noticed a long line of people standing on the sidewalk and wondered what was going on. His eyes followed the line to its abrupt end at a storefront in the middle of the block. A tattoo parlor.

"You have got to be kidding me," he said out loud. "Why do people have to overreact?"

The throbbing immediately morphed into an official migraine.

thirteen

March

Tara returned home again on Saturday instead of Sunday. Things were tense with her mother and she wasn't sleeping well. Her mother was convinced this would all blow over, despite the unending coverage and obsessive analysis on every talk show and news broadcast on air. By Saturday, most of the United States Congress as well as the President, his family, and, rumor had it, even their dog were now sporting tattoos. Tara was pretty sure that Rabin's dramatic death was the cause. But more than anything, she missed Noah. Though not completely convinced to run and hide, she felt safe when he was around and the constant coverage of the resurrection of Hitler was starting to wear on her nerves.

She had called Noah on the way home and asked if he would go to church with her the next morning. He agreed and on Sunday morning Noah picked her up. She was glad when she heard his car pull into her drive. That was the first positive event of the day. The second came when Tara and Noah walked into church. Knowing that her church's doctrine was more liberal than Noah's beliefs Tara cautiously looked around at her fellow congregants and then smiled. There was not a mark in sight. Granted, it had only been four days since the press conference, but already marks were showing up here and there.

As they walked into the foyer of the church, a young girl who was looking behind her as she ran, bumped into Noah's knees and fell to the ground.

"Are you all right?" Noah reached down and picked the girl up, setting her back on her feet. Tara saw her face as she looked up at him, and tears started to well in the little girl's eyes. "Don't cry. You have the prettiest green eyes."

With that the little girl smiled. Tara loved that Noah was gentle at heart.

"Do you see her parents?" Noah asked Tara, who started to look around. She spotted a man making his way toward them.

"That's probably her dad," she said, pointing in his direction. Tara knelt down and wiped a tear from the girl's cheek. "Are you hurt?"

"No, I just want my dad."

By then the man had reached them and he swooped the little girl into his arms. Turning to Noah and Tara, he said, "I'm sorry about that. Sometimes she gets away from me. Are you okay, Sarah?"

The little girl nodded.

"Do I know you?" Tara asked the man. "You look so familiar."

"I don't think we've met, but I've seen you over at Smith and Brumsby. Actually, I think I've seen both of you."

"We both work there," said Noah, extending a hand toward the man's empty one. "My name is Noah Greer, and this is Tara Warners. I work in accounting and she's up a couple of floors in personnel."

"Thomas Larson, acquisitions. It's a big firm, isn't it?" Thomas shook Noah's hand with a smile. "Actually, I think we may have a mutual friend. Charlie West? He told me his friend Noah worked at my firm. I mean, how many Noah's can there be?"

"Well, you've got the right guy! Charlie's a very good friend."

A petite blonde approached with identical green eyes to the little girl's, holding the hand of another daughter.

"This is my wife, Robin. And these are our daughters. You've already met Sarah," he pointed to the one he was holding, "and this is Christie. Robin, this is Noah and Tara. Noah is Charlie's friend who works over at Smith."

"Nice to meet you."

Tara smiled and shook her hand, but couldn't help notice a coolness about the wife.

"It's been quite a week, hasn't it?" Tara asked.

"No kidding," answered Thomas. "I was here Thursday night for Reverend Blackwell's meeting, but now that the dust has settled, it will be interesting to see what he has to say."

"We should get the girls to their classes, Thomas." Once again Tara noted the coolness in Robin's voice. "It's almost time for church to begin."

Suddenly, from across the foyer a small voice could be heard. "Mrs. Larson! Mrs. Larson!"

All four of them turned and a little, dark complected boy ran over to Robin, waving a piece of paper in his hand. Tara saw recognition on her face as Robin turned and said, more to her husband than to the others, "Oh, that's Isaiah Hamilton—the new boy I was telling you about." Then to Tara and Noah she added, "I teach fourth grade. He's one of my students."

The boy was out of breath by the time he reached Robin. She knelt down to speak with him.

"Good morning, Isaiah. I'm so glad to see you here at church."

Her demeanor had changed. Suddenly she was warm and kind.

"Mrs. Larson, I think I know who is trying to kill my cousin!"

Robin glanced around nervously and Tara looked at Noah.

"It's Hitler! Emma said the man would tell the world to worship him and that's what he did this week. I think Hitler wants to kill her because she won't worship him."

"Calm down, Isaiah. Where are your parents?"

"I have to go find them, but I brought this for you. It's one of her letters. It will help you understand."

Robin took the paper from his hand, and he turned and ran off. She stood, looking at the paper, which was covered with printed handwriting on both sides. The three other adults stood waiting for her to explain, and Tara instinctively cleared her throat. Robin looked up from the paper.

"Oh, I'm sorry. That was . . . just . . . a . . . well, it's just a child. He told me his parents think his cousin and her family are in a cult. Apparently they're hiding and he's worried about her."

"Hiding isn't such a bad idea right now," said Noah.

Tara looked at him, hoping he wouldn't start with complete strangers, but Thomas kept her from objecting.

"Charlie sure thinks so, too. You're part of the fellowship, right?"

Noah nodded.

"Charlie wants us to come, but we're just not sure about what's really going on."

"We really need to go," interrupted Robin. "It was nice meeting both of you."

She pulled on Thomas's arm and he added, "I'm sure I'll see you around the office." Then he was gone.

Tara turned to Noah. "That was strange. She had no interest in talking with us."

"My friend Charlie has told me about them. They're high school acquaintances of his. Apparently he's concerned and willing to consider hiding, but she'll have no talk of it."

"Well, we'd better get a seat. Church is filling up quickly."

They made their way into the sanctuary. As the congregation quieted down, the music began and Tara soon found herself struggling again. An anxiousness over the recent events was returning. As the songs were sung, Tara fought to focus on the words. When Reverend

Blackwell finally took the pulpit, she breathed a sigh of relief. Her favorite part of the service was the music, but today she just couldn't pay attention. There was too much at stake. She needed to be comforted by her pastor and though she knew it was selfish, she didn't have the strength to put her fears aside.

"We are living in difficult times," he began. "I must be honest with you, I don't like the things I am seeing. Over the past few days I have slept but a few hours and have fielded hundreds of phone calls and e-mails. Last night, I spent four hours with the pastors, priests, and leaders of the local churches here in Creston. We also invited Mayor Durbin to attend. The consensus is that we are heading into a time of international change which, unfortunately, will have direct impact on our daily lives here in Creston."

Tara reached over for Noah's hand and he readily took it. She looked at him, but he kept his eyes on Blackmore.

"Some feel we are in the last days. This is very confusing for me, as my understanding of the last days are very different from what I see going on today. But I was reminded that even the disciples were confused when Jesus was crucified, even though Jesus had clearly warned them of his purpose." Blackmore looked down at his notes, as if to find something he specifically wanted to share. "Perhaps the imam from the mosque on Ridder Street said it best, when he said, 'We cannot understand what is impossible to grasp. The will of God is exactly such a thing.' I don't know that we can fully understand what is happening, but we must walk in faith and press on."

Tara noticed some people near her nodding in agreement and she wondered if she was missing something. For the life of her, she couldn't figure out what Blackmore was saying. She squeezed Noah's hand and he glanced over at her. She raised her eyebrows and he nodded back toward Blackmore, as if to say, "Let me listen."

"I know you are looking for answers. The best answer I can find is that we need to keep our eyes on the heavens, for Jesus is coming soon." A few "amens" were called out from around the room. "But until that happens, I must encourage each and every one of you not to take this mark that Hitler has instructed the world to take. If you take the mark, you are buying into his system. I don't know if he is the Antichrist or not, but I am not playing a game and imprinting the number of Satan on my head."

A man from the back stood and called out, "But what about our money? I heard that we can't access our bank accounts without a mark!" A few more men called out in agreement. Tara was alarmed at the brazen manner in which the men yelled out their responses. This was still a church service and they should have been respectful of that.

"I understand. We have some time, though, to figure this out. In the meantime, stocking up on supplies in case we run into some problems probably isn't a bad idea."

"Supplies? For how long? How long until Jesus returns? We've got families to care for!" It was the same man who called out the first question. She was really getting annoyed with his tone, even though his questions were valid.

"I wish I had all the answers. I'm just not sure how much life will change here in Creston. Last night, Mayor Durbin listened to our concerns. At this point, the United States is on schedule to join the FWP and switch over to the One World Denomination system. It is unclear whether or not the mark will be associated with the banking system, but I know God is in control of this and will provide for us no matter what. We just have to wait a bit to see how this is all going to play out."

The question and answer format continued for another twenty minutes until Blackmore ended with a time of prayer. When it was all done, the people filed out of church rather quietly. Tara and Noah sat for a while in silence.

"He didn't really give any answers, did he?" Tara's heart sank. "I don't know what I was thinking he would say, but he really didn't say anything."

"He's unprepared, Tara. He had no idea something like this would happen. I am sure the counsel from other churches is even more liberal than what he is thinking. But Tara, this church is in big trouble if they don't come up with a plan. I agree God is in control and I think He was gracious to give people two months to prepare. But soon you'll be down to just weeks and counting."

"Noah, I just can't disappear. What about my mom?"

"Bring her along."

"I've asked and she thinks it's a ridiculous suggestion."

"And what happens to the two of you when you don't mark up?"

Tara shook her head. "I don't know."

"That's the problem, Tara. I do know. What did Hitler say? 'Follow me and live. Follow God and die.' He's not just talking, Tara, he's dead serious."

Tara could feel her chest tighten. Deep down she knew he was right, but it was such a rash decision to up and disappear. And she could never leave her mother. She was grateful for a couple of months to figure things out.

As Tara and Noah walked out of the church, the cold March air blew through Tara's open jacket, which she quickly zipped in response. Across the parking lot little Isaiah climbed into the backseat of his parents' car.

She wondered what was in that letter.

She wondered what his cousin knew that she didn't know.

Tara climbed into the passenger's seat and buckled her seat belt. She decided that if she ran into Thomas Larson at the office, she would ask about Isaiah's letter.

Mayor Wayne Durbin, on the other hand, was sleeping great. During the day, his mind raced with ideas and proposals, but at night he slept like a baby. Monday morning, bright and early, he drove to Indianapolis to the Indiana Government Center. Governor Slate had called a meeting of the 107 mayors in the great Hoosier state whose city populations were greater than 6,000 residents. The smaller town mayors would meet the following week, but Durbin knew all important decisions would be made by his group.

Actually, he had only been to one other meeting with these mayors, and they technically didn't make decisions. They listened and facilitated what Slate wanted them to do. Durbin had heard about the occasional mayor who had his sights on the governor's mansion and got too vocal for his own good. He was warned the mayoral conclave was not a wise environment to stump for future votes. Slate had been there for thirty years and he wasn't going anywhere soon.

Hitler's resurrection and demands would most definitely be discussed and Durbin was teeming with excitement. He was a student of Magorum, which now made him a Hitler fan by rote. Aside from the whole Holocaust debacle, Hitler had been a man who gave the people a voice. He was a powerful orator and had a remarkable track record of gaining the public's confidence. He just went overboard a bit. Durbin was sure he had learned from his mistakes—he even implied that in his revelation speech.

Durbin pulled into the Lincoln Street parking garage just down the street from the Government Center and quickly parked his car in the first available space. The meeting would start in the Conference Center at nine sharp, giving him some twenty minutes to find a seat and settle in. He recognized a couple of the mayors from a meeting a month and a half ago. None of them dreamed they would be meeting again so quickly.

Inside the Conference Center, Durbin was directed into the largest meeting room. It was set up as a lecture hall of sorts. Ascending tiers had tables and chairs set up all facing the front of the room where a single table with three chairs faced back toward the audience.

Durbin was pleased that individual microphones were in front of each seat, as well as nameplates, an empty legal pad, a bound notebook, a pen, and a cold bottle of water. Apparently they were going to be allowed to speak.

Durbin found his seat and settled in with the rest of the mayors as the digital clock at the front of the room changed to nine o'clock. There was a bit of excitement in the air, but not much conversation. Durbin didn't want to comment on last week's events and then find he was on the wrong side of the fence. Washing egg off your face wasn't as easy as it sounded.

At 9:04, Governor Slate entered the room and the mayors respectfully stood and applauded. Once seated again, Slate began the meeting.

"I appreciate you coming here on such short notice. I have spoken with many of you already and know your phones have been ringing off the hook, as have mine. The events of last week are of historic proportions that extend from Europe into our very own backyards. Today, your questions will be answered. Let me assure you, though many facets of this event were surprising by nature, this is a very well-thought-out, well-planned, and apparently well-executed program that has major world support."

Durbin glanced around the room. Slate had the mayors in the palm of his hand. No one moved, no one even touched his notebook.

"If you will open your notebook to page four, I want to start by reading the Federation of World Power's Consolidation Projection Statement, which was issued three years ago at a summit in Oslo, Norway. Yes, Norway. Though the big ten of the FWP is mostly eastern European and Middle Eastern, there are many nations who have been supporting the international movement of a one-world government and soon you will find that, as Americans, apparently we were not the last to know."

The forty-three page document laid out in generalizations the plan to form a united world. From leverage in the Middle East to opening the borders in North America, a system was set in place to make the world a much smaller place. Industry and trade regulations were standardized, benefiting both the service provider as well as the manufacturer. Medical co-ops were outlined, with the goal of bringing the greatest minds in the world together with the greatest equipment in the world. Research lab locations were determined, as well as health care provisions, with the goal of providing elite services at standardized costs. Everything was in this brief document: education, government, currency, manufacturing, trade, natural resource production, environmental care, as well as sustenance production.

That was the one that caught Durbin's eye. Granted, it was simply one paragraph long, but in those two hundred and thirty-seven words, Durbin found his niche. The FWP had high ambitions in every field, and Durbin was ready and willing to lead the way in milk development and production. Well, at least he could provide a great support system. But now he had to figure out how to tap into a system that had the same goal and focus as he did—to make the world a better place for all by working together.

After reading the short projection statement, Slate took a drink of water and looked up from his notebook.

"It is a very short proposal for a very lofty goal but it is not without years of discussion and planning. Turn to section B in your notebook and you will see the signatures and names of the men who have committed to this system over the past twenty years. World leaders, Americans included, have prepared for the day when the world would unite as one."

Durbin, with the rest of the room, flipped over to the signature page and scanned the hundreds of names.

"Now, let's talk about the elephant in the room. Hitler and his minions."

Durbin heard a collective "uh-huh" from the mayors, the first sound from them all morning.

"I'll be the first to admit, the sight of Adolph Hitler on the stage was alarming. Then came the . . . well, for lack of a better word . . . demons. I call them demons because Hitler himself does not claim to be from God. Instead, he is empowered by Satan and we all know Satan has demons at his disposal."

Durbin felt a bit uncomfortable with this part of the discussion, and though he was not a religious man, there really was no other explanation for the creatures that aided Hitler.

"The spiritual realm is no longer in question. It is a reality. And it is here to help us, not to battle against us. Look at the polls—before March fifteen, seventy-three percent of Americans believed in the spirit world and now it's one hundred percent. There is no denying its existence, since seeing is believing. And whether or not you are happy about this, in order to accomplish a one-world government, we need the help of the spirit world. Enter Hitler."

Durbin heard the mayors shift in their seats, but his own discomfort was diminishing. He knew where Slate was going and he completely agreed.

"In order to rule the world, one needs a unique set of skills. He needs to be a visionary. He needs to be charismatic and appealing. He also needs to have a firm grasp on reality and Adolph Hitler has been there. Even in his first life, his goals were right, he just communicated them improperly. It's not that he hated Jews, but the God of the Jews. Having now spent time in hell, he knows the wrath of a hateful God and has lived to tell about it. His true goal is to save mankind from God's wrath. And with the help of Satan, he will accomplish this."

At this point, Slate stood. He was wearing a wireless mike so he could be mobile. He walked from behind the table and stood before the room.

"As leaders of Indiana, the way you respond to this event will make all the difference for our state. We have been given huge incentives to get our cities on board with the new system. Wayne," Slate pointed to Durbin as he spoke, "the new equipment you have been drooling over for your dairy farms—it's all yours if you comply. Steve," again, pointing to another mayor, "that new bridge you've been asking for, it's a done deal if you comply."

Durbin felt the mood change a bit. He needed to know exactly what "comply" meant.

"As we speak, the Currency Act is being facilitated throughout America. The banks are receiving the new software and soon the dollar will be obsolete. On the federal level, chip implant systems are being delivered to banks, making it easy for your citizens to receive their identification numbers and account chips. But they will not receive anything until they get Hitler's mark. That's the cost. And it's a pretty cheap one, if you ask me.

"Once everyone in your town has taken Hitler's mark, the flood gates open and we quickly move into a whole new world. As mayors, you will be held accountable for your citizens. If your citizens don't mark up, then your city will not be able to access the funds for improvements. I know this seems a bit silly—does Hitler want us to mark up because he has a huge ego? The answer to that is no. It's so that we can see that we are all on the same team. It's like a soccer team. Everyone needs to be wearing the same color jersey, or else you don't know who to pass the ball to. The mark unites you with the mayor of Paris or the mayor of Barcelona—you belong to the same cause, the same purpose."

Slate turned back to the table and reached for his water. He took a drink and then, still holding the water in his hand, he continued.

"Give me just a few more minutes and then we'll take a break. After the break, I'll field questions. I know this is a huge responsibility as mayors of your cities. Rest assured, I am not leaving you alone. I spent the weekend with the heads of law enforcement, as well as the National Guard. We have decided to provide you with training facilities that will educate those in your town who refuse the mark. We believe with a proper understanding, everyone will want to be on the team. There are some brief schematics of our proposal behind tab C in your notebooks. Take a look at it and after the break we will discuss it further."

Monday turned into a very long day. Durbin had no need to be convinced of the process to get his citizens marked. He was well aware of the benefits and he also understood the terms were nonnegotiable. There were a few disgruntled mayors, however, who wanted to live in the past rather than look to the future. Eventually, Durbin knew if they didn't buy into the system, they would be replaced. The United States as a whole, let alone the world, was moving in a direction that would not be stopped. Either get on the train, or go to a training camp.

As the hours passed, Durbin grew weary of the discussion and decided it was born-again believers who were going to be his greatest obstacle. The four most outspoken mayors all claimed to be just that and every concern they voiced he had heard the other night at the religious forum he attended or from his buddy, Thomas Larson. So, to make the time pass more quickly, Durbin began to sketch out a plan for dealing with the Christians. He would have to get the Christian support in town—get a big name to mark up first and then the rest would follow suit. After all, Christians like the sheep analogy.

Durbin scratched a list of names that would help his cause, Reverend Blackmore and Thomas in the first and second place. The first would probably be a lot easier than the second. But in the end, Durbin knew it was in his power to make this happen. With a safety net in place, worst-case scenario would be putting the good old reverend on the first bus out of town to teach his congregation a lesson. And Wayne Durbin was willing to do just about anything for his little town of Creston.

fourteen

Late April

Three weeks after Hitler's announcement Charlie West quit his job with Chef Fredo and started working full time to fill the compound with supplies. The most important job on his to-do list was checking on the tunnels that led to the compound. The fellowship had dug two tunnels that led in opposite directions and surfaced on old dirt roads about four miles away from the compound. The purpose for these tunnels was twofold.

First, the tunnels could receive residents in a way that would not draw attention to the farm above the compound. The entrances were located in places that were inconspicuous but pretty simple to get to, depending on which town you were coming from. Since the compound was located about eight miles south of Creston, those coming from Creston could even go on foot at night and enter through the north tunnel. If people were coming from the south, there was the south tunnel. The plan had been for an east and west tunnel, too, but they ran out of time. Also supply runners, on the possibility that late in the game more supplies would be needed, could use the tunnels. The goal was to make the farm above the compound look dormant, so any activity had to be directed away from the farm.

The second purpose for the tunnels was for after the compound was in use. If for some reason the compound was discovered, there were two additional ways out, other than straight up. That purpose was rarely discussed but still a viable option.

Charlie spent the first week of his retirement running the tunnels. They were pretty rough and he spent a lot of time cutting roots from the walls and ground, to make them easier to traverse. There were no lights in the tunnels—another project that was never realized. So his work was done with a small generator and a construction light. By the end of a week, he felt it was as safe as he could make it.

The next project was supplies. The compound was quickly filling up with MREs and nonperishables. It had two walk-in freezers as well as refrigerators, all compliments of Chef Fredo who had closed down his business and planned to cook underground. His whole utility kitchen was being moved into the compound and Dave was overseeing that personally. Charlie purchased cleaning supplies, toiletries, extra plumbing parts in case of an emergency, hundreds of pounds of meat and frozen dough for bread, and gas for the generators. Residents brought bedding, clothing, kitchen supplies, books, games, televisions, video systems, personal toiletries, furniture, and more food. Charlie carried with him a list that he was continually adding to and crossing off.

One other ongoing project was getting Thomas and Robin to commit. The compound was slowly filling up, actually a lot slower than Charlie had expected, but Dave told him that the Lord may even use the compound for late arrivals. They just needed to be faithful in offering help and let the Lord do the rest. Dave and Charlie came up with a system to contact the compound without giving details of the location, so that late arrivals could make arrangements to come.

April fifteen came and went, taxes were paid and Charlie decided to call Thomas again. Less than a month away from the marking day, Charlie knew Thomas needed to be pushed into a decision.

"Thanks for meeting me." Charlie stood in the doorway of the local hardware store.

"This is a strange place to meet, don't you think?" Thomas shook his hand and followed Charlie into the store.

"Yeah, I wanted to show you something."

The men weaved their way to the back of the store. As they headed down the last aisle, Charlie stopped in front of a small generator.

"This one runs on about seven gallons of gas and will last you for about nine hours at a fifty percent load. Now this one," he pointed to one down further in the row, "this one runs on eight gallons of gas and will last about fifteen hours at fifty percent." Charlie turned to Thomas, enjoying the quizzical look on his face but not showing it. He scratched his head and furrowed his brow. "I don't think either of these are a good option for you."

"What are you talking about?"

"So, I was looking at one of these home standby generators. They are only a little bit more, but I was thinking that if you prepaid your gas bill—like for three years—then you could use this one at your house and get full electricity constantly." Charlie paused with a hand on his hip, the other rubbing his chin as if something had just occurred to him. "Then again, you could prepay your electric bill and not need a generator."

Charlie stopped and waited for Thomas to ask the next question but it never came.

"I get it. You have me meet you here at the hardware store for a little object lesson. Well, the lesson's over." Thomas turned to leave but Charlie grabbed his arm and pulled him back into the aisle.

"Last I looked, you didn't have a mark. The day is drawing near where you won't be able to pay for your utilities without one. So, what's your plan? Was it so wrong for me to do some thinking for you?"

"I've got a plan, Charlie," Thomas said as he pulled his arm away from Charlie's grip. "My church is stockpiling supplies in case things get bad. And Robin and I are storing up on food and household supplies, so I'm sure we'll be fine."

"Will your girls go to school without a mark?"

"No, Robin will teach them at home."

"So, she's quit her job."

"Well, not yet. Neither have I."

"How long do you think you can work at Smith and Brumsby without a mark? Will they just pay you in magogs instead of direct deposit?"

"I don't know. I . . . don't know the answer to that."

"Or maybe you want a little vacation to Camp Reconstruction. You know that's the plan—send the good citizens of Creston to a training camp to teach them the right way to think. It's very civilized. There are classrooms and bunkhouses and maybe even an incinerator in the back of the camp."

"Enough! You've made your point. I know this is serious, Charlie, but I think I'm ready for it. We'll just have to make do."

"And why can't you come with me? The girls would be safe and we'll all wait together."

"Robin is convinced we'll be raptured before anything bad happens. Any time I try to discuss even the slightest possibility of trouble, she leaves the room."

"Thomas, you're the head of your house. Make the decision. Save their lives. It's going to be a bloodbath and I'm telling you, these training camps are makeshift death camps!"

"When do you start living there?"

Charlie sensed a softening. "I'm already staying out there a couple nights a week. We have residents arriving with furniture and their personal goods, and we're trying to make places for everyone. By the end of next week, I'm sure I'll be out there full time."

"So, how would I get hold of you?"

Charlie suppressed a smile. "You've been a friend for a long time. You know my cell. When I make a run, I'll check my cell and call you back. I will probably make runs every day, or every couple of days initially. But eventually, I'll stop."

"Why can't you tell me where to go?"

"It's a protection for the people who are hiding. We can't just give the location away. Plus, we like to have runners bring you in through the tunnels so you don't get hurt. Right now families will be dropped off at the compound and cars will be taken away. It's really important that the property look abandoned. But once things get hairy on the outside, and that could be in a month, we'll only take people through the tunnels."

A man in his forties passed by and Charlie watched him peruse the aisle they were standing in. His heart began to race a bit, and something just felt wrong. He had seen him pass a few times now, but had been in deep discussion and ignored a possible danger.

"Let's go out to my car," he said to Thomas, as he motioned with his head toward the man in the aisle. "We need to talk where it's safe."

The two men headed out of the store and got in Charlie's car.

"Sorry, that guy just spooked me. For the safety of the whole group, I really shouldn't talk in public about the compound."

"I brought something for you." Thomas pulled his wallet out of his back pocket. He opened it and took a Post-it note out with a name and number written on it.

"There's a boy in Robin's class who just came from Michigan. He has a cousin in hiding and told Robin that she writes him letters. Robin asked to see one."

Charlie took the note and looked at the name. It read *Dan Dougherty*, followed by a phone number.

"What's this got to do with me?"

"I read the letter and it sounds a lot like your group—a bunch of Christians hiding in a cave system down in North Carolina. The girl who wrote the letter said that this man was a contact in Michigan, if her cousin ever wanted to come and hide with her and her family.

Apparently he stayed behind. I didn't know if you wanted to contact him. Robin doesn't know I copied the number."

Charlie looked up from the note at Thomas's face. "You're really afraid of her, aren't you?"

"It's not that . . . it's just that she has been so upset lately."

"I am sure she's worried about the girls, Thomas."

"I am, too. I just don't know what else to do. I guess I am holding out that things won't really change here."

"Except for the financial restraints, you might be right. But the American way of life has very cleverly been tied to receiving a mark. And whatever you do, you can't take that!"

"I know, I know. Robin and I have both agreed we won't let it go that far. I just wish I could contact you quicker. Once I get her to go, I think I will need to act fast."

"It's not that far from here—only a couple miles south of town. I'm sorry I can't tell you more. It's not that I don't trust you, but . . ."

"It's okay. I won't put you in a difficult position. Just pray for us. Pray she'll let me make this decision."

Thomas opened the car door and got out. He leaned back into the doorway and reached for Charlie's hand.

"Thanks, Charlie. I got your message loud and clear. I'm glad I have a little more time to think."

"See you around."

They shook hands and Charlie pulled out of the parking lot. As he drove away, he watched Thomas in his rearview mirror get into his car, and he wondered if he would ever see him again here on this earth. He reached for the phone number that he stuck to his dash and decided to make a call when he got home. If this guy really is doing the same thing he is, he might have some insight that Charlie had overlooked in the planning phase.

As he continued on his way, Charlie's mind raced with more details for the preparation of the compound. But no matter how long that list grew, he couldn't shake the despair that his friend was leading his family into a slaughter. He didn't know what else he could do. He just couldn't make him understand, so he finally laid his concern at the feet of his Master.

Father, I can't convince Thomas on my own. I'm out of ideas. Please intervene in a way that only You can.

Durbin looked around the room. All eight of the names on his list were in attendance—five pastors, a rabbi, a priest, and Thomas. A plate of muffins from Starbucks sat untouched on a sideboard near the door of the conference room. One of the pastors had helped himself to coffee, but the rest just sat and waited for the meeting to begin. There was very little conversation and after Durbin rounded the table, greeting each man personally, he sat in the sole empty chair. It bothered him that Thomas refused to smile and appeared angry from the moment he walked into the room, but Durbin didn't let that shake him.

"Gentlemen, I appreciate you coming on such short notice." Durbin scanned the room and tried to make eye contact as often as possible.

"In eighteen days our banking system here in Creston will permanently change over to the One World Denomination system. Let me explain how that will affect our town. Every store in town has already received software and systems that will only operate with a scanner. When a customer wants to pay for his groceries or dinner at a restaurant, his hand will be scanned and the amount will be taken from his bank account. If one of our citizens wants to purchase gas, he'll simply hold up his hand at the pump and it will scan his hand automatically, right through his palm."

Durbin continued to look around the room, speaking slowly and clearly. He wanted to make sure he was completely understood.

"As a testament to the efficiency and competency of the Federation of World Powers, this process of converting our monetary system has been remarkably smooth. I haven't heard of even one single hiccup in the process here in town. As a matter of fact, the new systems are already in place, accepting, for the moment, cash and credit cards. But on May fifteen, our current system will be obsolete. Only those with chips in their hands will be able to purchase anything in town."

The men sat remarkably still. Durbin stood and began to pace around the table, taking slow, deliberate steps. In his mind, he pictured DeNiro as he circled the table of mob bosses in *The Untouchables*, with a baseball bat in his hand. Thankfully, he didn't need the bat, but he had considered leaning one in the corner of the room, just for effect.

"You men have a lot in common. You are all religious. You all have families who need food. You all own homes. And still none of you have a chip in your hand." He stopped behind Reverend Blackmore and put his hand on his shoulder. "Why is that, Reverend?"

Blackmore pulled his shoulder a bit, but Durbin left his hand there for effect.

"Because none of us have taken Adolph Hitler's mark."

"Exactly. No mark, no chip. No chip, no money. No money, no food, gas, or utilities. So . . . I am curious." Durbin made his way back to his empty chair and stood in front of it. "You men are leaders in your respective churches, and Thomas, you're a good friend. I have visited most of your places of worship and I have noticed that your congregations are following your lead on this. Much of Creston is marked up and ready to go. I would love to hear what you all have planned, because in eighteen days, you are all going to find yourselves in a real bind."

Durbin added just enough sincerity to his tone that he was pretty sure the men were not completely offended by his words. Then he sat and waited for an answer.

"We've been telling our congregants to stock up on supplies." Rabbi Stone gave the first answer, and a few of the other men nodded as if that was their plan as well.

"Hmmm, supplies. Do you mean food?"

"Yes," Stone answered.

"And gas? What about gas?"

Stone sat quietly.

"How long will your people live on these supplies? A week? A month? A year? Five years? That would be quite a supply closet."

Reverend Blackmore cleared his throat. "Mayor Durbin, may I remind you of our meeting the night Hitler revealed himself. The religious community voiced our concerns of aligning with this man. That night you told us you would try to work out something for us, so that those of us with religious objections could still function. What have you provided for us, may I ask?"

Durbin leaned forward and rested on his forearms, fingers clasped in front of him. "The world has completely changed since that night, Reverend. Some things are no longer negotiable here in America. In the past, religious objections protected you from certain things, like vaccinations or even attending public schools. But this is not something you can avoid. No mark, no ability to function."

A pastor next to Blackmore spoke up. "We believe what we are seeing in the world is of prophetic significance. We believe it is a precursor to the return of Jesus Christ. So, our congregants are gathering supplies that will last until His return."

"And when exactly will that happen?" Durbin asked out of sheer curiosity.

"Well . . . probably sooner than later . . . I guess. But being a prophecy, we can't . . . exactly be sure of the day . . . but still, it shouldn't be longer than, say . . . umm . . . a few months or so . . . maybe a year or two . . ." The pastor was drowning at the table and Durbin was amazed that no life preservers were being tossed his way.

Thomas finally spoke. "Wayne, you know we're in a bind."

"So am I," Durbin shot back, not willing to go into the end of the world discussion he and Thomas had already had half a dozen times. "I know you all are devout believers, but you're missing the point here. We are talking about life and death. And it's not just you that this affects. You all have children and you all have congregations." Durbin stood again. As a small man, he found that when he needed to drive home a point, standing was usually more effective. "Let me make myself clear. In two weeks, buses are coming into town and if you don't have a mark on your head, you will be ushered onto the buses and taken away. Your wives will be taken to a women's facility with your children who eventually will be separated from their mothers. You will all sit in class, day after day, being educated in the benefits of joining the system. But it won't go on forever. A day will come where if you don't take the mark, you will not be allowed to return."

"Exterminated, you mean." Thomas's voice shot across the table.

"It's your choice." He ignored Thomas's comment, sat again, then softened his tone. "Someone explain this to me. All you have to do is put a little number on your head and you get a chip. Now life returns to normal and—no wait, it's better than normal because now you have afforded your children a future and an education. Your obedience has just afforded more jobs in our town and more jobs equate to a better economy. You can travel all over the world, you have a personal accountant who will balance your checkbook at the touch of a button. But for some reason you all think you'll burn in hell if you take it. You're willing to give up your homes and families because of it. I just don't get it. I really don't." Durbin leaned back in his chair and crossed his arms.

The men looked around at each other. The silence in the room spoke volumes, as Durbin assumed that his point was finally sinking in.

"What about the idol? Are you saying we don't need an idol in our homes?" asked the priest.

"As far as I know, there's no 'idol police.' Do what you want in your homes, just get a number so that you can access your bank accounts, feed your families, and get on with your lives."

Thomas leaned forward. "So we don't need idols. That's what you're saying?"

"What's the big deal with the idols? I have a picture of Hitler on my fridge. I don't pray to it or worship it, but it does remind me that the sooner my town gets marked up, the sooner I can access funds to update and improve our town. And you people are keeping Creston from receiving what we need because you won't mark up and tell your congregations to follow suit."

Silence again.

"Listen, guys," Durbin continued, "this really isn't a discussion. There's nothing to be negotiated. I just want you all to know what is right around the corner for you all. I would think being God-fearing men that you would want your congregations to provide for their families. Isn't being responsible pleasing to God?"

Pastor Richwell stood and excused himself. "Thank you for the information. I need to get going, however." He walked away from the table and Durbin called out to him.

"Eighteen days and the decision will be made for you. Consider yourself warned."

The meeting was over. The message was clearly given and there was no need for further clarification. One by one the men stood and left the room. Durbin sat with a disgusted look on his face. Thomas also stayed at the table. Once the room was empty, Thomas spoke.

"I told you not to take the mark. You're going to hell now, but I'm not following you there."

"What about Robin? Do you want to see her in an orange jumpsuit? She's probably smart enough to get the mark for herself and the girls once she gets away from you."

Thomas stood. "You're just being nasty, now."

"But I'm the one going to hell." Durbin raised his eyebrow and clearly made his point.

"Wayne, our allegiance is with Jesus Christ and He warned us about this time. We're not marking up and we may just disappear."

"There's nowhere to run, friend," Durbin said, as Thomas walked to the door alone. "A day is coming where you'll stick out like a sore thumb without a mark and everyone will consider you the enemy. They'll shoot to kill out there. At least here we'll take you, feed you, train you, and put you back in your homes. Outside of Indiana, you'll be on your own."

"We'll never take the mark."

"Our training camps have a way of being pretty persuasive."

"It won't matter."

"And you think your little girls will feel the same way?"

Thomas stopped in the doorway and turned back to Durbin.

"What has happened to you? How can a system be good if it will kill to have its own way?"

"For centuries man has killed for the good of society. We've done it here in America, too. Take the Civil War, for example. We were willing to kill our own citizens for the rights of slaves. In the end, it was a much better place to live. Once this time of adjustment is over, this world will be a much better place for all."

"Nothing is going to get better. It's only going to get worse, Wayne. Famine will become more severe and life is going to become nearly impossible to manage. Mark my words."

Thomas slammed the door behind him and Durbin sat alone in the conference room at Creston City Hall.

Thomas had been such a big help to him during the campaign. A true friend and supporter. Even when he expressed anger, Durbin still liked Thomas. He took a pen from his shirt pocket and jotted a note to himself. By next week he would finish his outline for the systematic identification of nonmarkers. Thomas lived on the west side of town, so to buy his friend some time, Durbin decided to start the inventory on the east side of town and work his way west.

The plan was to send law enforcement workers with last year's census data to interview each household. Initially, a record of those with jobs in a given household would be taken—marked versus unmarked. Obviously, the unmarked would no longer receive income, so logically, all employed residents would have to be marked. Any unmarked resident who held a job would be taken into custody. After a short stay in the county jail, they would be offered a free-of-charge marking service. If they still refused, they would be loaded onto a state bus and taken to the nearest training camp, which was about an hour southeast of Creston. Any other members of a household who were unmarked would be noted for a later round of arrests. Initially, the shock of a father being taken from a home, or a mother for that matter, should solve the issue of other law-breaking activity in any given household.

Durbin knew the plan wasn't perfect, but he had no choice. He had to get his citizens marked. Period. Once marked, the financial floodgates opened and his town would become a city. Or maybe a metropolis. And who knows, if a citizen or two slipped through the system, how would the FWP find out anyways? He'd do the best he could, show a respectable effort, and move on with life.

Durbin walked over to the sideboard and eyed the untouched muffins.

Everyone loves Starbuck muffins. You'd have to be crazy not to take one of these babies.

He picked up a sugar-encrusted blueberry muffin and lifted it to his nose. He took a deep whiff and let the fresh-baked aroma fill his nostrils.

This should be my insanity test. Have a plate of muffins sit out and when I meet with someone, offer them a muffin. If they refuse, I'll know I'm dealing with a lunatic.

Durbin pulled the paper away from the side of the muffin and took a bite. Crumbs fell on his chest and he brushed them away. He had about an hour before his meeting with the bronze caster. The life-sized statue of Hitler was complete and the caster was personally delivering it to City Hall that afternoon. Durbin had a stone pedestal made to hold the statue, and it would be placed in the center of the town, in Memorial Park. For decades the city council argued about who to commemorate in bronze for that park, and in a matter of mere minutes, he was able to convince them of the necessity of agreeing on the Hitler statue. It was definitely not permanent, and if the FWP did not come through with their promises, it could be replaced. But in order to access financial help for its citizens, Creston would have to prove compliance with Hitler's demands. Thus the statue. Eight "ayes" and one abstention, and it was done.

Durbin walked back over to the table, gathered his notes and headed back for the door. He glanced back down at the plate of muffins and he grabbed one more. After all, he had a long day ahead of him and he would need a bit of sustenance later in the afternoon. As he left the conference room, Thomas's warning still rang in his ears.

Nothing is going to get better. It's only going to get worse.

"Only for you, buddy. Only for you."

fifteen

May fifteen

Noah knew he was pushing it. His house had been emptied of anything that would be useful to the compound. Most of his furniture was gone, but his appliances were still in place. When the compound hit capacity in its food storage units, Noah had started to store food in his basement. It was cool and dark down there, and the food would store nicely. He had volunteered his home, because it was fully paid off, thanks to an inheritance check he received after the death of his grandmother. When supplies got low, someone would have to make a run to Noah's house and transfer the food from the basement to the compound.

Other than food, Noah still had some clothes in his closet, a desk in his bedroom, with a twin-size bed, a set of towels, and a lamp. He was sleeping at the compound regularly now, ever since his mother and sister moved in two weeks ago. He was so relieved when they agreed to come and stay at the compound. They really didn't have any other options. But last night he stayed at his house.

And today was Mark Up Day.

Charlie was pretty mad at him for staying in town, but as Noah weighed things, this would probably be the last safe day in town. Today all banking and merchant systems were changing over to the

One World Denomination system. He filled his car with gas one final time the night before and made a last run to the grocery store. The new cash registers were pretty high-tech looking, and were still accepting dollars as of last night.

But today, everything would change.

Noah promised he would be back at the compound before lunch. Hitler had a press conference scheduled for noon again, and he wanted to see it. The cable at the compound was up and running, and Dave hoped that paying for three years of service in advance would ensure an information flow during their time of hiding. So the plan was to secure the house, pick up Tara, and head to the compound with plenty of time. He was now sporting one of the compound supply vans, which would be stored in the garage at the compound, so he didn't have to add time to account for the four-mile run through the dark tunnel.

Noah arrived at Tara's house by a quarter to ten. He had been disappointed that she wouldn't leave sooner, but since her mother had refused to leave, Tara wanted to stay with her as long as she could. Her bed and dresser, as well as most of her clothes were already at the compound. She had spent the past two weeks at her mother's, but came home the night before to pack any final necessities.

Noah parked the van in the driveway and walked to the front door. Before he got there, it opened. Tara stepped out and closed the door behind her. She had an alarmed look on her face and Noah could tell she had been crying.

"What's wrong?"

"I can't do this." Tears streamed down Tara's cheeks and her voice cracked.

"Yes you can, Tara." Noah gave her an understanding smile. He already had this conversation with her multiple times and knew she was just struggling like everyone else to make the final move. "I know this is hard, but it's the right decision."

"No, Noah, you don't understand. I really can't do this. Everything has changed."

Noah hadn't seen her for two weeks and he missed her terribly. He had worried that spending a long period of time with her mother might cause her to change her mind, so he made sure he called every morning and every evening. They talked through what had happened each day, and he had no sense that she was faltering. He stepped closer and drew her into his arms. She was shivering and looked so frail.

"Tara, things are only going to get worse starting today. We've really got to"—

Tara put her hands on his chest and pushed away from him. Her voice, still shaking, was more forceful than before. "You're not listening to me. I can't go. Something has happened and I have to stay."

Noah was confused. "What happened? What could possibly have happened since I talked to you last night?"

Just then the door opened and a woman stood in the doorway, dressed in black slacks with an aqua sweater. She looked to be in her sixties, with dark, wavy hair, cropped in a stylish bob. Her makeup was smart but she did not wear a smile. Her face was unmistakably familiar.

"Mrs. Warners?" Noah addressed the woman.

"You may call me Sondra." She extended her hand but Noah never got around to taking it.

What Noah saw next nearly stopped his heart. Near the top of Sondra's hairline, just big enough to see, were three identical numbers.

Noah's eyes went from the numbers to Tara's eyes, which were immediately filled with tears again.

"What's going on?" His voice was steady, though his heart was pounding.

Tara turned to her mother, wiping the streaming tears from her cheek. "Mom, I told you I would tell him. Please let me do this. Go back in the house and give me a few minutes."

"Very well. It was nice to finally meet you, though regrettably under such difficult circumstances."

Sondra Warners turned and went back in the house, closing the door behind her. Her coolness left a chill in its wake.

"When did she take the mark?"

"She had it when I arrived at her house two weeks ago." Tara continued to struggle as the tears kept coming. "She refuses to believe God would allow us to go through this persecution. And she says she refuses to live in a hole like an animal. She honestly believes this is going to blow over and we'll all just go on with life."

"Why didn't you tell me two weeks ago?"

"Would it have made a difference?"

"But Tara, she knew not to take the mark!"

"I know, but her church said that God knows his children and a mark wouldn't change anything."

"But she was warned, just like both of us. Tara, how could she do this? Doesn't she understand that . . . ?" Noah's voice died away. The weight of Sondra's action hit Noah like a two-by-four to the face. He stopped midsentence and watched as Tara crumbled into his arms. Now he understood her desperation. The angel had said that taking the mark meant separation from God. Sondra had turned her back on God and chose to believe a lie. That choice would cost her eternity.

Moments passed and Tara once again pulled away. "I can't leave her now. I'll never be with her again if I leave now."

"She could have come to the compound. Why wouldn't she do that?"

"Mom loves the Lord, Noah. She really does. But she also loves her life. She didn't want to leave her home and friends. She is not convinced anything substantial will change. She needed the number to keep her life as she knows it. I didn't know she was going to do this, honest I didn't. I would have dragged her to the compound myself if I had known. But it's done, and I just can't leave her. Not yet. Please understand."

Noah reached up and held Tara's face with his hands. He looked deep into her eyes, searching for the words to say. "Tara, you can't stay. Your life is in danger."

"Mom can shop and pay for things. We transferred my bank account, or what's left of it, into hers before the system switched this morning. So, we're going to stay here for a bit and then go back to her house. She wants me to pack up and just move in with her until this is over."

"Until this is over. What does that mean. You know how this ends, right?"

Tara reached up and took his hands from her face. She stepped away from him and looked out across Memorial Park, which was across the street from her house. The trees were budding and everything was greening in the warm May sun.

"I just need some time, Noah. What if she is right? What if you've got it wrong?"

"Wrong? You've got to be kidding me!" Noah raised his voice, as he walked in front of her, blocking her view of the park. "Prophecy is coming true right before your very eyes and you can't see it. That's what you're telling me." He held up his fingers as he counted the signs. "Hitler raised from the dead. Six-six-six on foreheads. Increased famine and wars. Nations aligning into a one-world government. None of this sets off an alarm in your head?"

"This is all new to me!" Tara yelled back. "Don't you remember, even my pastor didn't think we'd be here for this. So, maybe this is just a precursor or something. Maybe we'll be raptured any day. I . . . I just can't leave her. Not now . . . because if you're right, she's going to hell and this is the last time I'll see her!"

Noah and Tara stood, face-to-face. He knew she wasn't going to leave with him. Behind her, Sondra Warners stood in the dining room window, arms folded, waiting for her daughter to return. Noah looked at her, and then back to Tara.

"Can I talk with your mom?"

"No, Noah. You just have to go." The tears started again.

"Tara, you can still come. It's not safe for you. Without the mark, you'll be targeted and taken away to one of the training camps. Please, come with me."

Noah was desperate and a lump was forming in his throat. He saw a softness in Tara's eyes, but her words continued to reject his suggestions.

"I can come later if things get bad. But I can't leave her now."

"Then I'll come back every week and ask you to come."

"What?"

"Every week I'll leave the compound and come find you."

"Don't do that, Noah. It will be dangerous for you."

Noah put his hands to his head and squeezed it, trying to make the ache that was growing go away.

"Are you even listening to yourself? You know it will be dangerous, but you still insist on staying. You can't live out here any easier than I can."

"Just go, Noah. If I change my mind, I will call your cell and leave a message. You can find me then. I won't even be here for very long."

Tara turned her back on Noah and walked back to the front door of her house.

"Don't do this, Tara!" Noah called out to her. "Don't stay here. Please. I love you and I want you with me."

She turned. He had never said that to her before. In desperation, he hoped it would change her mind. She reached up and wiped the tears from her face.

"I love you, too, Noah. Now, please leave." With that, she opened the front door, walked inside, and closed the door.

Noah watched as her mother turned away from the dining room window out of sight. He stood on the driveway and raised his hands in the air. Then they dropped to his side and he walked to the van.

Everything inside of him told him to sit in the driveway and wait for her to come, even if it took days or weeks. But after ten minutes he started the engine and put the van in reverse. As he pulled away from the house, Tara stood in the dining room, where her mother had been. He stopped the car and rolled down his passenger window. He could see her clearly now. He stretched out his arm and pointed a finger at her. Then he called through the window, "I'll be back for you."

Whether or not she heard, he knew he would.

Black Cap was relieved when Noah finally started up his car. He was beginning to become uncomfortable with how long it was taking him to leave. He felt a breeze on the back of his neck but when he turned, there was nothing there. As Noah's car rounded the corner and headed out of town, Black Cap turned his attention to the little park at the center of Creston. He walked down the sidewalk past the rows of tulips that had burst through the dead earth, bringing color back to the town. Sitting on a bench was a man and a woman, he with a mark, her without. They chatted casually and Black Cap noticed their wedding rings. They, however, didn't notice him.

Black Cap continued on into the park. The warmth of the sun apparently drew people there. Children on skateboards whizzed past him, as dogs caught Frisbees that were lofted across the reviving grass. It amazed Black Cap how humans lived so carefree. It interested him how many children had no mark on their foreheads. He wondered how Lucifer would deal with the children.

In the center of the park stood the newly erected statue of Hitler. Black Cap had been in attendance the day he was taken from earth the first time. As he strolled over to the statue, he smirked at the distinguished facial expression the sculptor had given Hitler—not a smile, but certainly not a frown. Black Cap had watched Hitler days before his death. He thought it cowardly that before Hitler pulled the trigger of his Walther PPK, he took a potassium cyanide pill to ensure his death. Then again, his true cowardice showed up when he opened his clenched eyes after pulling the trigger and saw Black Cap and his associates. There was no distinguished facial expression then, only terror.

He knew he would get to see that sight again, and this time Hitler would be imprisoned for eternity. Yahweh definitely had a unique way of handling things that sometimes he didn't fully understand, yet he never questioned. He only worshiped. And worship equates to obedience. Adonai had told him that one day His precious children would explain to the angels the great mystery and Black Cap looked forward to that day.

In the meantime . . .

There was an unusual shift in the aura around the statue. Black Cap looked around and observed that the humans continued with their frivolity. He stood, staring at the face of the statue. It was changing, moving, melding somehow. Then he recognized the hairless, bony face of the demon from the church roof. The statue was still intact, but the demon was somehow a part of it, moving and writhing within the bronze shell. He could spin around and see in all directions.

"Found a new home? The church didn't really suit you anyway."

The head of the demon spun around and quickly Black Cap was face-to-face with his nemesis.

"Oh, it's you. And I thought it would be someone important."

"So, what are you doing in there? I didn't think you guys liked being encased in nonliving structures."

"It's really none of your business." The hissing demon wriggled his nose and began spinning his head again, as if he were looking for something or someone. Then he stopped and spoke again.

"I know your ward didn't take a mark. Too bad, he'll have to die."

"He'll manage."

"You want to see something really cool?"

"Sorry, I don't have the time for this." Black Cap decided the longer he stayed around, the more this demon thought he cared.

"See that couple on the bench? Watch this!"

Black Cap looked over to the bench where the man and woman had just been laughing and talking. She bent over and reached for something in her purse. The man sat, staring off into space. Slowly he reached up and touched the mark on his forehead. The woman sat up again, reached for his hand, and offered a lovely smile. He pulled away and stood. He looked at his watch, spoke a few words, and turned to leave. The woman looked a bit surprised, but definitely disappointed. She gathered her purse and walked the opposite direction.

"I did that!" The demon was excited over the separation.

"Quite impressive, I must say. You made them get on with their day." Black Cap turned to leave and the demon lowered his voice.

"I filled his mind with thoughts of resentment. As those thoughts grow, his hatred for her will also. There is no room in this world for the enemy and today is the beginning of the end for them. Stick around and enjoy the show, my fellow being, it's going to be a doosie!"

Black Cap swung around and raised his hand. Knowing fire could flow from his fingertips at will, he held his temper and forced his hand back to his side. "I am no fellow being of yours, you disgusting excuse for a demon. We separated when you chose to follow a creature rather than the Creator. Your choice is made. Don't try to rise to my status, because your fall won't tolerate it."

"Your little boy and his girlfriend don't stand a chance. We have her mother and she will soon follow behind. If not, it will be a joy to watch her climb on the bus and go off to summer camp! Perhaps I will get a replacement so that I can escort her personally."

Black Cap had stayed too long. Yahweh was patient, therefore Black Cap was restricted in what he was permitted to do. But a day was coming when all restrictions would be lifted. He turned and walked away from the encased demon, who returned to spinning his head. Black Cap would have to keep Noah away from town for his own protection.

And knowing Noah, that would be harder than necessary.

sixteen

May

Elise lay with her head on her pillow, staring at the ceiling of her hotel room.

It had been a long week.

In the course of seven days Hitler held two televised messages and was magnificent, as usual, but completely unapproachable when they were over. He disappeared into his office, locked the door, and refused to answer his phone. But despite his lack of communication afterwards, both televised messages went off without a hitch.

Elise arrived in Jerusalem a few days prior to his arrival, to make sure the Israeli gift was perfect. The penthouse apartment and office that overlooked the Temple Mount would serve as a third headquarters, and was truly a surprise when presented to Hitler. His original headquarters in Moscow was now rarely used. Most of his time was spent in Iraq. Babylon was more magnificent than ever and not allowing the Israelis to outdo themselves, the Iraqi Arabs presented Hitler with a spacious palace in the heart of their glorious city. From there he chose to rule the world. However, Jerusalem had a special place in his heart, and he decided his most important statements would be televised from there.

Elise rolled over on her right side and reached for the extra pillow next to her. She pulled it into an embrace and wondered how in the world she had gotten so lucky to have the life she had. She smiled, as she thought about how beautifully furnished the penthouse and office were, solely due to her efforts with a talented decorator. Of course, having a boss who ruled the world helped to make the furnishings arrive ahead of time. And the quality was surpassed by none. She hadn't expected any hiccups and of course, she was right. The burgundy and navy overtones suited her employer to a tee and the gold accents were the finishing touch on a job well done. Elise found a wonderful hotel for herself just a block from the office, which made access to her work simple and easy.

The morning Hitler arrived, her alarm went off at four forty-five. She left the hotel by five thirty and had the first pot of coffee brewing by five fifty. Hitler and his entourage, protected by Agent Vasiliev, arrived an hour later. Elise stood at her desk when he entered the office. She knew Hitler would be pleasant but focused, since it was an important day. She convinced herself that if he didn't notice the fresh orchids or the Swiss chocolates in the Waterford candy dish on his desk or the cinnamon candles neatly arranged on his coffee table, it was because he would be distracted with the business of the day. After all, it was one week before May fifteen, the deadline for the world to make their allegiance to him, so he had much more important things on his mind.

But he noticed everything.

Because that's how incredible he was.

The rest of the day was a blur. After a quick tour of the office and penthouse facilities, the morning was filled with meetings. His travel staff quickly set up computers and hooked into the exterior copiers and fax machines in the conference room, making communication with the Babylon office continuous and seamless. Phones rang incessantly as communications from all over the world started to seep in. It would take months to determine which countries were using efficient methods to track the marking process, but if she heard him say it once, she heard him say it a hundred times, he really wasn't worried about human error—he had his own plan that would ensure accurate information. Elise was curious what that meant, but figured in time she would know.

Elise organized lunch in for everyone, but hardly anyone stopped to eat. By three o'clock, Hitler disappeared into his office with instructions for no interruptions. At four thirty Ferco Szabo arrived and was ushered into the office by Agent Vasiliev, who returned to his station, standing outside of Hitler's office door. He was dressed in a tailored black suit, giving him the appearance of a heartless security agent. He was still a mystery to Elise, a mystery she was determined to figure out.

Half an hour later a crew arrived from CNN. They took over most of the lobby, but when the time came for the televised statement only two men from the station were allowed into Hitler's office to film it, a cameraman and a technician.

The statement was rather short but spectacular as had become the pattern. Elise watched on a monitor in the conference room with the rest of the staff, minus Vasiliev whose continued presence was required in Hitler's office. Szabo and Hitler sat in the pair of wingback chairs. Hitler commended the world for their initial positive response and then Szabo demonstrated his unusual ability to grab the public's attention. The announcement was basically a seven-day warning that time was running out. At one point Szabo appeared on live television and described the nonmarkers as an infection which would spread to the whole world if not amputated. Then he stuck his arm into his jacket and pulled it out. It was immediately covered with leprosy, which was a miracle in and of itself. But then he lopped it off with an axe, only to have it reappear, completely healed and attached.

Remembering that sight turned Elise's stomach and she let out a disgusted laugh. What could possibly happen next? When those two were together, she never knew what to expect.

But that message was a mere warm-up for the announcement that Hitler had given today.

Elise let go of the pillow and rolled back over onto her left side in the king-size bed. The sheets were cool on her skin and she pulled the down comforter up around her shoulder. She folded her arm beneath the pillow that cradled her head and squinted at the digital clock on the nightstand. 1:34. She needed to sleep but her mind continued to stir. It raced with memories of the past two months. Beside her clock was her idol. She never traveled without it. It stood approximately six inches high and was a perfect likeness of Adolph Hitler.

He had given it to her himself. Wrapped in a box with silver foil paper and a large white bow. He gave it to her the morning they left Jerusalem after she had her forehead marked. She had been ushered into a limo outside the back entrance of the hotel by Agent Vasiliev and found Hitler waiting for her in the backseat. She'd proudly revealed her new imprint to him and then he turned to Vasiliev. He removed his hat, pulled back his blonde bangs that were matted onto his forehead and reveal his own set of numbers, set slightly off center over his right eye. Then Hitler handed both of them boxes. Elise gushed with delight but Vasiliev simply nodded approval.

It was a thoughtful gift. In the dark she could make out its small head and square shoulders. She liked that he was not in a uniform but in a suit. It wasn't an image from his past, either. It was a new one, the improved Hitler with all the charisma but without the stigma of a failed regime. She loved it.

Elise closed her eyes and the image of Adolph Hitler standing in the temple earlier that day returned to her mind. He made his second announcement from there. He stood before a single microphone. No longer would CNN cover his announcements. The newly formed World Wide News Network was the only camera crew permitted inside. When his face came on the screen, the awe and wonder in his eyes that she had seen before when he mentioned the temple was again present. He was so enamored with it. He greeted the audience but quickly got down to business, and the powerful leader forcefully addressed his world. Today he declared May fifteen World Independence Day. It was a defining moment for him and she could hear his words again as if he were standing in her room speaking with her:

"Today every government will receive a directive from the Federation of World Powers to begin to take into custody those who are our enemies. In a peaceful and prosperous world, there is no room for dissidents. Thus the mark system has separated those who desire peace and those who don't. This directive provides financial incentives to citizens who aid the government in collecting the enemy. They will be gathered, given the opportunity to join us, tried if they refuse, and disposed of."

His straight posture oozed with confidence. He had the armies of the world at his beck and call, and he would succeed.

"Hell is a very real place. Most religions agree on this point. I am not here to promote religion but reality. I desire to live in flesh and blood, but there is a spiritual realm that cannot be ignored. If we do not remove the enemy we will cease to exist. Our time is short to handle this matter, therefore the FWP will provide whatever incentive it takes to accomplish our goal. Together we will overcome the Enemy and usher in the greatest race of all," he purposefully raised his voice and his right fist. "One that is free from intolerance and judgment. We shall rule ourselves and be of one mind. We shall free ourselves from the merciless wrath of a loveless, empty God."

Whenever he spoke of this God, Elise got the chills. How a God could hate His creation was beyond her understanding, but it was that very fact that gave her the motivation to give her life so that the world could be free from this God's control.

Would you truly give your life?

Elise opened her eyes. The silence of the room overwhelmed her ears. Was someone in the room or had she started to doze? After a few moments, she closed her eyes again.

Don't be frightened, Elise. I am here to help you. I was given to you specifically by him so you can trust me.

Elise opened her eyes again but chose not to sit up, fearing the intruder in the room would hurt her. She strained in the darkness to see movement, but still the room seemed empty. Perhaps someone was sitting in the far chair or crawling on the floor. Her breathing became irregular as her heart raced, but still there was no movement, nor did she hear any sounds.

Then, movement. A slight motion near her alarm clock. The head of her idol seemed to tilt a bit to the right. Slowly she sat up in her bed and reached above the idol for the lamp on the nightstand. With a simple turn of the knob the room glowed with a warm yellow light. She blinked in the light and her eyes began to water a bit. Soon they focused on her idol. It blinked and she drew a quick breath.

"You? You're moving?"

"I can talk. That's all I really need to do."

"How are you doing that? Are you a robot? A fancy camera and mike system?" She cautiously picked up the idol and looked on the bottom of its stand, but there was nothing. No wires, no battery cases, just solid cast bronze metal. She quickly set him back down and he blinked again.

"I must have had too much to drink at dinner," Elise said aloud.

"No, you're not drunk, Elise. You're too disciplined to do that."

He was right. She would never . . .

"Then what are you?"

"I am a gift from Adolph to you. I am here to help you."

"But I've had you for two months now and you've never said a word before."

"That's because I couldn't until tonight. But now everything has changed."

"And you will help me by doing what?"

"Advising you, being a friend, helping you understand things that don't make sense."

"What if I don't want your help?"

"Remember, Adolph wanted you to have me. He gave me to you specifically, so I must have a purpose."

Elise was no longer frightened, and really, since the vision Hitler had allowed her to see in his office, nothing really scared or surprised her anymore. She knew there was an unseen force behind this man and his vision, but she chose to leave the supernatural alone and simply see to his administrative needs. This new turn of events could take her into a realm she didn't really want to visit.

"You're not going to show me hell or anything like that, are you? Because I've already done that and have no interest in doing it again."

The idol smiled. "He really does care for you, Elise, and he needs you to watch his back. There are many who want him dead and if he would die, the world would be lost."

"Well, he has his own security which handle matters like that, I simply keep his life in order so that he can accomplish greatness without worrying about what to eat, where to sleep, or how to get somewhere."

Elise knew her role and wasn't sure what the idol was implying.

"Elise, Adolph only keeps his most trusted friends at his side, and you have earned one of those positions."

Elise liked being considered a friend.

"But with that position comes great responsibility. Don't let your guard down. I am here to help you and together we will serve Adolph most effectively."

Elise sat in bed looking at her talking idol. He never moved his hands or legs and she was glad he couldn't walk. He appeared to be limited to just head movement.

"So, when exactly will you be able to talk again, because I hate to be rude, but I am rather tired and need to sleep."

"My presence here is now permanent, so we can talk whenever you please. I must say, I am surprised that you are not more alarmed at a talking statue."

Elise reached above the idol's head and turned off the lamp. "Nothing can surprise me anymore. I led a pretty sheltered life for my first thirty-two years on this earth, but in the past six months I have seen things that have no explanation. So, a talking idol? What's so frightening about that?"

She laid her head on her pillow and closed her eyes again. *Perhaps I'll awaken in the morning to find it was all a dream.* Truth be told, she was living a dream and she hoped she would never wake up. But if it's not a dream, she now had help in her role as personal assistant. As she dozed off, she wondered to what extent this idol would help her. She wondered if it could see into the future or provide her with information about people other than Hitler.

And then her mind drifted to Vasiliev.

Thomas pulled his car into the parking lot of Smith and Brumsby, his hands tightly gripping the steering wheel. Today would be a test. Yesterday Adolph Hitler gave the green light for governments to round up unmarked citizens. Mayor Durbin was ready and prepared to carry out that directive. And Thomas Larson was going to work without a mark. Up until now he had told himself that nothing would really change in Creston. Sure, some people got a mark on their head and there was a new statue in the park, but that was all fun and games. It was fashionable because it was European.

Thomas was never really the gambling sort. In college he never played poker with the guys because he needed every penny for his tuition. Risking it all to possibly double his money just wasn't appealing. He would rather know for sure he could pay his bills and go without extra spending money, than bet his luck and possibly go broke.

Well, today he officially became a gambling man. He gambled on the fact that he could work out an arrangement with his boss to be paid in magogs, without a mark. He gambled on the fact that the swift changes the entire world had made since March fifteen were simply a fad and life would return to normal soon. He gambled on the fact that his children could still attend school without a mark. And he gambled on the fact that if he was wrong, Jesus would swoop down and save his family in just the nick of time.

Thus the white knuckles.

As he walked into the building, everything appeared normal. However, all that changed as he rode the elevator up to the fifth floor where his department was located.

"So, you didn't have time to get a mark yet, huh?"

Thomas looked over at the boy in the elevator who was obviously addressing him. He considered him a boy, since he was barely over his teen-aged acne. In jeans, black Converses, an untucked button-down shirt and a skinny tie, this guy was definitely from the computer department.

"Excuse me?" Thomas acted as if he hadn't heard him and hoped the elevator would speed up a bit. Instead it stopped at three and two more passengers got on.

The boy pointed to his forehead and said, "No mark. What's up?"

"Oh, that. Yeah. I'm just not into the whole one-world government thing." Thomas tried to sound hip, but instead felt like a fool.

"It's people like you that are going to mess it up for the rest of us."

The woman in front of him had turned around and was now launching accusations.

"Pardon me?"

"You heard me. You nonconformists are just stubborn and ignorant. You're probably a Christian, too, aren't you?"

The elevator opened up on the fifth floor and Thomas pushed his way out the door without answering her question. As the doors shut behind him he heard her final comment, "Good luck getting paid!"

Thomas went to his office and closed the door. He took a deep breath and walked over to his desk. A white envelope sat on his desk, his name handwritten on it. He picked it up and flipped it over. He sat in his chair and opened the note.

"Thomas," it read, "It has been brought to our attention that you have not yet joined the new banking system here at Smith and Brumsby. This will make it impossible for you to receive your employment check. Please come to HR as soon as you get to work today and find me. We need to work something out." It was signed, Lyle Marconi.

Thomas decided to take the stairs down to HR to avoid more scrutiny. He found Lyle's door and knocked. A voice from inside called for him to enter. A middle-aged man, wearing a navy suit with a yellow tie sat behind the desk.

"I'm Thomas Larson from acquisitions. I got your"—

"Come in and close the door."

Thomas obeyed, but an uncomfortable tightness began to form in his chest.

"Have a seat. I see you're still not marked. Any reason why?" Lyle reached for a small stack of manila folders sitting on the bureau behind his desk. He fingered through the stack until he found the one he was looking for. Thomas saw his name on the tab.

"Um ... well ... I, uh, I'm a Christian and my faith won't allow me to take the number."

There. He said it.

"Your faith won't allow you to get paid for working? Your faith won't allow you to provide for your ..." he paused and flipped through Thomas's file until he again found what he was looking for "... your family?"

"I know it's hard for some people to understand, but I just can't take Hitler's mark."

Lyle set Thomas's file open on his desk, leaned back in his chair and clasped his hands behind his head. "Is there any way you could try to change your perspective here a bit and see this as a financial agreement. It's not really Hitler's mark, it's your banking identification mark. That's got a nice sound to it, doesn't it?"

"There have to be others here in my same position. What are you doing for them?"

Lyle grabbed the stack of folders and dropped them on top of Thomas's.

"The same thing I'm doing with you. Trying to convince you guys to get past any personal convictions you have about Adolph Hitler and get you to mark up so that I can pay you. I'm in a real bind here because there is absolutely no way for me to get money to you without it. You're not interested in working for free, are you?"

Thomas shifted in his seat. "Isn't it possible this whole fad is going to blow over? I mean, maybe we could work something out for a few months and then when things die down, it'll be fine that I don't have a mark."

"What are you suggesting?"

Thomas was thinking on the fly. "Well, let's say someone here at Brumsby, for a fee, mind you, would be willing to put my paycheck in their account and cash it out for magogs. We do this for a few months, he earns a nice little commission on the side and when things return to normal, I still have my job and my family still has food on the table."

Thomas waited for his response. Lyle rubbed his chin, deep in thought.

"You see, there's a bigger picture here, brother. If you don't have the mark, the FWP is going to withhold funds to our town. Mayor Durbin says that we're on the verge of a boom if we get the financial aid promised to us from the FWP. And what's good for Creston is good for its people."

"Come on, Lyle. Let's just try it for a month and see how it works. Maybe in a month, I'll have a mark. Who knows?"

"And maybe in a month you'll be living at one of those training camps."

Thomas looked into Lyle's eyes and knew he wasn't joking. Lyle opened the top drawer of his desk and pulled out a neon orange piece of paper. He handed it to Thomas, who took it and read it.

"You see, Thomas, Mayor Durbin is taking this very seriously. He is giving utility vouchers and free parking passes to companies who comply one hundred percent. Smith and Brumsby is a frugal company and they want their vouchers. So, I'm sorry my friend, no mark, no moolah."

Thomas stood. "Then I guess yesterday was my last day here." He turned and walked out of the office. As he walked toward the stairwell, he heard Lyle call to him from the doorway of his office.

"If you change your mind, come and see me."

Thomas went back up to his office and found an empty paper supply box. He filled it with his personal belongings and headed home. His garage door slowly opened. Robin's car was parked on her side of the garage. He was pretty sure what had happened. It was a good thing they had stockpiled supplies in their basement because it looked like they were going to have to buy some time until they figured out what to do.

He walked in the side door from the garage that led to the kitchen. Robin was sitting at the kitchen table, a cup of coffee in front of her and another one on the table.

"Expecting someone?"

"I saw you pull in. What are you doing home?" Robin's eyes revealed her concern.

"Probably the same thing as you. No mark, no job."

"I got pulled into Principal Sharp's office and told the same thing. Apparently your good friend, Durbin, is tossing incentives all over town to get people marked."

They sat in silence for a moment until Thomas remembered the girls.

"Where are the girls?"

"They're still at school. It's crazy but none of the kids at school are marked."

"None?"

"Nope. Several of the kids told me their parents had numbers put on their heads and the next morning they were gone. A couple said they rubbed them off, but others said they just disappeared. What do you make of that?"

"Looks like some kind of special protection. I wonder what Durbin will do about that. I don't think there was a child exception clause in the FWP's directive."

Thomas smiled. It was the first one all day and it felt good.

Robin reached for his hand. "What are we going to do, Thomas?"

"We knew this might happen. We've got enough food to feed an army for a couple of months in our basement and some gasoline in the garage. That won't last too long, so we'll have to use our vehicles sparingly. But gas doesn't store for long periods of time, so we didn't have much of a choice. I guess we will just have to keep in contact with the church body and hunker down for the time being. The mortgage is covered for the next six months and I prepaid phone, gas, and electric bills. So, this is it. We just wait. We should be okay for a while, unless . . ."

Thomas tried to feel out whether Robin would be open to another option.

"Unless what?"

"Unless Wayne is serious about sending people to the training camps. Then, we may have to leave town. Or even call Charlie and see if there's room at the"—

"I called my dad. He said we could stay with them. Things are pretty much the same by him also. His church is really getting hassled. He's sure things will get worse. And this is just day one."

"So, what about the compound?"

"No, it would be foolish to go now when we have so many supplies here. We should wait."

Thomas pulled his hand away and pushed his chair away from the table. "What is your hang-up about the compound?"

"We don't even know who's down there. How safe is it? And do they really have enough food?"

"Charlie's there and other Christians. When it's a matter of life or death, why does that matter?"

"Did they screen people? Are you sure there's not some child molester down there?"

"Good grief, Robin! It's seventeen Christian men and their families and friends. You know they've stockpiled food and there are only a couple of ways in and out. These guys knew this was coming and they were prepared. They were generous enough to offer us a place and we turned them down. I think we should rethink our decision."

"I can't do it, Thomas. You know I get seasonal depression—living underground would kill me!"

"Living above ground may kill you sooner." Thomas stood and walked to the garage door.

"Where are you going?"

"To get the girls. They're safer here with us."

He shut the door behind him without waiting for a response. He climbed in his car and a helpless feeling enveloped him.

"Why is this happening, Lord? Have You forgotten Your children?"

Thomas shook his head and started the car. Slowly he backed out of the drive. As he headed toward school Thomas passed a large grey bus heading in the opposite direction. The words *Federation of World Powers* was painted in large black letters across the side. Beneath the title were two words that sent chills up his spine. *Training Facility.*

His anger dissipated and fear quickly stepped in. "I'm sorry, Lord. Please tell me what to do." Thomas picked up his girls and quickly returned home.

seventeen ‖

July

Noah woke to the sound of footsteps in the hall. He pushed the LED button on his watch. It was already after seven in the morning. That was a pretty good night. He remembered waking up once because he heard someone coughing in the hall, but that was it. A full night's sleep. Noah sat up and swung his legs off the side of the bed, resting them quietly on the floor. There wasn't a sound out of Charlie over in his corner, but his third roommate, Cal Moeller, was still snoring.

Noah shook his head. He was amazed at how much later he was sleeping these days. Dave thought that living below ground was developing a sort of hibernation amongst the residents. Each night lights were out by ten thirty or eleven and each morning everyone slept in a bit later.

Noah grabbed the towel at the end of his bed and made his way to the door. Every room had a small night-light in the outlet near the door so he found it easily. Because of the lack of natural light, even during the day it was pitch black. He opened the door and went into the hallway, closing the door quietly behind him. He made his way to the men's community bathroom and there were several showers already running but still a few open. He grabbed a quick shower and headed back to the room.

The compound was long and narrow. In the center were two rows of twenty-four small sleeping units with two bathroom/shower facilities located on the perimeter, one for men and the other for women. At the far north end was the kitchen and eating area, and at the south was the massive living room. There, multiple sitting areas were set up around a couple of televisions, hooked up to video games and DVD players. Game tables sported puzzles and decks of cards where continuous games were held. Three treadmills and an elliptical machine were in one corner and in constant use. The only cable television was located near the kitchen and the adults typically gathered there to catch the daily news. Chef Fredo had an efficient and helpful staff, as there was not a whole lot to do to pass the time. The few children at the compound did schoolwork on a daily basis in between breakfast and lunch, mostly just to keep them busy and keep their parents' sanity intact. There was nothing overly exciting about compound life, but it would have to do.

When Noah got back to the room, the light was on and both Cal and Charlie were sitting up.

"Any hot water left?"

"That's not going to be a problem any time soon, Cal." Noah hung his towel at the end of his bed and sat facing the other two. "We have water heaters big enough to fill an Olympic-size pool twice over. I guess Dave really loves his hot showers."

"So, did you try again?"

Noah looked at Charlie. "I tried four times yesterday alone. Her phone is dead. Gone. She was planning on being here so she didn't prepay her bill. But her mom's phone just rings and rings."

"You're going to go again, aren't you?" he said with disbelief.

"I could go at night this time, wear a hat in case I ran into anyone. We've got tanks of gas we're not even using."

Charlie stood and grabbed his towel. "Where would you even look? Her house was locked up tight and you don't even know where her mother lives."

"I just want to see if there's been any movement at her house. I could ask around a bit."

"Oh, that sounds safe. She could call you, you know. You've had no messages from her. Maybe she left the state."

"She has no other family."

Charlie walked over to Noah and put a hand on his shoulder. "She could have been taken to a camp, Noah. You have to face it. You've seen what they're saying on the news. The camps have been filling up and the Stepford Wives they send back are completely different people."

Noah stood and pulled Charlie's hand off his shoulder. "She would never take the mark, Charlie, so don't even imply . . ."

"Whoa, you two!" Cal stepped in the middle of the men. "I've only been here a week but I thought you guys were like best friends."

Noah took a step back. "I'm sorry. I'm losing my mind about this, when I should be leaving it in God's hands. It's just that the way we left things was so vague. I could tell she wanted to come, but her mother taking the mark had completely thrown her for a loop."

"Go find Dave. See if he thinks a run to town would hurt. I'm making a run to Indianapolis this morning to pick up another family—relatives of Mary Wilson. We could go into Creston first and take a look around."

"Heard anything from your friends in town?"

"The Larsons? No. I check my voice mail regularly but I haven't heard anything. I wish we had phone service down here, but for now I'll just wait until nighttime and go above ground to check. I've tried calling but I think their phones must have been turned off."

"That's what happened to mine," Cal added. "Durbin is systematically working his way through town and if he finds a family without the mark, he shuts everything down. It doesn't matter if you prepaid. Your electricity gets turned off, no gas and no phones. That's phase one. I lived without those things for a couple of weeks. Since it's so warm out, I didn't really need gas and I just kept the windows open."

"What's phase two?" Noah tried to picture Tara without electricity, but since her mother was marked, maybe she would still be okay.

"He waits a couple of weeks and then sends an officer to see if you want a ride over to the local tattoo parlor. When you refuse, you end up taking a ride to the station. A few days there and it's off to the training facility. Durbin said he thought that by September first his town would be eligible for FWP funds. So he must be working overtime to get it done."

Noah looked at Charlie and made up his mind. "We've got to go. If I can get into Tara's house, I think I can find an address for her mom. As long as you are going to Indianapolis, we might as well try to find her. I'll meet you in the kitchen."

Noah grabbed his baseball cap from his dresser and shoved it on his head. He ran down the hall toward the sitting room. Dave could usually be found there in the mornings, scanning the *Internet* for world news or reading his Bible. Noah spotted him at a far corner table, coffee and muffin in front of him, Bible open on the table with a notepad next to it.

Noah slowed himself down and walked over to him.

"Good morning, Dave. Can I join you?"

"Have a seat." Dave pointed to the chair next to him.

"I need to talk to you a minute."

"One hundred thirty-seven. Did you know that's how many we're up to?"

"Excuse me?"

"We're up to a hundred and thirty-seven residents. Slowly but surely they're coming, but I'm worried about security."

"What do you mean? Everyone who comes was invited by one of the fellowship. We have to trust that they were careful who they invited. Why are you worried now?"

"Look at this." He slid his laptop over toward Noah. He clicked through a series of pictures, each one showing bodies piled and being burned in different countries around the world. Cheering people standing beside the burning mounds filled each picture, as if it was a cause for celebration. Noah looked up at Dave.

"We're trying to be orderly and civilized in how we handle this, but things are going to change. It's going to turn nasty and I just worry that not everyone who walks through that door is truly looking for a refuge. What happens if we find someone who is marked down here? What do we do then?"

"Dave, you worked hard to provide this protection and God guided you the whole way. You can't worry about something that hasn't happened yet. We're all being careful."

"People go above ground every day. Every day some of the mothers take the kids out into the cornfield."

"To gather the fresh corn and potatoes. The stalks are high enough that they aren't seen."

"Not by anyone on the ground, but what about satellites?"

"So we'll pick at night."

"There's just a lot to oversee. I think tonight I'm going to meet with the men and go over some of my concerns."

Noah decided it was time to tell him he was leaving.

"I just wanted to let you know I am going to go out with Charlie today." Dave raised his eyebrows so Noah added details. "He's picking up a family in Indianapolis and I'm riding along. We're going to run into Creston first."

"Trying to find Tara?"

"It's that obvious?"

"I understand. I was young and in love once."

"You were married, weren't you?" Noah asked cautiously, pointing to the wedding ring on Dave's left hand.

"Yeah. There are times I wish she was here, but as things get harder, I'm glad she didn't have to go through this. She went through enough as it was."

"How did she die?"

"Colon cancer. It was a short battle. She died six and a half years ago. You know, this whole compound was her brainchild."

"Really? I thought you . . ."

"It's a long story and you probably should run. I'll tell you some other time."

Dave stood and shook hands with Noah. "Be careful, especially when you return. And be sure to cover your tracks outside the barn when you get back."

"Okay, Dad."

Noah tossed him his patent half smile and Dave punched him in the arm.

"Let me know when you get back."

Noah ran out of the room and found Charlie in the eating area with the keys in his hand. They walked through the back of the kitchen and caught the fresh blueberry muffins Fredo tossed to them on their way out. At the back corner of the kitchen was a door that led to the stairwell. The stairs ascended into the garage of the farmhouse above the compound. This entrance was rarely used, except to access the vans stored in the garage and in one of the barns. Charlie pointed to the van on the right and Noah jumped into the passenger seat. Charlie stepped outside of the garage using a side door and the next thing Noah knew, the door was opened and Charlie was in the driver's seat.

As they pulled away from the farmhouse, there were no other cars in sight. Charlie and Noah pulled their baseball caps firmly over their foreheads and headed for town. It only took a couple of minutes in the van to reach civilization and soon Noah started to see people. He pulled his cell phone out of his pocket and checked for messages. Nothing. Then he tried Tara's house and cell. Still no ringing, just a recorded message that he had misdialed.

"Turn left on Washington. She lives across the street from the park on Harrison." Noah dialed the number for Tara's mom's house and got a busy signal. "It's busy, but at least someone's home." As Charlie slowed the van onto Harrison, Noah pointed to the beige house. Charlie pulled in the drive and put the van in park.

"Let's try the front door. If there's no answer, I'll go around back and see if there is a window I can open."

The two men got out of the van and went to the front door. Noah knocked and looked through the window. There were no lights on in the house and no signs of life. They waited a moment and a voice called to them from the house on their right.

"You from the bank?"

Noah and Charlie stepped back from the door and looked over at a man in his fifties, who stood on his porch with his hands on his hips.

"Uh, no, we're not," answered Noah.

"Haven't I seen you before?" the man asked.

"I'm a friend of Tara Warners. She owns this house."

"You mean 'owned' it. She's been gone for a month. The utilities were shut off and she just took off. I think the bank will take it over now."

"Why were things shut off?"

"She wasn't marked, so her house was turned off. My wife and I warned her it would happen, and just like everywhere else, she got shut down and she disappeared."

Noah felt his heart race a bit and he tried to speak calmly. "Was she taken away?"

"You mean to a training camp? No. They came to get her and she was already gone. But it's been a month now."

"Well, thanks for the information," said Charlie, grabbing Noah by the shoulder and pushing him toward the van. "I guess we'll get going."

"It's a pity she'll lose the house. She was a good neighbor, too." The man rubbed his chin, then turned to go back into his own house.

"If you see her, will you tell her to call Noah?" He couldn't help himself. Charlie threw him a look of alarm, but what harm could there be in a first name.

"N N N N O O O O A A A A H H H H H GRRRRRREEEEEEEEEERRRR!"

The screech came from across the park. Charlie and Noah looked to see who or what had screamed his name, but couldn't figure out where it was coming from. People in the park stopped walking and looked around. The man on the front porch turned back to the men.

"HE'S ONE OF THEMMMMMMM!"

The wail was loud and clear.

The man started down the front steps of his porch. "You're not marked either?"

It was a question that neither Charlie nor Noah wanted to answer. They weren't sure what he planned to do but Charlie had already edged his way to the door of the van. He looked through the window at Noah and yelled at him to get in. Noah leaped into the van and slammed the door shut. They peeled out of the driveway and headed down the street. Charlie looked in the rearview mirror and realized what the man was doing.

"He's got our license number. We shouldn't have come."

"But I didn't get inside. I don't have her mother's address!" Noah struggled to breathe and searched his mind for a solution. "Maybe if we come back at night . . ."

"We're not coming back. We're marked in this van now. I don't even know if it's safe to go to Indianapolis."

"Well, we have to. People are waiting. Who was screaming my name anyway? Did you see anyone?"

Noah noticed Charlie's white knuckles on the steering wheel as they headed out of town. The whole scene must have shaken him up more than he was letting on. Noah sat in the passenger seat, not sure what to do next. The drive to Indianapolis would take an hour and that gave him time to think. Then he remembered the busy signal. Maybe he'd find Tara with her mother and everything would be fine. He pulled the phone out of his pocket again and tried her mother's number again. This time it rang. Sonda Warners finally answered on the eighth ring.

"Hello, Mrs. Warners. This is Noah Greer. I've been trying to reach Tara. Is she with you?"

After a slight hesitation, she answered, "No. I haven't seen her since she went to Nashville with some friends."

"Nashville? With friends? Who did she go with?"

"The daughter and son of one of my friends."

"But can she travel without a mark? How is she getting around?"

"Noah, I know this will be hard for you to understand, but Tara has been able to clear her head since you've been gone. She is thinking much more clearly and she no longer believes the way you do."

"What do you mean?"

"She's not playing these little games of rebellion to the government any longer. I was able to convince her that we are called to submit to the government that the Lord has placed over us. It is our obligation. That's from Romans 13, in case you were wondering."

"What are you saying, Mrs. Warners?" Noah could feel his hand start to shake and he braced himself for her next words.

"Well, I don't know how else to tell you. Tara has taken the mark and gone on with her life. You don't need to try and call her any longer. She's not interested in your end-of-the-world games. And Noah," she waited for a response.

"Yes?"

"May I suggest you do the same."

Click. And that was all.

Noah pulled the phone from his ear and stared at it.

"What?" Charlie wanted to know what she had said.

Noah could hardly process the information. It couldn't be true. If he had made one thing clear to her it was not to take the mark. A tightness began to form in his chest and suddenly Noah found himself struggling to catch his breath.

"Come on, Noah. What's going on?" Charlie's voice cut into his thoughts.

"Uh," he stammered, "She said that Tara took the mark." Noah reached up and rubbed his forehead. "She said that she was going on with her life."

"No way. Do you think she's telling the truth?"

Noah slammed both hands on the dash of the van. Thoughts raced through his head. Was this part of the plan all along? Did she have a mark when he saw her? She couldn't have, but why now? Did her mother have this much influence over her or is it someone else? Who would she be talking to?

It just didn't make sense to him. If she had the mark, why wouldn't she be in her own home. He had told her he would come back for her. Was she hiding from him?

"Why wouldn't she be back in Creston then?" Noah reasoned out loud. "I just don't get it, but I need to see it for myself."

"Settle down, buddy. You may never get to see it. How will you ever find her? And if she has the mark, it's over. You can't bring her down to the compound."

Noah held his head in his hands. That last statement was like a slap in the face. If she had the mark, not only was her future set, but Charlie was right. She couldn't come to the compound and it was over between them. He couldn't believe it was true, but it would explain why she hadn't gotten ahold of him for two months. He turned and stared out the window, as Charlie turned on the radio. The next hour was spent in silence, though the thoughts in Noah's head drowned out the radio at times.

Would she really take the mark? How could she have done that? I have to see for myself. I can't believe unless I see. I won't believe it until I see. But how? How am I going to find her? It just can't be true . . . but then again, it does make sense . . .

Noah had no idea how he would pull it off, but the only way he could deal with Sondra Warners words would be to verify them for himself.

Thomas slept better. Perhaps it was because he had gotten used to his new schedule or maybe it was because he had tried to get up earlier and go to bed later so he was more tired at night. Initially, he would lie awake for hours, his mind racing, and try to figure out how to keep his sanity just staying in his house day after day. Every time he left the house it brought scrutiny and judgment on his family. Even a walk through his neighborhood for fresh air brought sneers and ridicule. No longer did a baseball cap hide the fact his family wasn't marked—caps were the mark of rebels.

He had to hand it to the mayor. Durbin had done a good job creating incentives for Creston to mark up and become their brothers' keeper. That man had tunnel vision and he wanted to be the first town to get a hundred percent on the test. But there were too many believers like Thomas who refused to conform and that had to be eating away at Durbin.

In the meantime, Thomas spent day after day in the house with Robin and the girls, computing the rations in his basement and watching CNN for a hopeful sign of relief. But no relief ever came. Three times over the past two months, the Larsons were able to get together with a family from church, but the rumor mill said that most unmarked church members had disappeared. They could no longer meet without being harassed by the community and to top it off, Reverend Blackmore was on the first bus to the training camp on May sixteen. It had been two months and he still wasn't back.

Thomas stared at the ceiling, wondering what the day would bring. He noticed movement out of the corner of his eye and saw Robin coming out of the master bathroom with a towel on her head. "You're sleeping in late today."

"I slept well last night," he explained. "It's so hard to turn off my thoughts at night."

"I know, but for the sake of the girls, we need to try to keep things as normal as possible."

Thomas sat up in bed, and ran his fingers through his hair.

"Normal? What exactly is normal about anything in our life?"

Robin picked up the remote for the television from the night-stand next to Thomas and turned on the television. "Here, get some news. That should get you going. I've started the coffee and you need to get in the shower."

Robin pulled the towel from her head and tossed her wet hair with her fingers. Thomas watched her leave the room before he slowly got out of bed and headed into the bathroom. He turned on the shower and walked over to the sink. His chin was dark with stubble from four days of neglect and he decided to shave after his shower.

"There. Something to look forward to."

Then the lights went out in the bathroom. Thomas reached for the light switch and flipped it a couple of times. He realized the TV was off in his bedroom, too. He reached to turn the shower off , but the water pressure was diminishing and soon it stopped. Thomas ran out into the hallway, down the stairs, and into the kitchen. Robin had the girls at the table, eating breakfast. All the lights in the house were off and she threw him a frightened look.

"What about the phone?" Thomas asked.

"I didn't check yet." Robin picked up the telephone and put it to her ear. "Nothing. No dial tone. It's dead."

Thomas ran to the den and grabbed his cell phone. He flipped it open and read the screen. It indicated no service. He carried it into the kitchen where Robin was checking hers.

"They've cut the phones off." Thomas felt a knot forming in his stomach.

"Who's cut the phones off?" Sarah asked, with a mouthful of toast.

"Don't worry about it, honey. I'm going to talk to daddy in the other room, but you finish your breakfast and then go get dressed."

Thomas and Robin headed into the living room, and Thomas put his hand on Robin's shoulder. He could feel her muscles tense and knew she was frightened.

"We knew this was coming. It's happened to everyone. I'm surprised it hasn't happened sooner." He tried to keep his voice calm.

"Thomas, I can't keep the food in the fridge cold! And the house is going to heat up like a furnace without any air-conditioning. And what about toilets? We can't live like this!"

"Then we'll have to leave. I've got the car full of gas, so we've got enough for one trip somewhere. We'll just have to pick wisely."

"Where? Where can we go?"

Thomas sat on the couch and Robin followed suit. "Give me a minute here. If we panic, we'll make a mistake that could be avoided. Now, let's think this through." Thomas stared at the floor as he laid out a plan. "We have plenty of food still, and about fifty gallons of stored water. If we limit the use of bathrooms to just one in the house, I can go out at night and siphon some water from the neighbor's spigot. We can just flush once a day." Robin cringed and Thomas grabbed her hand. "I know it's gross, but it will work. I will try to get a couple of buckets of water and we can use the extra to clean up with. We just need to buy some time until I figure out what to do."

"How will I wash clothes? And the girls' hair? This isn't going to work!"

"Yes, it is. It has to. We can call your parents and see if they still have utilities. Or we could get ahold of Charlie. I'll bet we could still get to the compound."

"We don't have a phone and my parents only have a two bedroom house. We can't move in there."

Thomas ran through several scenarios in his mind, but each option ended up with a trip to the county jail and then off to a training camp. That was the three-step process—cutting off utilities, a short stint in jail, and then the camp.

"How about this: we head over to your parents' house and bring food with us. We can stay in the basement. We'll stay for just a couple of weeks. If things start to get bad there, we'll move around a bit, until we think it's safe to come back here."

Robin gave him a confused look. "How will it be safe to come back here? We'll never get our utilities back and if they find us, we'll be separated and sent to the training camps. I couldn't handle that, Thomas!"

"Well, what if they come to get us and we're gone? They search the house, we make it clear we're really gone—make it look like we left in a hurry. Then after they mark the house with the yellow tape that's on everyone's house who are sent to camp, we come back and live in the house. We just don't let anyone know we're back. We'll return late at night, we leave the tape on the door and we'll live on the food here until . . ." Thomas struggled with his own words ". . . Jesus returns, or this blows over."

"Do you think it'll work?" Robin sounded hopeful.

A knock at the door interrupted their conversation. Robin looked at Thomas and her trembling returned. He reached up and tried to force his mussed hair into place.

"They don't take you the first day. It's probably a warning. Get the girls and stay in our bedroom until this is done."

Thomas watched as Robin ran into the kitchen and grabbed the girls by the hand. She practically dragged them up the stairs and when he heard the door close, he walked to the front door. Glancing down, he remembered he was still in his pajamas. There was nothing he could do about it, so he opened the door. Relief poured over him when he recognized Reverend Blackwell standing in the doorway.

"I'm glad to see you, Reverend." Thomas extended his hand and the Reverend willingly took it. That's when Thomas saw the mark. High on his forehead in miniscule numbers was the mark of the Antichrist. Thomas's spirits fell.

"May I come in?"

"Sure." Thomas stepped out of the doorway and the Reverend walked past him into the living room. His head turned and he looked into the kitchen.

"Are Robin and the girls home?" Reverend Blackwell sat on the couch but Thomas remained standing.

"What's going on here, Reverend? When did you get back?"

A smile came over the Reverend's face. "I've been back for two weeks now."

"Really? No one has said a word to us that you were back." Thomas could feel anger welling up inside of him, as the implication of the mark on his pastor's head filled his mind. "I've got to ask, sir, is that really the mark of Hitler on your forehead?"

The Reverend reached a hand up to his forehead and lightly touched the mark.

"Sit, Thomas. Let's talk a bit."

Thomas obliged, but kept his guard up. It made no sense that his pastor had a mark on his forehead, not after instructing the whole congregation not to take one.

"Yes, it's the mark. Now, I know what you're thinking, Thomas, but please hear me out. I'm here as your pastor and your friend. You can't let your family go to the camp. You'll never see them again and they'll do terrible . . ."

The Reverend reached up and wiped his eyes. They were the eyes of a tired man and for the first time Thomas carefully studied the face of his pastor. Deep wrinkles creased his forehead and his cheeks were gaunt and worn.

"I had no idea this was going to happen. No idea at all. They picked me up on a Wednesday morning, at four thirty in the morning, mind you, and that was the last time I saw Carol alive. They put Carol and the boys in one squad car and me in another. At the station, I sat for ten hours alone—no food, no phone, not even a chair. I sat on the floor. By the time they came to get me, they said that my family had taken the mark and were already back home. I knew it wasn't true. I spent the next four hours being questioned, still no food. It went on like this for days. Occasionally they would give me a glass of water and eventually they gave me an apple and a dinner roll. But I slept on a cold floor and was completely isolated for the first four days. Then it was into the general population of the jail for three more days. There were five of us who were used for sparring practice by the rest of the inmates. I ended up with bruises all over my body." After a week had passed, they sent me to the camp."

Blackmore leaned to one side and slid his hand into the pocket of his khaki pants. He pulled out a wad of Kleenex and blew his nose.

"At least the camp had beds. We were deloused upon arrival and I thought I had endured pain and embarrassment at the jail—this was dehumanizing. Then we were put into the program—breakfast/class/work, lunch/class/work, dinner/class/work. Day after day after day. Three times a day they offered the mark. After four weeks of class they stopped offering and they told me that they would only offer it one more time. I continued to refuse on the grounds that it was aligning with Satan and my allegiance was with God. Then, one by one, the men who I had spent the last month with started to disappear. One day they called me out of lunch."

Reverend Blackmore wiped a tear from his eye and seemed to look around nervously. He was but a shell of the man who stood in the pulpit each week teaching tolerance and love.

"They took me to a room that looked out on a back lot at the camp. I will never forget what I saw. Mounds of burning bodies. Men and women who refused the mark were being burned. I pray they died quickly, but that's how they are disposing of the people—they are just burning them. And then I saw her."

He paused again and put his head in his hands. His shoulders began to shake, as he sobbed into his hands. Thomas waited, not knowing what to say or do. He glanced toward the stairs, and hoped Robin and the girls weren't listening.

"It was Carol. She was dead. I started to scream and they hit me with a baton across my back. I fell to the ground and they stood me back up. When I asked where the boys were, they told me that if I took the mark they would return the boys to me, unmarked and unharmed. That night, I spent a long time in prayer and I came up with two conclusions. First, this is not of God. Something has gone terribly wrong, but I know with confidence this whole thing is not of God. Perhaps He is finally fed up with sin, but for some reason He has turned His back on us. Second, I am a father first and I have an obligation to protect my children. I should have protected Carol, but I can't change what happened to her. But I could save my boys' lives, so I did it. I took the mark."

Thomas winced at the reality of Blackmore's predicament. "Are the boys back with you?"

"They are supposed to be coming home in the next week or so." Reverend Blackmore looked even more weak and insecure.

"Why didn't you get them back immediately?"

"I don't know, but I have talked with them and they are fine. So, for the past two weeks I have been trying to go to every congregant's house that I can to tell them to protect their family. That's why I'm here, Thomas. You can't let Robin and the girls be taken to the camp. You have to mark up your family and continue on with life. Once you take the mark, all this is over. You can work again, you can take your family to restaurants, the kids go back to school, and you will live to a ripe old age."

Despair filled Thomas's heart. He knew that he may well have to face the very same choice. "What about the rapture? You said it was right around the corner."

"This was not in God's plan, Thomas. He has turned from His people and I don't know what else to say. I love Him, but right now

I'm on my own. And I could sit here and show you plenty of Scripture that obligates a man to provide for his family. Why I didn't do this sooner, why I allowed so many of my people to die for this . . . I'll never be able to explain it, but that is the burden I must bear."

Thomas became more and more uncomfortable with the conversation. His mind raced with questions, but Reverend Blackmore's frailty stopped him from asking them. The Reverend stood and Thomas followed suit.

"I have to leave now, but Thomas, they're coming." Blackwell looked around the room. "They've shut off your utilities and soon they'll be here. Don't let them kill your family. You have a choice. There's no need to be a martyr, especially when God seems to be on vacation. Take care of your family and don't bear the guilt of sending them to their deaths."

They walked to the door and shook hands.

"I appreciate you coming by, Reverend. You've given me a lot to think about."

Thomas watched Reverend Blackmore pull out of his driveway. He stared at the car as it slowly headed down the street until it turned out of view. There were few men in Thomas's life that he looked to for spiritual guidance. One just drove away. The thought of this godly man being forced to chose the mark or the life of his children was unbearable. It hit too close to home. What would he do if he was faced with the same decision?

It probably was not a matter of "if" but "when."

"Robin? Robin! Bring the girls!"

Thomas heard Robin open the door of the master bedroom. He met eyes with her as she looked over the banister.

"We're leaving in an hour. Pack bags and I'll put food in the van."

"But Thomas—where will we go?"

"We'll try your parents' house first. If that doesn't work, we'll try to get ahold of Charlie, but we can't stay here."

"What did Blackwell say?"

"There's no time! Pack and we'll talk in the car."

Ninety minutes later the Larsons were on the road. Thomas glanced into his rearview mirror at his disappearing house. He had a lot to process, but to do it at home was no longer an option. Blackmore may be convinced that God was gone, but Thomas sure wasn't. There was specific Scripture that Charlie had tried to get him to read and before he decided the best course of action, he had better figure out what God's take on this whole thing was. Thomas put his hand on his Bible, which was on console next to him. It was time for him to step up and lead. He needed to make the decisions now. He would answer to God.

Now, if I could only remember where Charlie told me to read . . .

"Do you think he heard you?" Durbin leaned forward in his chair waiting for the answer.

"He listened closely and thanked me for my advice. It may take some time, but he loves his family. He'll mark up."

"Well, he's on the run now, but since his car is traced, we'll be able to find him when we are ready. I'll give him a week or so to think about your conversation."

Durbin picked up the phone and pushed a button. "Send them in."

Two minutes later the door to Mayor Durbin's office opened and a woman with two boys, age nine and twelve entered the room. The boys ran into their father's arms, as the woman noticeably fought back tears. Reverend Blackwell, hugging his sons, turned to Durbin.

"Thank you for keeping your word."

"No, Reverend, thank you. You can rest your head tonight knowing you saved the lives of twelve families over the past two weeks."

"Even though I had to lie to do it?"

Durbin ignored the comment.

"And with your wife home, your life should be back to normal in no time."

Reverend Blackwell embraced his marked wife, and then he and his family left, arm in arm.

Durbin leaned back and crossed his feet on top of his desk. "I love happy endings. I hope Thomas chooses one."

eighteen ‖

August

Elise sat at her desk, acting as busy as she could but keeping one eye on Agent Vasiliev who sat on the couch in the foyer of the Russian headquarters office. Occasionally he glanced her way, but she acted as though the information she was inputting on her computer was of greatest importance. He was flipping through a file that he had carried in with him fifteen minutes earlier. He had an appointment with Hitler, but her boss was running a bit behind schedule.

Elise noticed a rustling from near her feet and she glanced down at her purse. It was unzipped and propped open, and she could see her idol lying on the top. He smiled at her and she furrowed her eyebrows at him, hoping he would keep quiet. She'd started carrying him with her because she found his information useful. Because of that she was becoming more dependent on him every day. Every time she asked his advice, he knew the right thing to do. Would Adolph rather take the Mercedes or the Jaguar to the theater? Would he rather have beef or salmon for lunch? What would Adolph like for his birthday? What kind of mood would he be in when he arrived? And yet, the advice her idol gave was rather trivial by nature. Elise wondered if its sole purpose was to make Adolph's life easier or if there was a greater use that she hadn't quite tapped into yet. He was completely clueless whenever she asked even a general question about Agent Vasiliev, so she gave up on that weeks ago.

Elise heard a loud noise that startled her. It sounded like glass shattering. She looked to Hitler's closed door and then to Vasiliev, who stood up alarmed.

"Don't go in," she warned. "This happens every once in a while. He's been known to throw things lately. I'll sweep it up once he comes out to get you."

Vasiliev sat but said nothing.

"You wouldn't happen to know why he has been so angry lately?" Elise decided to try some small talk.

"If he wanted you to know, wouldn't he have told you himself?"

Elise sat quietly for a moment, then pushed away from her desk and stood. She walked over to the sitting area and sat on the edge of a chair, facing Vasiliev.

"You just don't like me, do you?"

"It's not my job to like you."

"But considering our paths cross on a daily basis and our lives are completely absorbed with the same man, I was hoping we could be friends."

"I don't need a friend."

"Well, what do you need, Agent Vasiliev? Do you need a cup of coffee or a glass of water? I can easily get you either of those without being over friendly now, can't I? I would hate to think you were thirsty and I didn't offer you anything to drink."

"I am completely capable of getting a drink myself."

Elise scooted back in the chair, leaned back, and folded her arms. "That's good to know. Heaven forbid I give you a drink and then you might actually have to say thank you to me. That might just do you in."

"What's your point?"

Elise stood. "My point is that we have been working together for almost five years now and I don't think I even know your first name.

Perhaps it is just 'Agent' but I would think that is a silly first name. Would it kill you to be polite enough to make small talk when we are alone? Or if it's not in your job description, you just refuse to extend yourself?"

Perhaps it was her tone, but she definitely struck a nerve. Agent Vasiliev stood with a fire in his eyes and opened his mouth to speak, just as Hitler's office door opened.

"What's going on here?" Hitler looked at his personal assistant and the head of his security.

"I was just asking Agent Vasiliev if he would like a glass of water while he waited for you to finish up your phone call."

Vasiliev looked at Elise, the fire still there but the mouth now closed.

"Did you bring the latest report?" Hitler asked Vasiliev.

"Yes, sir."

"Then let's take a look."

Hitler turned and walked back into his office. Vasiliev followed behind and as he passed Elise he said, under his breath so that only she would hear, "Yakov." Elise smiled and watched him close the door. Perhaps the outburst paid off. Either way, at least she now knew his name.

She returned to her desk and continued on her computer. From her purse below she heard a small voice.

"I don't like him."

"What?" Elise looked down at her idol.

"I don't like him and I don't trust him. I need to see him."

"You need to see him. For what reason? I don't want you to sit on my desk."

"Why not? I can be a much better help if I can see around your office."

"Because I have the real thing ten feet from me in his office, and I don't need an idol of him sitting on my desk. I don't want him to think I'm crazy."

"He gave me to you. He'll be happy to see that you carry me around."

Elise reached down and zipped her purse shut. "Enough. You need to be quiet now."

Her phone buzzed and Hitler asked her to come into his office. She grabbed her calendar, a notebook, and a pen and hurried in. Hitler was behind his desk, sitting upright, and Agent Vasiliev was in one of the wingback chairs facing him. She quickly scanned the room for broken glass, but saw nothing out of place. *Perhaps he cleaned it up himself?*

"Yes sir?"

"When do you leave for Jerusalem?"

"I leave tomorrow morning, sir, and you will arrive three days later."

"I need you to put Agent Vasiliev on that flight with you."

"I think we're full, sir." Elise quickly thumbed through her organizer and found the list of passengers on the eight-seat Citation X.

"Bump someone. I want him there tomorrow. You will be doing some research with him for me. He'll fill you in on the plane. When I arrive, I want it complete."

Elise glanced over at Vasiliev. He didn't look overly thrilled at the assignment, so she smiled and said, "Why, thank you for this opportunity, sir. We will be thorough and waiting for you when you arrive." She turned and left the office, closing the door behind her.

Well, well. An assignment with Yakov. Sounds interesting.

She glanced down at her purse and considered not taking the idol. He was a bit annoying earlier. Then she decided to just not keep him in her purse, but to pack him in her suitcase. He could stay at the hotel and then still be available for counsel when needed. The door to Hitler's office opened and Vasiliev exited.

Elise kept her eyes on her computer screen and said, "Be at the airport at six."

"Okay." He turned to leave.

"Be sure to pack your smile."

She lifted her eyes. He stopped walking, as if he was going to respond, but then continued out the door.

This is going to be fun. I think I'm getting under his skin.

The flight to Jerusalem was uneventful. Because of the other six passengers, Vasiliev chose not to share their assignment with Elise, which increased her curiosity, as well as annoyed her. However, Elise was able to adjust her schedule to free up time for the assignment, as she allocated various responsibilities among the other staffers. She prepared e-mails which would be delivered upon her arrival in Jerusalem, at which time she would be free to focus one hundred percent of her attention on the project.

At the airport, two limousines sat on the tarmac, one for the other six passengers and one for Elise and Vasiliev. When the door closed and they were finally alone, Elise decided to let him begin the conversation. In true Vasiliev fashion, however, he just sat and stared. The driver didn't move the car, apparently awaiting instructions. Elise tilted her head and furrowed her eyebrows at Vasiliev, wondering if he was going to step up and speak, or if the day would be spent at the airport.

Yakov removed his suit coat and rolled up the sleeves of his starched white dress shirt. He loosened his tie and sat back in the seat.

"Now that you're comfortable, would you like to instruct the driver?"

Yakov thought a moment and then said, "Take us to the Wailing Wall at the Temple Mount."

The driver put the car in drive and slowly headed to the driveway.

"The Wailing Wall? So, what's the plan?"

Elise tried to be perky, though she was tired of the silent treatment. He could pull off the tall, blonde, and handsome thing, but the strong, silent type was boring her. Yakov opened his briefcase and pulled out the file he had been holding outside Hitler's office the previous day, and handed it to her. She opened it and thumbed through a series of pictures. The subjects of the photos were two elderly men, definitely Jewish, but not dressed in traditional orthodox garb. Each picture was taken near the temple, for Elise knew those steps and that architecture well. One of the pictures showed a closer image of their faces and there were no marks on their foreheads.

"So, who are these guys?"

"Ever since Hitler revealed himself at the temple, these two guys have come to the temple every day and spoken boldly against him."

"Every day?"

"Yep, they haven't missed a day yet."

"So, why haven't they been arrested? I see they don't have a mark."

"No one can get near them. They draw large crowds and spend all day prophesying the fall of Hitler and Satan. But when officers attempt to touch them, it's like there is a magnetic field or something protecting them. They can't get near them. They've tried to shoot at them and the bullets fall to the ground."

"Strange. Where do they stay at night?"

"No one knows. They just disappear and reappear in the morning. But that's not the half of it. They claim that for the past two months, they have asked God to withhold rain from Russia and Iraq, where Hitler has two of his headquarters. And we have had record drought for two months in Russia and Iraq but no where else on earth."

"So, you think they have been sent by the Enemy?"

"It looks that way. The other day, one had a bottle of water in his hand, and when he poured the water onto the ground, it turned into blood. He said that the blood of the Jews would be spilled in their land, but God would soon bring His wrath and avenge the blood of His children. It might have been a cheap magician's trick, but the only other person that I've seen do something like that for real is Szabo. The power of these two men may be giving Szabo a run for his money."

Elise looked at a color photo of the two men. Both looked to be in their late sixties or early seventies. They weren't very tall and one was completely gray, while the other had dark, black hair with gray at his temples.

"Do they have names?"

"They call themselves the witnesses of God. They say they are here to warn the world. So far, they haven't caused enough commotion for most of the world to notice, but Hitler fears they have the potential to stir up trouble."

Elise closed the file and handed it back to Yakov. "So, what's our assignment? What could we possibly do that hasn't already been tried? I mean, it's not like I'm going to kill them or anything."

Yakov didn't even smile.

"Apparently Hitler doesn't think you are being used to your full potential. He thinks you're smarter than just ordering lunches and picking up his dry cleaning."

"I do more than that." Elise was anxious to hear what else Hitler had to say about her, but she wasn't happy that Yakov had such a low opinion of her job.

"I'm sure you do. He wants you to research these guys. Find out if there is any background information you can find. Do they have families? If they do, we can use them for leverage to get rid of them. I guess you should talk to the bystanders and find out what they know. Since you are not military, you, being a female, won't seem offensive or threatening."

"And what are you going to do?"

"I'm going to simply follow them. They have to go somewhere at night—maybe they're being hidden by the Temple Mount Institute or some other orthodox group. Hitler is counting on us to figure out how to get them to shut up."

"Well, three days is not very much time."

"Tell me about it. That's why he's been in such a bad mood lately. Any bump in the road makes him panic. I don't think they're that big of a deal, but Hitler's very nervous about them. Here, the whole world needs to mark up and he's worried about two old, Jewish men."

"Okay, well, we have three days and we'll have to use them wisely. You have my cell number. We can contact each other every couple of hours. Let's see what we can find out on day one and then we can plan from there. I will go with you tonight when you follow them."

"No, you won't."

"Yes, I—"

"No, you won't. I will call you when I have a chance."

The limousine came to a stop near the plaza in front of the Wailing Wall. Elise noticed a small group of women at the right side of the wall, but other than that, the area was rather empty. Yakov opened the door and got out. He reached for Elise's hand to help her, but this time it was she who gave him the cold shoulder. Two could play his game. If he didn't need her help, she surely didn't need his. She got out on her own and turned to him.

"Keep your cell on and I'll talk to you later. It's probably best that we don't go on the mount together."

She turned and walked toward the base of the wall, into a tunnel with a stairway that led to the Temple Mount. Armed guards scanned her for weapons and then she was permitted to proceed. Once on top of the mount, she scanned the platform and noted her surroundings. She remembered Hitler's struggle with the Arabs on the location of the temple. It was hard enough to get them to allow the construction, but when the Israeli government revealed the site, the Arabs went through the roof. In the end, the Jews got their way, thanks to her boss.

The temple was placed on the north side of the Dome of the Rock, with the Al-Aqsa Mosque on the south. But what angered the Arabs was how close the temple was in proximity to the Dome of the Rock. A mere six feet separated the two. The Jews were insistent that the temple be placed where the original Holy of Holies would have sat. Back then, as Magorum, Hitler had a drive to appease the Jews that Elise didn't quite understand, until he revealed himself. Then everything fell into place. The God of the Jews was a very particular god, demanding nothing short of perfection. She had read His law and considered it outrageous. In placing the temple exactly where He had wanted it, Hitler was now able to claim superiority over this god. His image now stood in the place where this god used to sit on His mercy seat. Nothing short of the precise location would be tolerated. Hitler was now god.

Armed soldiers from the FWP protected the mount. Initially Arabs were allowed access to the Dome of the Rock and the Mosque for worship, but the Jews were only allowed in the courtyard of the temple. Now that it was a place of worship for Hitler, anyone could freely flow through the doors of the temple to gaze on the statue of his likeness, making him far more accessible than the Original Inhabitant. A large group of people had gathered near the steps of the temple and Elise determined that must be the location of the two supposed witnesses. She made her way over to the crowd and did her best to blend in. Several soldiers were standing near, apparently allowing the gathering, though Elise knew they couldn't stop it.

The two men were dressed in strange attire, one in black pants, the other in khaki, both wearing shirts made of flax or hemp, like potato sacks. It looked uncomfortable and both men had rashes where the material was rubbing against their skin. As she approached, the man on the left spoke.

"The days of His wrath are quickly approaching. For those who have not already aligned with the Antichrist, there is still time to repent."

Elise looked around. As far as she could tell, there were marks on everyone's foreheads. She spotted Yakov across the crowd.

"For the rest of you, there is no hope. You have called judgment down from heaven and there is no escaping the wrath of God."

From the back, the voice of a man called out, "It's getting old, rabbi. We've heard this message every day. Do one of your tricks. That's why we're all here!" The crowd laughed and nodded in agreement.

Elise watched as the witness on the left spoke, looking directly at the heckling man. "It is a sad generation who desires to see the handiwork of God, yet does not fall in fear before the very One Whose power is displayed. If I blot the sun from the sky or if I make hail to fall with fire from heaven, how will that change your condition?"

The man responded, "It probably won't, but it would be entertaining!" Again, the crowd laughed in agreement and Elise suppressed a smile.

Elise saw a bead of sweat appear on the brow of the first man as he continued to engage the audience. "Woe to you, men of Jerusalem. Your king has been usurped and you laugh. But what you don't see is the very hand of God writing the script before it happens. He is sovereign and He is not usurped. He will allow your deception to continue for a short time, but soon, He will be revealed in might and power."

The argument continued between the witnesses and the crowd, with the crowd begging for supernatural signs. But the men simply responded with dialogue and forty minutes after she arrived, the crowd started to break up. Not wanting to draw attention to herself, she wandered past the men to enter the temple to plan her next step. As she passed the prophets, one intercepted her and touched her on the arm. She turned and they met eyes.

"Your investigation should start in the Word of God. He has planned this and it shouldn't be a surprise to your master. But your master is an unstudied man who refuses to humble himself and read the plan book. It is all in there. Even Satan knows what the outcome will be, but he insists on ignoring the truth. Everything you need to know about us you will find in the Word. Oh, and one more thing. Tell your friend he can't play this game much longer. Fence riding only gives you splinters."

He let go of her arm and she averted her eyes. There was something about his stare that sent chills up her spine. When his hand touched her arm she felt a power and a warmth that frightened her. Without speaking she ran up the stairs and stopped short of the temple door. She put her hand on the outside wall to steady herself as she caught her breath, and saw Yakov walking toward her.

"He touched you. No one has been able to get that close to them. What did he say?"

"He told me to look in the Bible to find out about them. He referred to my master, as if he knew who I was and what I was doing there."

"But he told you to read the Bible?"

"He kept saying the Word of God, and I assume that's the Bible, at least the Jewish writings of the Old Testament. I don't think the Jews follow the newer writings."

"So he just said, 'Read the Bible.'"

"Yes, and that Hitler was uneducated and could find out everything if he'd read the Bible, too. I really didn't like his tone."

"Where can you get a Bible?"

"I can pull one up on my computer, I would think. He also said something about a friend of mine playing a game—I think he was talking about Hitler again. That man was scary, Yakov. He really gave me the creeps. His touch was"— Elise hesitated. How could she explain the power that flowed through her body at his touch? Would Yakov understand?

But Yacov had already moved on. He pulled his eyes from hers and was looking back at the men at the bottom of the stairs. "I'm hoping to get some answers tonight. I'll call you later." He moved away and she watched him head back down the stairs and blend in with the crowd. She made her way back down, too, and put some space between her and the men. The pristine white temple towered over the Arab Dome of the Rock and as shadows from the afternoon sun began to stretch across the courtyard, a new crowd had gathered, but the message of the two old men was still the same—repent or prepare for God's wrath, whatever that meant.

Elise made her way off the Temple Mount to the limousine, which sat parked across the street from where she had been dropped off. She climbed in the back and lowered the sound proof window between herself and the driver.

"Please take me to the hotel. Thank you." Elise leaned back in the seat and closed her eyes. It was a short drive, but her head was swimming with the details of the afternoon. Perhaps she could doze . . .

Once at the hotel, Elise was back to full strength. The driver offered to roll her bag into the hotel for her, but she insisted she could handle it. She waved at the woman behind the front desk, who nodded and smiled back at her. Elise was now a regular and she had a permanent key. She even left clothes in the closet, so travel was light. Her suitcase only carried clothing for special events and her idol. When she got to her room, she put it on the bed and unzipped it. She took out two formal gowns and two pairs of dress shoes and put them in the closet. Then she took her idol and set him on the desk by the window.

"It's about time you took me out. You've been with him, haven't you?"

"I think you're jealous." Elise was amused that a talking idol could be that attached to its owner.

"I am not jealous. I am here to protect him. And I don't like Vasiliev. I need to see him."

"What are you worried about? He is as loyal as I am, so harming Hitler is the farthest thing from his mind. He protects him. You're not thinking straight on this one."

Elise grabbed her attaché case and brought it over to the desk. She took out her computer and powered it up. Then she started to search for copies of the Bible. While she searched, she caught her idol up to speed. There was a strange comfort in its counsel and she even found the memory of the man's powerful touch was fading. Her idol didn't have any idea who either of these men were, but said they were vaguely familiar in his memory.

"What do you mean, your memory?"

"I had a life before I occupied your idol."

"So that makes you a what? A ghost? A spirit? I thought you were a gift."

"I'm a demon, a loyal follower of Lucifer. There. Now you know."

"Really? A demon. And I thought demons were a bit scarier." Elise glanced up at her idol, who returned her smile with a disgusted look. "So, how old does that make you?" She returned to her search at her computer, but was coming up with nothing.

"I've seen a lot of things you couldn't even imagine."

"So you've seen God."

"Do we have to talk about Him?"

Elise smiled again. What a funny, little idol. "Is He really as bad as Hitler makes Him out to be?"

"He's ruthless. Christians walk around saying He's the God of second chances, but He never gave me a second chance."

Elise stopped typing and looked at her idol's face. "So you're saying you wish you were back on His team?"

"No. I just don't think 'merciful' is really a word to describe Him. Angry, maybe. Vindictive, definitely. But we have a pretty good plan in place and we're going to throw a wrench into His plan. I can't wait to see the look on His Son's face . . ."

Elise continued to search but couldn't find anything. "They said it would be here, but I can't find it."

"You are looking in Revelation, right?"

"Revelation? No, what's that?"

"It's the last part of the book. It's all about His supposed plan. But no one can even understand it, it's so cryptic. You should see the people argue about it. It's hysterical."

"I thought the Jews didn't read the second half of the Bible."

"They don't, but the Christians do. These two guys must be trying to fulfill a prophecy or something."

Elise typed in "witnesses" and Revelation 11:3 popped up. She started at the beginning of that chapter and read it through. Suddenly she understood.

"So these guys think that if they dress like they are in mourning and spew Old Testament sounding prophecies, then God will give them power. They got lucky with the drought, but I don't think they'll be able to spit fire from their mouths any time soon. I think they are just delusional."

"But you said the FWP has tried to kill them and the bullets are deflected."

"That could be a number of things. Magnetic fields or bad aim. I don't know, but there is nothing supernatural about these two. They are just two fanatics trying to get attention. Even the prophecy here says they are going to be killed. Why they chose these two guys to imitate, I'll never know."

Elise spent the rest of the afternoon organizing her theory, quoting from the Bible to show these men were trying to fulfill an ancient prophecy. Later Yakov shared that he had struggled to follow the men, but believed they disappeared through a false door in the Jewish shopping district near Old Jerusalem. He and Elise spent the next two days asking the bystanders questions about the men, noting the fact that they never stopped to eat. By the time Hitler arrived, they had concluded that while the men were an irritant, they weren't shooting fire from their mouths yet, so most likely their fervor would soon die away.

Elise felt that Hitler was pleased with her thoroughness, but what brought her even greater pleasure was the fact that Yakov was finally speaking to her. Perhaps he even trusted her now, and that could only lead to a deeper relationship. Or friendship.

Well, only time will tell . . .

nineteen

Noah was losing his mind. No matter how hard he tried, he couldn't concentrate. When the residents of the compound had devotions and worship, he couldn't sing. He hadn't finished a plate of food in weeks. Even when it was his turn to hang out with the kids at the compound, he completely forgot and someone had to come and wake him up to remind him.

And it was because of Tara. The more he thought about it, the harder it was to believe that she had truly taken the mark. Sure, they had their differences, but he was confident she was in complete agreement not to take the Antichrist's mark. Three times he was able to find an excuse to return to town. He would go at night and he always took a drive past her house. He simply wanted to see if there was any sign of life. But each time her house was exactly the way she had left it. Nothing was moved. The grass wasn't mowed, and to make matters worse, the last time he went, there was yellow police tape across her front door. That normally meant only one thing in Creston—that she had been taken to a training camp. But that wouldn't have happened if she had taken the mark, so Noah was completely bewildered.

He tried to cast his cares at the feet of his Savior, but the worry was too great. When he first awoke, he would ask the Lord to carry his burden and by late morning, he was back to bearing the load. He had spent some time in prayer with Dave and Charlie, but that didn't even seem to help. His concern had turned to desperation and all he could think about was finding her and seeing for himself whether or not she had a mark on her forehead. But in the end, his desperation turned into sorrow and he grieved the loss of his friend. No, she was more than that. He'd told her he loved her, and he'd meant it.

"Hey, Noah. You need to come and see this." Noah jumped as Cal Moeller stuck his head in the room and called him out of a daydream.

"What's going on?"

"Hitler has another big announcement." Cal disappeared and Noah reluctantly headed toward the eating area to watch the announcement. The last time Hitler had made an announcement it was to tell the world he had given the gift of language back to the world. Overnight, all language became understandable. It wasn't that everyone spoke the same language, but everyone could understand all languages. Truly a supernatural occurrence that bothered Noah. Why would he, as a believer, benefit from a gift from Satan? It bothered him, but he still headed to hear the latest rant from Satan's minion. As he entered the eating area, most of the adults were already there. There was a woman anchor with a picture of the FWP headquarters behind her, complete with ambulances and a large crowd in the distance.

"Today, Adolph Hitler again turned the world upside down by replacing the president or premiere from every country except Hungary, with its assistant president or premiere. And he did it in a way that only Hitler could pull off. Mike Morrison is at the FWP headquarters in Moscow with the latest."

A middle-aged reporter stood on the sidewalk across the street from the crowd in front of the FWP building.

"Thanks, Rachelle. It has been quite a day here in Moscow. It began with a nine o'clock meeting this morning of all the leaders of the

FWP. Reporters were not allowed in. We were kept here, across the street, and the building was cordoned off by FWP security guards. At 10:13 we heard a loud crashing sound and looked to the buildings. The windows had broken inward, as if a strong wind had shattered through from the outside. No glass fell on the sidewalk. Apparently it all fell inside."

The camera panned away from the reporter and zoomed in on the FWP building. Large window panels were missing halfway up the building, just as he said, across the whole front of the building.

"This obviously caught all of our attention and we instructed our cameramen to lock in on those windows. The following footage is disturbing and may not be appropriate for younger viewers. Five minutes after the windows shattered, the dead bodies of every president and premiere in the world were hurled through the windows and piled on the sidewalk as a testimony to failed leadership. No human hands had murdered these men—the way they were thrown from the building all at the same time proved that fact. But eyewitness testimony consistently gives responsibility to Lucifer and his demons. Apparently, Adolph Hitler is not pleased with the progress that the nations have made marking their citizens. I spoke with Aleksander Macheila, the new president of Belgium and he described the scene like this . . ."

The picture rolled to a previously taped interview. The face of the new president filled the screen. Noah thought the guy looked a bit pale, but he'd had a long day.

"Uh . . . it was a display of power I will never forget. One moment we were all asked to stand behind our presidents and then next thing we knew the windows were crashing down on our heads. A wind had entered the room and was sweeping around the sitting presidents— it kind of formed a wall between the presidents and us. When the wind stopped, we watched as Hitler was lifted from his place and, carried by a spirit, set into the middle of the room. Lucifer himself was indwelling him and he told the sitting presidents that they had failed. Then demons appeared, standing behind each president. They reached around the men and picked up shards of glass which were on the table and pierced each president through the back. All at the same time. It was chilling. The next thing I knew, my president's body was being pulled from his chair and thrown out the window and Lucifer told me to sit in his seat. At that point, none of us was in a position to argue. Lucifer made his point loud and clear. We need to finish up this marking project and move on. Each country must have one hundred percent participation, or new leadership will once again be forced into place. What I saw gave me the motivation I need to get the job done, believe me."

The scene changed back to the reporter in Moscow. "Adolph Hitler informed us he has a prerecorded announcement which will air at one thirty, Eastern Time. That's the next thing on our agenda. This is Mike Morrison, reporting from Moscow, Russia, for NBC News."

"Thank you, Mike," the anchor in the studio continued. "We're going to take a quick commercial break and then return for coverage of Hitler's announcement."

When the television broke to a commercial, Noah looked around the room. The adults were quiet, absorbing the latest information. The feeling of being trapped fell over Noah. Whatever this news was, it was only going to make things more difficult for the group in hiding. Charlie made his way over to Noah from across the room.

"Pretty nasty stuff."

"No kidding. I don't like the sound of this." Noah pulled a chair away from one of the dinner tables and sat. How much worse could things get?

"I was talking with Dave this morning. We were thinking that we should go get the food from your house. We have the room now, and though we're not low on anything, we may not be able to go out much longer. Are you up for a run in the next couple of days?"

"Sure. I can run tomorrow night. I'm helping Fredo after dinner tonight with his mixer. It's broken and we're going to take it apart."

"I can get someone to go with you, maybe Cal. I'm teaching tomorrow night at Bible study so I can't run."

"Don't worry about it. I can do it by myself. It won't take too long." Noah wouldn't mind the time alone.

He glanced back at the screen and the news was back on. Adolph Hitler was standing in front of a podium, the flag of the FWP behind him on the right, a picture of himself on the left.

"Thank you for your support and attention." He gripped the sides of the podium and Noah wondered if it was nerves or just habit. "Though much of the world has willingly joined the Federation of World Powers, we have not completed the task at hand. Never before in the history of mankind has a global initiative been put in place to unite the world under one cause. Perhaps that is why our struggle is so great. Today was a momentous occasion. It is never my desire to take life for granted, but incompetence cannot be rewarded."

The camera slowly zoomed in on Hitler. The steel resolute in his eyes was eerie. Noah thought for a moment he might be looking into the eyes of Satan himself.

"Our Enemy has suffered a major blow, but one strike is not enough to do away with Him. We must be thorough. We must wipe Him out. Stopping short of complete victory has been the actions of past world leaders who have failed. We must finish the job. Because your government cannot do this alone, I am announcing today that if you as citizens will help us rid the world of nonmarked people, you will be compensated generously. Seven days from today, on September twenty-first, you will be allowed to receive all properties and possessions of any unmarked person whose life you terminate. When you deliver the head of this person to your local authorities, you will receive a voucher that will give you ownership of this person's land and possessions. I am giving your governments seven days to prepare for the Day of Destruction, but mind you, on September twenty-first, we will be the victors! I am completely confident that with your help, we can deliver the final blow to our Enemy and wipe His presence from the earth. His followers are a plague to society. They cannot provide for their families so they steal from you, and yet they think they have a right to exist. The sooner we destroy them, the sooner the disease is gone."

A drop of sweat started to form on Hitler's brow, near his hairline. The camera began to pull backwards as he spoke his final words.

"The Day of Destruction is a day you will be rewarded personally for your loyalty to me. You have seven days to target the enemy. I am counting on you."

The woman anchor reappeared. "This decision comes on the heels of the murder of an FWP officer on the Temple Mount in Jerusalem. The two witnesses have turned from passive prophets to aggressive, fire-breathing murderers."

The sound on the television was lowered and most of the adults began talking amongst themselves. Charlie looked back at Noah.

"Looks like our running days are just about over. I wonder if we'll get an influx of people over the next week. I should try my friends again." Charlie got up from the table and wandered back toward the bedrooms.

When Noah heard Hitler demand the heads of the unmarked, all he could picture was Tara's face. If she was marked, she was safe. If not, where could she hide? The thought of her being hunted and beheaded was too much for Noah to bear. He decided he would take one more trip to Tara's. He prayed that she would somehow be there, but deep down he knew she wouldn't be. Not unless she was going on with her life like her mother had said.

Now he just had to kill some time for a day and a half, and then make his final attempt to find Tara. What if she was home? What if she was marked? Noah shook his head and went back to his room.

Thomas and Robin slept in their own bed for the first time in two months. And though it was far more comfortable than Robin's parents' pullout in their basement, Thomas still didn't sleep well. They had returned home around two in the morning. There was yellow tape on their front and back door, but Thomas had left a basement window open, so they didn't disturb the tape. He climbed into the window well, opened the window and then Robin handed the girls down to him. Then he went up through the house and into the garage. He detached the garage door and quietly opened it manually. Robin then pulled the car into the garage while Thomas filled a couple of buckets of water from the neighbor's spigot. He cringed as the water flowed from the house, but there was no movement and it only took him a few minutes. He went back through the garage and he shut the door again.

The girls wanted to sleep together, so Robin put them in Christie's bed and they were asleep in just a few minutes. Thomas and Robin were worn out and didn't talk much when they went to bed. Before he went to sleep he asked the Lord for wisdom and protection and then dozed into a fitful few hours of sleep.

A sudden noise woke Thomas from a deep sleep. He glanced at the clock. It read six on the dot. He heard voices yelling and could make out the sound of feet running up the stairs. Thomas reached over and touched Robin, who laid eyes wide open in the bed. Fear froze Thomas's body as his bedroom door swung open and the room filled with police officers, guns drawn, pointing right at him and his wife. A man stood in the doorway and gave orders.

"Take these two and we'll get the children." As he turned to leave, Thomas felt Robin move.

"No!" she screamed, as she jumped from the bed. Immediately an officer grabbed her arm and pushed her into a sitting position on the bed. "Please! I beg you! Let me get the girls. Please, don't do this!"

Thomas sat and immediately there was a hand on his shoulder, too. There was no way out—too many officers and way too many guns. This was it. The running was over. All Thomas could think of was Reverend Blackwell's face and his ominous warning.

As Robin continued to sob, the officer in the doorway stood quietly for a moment and then pointed at Thomas. "Get him dressed and bring him outside." He turned to the officer next to Robin. "You go with her." And then he addressed Robin. "Get your daughters. You've got five minutes."

She jumped from the bed and hurried out of the room, her escort close behind.

Thomas pulled on jeans and a tee shirt. An officer threw him a pair of tennis shoes and then he was cuffed and led out to his driveway. Behind him he heard the girls crying and he turned to see Robin and the girls being brought outside. Tears were streaming down Robin's face and Thomas was at a loss for words. He was forced into a squad car and the door was shut before he could even call out to his girls. His family was put in the backseat of a second squad car. Thomas watched as long as he could but soon his eyes blurred with tears and he turned his head from the window.

At that very moment Thomas accepted responsibility for what had just happened. He had been warned and he chose not to prepare. He ignored his friend's charge to search the Word and now his family would pay the price for his sin. A pain shot through his chest and for a moment Thomas thought he might throw up. The tears flowed freely and without a free hand to wipe his face, he bowed his head in agony and shame. He knew the end of this story and the thought of these men killing his daughters and wife was unbearable.

"Cry all you want, but there's only one way out of this mess." The officer in the front passenger seat was turned and looking at Thomas. "We're not overly patient any more, so you've got a day or two to decide whether or not your family will go to the training camp. Then again, in six days it won't even matter anymore, since the Day of Destruction is going to eliminate the need for camps." He turned back around and elbowed the officer who was driving. Both men laughed.

Thomas fought back the tears enough to ask a question.

"How did you know we were back?"

The officer turned again and locked eyes with Thomas. "The Memorial Park idol has been screaming your name ever since you pulled into town. We came at six to shut him up so everybody else could get some rest."

Again the men laughed and Thomas sat, completely confused in the backseat of the squad car, but also completely defeated.

Noah left the compound at eight. He had been ready four hours earlier, but it had seemed to take forever for darkness to cover the farm. He pulled out of the barn, got out of the van and shut the door of the barn, then headed into town. His heart pounded, more from his concern for Tara than for getting caught. Two blocks away from her house, he pulled the van into an empty parking lot of a small elementary school and parked. It was eight thirty and no one was walking around. He got out of the van and started on foot to Tara's house.

As he neared the house, there was a little more activity, since the park was directly across the street from where she lived. A man walking a dog or a jogger occasionally passed him, but nothing to cause alarm. He had pulled his dark bangs down on his forehead before he put the cap on, so that someone might think they saw markings on his head and not question him.

As he neared the house, his heart sank. There was a FOR SALE sign in her front yard and the yellow tape was no longer across her front door. It scared him to think she was selling her house, because that would mean she was functioning in society, which meant she truly was marked. The lights were off but he went to the front door anyway. He looked through the window and saw no movement.

"NOOOOOOOOOOAAAAAAAAHHHHHHH!"

The screech of his name almost knocked him to the ground. He spun around to try to identify where the voice was coming from.

"N O O O O O O O O O O O A A A A A A H H H H H H GRRRRRRREEEEEEEEEEERRRR!"

He didn't see anyone yelling but it continued.

"NOAH! NOAH! NOAH! NOAH GREER! NOAH GREER! NOAH! NOAH! NOAH!"

Noah heard the door of the house next to Tara's open and the light on the porch turn on. Noah was surprised by a shove on his shoulder and he fell behind a row of bushes in front of Tara's house. The man he and Charlie had spoken to came out on his porch. He looked around to see if anyone was outside. His wife came out a few moments later and handed him the cordless phone. He dialed something and then through the screeching, Noah could hear his conversation.

"Hi, the statue is yelling again."

He paused as he listened to the other party on the phone.

"The name is something like 'Noah Green'"—

His wife interrupted him. "Greer, dear. It's saying Greer."

"Noah Greer. I think it's the guy who used to date my neighbor, but I don't see anyone around. I'll keep an eye out until you guys arrive." Then he pressed a button and that was the end of the call.

Noah knew he had to get out of there, but until the man went back inside, any movement would draw attention. Then he felt a hand on his shoulder and he turned quickly, but no one was there. There was a pull and though Noah fought to stay crouched behind the bushes, he was pulled into an upright position. He stood, just feet away from the man and yet the man didn't see him. Then he felt a shove on his right heel and his foot moved sideways. Then a kick to his other foot and before he knew it, he was being forced out from behind the bushes.

Noah struggled against every step. He knew it was most likely a demon bringing him into the open. When he made it to the sidewalk, the screeching of the idol intensified and changed.

"THERE HE IS, YOU IDIOT! CAN'T YOU SEE HIM?"

Noah continued to walk down the sidewalk, away from Tara's house, right in front of the neighbor, but the neighbor still looked around confused. Noah felt a shove on his back again. When he realized he was apparently invisible to the man, Noah stopped struggling and took off in a full sprint to the van.

"HE'S RUNNING! GET HIM! NOOOOOAAAAAHHHH GR-RRREEEERRR! YOU'RE LETTING HIM GET AWAY!"

A squad car passed Noah but didn't even brake. He couldn't believe his luck as he raced back to the van. Once inside, he fumbled to get the key in the ignition. The van started up but Noah didn't put it in drive. Instead, he closed his eyes and spoke out loud.

"Forgive me for thinking a demon was pushing me. And I know better than to believe in luck. You are Lord over all. I know Your goodness and I can't explain why You would spare me, but all I can say is thank You. You are unbelievable! Thank You."

He pulled out of the elementary school parking lot and headed to his house. He had a peace that he could accomplish the mission, especially after his protection was in place. As he pulled into his own drive, he hit the garage opener without thinking. The door opened, turning on the garage light, and Noah's heart leapt. He was pushing it now. As soon as he got the van inside, he shut the door and went into the house. He leaned back against the door and took a deep breath. Sweat dripped from his brow and he pulled up his shirt to wipe it away.

Then he heard it. A noise in his living room. A footstep and then another.

They were waiting for him. His hand went to the knob on the door he was leaning against when he heard a small noise, like a squeak. Was it a mouse? How could a mouse make the sound of footsteps?

He decided to find out for himself. There were no squad cars outside, so the thought of a policeman hiding in his living room, waiting for him, and . . . was that crying he heard?

Quietly Noah walked down his back hallway. The noise was a bit louder. Someone sniffled.

Then he saw her. She stood in the middle of his living room. In the glow of the moonlight that shone through the windows, he could see her shoulders shaking. Her hands were over her face, but he would know her anywhere.

Tara.

Like a magnet, he felt the urge to hold her. He walked over to her and wrapped his arms around her. She buried her head in his chest and sobbed. Noah didn't say a word, but his heart burst with joy and ached with pain at the same time. She was in his arms, but he needed to see her face. For minutes he just held her and she cried. Then slowly she pulled her head from his chest and looked into his eyes. Her dark curls lay on her forehead, but he had to know. He lifted his hand and gently brushed them aside.

Relief flooded his whole body and he began to cry. Now it was her turn to hold him.

"You didn't take the mark!"

"No, what are you talking about?"

"I've been so worried! Your mother told me you had taken the mark!"

"Oh, Noah, it's been horrible!"

Minutes passed as Noah and Tara wept in the darkness, holding on to each other tightly. Without knowing her story, Noah thanked God aloud for sparing her life and bringing them back together. Then they sat on the couch and she poured out her story.

"After you left me at my house with my mother, she insisted I return to her home. I felt so guilty that she had taken the number that I convinced myself I should stay with her to the end. But she changed,

Noah, right before my eyes. She became irritable and angry. Even just buying groceries put her in a bad mood. It was as if I had become a burden to care for and within just a few weeks, she was begging me to take the number, too. She said it wasn't fair for me to ask her to provide for me, just because I was stubborn about taking the mark. She would belittle me and tell me I was worthless."

"So what made you finally leave?"

"One day she told me her friends had threatened to turn me in. They thought I was taking advantage of her and they were going to put a stop to it. By then, she was lying to me all the time, I didn't know if she was telling the truth or not, so I left."

"Why didn't you call me?"

"My cell was shut off and she removed all the phones in her house except for the cordless, which she kept with her at all times. She slept with it and if she left the house, it went with her. She said you had put wrong ideas in my head and once I cleared my mind I would think straight again."

Noah held both of her hands in his own. They felt so small and cold. It was warm in the house, nevertheless her skin was chilled. She had been through a lot.

"So you left? Where did you go?"

"All I could think of was getting a hold of you. I know you would have come for me if I could have called you. But I couldn't get to a phone. I made my way home at night, hiding in abandoned sheds or even lying in cornfields during the day so I couldn't be seen. The corn is dying but some of the ears are still edible, so I ate corn. I would walk or run all night. It took me a week, but I made it back to my house. When I got there, the phone was dead. Next I went to the church. That was two nights ago. There was something going on there and I was hoping to find unmarked members, but I hid in the parking lot until I could see what was happening. The people going in and out of the church were all marked and soon I realized they were carrying books from the church and piling them on the street. This went on for about forty-five minutes. There were hymnals, Bibles, books from the library—even Sunday School material, because the loose papers would just go flying when they threw them on the pile."

"Who was doing this?"

"The police were there in addition to the crowd. Once they were done piling the books up, one of the officers stood on the front steps of the church, like he was Hitler at the temple, and declared the religion of that church dead. The people cheered and gas was poured on the pile. Then a match was thrown on and a roaring bonfire like I had never seen blazed in the street."

Noah waited as Tara couldn't speak for a moment. He put his arm around her to comfort her, but she continued to cry.

"It was just terrible, Noah. As the pile burned, there was this horrible scream from across the park. It was screaming a name and the people started to scatter. A few ran toward me and for a moment I thought they had found me. But just as they got close, someone yelled that they had found them and everyone ran to the other side of the parking lot. From where I was hiding, I couldn't see everything, but three people were dragged up to the main officer. And I knew who they were."

"Who?"

"It was that little boy from the church, Isaiah. Remember the one with the letter?"

"Yes. The letter mentioned a man in Michigan and Charlie actually talked with him some time back."

"He and his parents were brought up front and then the crowd quieted. The officer yelled at this family, taunting them, asking them why they thought they were better than everyone else. The wife just cried and the husband didn't answer. Then the officer called over one of his buddies who was standing with the crowd. He pulled on Isaiah's arm, trying to get him away from his father, but Isaiah fought and held onto his leg. He pulled so hard that eventually Isaiah had to let go and he fell down the steps. His little body didn't move. It just lay there. There were two shots and the parents fell to the ground. And then, Noah, then the people cheered. They picked up the bodies of the parents and threw them on the fire, but I saw someone run into the church and bring out a white sheet or tablecloth. They laid that on Isaiah. I don't know why they didn't burn him, too, but I didn't stay around to see what would happen. I started to run and I came here. I broke your back garage window and I've been here for a day."

Noah looked at Tara's tear-stained face in the moonlight. He held her face in his hands and wiped the tears with his thumbs.

"I never should have left you. I should have put you over my shoulder and thrown you in the van. I'm so sorry."

"It's not your fault, Noah. I was stubborn. But we're together now."

Noah could not even think of what else to say to comfort her. She'd been through so much and his words seemed to fall short. Though having her in front of him was a dream come true, the reality of what she had been through broke his heart.

Suddenly, the living room of Noah's house was filled with red and white flashing lights. The police were outside the door and Noah could hear them pounding to break the lock. The voices and pounding brought him back to his senses and he quickly stood.

"Go out the back way. You've got to get to the compound."

"No, Noah. Don't make me leave you!"

Her eyes darted from his face to the door and Noah could tell she was deciding what to do. He had to make this decision for her, so he grabbed her hand and ran her to the back door. "I will stall the police, but if we run together, they'll find us for sure." Another crack sounded at the front door and Noah knew the wood was giving way.

"Take 31 south until you get to 35. Head east on 35 and about three miles past that intersection is an abandoned barn. That's where I'll meet you. And if I don't get there you'll have to find the compound entrance in that barn. Look in the back corner. And don't wait too long for me. Now go!"

Another crack at the front door. Noah knew there was no more time.

"But Noah, come with me! You'll never get out of here alive! I've seen what they do!"

"I have to give you time to get away. I'll be there. Don't worry, I'll make it!"

Noah took Tara's face in his hands again and kissed her. A lump formed in his throat, but he had to get her to safety. He might even be able to catch up with her. But he couldn't let them take her. He pulled away and opened the door.

"Go! Run at night and I'll meet you at that barn."

He shut the door before she could argue and ran through the living room to his den. He pulled the chair out and sat down, opening desk drawers, looking for a letter opener or scissors. All his cutlery was at the compound already. There was another crack at the front door. Men's voices grew louder. Suddenly the front door gave way and the men were rushing into his house. They had high-powered flashlights and were lighting every nook and cranny in search for him. There was nowhere to hide. There was no weapon to protect himself. He was out of options.

At least he could stall them and give Tara time to get to safety.

Black Cap stood between Noah and the officers. His instructions had been to protect this man, no matter what. Again, the girl had led him into danger, and now she was gone, and it was just him and Noah. The darting flashlight beam of one of the officers stopped on Noah.

"I found him! He's in here," he called to the other officers. Within seconds the den filled with agents. "Are you Noah Greer?"

Noah stood, speechless.

Another officer ran in. "Dispatch said the idol stopped yelling, so this must be him."

That stinking demon. I hate that thing. I should have shut him up myself. Well, I guess now is as good a time as any.

Black Cap took a deep breath and his presence suddenly filled the room. He enlarged himself to almost full height, reaching all the way to the nine-foot ceiling, easily towering over the largest man. His human garb disappeared and his heavenly attire began to glow. A flaming sword appeared in his hand, as he unfurled his enormous wings behind him. It felt good to give them a stretch.

He stood between Noah and the officers and watched.

"Are you Noah Greer?"

Just stall, Noah. Just stall.

Noah looked at the officers, not sure whether to answer or refuse to talk. Then another officer ran in the room and said, "Dispatch said the idol stopped yelling, so this must be him."

Noah's heart skipped a beat. *I guess that's one question I won't have to answer.* He waited for one of the officers to make the next move. The electricity had long been shut off to his house, but in the moonlight, Noah could see them pretty well.

None of them said a word.

As a matter of fact, no one even moved.

They hardly breathed.

It was like a standoff. Here was Noah, no weapon and nine police officers, all with guns drawn. And they were waiting for him to make the first move! Noah shut his eyes, fully expecting them to unload their guns directly into his chest. Minutes passed and there was nothing. He opened his eyes again and they were all still standing, frozen. Noah's eyes darted from left to right, wondering why they hadn't done anything yet. Still, he didn't have the courage to say any-thing. Then it hit him. Maybe he was invisible again.

Black Cap decided to speak.

"If you want him, you're going to have to get through me. And I make those guys at the temple who shoot fire from their mouths look like preschool teachers."

The officers still remained frozen, eyes bulging in their heads, ter-ror seizing their hearts.

"Why don't you guys just go now?"

Suddenly the officers all moved at the same time. They turned their backs on Noah and fought to get through the door. No one spoke. It was as if they had seen a ghost. Noah remained in the den long after the last police cars sped away from his house.

For the next hour he talked with his Father. They had a lot to discuss.

When that was done, Noah went back to the garage to open the back of his van so that he could fill it with supplies. All four of his tires had been slashed and he realized he was going to have to get to the barn on foot to meet Tara.

Noah headed out the backdoor of the house. In a day or two he would be safely at the compound with Tara, and the wait would fi-nally be over. His heart soared with gratitude and anticipation for the moment when he could introduce Tara to Charlie and Dave, and tell them he didn't ever want to leave the compound again.

Part three

Present Day Continued

"For then there will be a great tribulation,
such as has not occurred
since the beginning of the world until now,
nor ever will.
Unless those days had been cut short,
no life would have been saved;
but for the sake of the elect
those days will be cut short."

MATTHEW 24:21, 22

twenty

September

Elise heard the knock at her door and looked at her watch. It was early evening, and though she was back at the hotel, her workday was not finished. She had set out her notes to transcribe, ordered up a chef salad for dinner and took a quick shower. But the knock was too soon for dinner, unless the kitchen was having a slow evening. She had thrown on a pair of sweat pants and a long-sleeved tee shirt, so she was at least presentable.

When she opened the door, Yakov Vasiliev held a silver tray in his hands with a chef salad and a Diet Coke in the center.

"Are you moonlighting? Does Hitler not pay you enough?"

He stammered a bit and Elise thought she saw a hint of redness in his cheeks.

"I rode up the elevator with room service and when I realized they were delivering to you, I offered to bring it in for them."

"I suppose you'll want a tip?" She smiled and took the tray from his hands.

"We need to talk." He followed her into the suite. She walked over to her coffee table and set the tray down.

"It's kind of late, Yakov. This can't wait until morning?"

"There was another incident at the Temple Mount with the witnesses today. Seventeen FWP soldiers died."

"You have got to be kidding. That's three days in a row. And was it fire again?"

"Somehow these guys are spewing flames from their mouths and no one can figure it out. They must have some kind of an aerosol can that they light."

"How did Adolph take the news?"

"He's furious. He can't figure out why Lucifer won't handle these guys and I think he's mad at us."

"Us?" Elise sat on the couch and threw her hands in the air. It made no sense to her that Adolph would hold her responsible for this. "How this is our fault is a mystery to me!"

"He said we told him not to worry about these guys. But now they are fulfilling the Revelation prophecy, which only makes them more credible."

"Remember, they get killed in the prophecy, too. So what are we worrying about?"

"Well, I just wanted to let you know what you are walking into tomorrow morning. He's more agitated than ever. Just wanted you to know."

Elise paused a moment and gave Yakov a curious look. "Why Agent Vasiliev, with a warning like that, a girl might be led to believe you actually care about her."

"It's just that I don't think either of us deserves to be fired over these guys. You have a way of calming him down, so I thought I'd warn you."

She smiled at him. "I do appreciate it. It's nice to have someone looking out for you."

"Well, don't get any ideas or anything like that. I'm just doing my job."

Yakov turned and headed back toward the door. "So, I think I'll get going now. I'll see you in the morning?"

Elise followed and opened her hotel room door. Yakov walked out and turned back for her response.

"I'll be there, and thanks for the warning." She gave him a warm smile, closed the door, and headed back to eat her salad.

"Oh, you've really got a big problem now."

It was her idol. Elise was used to him eavesdropping on her conversations at home, so his two cents were expected.

"It's nothing. I know how to handle him. These witnesses can spew all they want, we just need to figure out how to keep people away from them."

"That's not what I am talking about."

"Then what's the problem?" Elise sat down on the couch and picked up the small pewter pitcher of salad dressing.

"It's him. Vasiliev. He's your problem."

She poured dressing on her salad and set the pitcher back down on the tray.

"Oh, so you're jealous, now, are you?"

"No, I'm not jealous. But you have a problem."

"And what would that be?" Elise twisted off the top of her Diet Coke.

"That good-looking security guard you have a crush on?"

"Yes . . ."

"He's not marked."

"What do you mean?" Elise took a sip of her Coke. "Of course he's marked. He showed it to me the morning in the limo that I was given you as a gift. I see it every day."

"I'm telling you, he's a fake. He's not really marked."

Elise put down her drink and stared at her idol. She got up from the couch, walked over to the bed and sat.

"Are you really that obsessed with me that you'll lie about someone I care about?" Elise was a bit angered by the idol's accusation.

"I'm telling you, his mark is not permanent. One of my gifts is knowing a permanent mark when I see one, and that one is a fake."

Elise stood. "This is outrageous. He is the head of Hitler's security. How can he not be marked? That's enough."

She picked up the idol, opened the drawer of her nightstand, laid him face down in the drawer and slammed it shut.

"I don't need this ridiculous talk. I've got enough on my mind."

Elise stormed back to her salad and grabbed the remote. Before she turned on the television, however, she heard a faint voice from the drawer say, "I'm warning you, he's not marked. If you don't do something about this, it could be dangerous for both you and Adolph." She pressed the power button and turned the volume up high, thinking the sound of the television would drown out the sound of the idol's voice.

Up until today, her idol had never lied to her. His advice was always up-to-date and relevant. Why would he lie to her about Yakov? Earlier he had asked to see him. Perhaps he could check the mark in a different way than she could. She put her fork down and slumped back in the couch.

After a few moments, she sat back up, finished her salad and headed back to her computer. She had work to do and she wasn't going to let the silly rantings of a pile of bronze wreck her evening. He was simply jealous, that's all. She should be flattered.

But deep down, she wondered if he could possibly be telling the truth.

Durbin watched as the police officers loaded Thomas onto the bus. Two days ago when he was brought in, Durbin personally went to the jail and pleaded with him. But Thomas wouldn't even speak. Now he was on his own. It really wasn't Durbin's problem anymore, and yet, seeing Thomas climb onto that bus made his heart ache a bit. Thomas was a good man, messed up by religion.

When the bus pulled away from the curb, Durbin headed down to Memorial Park. This had become a habit he hadn't looked forward to, but it was his most accurate way to find out if he was getting close to completing the task at hand. He hated that idol because it had no social graces, but then again, Hitler wasn't that polite either.

He walked down the sidewalk. It was a nice day for September. The leaves had started to change their color and the sun was high in a cloudless sky. There were a few people in the park, but not many children anymore, since school was back in session. Children were becoming a real problem. They were nearly impossible to mark. Only the ones who asked for a mark could get one, but if a parent decided for the child, the mark wouldn't adhere. It really was the strangest thing.

Apparently Governor Slate was wrestling with the same issue. He had a team of researchers pore over various solutions to this problem, because in Hitler's mind, no mark meant death, child or not. But Slate just didn't feel right about it. Over the past six months, he had been mulling over his options and decided that boarding school was the best one for unmarked children. If a child hadn't willingly asked for a mark, they would be put in a school where they would get their education and eventually make the choice to be marked. That way, they weren't wandering the streets, but were in a controlled environment. Of course the school was conveniently located on the grounds of the training camp in southern Indiana. Eventually, if a child refused past a certain age, they would have to be terminated. Slate hoped this solution would fly with the FWP. At this point, he figured what they didn't know wouldn't hurt them. The inability to mark children was plaguing his whole state, so he offered this solution to his local governments and for now, this was the option they chose to follow.

Durbin could tell the idol was asleep, because it was quiet. When it was awake, it never was quiet. He carefully approached it and cleared his throat.

"A-hem. Excuse me? Hello?"

He waited a moment until a response came.

"What now?"

"I just sent nine more unmarked citizens to the camp. A few women and children will stay here for another couple of weeks, since we have a pretty good success rate with them right in our own jail, but the men will be disposed of rather quickly, due to your master's Day of Destruction plans. The guards at the facility want the men's properties, but I think it is only fair that the government gets half, since we're the ones who rounded them up. So, we're going"—

"I couldn't care less about you stupid humans and your greed. All I know is that you are nowhere near finishing. I don't know what you have been doing all this time but you have well over a hundred still unmarked."

"What? Where?" This was impossible. Durbin had a better grip on his town than this idol. "I don't know where you get your information, but it's not accurate. We have swept this town thoroughly and it's nearly empty of nonmarkers. How can there be one hundred?"

"I said over a hundred. I think the number is one hundred and thirty-seven. And they are all together, but you just haven't looked hard enough. Until you find them, you will get nothing. Nothing! Do you understand me? You will receive no funds until you're job is complete, and after what happened to the premieres of the world a couple of days ago, you need to understand that you are not irreplaceable."

Durbin squirmed a bit, fighting back the urge to remove that idol and end his torment, but he knew that would be the death knell for his town. So he politely thanked the idol and went back to his office. He would make a few calls and turn up the heat. Somewhere within his city limits was a large group of unmarked people and he was going to find them no matter what the cost.

———�֎———

When Noah didn't return on time, Charlie became concerned. When he didn't return the next day, he became downright worried. He went above ground into the garage and powered up his cell. He was amazed he still had service. There was one voice mail and he quickly retrieved it.

"It's me. Noah. You won't believe it, Charlie. I found Tara! She was in my house, of all places. You're going to love this story. We ran into some trouble, though, and got separated. She's meeting me at the north tunnel, but both of us are making our way on foot. I didn't get the food either because my tires were slashed in the garage. But anyways, could you make sure there is a flashlight at the front of the north tunnel? It may take us a day or two . . . but we'll see you soon."

Charlie was relieved and went back down to the compound. He found Dave playing Scrabble with one of the young teenagers.

"Noah's on his way back."

"Oh, that's great. What happened?"

"He left me a message and didn't give many details, except to say that Tara is with him."

Dave looked up from the game. "You're kidding!"

"His tires were slashed so he's on foot. He's going to come through the north tunnel. I'm going to run a flashlight to the ladder and then come back."

"That's a good idea. They'll need it. I doubt we'll make many more runs after the Day of Destruction."

"I was also thinking of trying to get that food tonight. In a couple of days we won't be able to get that either. I can go tonight and fill up the other van. I could take someone with me and it will go faster. We could change the tires on the other van and fill them both." Charlie knew his roommate Cal wouldn't mind a trip out of the compound. Nearly anyone he'd ask would love some fresh air. But it would be dangerous.

Dave rubbed his chin. Charlie didn't know if it was in consideration of his suggestion or if he was working on a word.

"I think you might be pushing it. We don't know what trouble Noah got into and sending someone right back over there may be a foolish move."

"I'll circle the house a few times, if you want. And I'll go alone. I just want that food, Dave. We have no idea how long we're all going to be down here and that extra food could be the difference between us starving to death or not. Plus, he has a large stash of batteries and candles we could need in the future."

Dave looked up from the game. "Then I'll go."

"No, you're more valuable here at the compound. I'll go." Charlie pointed to Dave's row of unused letters. "Now, you'd better use that x or it's going to hurt you when the game's over." Charlie winked at Dave's young opponent and Dave threw his hands up in frustration.

"Great! Thanks a lot! Get out of here and be safe. If you sense danger, leave the food behind."

It took Charlie an hour and a half to get the flashlight to the start of the north tunnel and then back to the compound at a full run. He'd done it so many times by now, he knew where all the dips and bumps were. During that time, he convinced himself that he'd better just go alone and get the food. He didn't want to spend one minute longer than necessary in Noah's house and they really didn't need the other van anymore.

By eight o'clock he was making his way to Noah's house, closely watching the road for pedestrians as he drove. If he could spot Noah and Tara, he could just run them back. As he drove, he powered up his cell again to see if there was another message from Noah.

There was one new voice mail. Charlie called the message center and listened. At first he didn't recognize the voice, but then he realized who it was. He slammed on his brakes and did a quick U-turn. Thankfully there was no one on the road. He looked at his watch. It had been almost five hours since the message was sent. No doubt the state police would be combing the highway. He would probably be too late, but he had to try.

He hit the gas and prayed for a miracle.

When Noah found her at the abandoned barn as he had instructed, Tara was cowering in the corner. They found the door in the floor and headed down into the tunnel. Noah had seen two cars drive into the driveway by the barn and slowly shine high-powered flashlights around the area. He was relieved when they left. Perhaps they had seen movement or maybe they followed Tara. Either way, he wasn't going to stay above ground for long.

Noah held the flashlight and kept the pace moving as he and Tara made their way through the dark, dirty tunnel. Again and again he thanked the Lord for bringing them safely to that place. Only a few minutes more and they would be at the compound. Tara held on to the back of his shirt, stumbling here and there, but keeping up.

It helped that it was so dark, because claustrophobia could have easily overtaken anyone in a tunnel like this and Noah was worried about Tara. She had been through so much lately. Twenty feet below ground, barely six feet of standing space and only about three feet across, this tunnel could wear on the nerves of even the most stable person.

It took them just over an hour to reach the compound. It was about nine thirty when they arrived and entered through the kitchen. Chef Fredo was working on prepping food for the following day and jumped when the back door of his kitchen opened. Then a big smile spread across his face and he extended a floury hand to Tara.

In a heavy French accent he said, "You must be Tara. I've heard so much about you."

Tara, squinting in the brightness of the lights, smiled and returned his handshake.

"Come on. I want you to meet a couple of people."

Noah led her out of the kitchen to the eating area. It was relatively empty, except for a few adults in a corner playing cards. CNN was on the television, volume muted. Noah hung on to her hand and nearly ran her down the hallway to the living area.

"Noah, slow down! I'm exhausted. Can't I clean up somewhere first?"

"It will just take a minute, Tara. They need to know we're back."

"All right, but first impressions can take a while to forget."

As they entered the living area, small groups of people sat on couches, and there were a few children still awake, playing video games. In the far corner, Dave sat with several adults and immediately stood and left his friends when Noah entered. He made his way over to the couple and gave Noah a warm handshake.

"We were really worried about you." He turned to Tara. "You must be Tara. I'm Dave Conover and we've all been praying for you." He looked back at Noah. "So, where've you been and what took you so long?"

Noah smiled and wiped his brow. He looked at his hand and realized just how dirty they both were.

"We need to get her set up in a room. A hot shower will do both of us good. Then we can talk."

Noah's sister Tami had jumped up from her seat and joined the conversation.

"I know where we put all your stuff. You actually have a room ready for you already. I'm Tami, by the way, Noah's younger sister." She then glared at Noah. "You know, the one who is supposed to meet a girlfriend before the rest of the world does." Her head turned back to Tara. "Come with me, Tara. I'll take care of you."

Tami put her arm around Tara's shoulder and led her out of the room. Tara looked back at Noah and he shrugged his shoulders. His sister had always had a way of taking charge and Tara should probably just get used to it. He added a wink and a smile, then she was gone. An hour later, Noah was informed that Tara was set up in her bedroom and had taken a hot shower. When she walked out of her room, Noah was leaning against the opposite wall, waiting for her. His heart skipped a beat when their eyes met. Her hair was pulled back and her cheeks were rosy from the hot shower. Her eyes twinkled when she smiled at him and he thought his knees might give out from under him.

"Fredo has some soup and bread for us in the kitchen."

"Thank goodness, I'm starving." As Noah turned to lead her back to the kitchen, Tara touched him on the arm. "Noah, my head is really spinning. When I think of my mom, I want to cry but when I look around the compound, I want to shout for joy. This is the first time in months that I've felt safe. I'm so sorry I didn't believe you. I'm sorry I didn't come with you. I thought I had it all under control, but I was living a lie. My church was a disaster and I was too weak to see it." Tears streamed down her face and Noah pulled her into his arms.

"It's okay, Tara. That's all in the past now."

"But I don't know why you put up with me for so long. I was such a fool. I look around this place and know I shouldn't really be here."

Knowing what was happening to the world above ground, Noah often was humbled at God's provision and goodness in his own life. Tara was no exception—she was simply protected by God. Her road was a bit rougher but the end result was the same as his. Safe in the hidden compound.

"Tara, there's not a single one of us down here that deserves to be protected. God has provided for us and He's the One at the center of all of this."

"But you tried to show me—we even studied it in the Bible and I did nothing. I wonder what else the Bible says that I blew off."

"You're here and that's what matters now." Noah pulled away and wiped a tear from Tara's cheek. "And the good news is, there's not a whole lot to do down here, so we study the Bible a lot. You'll learn more than you'll know what to do with in no time flat."

Tara smiled and the twinkle returned. "Let's eat."

They headed into the eating area where Fredo had set out their dinner. Dave, Noah's mother, and Tami joined them, and the next hour and a half was spent hearing Tara's story of the time at her mother's. Noah was amazed at the fact that there was not more resistance to Hitler by the world. Satan's foothold was strong and in a few days, the Day of Destruction would raise the insanity to a new level.

"Hey," Noah suddenly realized he hadn't seen Charlie yet. "Where's Charlie?"

"He got your message and took the van to your house to try to retrieve the food." Dave looked at his watch. "He left at eight and I think he should be back in an hour or so."

Noah didn't like that news. He barely escaped with his life and he still wasn't sure how that had happened.

"Oh, man, it's not safe out there. When I went to Tara's house, as soon as I got out of the van, someone was literally screaming my name. And he was loud. He was yelling that I wasn't marked. I jumped in the van and took off. I couldn't hear him at my house, though."

"That was the Memorial Park idol," explained Tara. "He can identify unmarked people. He screams the name until the police arrive and arrest the person."

"An idol that talks? You're kidding me. I hope Charlie doesn't run into any trouble. I had officers at my house when I left, so I hope they aren't watching the house."

Noah took a drink of water as Dave shook his head and glanced down at his watch. "He said he would scope it out and if there was anything suspicious he would leave. I'm assuming since he's not back that he's getting the food."

Noah didn't like the fact that Charlie was doing this alone. It wasn't safe out there anymore. He knew he wouldn't sleep until Charlie returned so he went to the kitchen and started a pot of coffee. The only thing that distracted him was the sound of Tara laughing with his mother and sister. That was music to his ears. He quietly thanked the Lord for sparing her life, then rejoined the group to find out what was so funny.

The bleeding had finally stopped. It took a couple of hours, but the strip of cloth torn from his sweatshirt and tied tightly around his head had done the job. Thomas was grateful for nightfall, because since the accident, the state police had been combing the area with helicopters as well as with men on foot, and he knew they were looking for him. Thomas had seen the SUV blowing through the stop sign at the intersection of the highway and the old dirt road. He had braced himself, but was unprepared for the fact that the impact would tip the bus, causing him to lose consciousness when he hit his head on the window. When he came to, the bus was on its side and no one was moving. He didn't know how long he had been unconscious, but he struggled to wake himself up and then climbed over the bus seats to check on the others. A couple of guys he couldn't find a pulse on, but the rest were just knocked out. There was a lot of broken glass and blood, and interestingly enough, when Thomas went to check on the driver of the SUV, he was dead and didn't have a mark on his head. It made him wonder if he had purposefully hit the bus. Sooner than later he might be able to ask him in heaven.

Thomas had found the keys to his handcuffs along with a cell phone in the pocket of one of the guard's pants. He called Charlie and left a message. At that point, he knew what highway he was on and was going to make his way north. There was a rest stop about twelve miles back and he was going to try to make it there. Not knowing when Charlie would check his messages, Thomas told Charlie he would wait a couple of days in the cornfield behind the rest stop, but then he would move on. He had no idea where he would go next, but he also knew that he had probably just put Charlie's cell out of business. When the state police realized the guard's phone was missing, they could check the account and maybe even trace Charlie's line. He passed along his concern to Charlie and hopefully Charlie would toss the phone and pick him up. Then he stomped on the phone, shattering it and kicked it into a ditch. He didn't know what else to do.

As he made his way carefully through the late September fields, he had to stay hunched over to keep hidden. His head pounded and his stomach rumbled but he kept moving as best he could. Every once in a while he would lie down to rest his back and try to relieve his pounding head. He had counted seventeen state police cars heading toward the crash site behind him, lights flashing and sirens blaring, and was grateful for the warning sound so that he could drop on his stomach to avoid being seen. Often his mind strayed to Robin and the girls, but for now there was nothing he could do for them but pray.

So pray he did. Continually and without ceasing. Talking to the Father was the only thing that kept him from passing out from the pain in his head. It was also the only thing that kept the fear of what was happening to his wife and children from completely overcoming him.

After a few hours of working his way back north, Thomas could see the lights of the rest stop in the distance. His heart lifted and his energy was boosted. There were no cars at the stop and none on the road, as far as he could see, so he stepped out onto the pavement and began to run. He had taken a few magogs from the officer's pocket, something that was a rare find, and was hoping to find a vending machine where he could get some food. That food might have to last him a while so he would have to control himself.

As he neared the stop, he saw lights in the distance. The fluorescent orange sweatpants and tee shirt were a dead giveaway that he was an escaped convict. He didn't even consider trading clothes with an officer but now that he was thinking more clearly, he kicked himself for overlooking that detail. He ducked behind the rest stop and hid in the shadows until the car lights passed. It was another state police car, most likely going to help in the search. Why the officers weren't searching north was a mystery to Thomas, but he counted it a blessing.

Inside the rest stop, he quickly bought a few candy bars and a can of Coke. He glanced out the front door and there were still no cars around, so he headed into the bathroom. Carefully he untied the cloth from his head. The cut above his left eye was about two inches long and it was rather deep. The skin around the edges was a sickly white, as if the blood loss was killing the skin. He took the sweatshirt that he had tied around his waist and tore off another piece. He used the end of the first bandage to carefully wash around the wound and then tied a fresh bandage around his head.

Suddenly he heard footsteps. He glanced into the sink. The blood stained bandage had made a mess, but there was no time to clean it up. He wiped around the inside of the sink with the used cloth and ran to a stall. The footsteps were coming closer, almost at a running pace. Thomas shut the door of the stall, locked the door, and climbed up onto the toilet. He heard the door to the bathroom open.

"Thomas?" a voice loudly whispered. "Are you in here?"

Thomas started to cry. He never considered himself an emotional guy, but the sound of Charlie's voice pushed him over the edge. He stepped down and unlocked the door. At the sight of his long-time friend, Thomas felt so overwhelmed that words wouldn't come. Charlie turned, took one look at his friend, and ran to his side. He put an arm around his waist and said, "I'm here, now. I'll get you to safety. Can you walk?"

"Barely, but I'll be okay."

Thomas let his weight fall onto Charlie's side as they made their way to a van outside, just as another car's headlights were seen up the road. Charlie shut the door and Thomas hoped that no one saw his prison colors. But again, the car passed without stopping and he breathed a sigh of relief.

Charlie jumped in the driver's side and hit the gas. Thomas heard the tires spin and quickly glanced around again to see if there was an audience anywhere.

"Don't worry, Thomas. You're safe now. We're about forty-five minutes away from the compound. Have you eaten anything today?"

Thomas took a deep breath and tried to calm himself. He pulled the Coke and candy bars from the waistband of his pants. "It's my dinner. Want one?"

Charlie smiled and took a Twix bar. "Were there any other survivors?"

"At least two of the guards were dead and the driver of the SUV was dead. The others were breathing but unconscious. I figured it wouldn't take long for the state police to arrive, so I took off pretty quickly. I haven't seen anyone else, but the number of cops that passed me probably indicates there are others who escaped."

"This is unbelievable. Have you been at your house all these months?"

"No, we were at Robin's parents for a month or so, but the morning after we returned to our house we were arrested. That was just a couple of days ago." He paused and put a hand to his head. "It's getting really bad out there. I can't believe that people are just going on with their lives while Christians are being hunted like deer."

"And it's going to get worse in a couple of days. Where are Robin and the girls?"

The lump in Thomas's throat returned and he fought back the tears. "We were separated at the house and I don't know where they are. Right before we left to go to my in-laws', the pastor of Creston Bible came for a visit. He had been taken to the camp and shown piles of bodies dumped behind the campsite which were being burned. If they're at the camp, they're probably already dead." Thomas dropped his head into his hands and sobbed. The mere thought of it was unbearable.

"I know this is no consolation, but if they were killed, they are free from this mess and with the Lord right now. You have to find comfort in that."

"I hear you, but what if they're not dead? What can they possibly be going through?"

For a few minutes the two men rode in silence. Thomas had no more words, and fought to keep his mind from imagining the worst. He needed to get his bearings. A good night's sleep would help clear his head.

Then he could decide what to do about the girls.

twenty-one ‖

November

For two months now, Elise had closely watched Yakov, noting his words, his actions and his forehead. His floppy blonde bangs always covered his forehead, but occasionally she saw the rounded bottoms of three sixes. He loved his wool felt hat and wore it in almost any weather, but now that the weather was heading toward the cooler temperatures, his hat was a constant part of his wardrobe. As far as she was concerned, her idol must be mistaken and that was the end of that.

The two witnesses in Jerusalem continued to decry the Federation of World Powers and prophesy of impending doom. Occasionally they blew fire from their mouths, or took responsibility for the continued lack of rain in Russia, Iraq, and of late, Israel. Once they supposedly caused a minor earthquake near the mount and another time they claimed to ask God for hail to rain down on Moscow, but considering it was the rainy season, that was hardly a difficult call to make.

Her working relationship with Yakov was continuing to warm up. Once they had lunch together out of convenience and another time he invited her to join him at the ballet because Adolph had given him two free tickets. Though technically he hadn't spent any money on her, they were still growing in their friendship and she was pleased with that.

It had been two months since the Day of Destruction and the central office in Babylon was busy receiving the latest numbers of fully marked countries. Of the one hundred and ninety-two nations of the world, only seventeen were completely marked up. Another thirty were at ninety-seven percent and the next twenty-seven were right around ninety-two percent. Fifty were at eighty percent and the remaining sixty-eight were below that mark. Hitler projected that in a month, another fifty would reach the goal, and within three months he would have nearly one hundred percent participation.

Elise often wondered what percentage of the population had been killed off to get to the goal, but she never asked. The Day of Destruction left carnage all over the world, except in third world countries, where there was nothing to gain by murder. Those countries, however, in desperate need of relief supplies, had responded early for the much-needed help Hitler had to offer. New medical facilities were already being constructed and supplies were just waiting to be delivered to the good people of Africa. Hitler continued to be a hero around the world, the Uniter of people, Lord of the New World Order. And as his personal assistant, Elise was relishing the ride.

As she sat at her desk in Jerusalem, she watched the clock. Agent Vasiliev was to arrive that morning with Adolph. She, of course, had come a couple of days early. It would be a busy week of meetings and Adolph would not be in the office much. Rather, he would be on-site at several FWP building projects that were spread throughout Israel. It was a quarter after eleven and they should have arrived twenty minutes ago. Elise picked up the phone to call the limo driver, when the door in the foyer opened and Adolph Hitler, followed by Yakov, entered the room. She could tell immediately he was in a dark mood, and she stood to greet him.

"No calls. No interruptions. Put the phone on the answering machine and leave the office for two hours. When you return, we will begin our day."

Elise knew better than to argue with him and in five minutes she had cancelled his appointments and was ready to leave. She grabbed her purse and jacket and headed for the door. Perhaps she'd just go back to the hotel for lunch. She took the elevator to the lobby and when she walked out, Yakov stood at the desk, and looked her way. He motioned her to come over.

"Thanks for the heads up on that mood," she said, half joking, half serious.

"There was no time to get a call to you. Let me make it up to you by getting lunch. Have you grown to appreciate falafel yet?"

Elise was surprised at his forwardness, not that it wasn't a pleasant surprise, just out of character for Yakov.

"Sure. Do you have somewhere in mind?"

"Well, last I heard we have two hours to kill, so let's catch a show at the same time."

Elise gave him a quizzical look, but answered, "Lead the way."

He took her to a small falafel house near the Temple Mount. The show he was referring to was the dependable and yet still entertaining witnesses. As they sat at a table under a sun umbrella, Yakov turned the conversation personal.

"Does it ever bother you?"

"The witnesses?"

"No, all the killing."

"What are you talking about?"

"All the people who have died under Hitler's regime."

Elise was a bit taken aback with his question. "Regime? I haven't heard it called that yet, at least not by you. Why do you ask?"

"I would just think that as a woman, to see the carnage day in and day out on the television, knowing your employer was responsible for it would wear on you."

"What does my being a woman have to do with it?"

Yakov stirred in his chair. "I'm just saying, I have seen a lot of death. It's part of the job. I was in the military before I was pulled into security. But you haven't seen that much. I was just wondering . . ."

"No, it doesn't bother me. Partly because I don't watch the news much. But the other part is because I can balance the deaths with the benefits he has provided the world. Medical technological innovations which never would have been realized if he hadn't brought the world together, free trade and commerce between nations which has brought stability to ravaged economies, hunger relief and peace to war-torn tribes in Africa"—

"Whoa! Hey! I've seen all the commercials. I know the taglines." Elise hated to be interrupted, but apparently Yakov didn't see it in her eyes. "I know what he's done, but you're telling me you never stop and wonder if it was right to kill tens of millions of people to accomplish it."

"Tens of millions. Is that what you think the number is?"

"Yeah, it's big. A lot more than the Holocaust."

Elise did not like where this conversation was going. "I resent you throwing that in my face. He is not the same man he used to be. This time he needs to know the world is behind him. Without full cooperation he couldn't do all this good for the world. And I think you are questioning the very man who puts food on your table. Besides, I don't necessarily believe your numbers."

Elise felt uncomfortable as Yakov leaned forward, his eyes narrowing in on hers. He lowered his voice. "Do you really believe that is what motivates him? The good of the world? You tell me why he couldn't unite the world with the Christians and the Jews still living in it."

Elise stood. She could feel the heat rising in her face, though she was still in the shade. "There are many Christians and Jews still on this earth. But there are those who refuse to honor the man who is saving the world. Don't you believe him when he warns us of hell? Is that where you want to go?" A thought suddenly occurred to her and before she knew it, she was saying it out loud. "Maybe my idol was right. Maybe you aren't on our team."

With that, she reached across the table and pulled Yakov's wool hat off of his head, revealing his marked forehead. But something was wrong. Only half the numbers were showing—the bottom half. Elise's heart skipped a beat and she dropped the hat on the ground. Yakov reached down and placed the hat back on his head.

"I can explain, Elise. Please sit back down. I can explain everything."

Elise couldn't decide what to do. His mark wasn't real. It wasn't permanent. She could not imagine what explanation he could give, but she chose to hear him out.

Suddenly, in the distance someone started to yell and Elise looked up at the mount. A man, fully on fire was running, then he fell and rolled on the ground. People ran to him and tried to put out the flames with their jackets.

"What is happening to this world?" She looked back at Yakov. She really liked him, and in secret, she had imagined a future with him. But that dream was over. When Hitler finds out about the fake numbers, Yakov would be killed. "What explanation could you possibly have?"

Yakov stared at the table between them for a moment. Then he raised his eyes and locked them on to hers.

"The night of Hitler's announcement, I took him back to the hotel. I was the only one with him. He was exhausted and I suggested he have a drink to relax, but he wanted to stay focused. We discussed many things that night, many things that I could never repeat. But in the end, he asked me to not take the mark."

"What? For what reason?" This was completely unbelievable.

"Lucifer believes that the ancient writings of God tell of large groups of rebels that will successfully hide until their Messiah returns. Hitler is in a panic about that, because if their Messiah returns and there is a remnant still on earth, then Lucifer loses and we all go to hell. That is the plan in a nutshell and that is what we have to stop. Soon I will be leaving and searching for this group. Supposedly, according to the writings, they are hiding in the wilderness. I couldn't infiltrate this group with a number on my head, so he asked me not to take the number so that I could spy on them and reveal their location. I already have underground connections. For example, I know where the two witnesses stay at night."

Elise struggled to accept this explanation. "Why wouldn't you share that information with me? We researched it together. And why wouldn't Hitler tell me about you? He confides nearly everything to me."

"I couldn't tell you because you would have wondered how I got this information and I would have had to tell you that I wasn't marked. Most of the time I don't wear a mark at all. Some days it wears off because I wear the hat all day. Rarely, when I know I will be inside all day, I'll put the number on and off as the situation demands."

Elise sat and stared at Yakov. There was a small glimmer of hope in her heart that he was telling the truth, still so much didn't add up.

"I'm still confused. If you are sold on following Hitler, how can you question his methods?"

Yakov looked down at his half-eaten plate of food. He fumbled a bit, then answered. "He asked me to question you. He wanted to make sure you were loyal. And you are. That's good news." He raised his eyes and met hers.

"Test me? Test me? This is really unbelievable, Yakov. Why would he test me?"

"For all his success, he's still very insecure. He tests all those around him. Don't be hurt. He just needs reassurance that you're loyal. And by this afternoon, he'll have all the reassurance he needs." Yakov hesitated. "But there's one more thing."

"What's that?"

"Hitler would be furious if he knew that you had found out that I don't have the mark. It's supposed to be only between him and me. You can't tell him you know, or I could be put away. You know what I mean?"

"He would kill you because I found out?"

"You saw the mood he was in. I just don't want to risk it. But you know everything now. There are no more secrets."

Elise needed time to absorb all this new information. In her mind, it was rather convenient that he asked her not to tell, especially if his whole story was a lie. On the other hand, there could be projects she wasn't aware of and accepting his explanation would keep him safely in her life. She just didn't know where to go with this. She needed time.

"I'll be back to the office by one thirty. I'm going to take a walk." She stood to leave and Yakov grabbed her arm.

"You don't believe me. I can see it in your eyes." His voice revealed disappointment. "And I was hoping our friendship would continue to grow." His square jaw and blonde hair were suddenly more irresistible than ever and she failed to fight back a smile. Was she really this gullible or was there something between them?

"I'll be back in an hour." Elise pulled her arm away and left Agent Vasiliev standing at the table. Then it suddenly dawned on her. She didn't have to make this decision alone; she had a very attentive advisor sitting on her dresser back at the hotel. She ran to the curb and hailed a taxi. Perhaps he could shed some light on the situation. Elise felt relief as she headed back to her room.

Durbin woke up cranky. He sat at his kitchen table, drinking a cup of coffee in silence. His wife had taken the children to school and was getting groceries, so the house was unusually quiet. Since the day of the accident, all but two of the escaped prisoners were apprehended. That was a couple of months ago. Deep down he hoped that Thomas was out of his state and someone else's problem. It made him sleep better at night to think he wasn't responsible for the death of his old friend. But the idol in the center of Memorial Park was a glaring, obnoxious reminder that he still hadn't succeeded in his mission. His goal of being the first fully marked town was long dead. In fact he was in the running to be the last one fully marked and this was not a badge of honor he enjoyed wearing.

The Day of Destruction proved relatively valuable with seventeen heads delivered to City Hall. Durbin fought back nausea looking at the severed heads, but that was the deal. One head earned the bearer a voucher to receive the dead man's possessions. There were seventeen families in Creston who bumped their tax bracket that day. But there was still a large group in hiding, and according to the loudmouth outside, the number was growing. It had mysteriously jumped two digits to one hundred thirty-nine and Durbin was suspicious his two escapees had found refuge with the group. But this group completely eluded captivity. The state police even jumped into the search and came up with nothing. All Durbin knew for sure was that they were within his city limits, so they were his problem.

"Where could they be?" he asked aloud. His voice echoed off the tile floor and the kitchen cabinets.

"I've been waiting for you to ask. What took you so long?"

Durbin jerked in surprise in his chair, almost falling onto the floor, but he caught himself. He quickly stood and looked around the kitchen to see who was talking. But no one was there.

"Who's there?"

"Over here, Wayne. On the fridge."

Durbin looked at his picture of Hitler, which was taped on the fridge. The voice was coming from the picture. As a matter of fact, the picture was 3-D. It was like a tiny window with a man looking out of it.

"Oh, come on, Wayne. You can't be surprised. You talk to the idol in Memorial Park every day."

Wayne cautiously walked over to the picture. Originally, it was a head shot of Hitler. Now it looked as if Hitler was leaning on an open window, his forearms resting on the picture edges, hands hanging over onto his refrigerator. His hands were clasped together and he was actually twittling his thumbs.

"You've got to be kidding me. Every idol talks? Not just the big one?"

"We all can talk."

"Why haven't you spoken sooner?" Wayne was nervous, because his relationship with the Memorial Park idol wasn't the greatest.

"Technically the only one in this house I would even want to talk to is you. And you're never here. And when you are home, there are kids everywhere and that dog is always barking. But today, it's quiet, we're alone, and you asked a question I may be able to answer."

"How could you know where they are hiding if the idol in Memorial Park doesn't."

The picture of Hitler smiled and motioned with his finger for Wayne to come closer, as if he had a secret to tell.

"Between you and me, he's not the shiniest magog in the bunch. Me, on the other hand, I've got a great mind and between the two of us, we can figure this one out."

Durbin kind of liked this idol. He was upbeat, a little bit funny and a lot kinder than the other one.

"Do you only speak here at home?"

"Nope, I can come to work with you, too. I just choose to communicate with you and no one else."

Wayne carefully pulled the picture from the refrigerator, with the tape still on its edges. He brought it over to the kitchen table and taped it to his coffee mug.

"So, where could they be?"

"I think a better question would be, who are they?"

"What do you mean?"

"Well, these are your citizens who are hiding, so there must be some kind of record of who has marked up and who hasn't. I know you've sent many to the camp, but there has to be a group of people who didn't go to camp, but you can't locate them at their homes.

Maybe they sold their homes or relinquished them to the bank. Or maybe they prepaid mortgages and utilities and just don't answer the door. But I would think if you looked at your list, you might find out some strange behavior patterns that will at least help you identify who might be hiding. Once we have that information, we can start investigating other aspects of their lives. Where they went to church, if they have family in the area, were they talking strangely or trying to convince neighbors to hide with them. You know someone slipped up. And sooner or later, we'll find them."

Durbin sat in utter amazement. In thirty seconds this little picture had just laid out a plan to find the missing nonmarkers that was better than anything he or his staff had brainstormed. He just had one more question for the idol.

"Do you mind traveling in my wallet, or would you prefer a window seat?"

Creston's city Web site had a link to the training camp. You could click on the link and take a virtual tour of the camp, minus the burn pit in the back. There was also a current list of residents. It was a way for family members to find missing relatives and check on their "status." That's what the site said. From the day Thomas arrived at the compound, he checked the list. Robin's name was never posted.

He could also access live feeds into the schoolrooms where the children were studying. This was a way for parents to see their children, if they were in the boarding school program. Over three thousand children were in this program, with additional facilities being built to hold the nonmarked children. Thomas searched by age groups and tried to find his daughters to no avail. He was pretty sure his family was not at the camp.

So the question became, were they still at the jail or had they already been killed? This question haunted him day and night. Thomas could hear the voice of the news anchor droning as he sat picking at a plate of pancakes.

Charlie sat down at the table next to him, a full plate of breakfast in one hand and a hot cup of coffee in the other.

"Good morning. How did you sleep last night?"

Thomas snapped out of his trance and looked at Charlie. "I slept okay. How are you doing today?"

"Same old, same old. Anything interesting in the news this morning?"

"Haven't been paying attention." Thomas flipped over a heavily saturated half a pancake on his plate.

"Well, if it's any consolation, you look like death."

Thomas looked up from his plate. "Thanks."

Charlie shook his head. "You're not sleeping, are you?"

"I haven't slept well since I arrived. If I don't do something, I'm going to lose my mind. Last night, I actually had myself convinced it would be better to turn myself into the police and just be done with it, rather than sit here without my family."

"Thomas, you're not thinking straight. I can't imagine what you're going through, but you've got to get your eyes on the big picture here. The accident that brought you here was not a mistake. God put you here. Why did I go out that day and check my phone, just hours after you called? And I had a van to get you? And we met up as easily as we did? Is all that coincidence?"

"No, but why hasn't He saved my family?" Thomas was actually surprised that he verbalized what he had been thinking, but there was no point in hiding his feelings.

"I can't answer that. I don't know what is happening to your family, but I want you to listen to me. I have a clear head and this is how I reason through where your family might be. First, we know they are not at the camp. You check daily. Second, they won't kill the girls.

Durbin hasn't allowed that yet or there wouldn't be buildings full of children at the camp. So, the fact that the girls aren't at the school leads me to assume they are still with Robin somewhere."

"In the jail? Then maybe I need to go there and get them!"

"But we don't know they're there. And how are you going to get them back?"

"God worked a miracle for me . . ."

"So you're going to force His hand for a miracle for them? It doesn't work that way. If He wants them here, He'll get them here. In the meantime, we're obediently hiding and waiting for Jesus to return. You can't go into town anymore. The new motto is shoot first and never ask questions. You may think you can help them, but most likely you'll just get slaughtered, and who have you helped then?"

Thomas slammed his hands down on the table in frustration. The eating area was instantly silenced. He looked around and his face flushed with embarrassment.

"How do I live with this? What if they mark my daughters?"

"Didn't Robin say that the kids at her school weren't being marked? Didn't she tell you that when parents tried to mark the children, it wouldn't stay on their heads? God won't allow it, Thomas. It has to be the child's choice. You need to trust Him."

"I've just never been in this place before. I've always been able to control things. And this is just so much out of my control that at times I think death would be a relief from my thoughts! Why is God doing this to me?"

Charlie stood. "You need to talk with Dave. His wife died from cancer and he knows what helplessness feels like. But he never was angry with God. He learned to take every thought captive to the will of God and simply trust. Come on, let's find him."

Thomas shook his head. "I feel like an idiot. I've already become the compound leper. No one will even talk to me. I don't need to bother Dave with this."

As Thomas dropped his head, he felt a tug on his arm. Charlie pulled him to his feet.

"Enough of this. People don't know how to comfort you right now. But you don't have to bear this burden alone. We're talking with Dave, whether or not you feel like it."

Thomas felt tears welling up in his sleep-deprived eyes. "I just feel so responsible. You warned me. God warned me. But because I was not the man God would have me be, I led my family to be slaughtered."

"If your family is dead, they are with the Lord. Whatever they went through to get there is not even a memory anymore. Thomas, Christ said this tribulation would be the worst the world had ever known. There have been slaughters throughout the ages, but they pale in comparison to this. This is a supernatural event that has caught most Christians unprepared. It doesn't mean you were a bad husband or father. Now is not the time to question God or your intelligence, it is the time to thank the Lord for sparing you and wait. It won't be long. A year or two and it's all over. But we're all in the same boat here. We're just waiting and making the best of our last days on earth."

"And going to find my wife wouldn't be wise because . . ."

"Because God specifically pulled you out of that bus and put you here. You need to be grateful and stay."

"Grateful that He's put me into a living hell because of my thoughts!"

"Your thoughts are not His thoughts, Thomas. You're ways are not His ways. If you want to do this your way, then go ahead and leave. But if you stay, you've got to change your way of thinking. Immerse yourself in His Word. Recognize God's role in your escape and submit yourself to His plan. I'm not saying it will be easy, but blaming Him for saving you seems awfully twisted."

Thomas stood quietly for a moment, his mind racing faster than he could ever imagine. "Staying makes me guilty. How can anyone down here even talk to me after what I've done to my wife and daughters?"

"He bore your guilt and shame on the cross. You can't pay extra for that—it's already been paid for. Half the people down here were unprepared for this, too. They can relate to your situation because many of them lost family members. But up till now, you've been unapproachable. If you lift your head, you'll find many brothers and sisters in Christ just waiting for the opportunity to help you."

"I don't know if I can do this."

"Sure you can."

"Well, if I have the choice of beating myself up for another day or talking to Dave, maybe I should try something new." Thomas lifted his eyes to meet Charlie's. "Let's find him."

As Charlie turned to head back to the living area, Thomas felt a hand on his shoulder. He turned to see a man, around his age with a smile on his face. He reached out his hand and Thomas took it.

"I couldn't help but overhear. I just want to say, you're going to get through this and we're all here to help you."

He pulled Thomas into an embrace and Thomas felt his face flush again. He didn't even know this guy. But immediately there were more people there, hugging him and saying words of encouragement. Thomas felt his heart break and soon the tears were flowing, not only from his eyes but from those comforting him. They told him he wasn't alone, that they were praying for him and that God was in control, even though he didn't understand. For the first time since that horrible morning when he was separated from his family, Thomas felt encouraged and that perhaps a bit of the burden was being lifted.

Thomas retired to his room and sat on his bed, his mind still racing. He had spent so much time questioning God, questioning himself, that it was going to be hard to change that mind-set. If only he could hang on to Charlie's encouragement. If only he could believe he was where God wanted him. Then he could stay and get through this ordeal. He could sleep each night and dream of reuniting with his wife and children in heaven. He could be personable and get through the days until the Lord returned.

But deep down Thomas knew what he had to do. He wasn't sure how he'd do it, but he had plenty of time to figure it out.

twenty-two

March

Noah paced outside Dave Conover's bedroom door. Occasionally he mumbled a few words but then would quiet back down. When Dave opened the door, Noah stopped and took a deep breath.

"So, what's so urgent?"

"Um, I really need to talk to you."

"No kidding. What's up?"

"Well, you know that Tara has been here for almost six months now. And I was thinking, I mean, we could be here for another couple of years, right? And well, we're not really at capacity down here, so there are extra living spaces. And so, um, well, I was thinking . . ."

"Get to the point, Noah."

"Do you . . . do you . . . think Tara and I . . . could get married?" Noah waited anxiously for a response.

"Married?" Dave smiled.

"Well, yeah, I mean . . ."

"Okay, enough." Dave put up one hand to stop Noah from talking. "Let me ask you a few questions. Do you love her?"

"With my life."

"Does she love you?"

"I'm pretty sure she does."

"Have you talked to her about this?"

"No, I wanted to make sure we could do it before I asked." Noah raised his eyebrows and waited for the next question.

"And hanging out with her during the days just isn't enough?"

"Nowhere near enough."

Dave grinned, shook his head, and suppressed a laugh. "Okay, get her to agree and we'll handle everything else. It'll give us all something to look forward to."

Noah bit his lip, imagining her face when he asked her. He turned to leave when Dave called out to him.

"Oh, wait! Do you have a ring?"

Noah frowned—the one detail he had forgotten.

"No, but I can probably get something from my mom."

"Hold on a second." Dave reached into his back pocket and pulled out his wallet. He opened it and from the fold pulled out a small square piece of tissue paper. It was folded multiple times and he opened it, revealing a beautiful, solitaire diamond ring set in a white gold setting. He held it out to Noah and Noah took it from him.

"It was my wife's. I've been carrying it with me ever since she died."

"It's beautiful."

"Give it to Tara."

Noah looked up and met eyes with Dave. "No way, Dave, I couldn't."

"What do I need it for? Is it going to buy me anything I need? Seeing it used, especially on the hand of my good friend's new wife, it'll do me some good. It's what Beth would have wanted."

"I don't know what to say. Can I pay you for it?"

Dave chuckled again. "Think about how stupid that comment just was."

"Oh, yeah, I guess you're right. Well, I owe you, Dave." Noah turned to run down the hall and find Tara. Over his shoulder he added, "Big time!"

Tara sat at a table with three teenaged girls playing the game of *Life* when Noah came running into the living area. She looked up and their eyes met. She smiled at him but he didn't return the smile. His face looked concerned and Tara could tell he had something on his mind. He ran over to her and interrupted the game.

"I'm sorry, girls, but I need Tara for a minute." He reached down and grabbed her hand to pull her up. His hands felt sweaty and Tara noticed a bead of sweat on his forehead.

"But we're just about done. Is something wrong? Are you feeling all right?"

"No, no, nothing is wrong, I just need you for . . . well, go ahead and finish and I'll wait." Their game table was in the far corner of the room, so Noah leaned against the wall and crossed his arms.

Tara cautiously sat back down, giving Noah a strange look, wondering what was up with him. Seven minutes later the final car full of family pegs made it to the end of the game and it was time to count the money. Not that she enjoyed the end of the game, since Noah's fidgeting and shifting his weight from one foot to the other was so distracting.

"Um . . . they can count your money, Tara, don't you think?"

Tara turned to Noah. "It will only take a minute, Noah. Good grief!" She was pretty sure by now there was nothing wrong or he wouldn't have let her finish, but Noah's impatience was getting the best of her. A few minutes later, she conceded defeat to one of the girls and then asked if they would clean up the game for her. She stood and turned to her impatient friend.

"So, what's going on?"

"Come with me."

Tara thought maybe he didn't want the girls to hear what he had to say, but when they passed the bedroom units and bathrooms and he didn't stop, Tara really started to wonder. They made their way to the eating area. As usual, CNN was on the television and a few adults sat at tables here and there. Noah pulled her toward the kitchen, where Fredo and a couple women were preparing dinner. He looked around, as if he had lost something and then continued into the kitchen, dragging Tara behind him the whole time. Tara went from concern to amused and back to concerned in just a matter of minutes.

They went through the kitchen and Noah opened the door that led to the stairway leading to the garage above. Once in the stairwell, he shut the kitchen door and turned on the light. A bare lightbulb dimly lit the small stairwell. Tara felt a bit chilled.

"I should have grabbed my sweater. I didn't know you were taking me here." Tara put the emphasis on the word "here" to make a point, which was . . .

"It's okay, we won't be here long."

He faced her and took both of her hands in his, and then just smiled. Tara couldn't help but return his goofy smile because the whole situation was so awkward. She breathed a sigh of relief that their run through the compound was over and decided to just wait for Noah to speak. Obviously something was on his mind, but for the moment the dark, quiet stairwell was actually peaceful. Time alone was rare, so if she could stand the chill, she'd cherish the quiet.

After a minute, he finally spoke.

"I'm really so proud of you, Tara."

Tara smiled. "Why?"

"You've adjusted to life down here so well. You help the women in the kitchen and play with the kids, you seem to love the Bible studies, and you're a great card player."

Tara winked one eye in thought, as she furrowed her brow. "So that's what was so important that I had to drop everything and come into a cold stairwell for you to tell me? That I'm a good girl?"

"No, it's more. It's just that, Tara, I love you so much. Every day I love you more."

"I love you, too, Noah."

With each day that passed, Tara loved him more. He was kind of quirky and this little conversation in the stairwell would definitely be filed in the quirky category. She shivered in the coolness of the stairwell and Noah must have noticed because he put his arms around her and then kissed her.

"We don't know how long we're going to be down here. Only God knows, but it could be a couple of years. And I just think that, considering how we feel about each other, I think that . . ." His voice died away and Tara leaned in, her brow furrowed again, waiting for the end of his sentence.

Noah stepped back and in the dim light, dropped to one knee, still holding her hands in his.

In an instant her heart skipped a beat and a wave of chills flew up her spine. She struggled to catch her breath and could feel a lump form in her throat. She felt tears form in her eyes, and she looked down at this precious face which was looking up at her.

"I know the world has turned upside down, but I believe God has brought us to this place safely. I love you and would give my life for you, Tara Warners."

In the near darkness, Tara could see Noah's eyes glistening. The smile was gone, but his face shone with sincerity. She couldn't speak. All she could do was wait for his next words.

"I know we're stuck down here together, but it's not enough for me. I want to fall asleep with you in my arms and wake to your beautiful blue eyes every morning. So, I was wondering, whether it's for a day, a month, or a year, will you marry me?"

The words hung in the air. Tara felt a wave of emotion flood over her whole body. Joy? Was it joy? Or shock? Or was this love, true love? Tara fell to her knees and into his arms, and she began to cry. Softly, she forced out the word "yes," so he would understand her tears. He held her tightly and kissed away the teardrops. Then he took her hand

and slid something onto her finger. Tara held it up to look at the ring and turned it so the naked lightbulb would give her the best view. It was a perfect fit and the solitaire diamond sparkled even in the dull light. She couldn't believe her eyes.

"Where did you get this? How did you know my ring size?"

"God knew, Tara. He provided the ring through Dave."

"What do you mean?"

Noah stood and pulled her to her feet. "I talked to Dave about getting married and he gave me his wife's ring. He said it would bring him joy to see it on your finger."

Tara loved Noah more than life. It was a growing and maturing love, since they had such a rough start, but God had a plan from the start. She wrapped her arms around his waist and squeezed tightly. More tears and kisses followed until reality set in.

"When are we doing this?" She looked at Noah, a bit concerned he had made more plans than she had realized.

"Don't worry. I haven't gone beyond talking with Dave about this. But my vote is sooner than later."

"What about your mom and sister?"

"Oh, yeah. I suppose we should tell them."

Tara reached up and wiped another falling tear, aware that her makeup was most likely running off her face by now. She laughed and said, "Noah! They're going to kill you! Let's go now and they can help us plan the wedding." She looked at her hand and saw streaks of mascara.

"I think you're going to have plenty of help—the guest list is already done! And I'm sure Fredo will figure how to make a feast out of powdered potatoes and Spam!"

Tara suddenly thought of her mom. It was like running into a brick wall. They had talked often about her wedding day, though never in this context. Hours of laughing and dreaming and now, she'd never know about it. Tara fought the sadness, because it was a joyful day and she was determined not to dampen the excitement.

"I love you, Noah."

"I adore you, Tara."

He kissed her again and her sadness melted away. Holding her close, he whispered a prayer of thanks to their Heavenly Father for this precious and unexpected gift. Then they were off to make plans.

The package on her desk was beautifully wrapped with a large, white bow on the top. There was a card tucked underneath the ribbon with her name on it. She had just returned from lunch, and Elise walked around her desk and sat in the chair. Of course she recognized his handwriting, but a gift? This was unusual indeed.

She removed the card from the gift, opened the envelope, and pulled out a small, yellow, flower-shaped card from inside. She opened the card and read the note.

Your safety is very important to me, Elise. Please accept this as a gift of love, concern, and protection. Adolph.

Her heart skipped a beat or two. Such a personal note from such an impersonal employer. She picked up the package. It was heavy and actually cold to the touch. She slit the folded and taped sides with her letter opener and slid the paper off the box. It was an aluminum box with gold hinges, a gold handle, and center clasp, about the size of a lunch box. She unhooked the clasp and opened the lid. Lying on a bed of gray foam was a small handgun and a clip.

Hmmm . . . a gun.

Adolph was an intentional gift giver. He never left gifts up to her. He knew various world leaders and what their hobbies and preferences were, and the gifts he chose to give away were done with great thought. Then she imagined him at his desk thinking through this decision.

For Elise? Let me think. A gun.

Elise didn't know much about guns, so whether this was a pistol or a revolver or if it had numbers in its name, she couldn't say. She carefully picked up the gun and could see that the handle was empty. Apparently that's where the clip would go. She looked to see if there was something to cock back, but there wasn't, however she did see a button on the handle, which was presumably a safety of sorts.

She returned the gun to its bed and picked up the clip. It was heavy and she turned it over in her hand. Engraved on the side of the clip were these words: *Given to my personal assistant, Elise Orion, for her years of faithful service and companionship. Adolph Hitler.* She understood the faithful service part, but she wasn't sure where the word "companionship" came in. Adolph didn't have many friends, so perhaps the little they did talk was considered friendship to him. She laid the clip back in the case and closed the lid and the center clasp. Then she stared at the gun, trying to figure out exactly why Adolph would give her a gun. He was in Iraq at the moment, and she was in Russia, so he must have prearranged the delivery. She set it on the floor, sliding it under her desk and out of sight. This is one mystery she would have to sit on for a while.

Then she wondered if Yakov knew about it. Most likely he arranged it. But should she ask him? Ever since he explained his unique situation to Elise they had become much closer. He felt that at any time he would be sent off for his secret mission. But the days came and went and he was still around. Three days earlier, their relationship entered a new phase. He actually kissed her goodnight after a late dinner. It wasn't anything out of a movie, but there had still been fireworks . She was slowly but surely breaking down his tight-lipped veneer and finding he was rather interesting and engaging, someone she could potentially spend her life with. But if Yakov knew about the gun, why wouldn't he have told her about it? Perhaps he didn't know.

And maybe Adolph didn't want anyone to know about it. He wasn't really the gift-giving type.

Two days later, she started to piece together the puzzle.

Robin sat in the chair opposite Wayne Durbin in her orange sweat suit. She was being transported from the jail to the camp today, but had thrown such a fit, demanding to see Durbin that one of the guards finally put a call in to his superior who contacted him. Out of respect to his past friendship, Durbin had left her and the girls in the local jail much longer than usual and now he agreed to meet with her. He was finishing a phone call when she was ushered in. Durbin noted how pale and thin Robin looked. When he hung up, however, she was the first to speak.

She sat on the edge of the seat and folded her hands in her lap. "I can help you, Wayne. I know things that would be valuable, but I need you to help me."

"Robin, I hate seeing you like this."

"No, you don't, Wayne, or you would have let me out months ago."

"Don't put me in the position of explaining this to you again. You never had to be put in jail if you'd have marked up like everyone else in Creston." He was tired of the argument. "You know, it's people like you who are stopping the advancement of this town."

Robin set her jaw and her eyes didn't show fear, but exhaustion.

"All I want is a car full of gas and food, and my daughters and Thomas, if he's still alive. I'll tell you what I know and then you let us just disappear. We'll leave the state so you are not responsible for us."

"I don't even know what information you supposedly have, but I'm not cutting any deals until you prove to me your information is relevant."

"You're struggling to find all the nonmarkers, right? Word in the jail is that the idol in Memorial Park says there's a large group still hidden that you haven't found yet. So you can say it's people like me who are stalling things, but there's a whole group you haven't found yet."

"We're working on it, but you're right, there is a group I haven't found yet."

"I think I know who they are."

"I don't care who they are. I just want to know where they are."

"Well, I don't know exactly where they are, but—"

"Then you really can't help me at all." Durbin stood and pointed to the door.

Robin jumped from her seat. "Wait! I am sure with my information you'll find them quicker. They wanted Thomas and me to come with them. They didn't tell us exactly where but I know more than you. I'll stake my life on it."

"Funny choice of words, Robin, since you've already given up your life by not taking the mark."

Hear her out, Wayne.

Wayne glanced at his top desk drawer. His idol lay inside the closed drawer. He could hear it plainly, but could Robin? She wasn't startled, so he assumed she couldn't hear it.

"Charlie West is the first name for you to look into. He was the one who initially invited Thomas and me to hide with him."

"When did he talk with you?"

"He actually spoke with us before Hitler revealed his plan for the world."

Durbin found that fact interesting. "Before? Why? What did he know that would cause him to want to hide back then?"

"He based it on some verses in the Bible. I guess he just saw signs that this was coming that we hadn't seen. He studied the Bible a lot and had a different bend on the Scriptures than we had."

"So all of this is more than just an unwillingness to worship Hitler. Thomas told me he would never align with Hitler, but you're saying there is fulfilled biblical predictions going on here?"

"Oh, come on, Wayne, you know what the church has been saying. It doesn't matter to you anyway. The Bible has never been an authority to you. But Charlie saw this coming and tried to warn us."

"Why didn't you go with him?"

Robin was quiet for a moment and she seemed to struggle as she answered. "My pride. Thomas wanted to go, but I refused to believe." She drew in another breath and then pulled herself together. "Another name is Noah Greer. He was a friend of Charlie's who worked at Smith and Brumsby. He was part of the group that prepared the compound, as they called it."

"But you don't know where the compound is?"

"The location was a secret in case something like this would actually happen."

"Something like this? Like someone telling to save their own life?"

"To save her children's lives."

Robin's jaw was set again and he knew this woman had tunnel vision at the moment.

"So, what do you know about it?"

"I know it's south of town, with underground tunnels right off the highway that feed into it. The tunnel entrances are close enough that you can walk to it in a day or so from town."

"And where are these entrances? In houses?"

"I don't know. I just know they dug a northern tunnel and a southern tunnel. The compound itself is underground, under a farm or something."

"So, how is this information going to help me? Two names and hidden tunnels?"

"Charlie had a cell phone that we were given his number to call. Thomas had it in his wallet. Maybe you can track his cell. I don't know,

Wayne, maybe you can have the police check houses and barns along the highway for tunnel entrances."

"There's nothing else you can tell me?"

"Where is Thomas, Wayne? Is he still here, too?"

Durbin knew this question was coming, but he quickly changed the subject.

"He's safe for now, but you don't have anything else that would help me? This really isn't much to go on."

Robin got up from her chair and went around to Durbin's side of the desk. She got down on her knees and took his hand. "I'm desperate here, Wayne. I know I am just days away from death and I don't fear my destiny, but I can't bear the thought of my daughters being hurt or brainwashed. Please, let us go. I am begging you."

Two names are not enough, Wayne. Get rid of her. She knows nothing. Keep your focus on the prize. Without the mark she's going to die anyway.

Durbin pulled his hand away from Robin's grip. "Get up." He stood and she followed suit. "It's not enough, Robin. You've got to go now."

What little color was in her face drained away and fear replaced exhaustion. "Please help me, Wayne. If you won't help me, just help my girls. Get them to Thomas, so I can die in peace."

Wayne grabbed her arm and led her to his office door. "I don't get you Christians. Here you are, willing to slaughter a group in hiding who was apparently prepared enough to see this coming, but you're not willing to take the mark to save your children. It's a strange religion, rather self-serving, wouldn't you say?" He pulled her closer to his face and lowered his voice. This was her last chance. "If you just take the mark, your girls move into the boarding school until they're marked and very soon your life goes back to normal. But you know all this. There's only one way to save yourself and that's get the mark." He opened the door and nodded to the guard in the foyer. He pushed her out the door and closed it behind her before she could say another word.

Durbin sat back at his desk and opened his drawer. His small picture of Hitler stared back at him.

"West and Greer. Check them on your master list. Find out if they have active cell accounts. Also, check abandoned farms along the highway that still have utilities—gas, electricity, cable—and shut them off. We'll force them out of hiding. We may force them above ground before we ever locate their compound, so increase your patrol teams on that stretch of highway."

Wayne quickly listed out the instructions on a legal pad and shut the drawer. He wasn't used to having a boss, but this one was pretty competent. He was getting close and he could feel it. The idol had told him to stay focused and more than ever, there were several things that were crystal clear to him now. First, he was close to having one hundred percent participation for the FWP's approval for the funds. That had been a long task, but he could see the finish line. Second, once the funds were released to his town, the people were prepared to roll up their sleeves and get going. The farmers had already finished the blueprints for the research facilities they needed, locations were chosen for new wells, improvements were targeted at the dairy facilities and even the increased labor force was waiting in the wings for the green light. His town was ripe for change. And third, the group stopping this progress was a cult his town would not miss. If Robin was a taste of what true Christians were all about, they were a bunch of self-centered losers. The mere fact that their hiding was hindering the advancement of the rest of Creston was evidence of their selfishness. Wayne won't miss them at all. Not even Thomas. He had no idea that Thomas was so ignorant to fall for a cult, but he could no longer feel bad it ended this way. The FWP said those who wouldn't mark up weren't worth keeping around and they were exactly right.

Elise had lunch waiting when her boss arrived from Iraq. He entered the office and stopped at her desk.

"Good day, Elise," he said, pleasantly. She stood and reached for his hand, a typical greeting after a separation.

"Welcome home, sir."

"Is lunch ready?"

"Yes, sir. It's on your side table."

"Is there enough for two?"

Elise stammered a bit. She had not been informed that he would be having a lunch guest.

"I am sorry, sir. I must have"—

"For you to join me."

"Oh, well, I do have mine here. Should I bring my notepad?"

"No, I want to talk." He turned and headed into his office. Elise grabbed her sack lunch from the bottom drawer of her desk and followed him in, closing the door behind her.

Adolph had taken his lunch and placed it on the small round table by the window of his office. He stood behind the chair where Elise would sit, apparently waiting to help her. Elise was a bit flattered, since he had never really paid attention to her needs before. She sat and watched him as he sat opposite her.

"Have you been busy while I've been away?"

"Yes, sir. I have your arrangements finished for next week's trip to Jerusalem and the books for your summit meeting are at the printer."

"Very well, very well." He took a sip of water and placed the cup back on the table, but didn't touch his food. She waited for him to speak but he just stared at her for what felt like forever.

"Sir, is something wrong?"

"Did you receive my present?"

Elise's face lit up. "Oh, yes, sir! I am sorry I didn't mention it sooner. What a lovely surprise! I've never had my own gun before. It really was an extravagant gift."

"Have you ever shot a gun before?"

"No, I am afraid I haven't."

"Then we will go shooting this afternoon." Adolph smiled and took a bite from his sandwich.

"This afternoon? But sir, I am sure you have better things to do. Prime Minister Szabo is arriving in an hour and he will come directly here."

"He can wait. This is important to me."

"Sir, I don't mean to be ungrateful, but a gun is a very unusual gift. May I ask, do you have a specific concern in mind?"

Adolph smiled warmly at her, almost fatherly, Elise thought. He leaned forward and touched her hand that was resting on the table.

"We have known each other for years now, Elise. It has just come to my attention that I have taken you for granted. I once believed that highly intelligent men should surround themselves with primitive and stupid women, but I listened to great advice in hiring you. You are hardly primitive and you yourself are highly intelligent. You have made my life run much smoother because of your ability and devotion."

Elise struggled to look into his eyes, for there was a bothersome quality about his stare that was making her uncomfortable. His hand stayed on hers and she could feel his fingertips tremble.

"Though the world is close to peace, there are still those who want me dead, and being close to me can be a dangerous occupation. I will teach you to use your gun, and then you can carry it with you at all times. Then I will trust that you are safe."

"But sir," interrupted Elise, her hand still under his, "I am rarely without your protection. The security force watches over me well."

Adolph pulled his hand away and the smile faded. "I have noticed that you are spending a lot of time with a certain agent. Is there more than a working relationship between you and Agent Vasiliev?"

Elise felt her heart begin to race and she was unsure how to answer this question. Adolph's question was pointed and she didn't know why this would bother him. She carefully chose her words.

"Your generosity in both our lives has caused a friendship to develop, but that is all."

"It is important to me that you not be distracted from your responsibilities."

Elise became defensive. "Have you seen a change in my work, sir?"

"Of course not, I am just warning you that appearances can be deceiving. A devoted employee one day can be a traitor the next."

"Is there an issue with Agent Vasiliev?" Elise couldn't help but feel he was suggesting something.

Hitler stood and dropped his napkin, leaving his half-eaten lunch. "We had better get to the shooting range. May I ask you a question, Elise?"

"Yes, sir."

"If I teach you to shoot, would you be willing to kill for me?"

"Sir?" Elise stood, unsure of his question.

"There are dangers amongst us, Elise. That gun could protect both of us. Do you believe in me enough to protect me?"

Elise forced a smile. "I already protect you daily with the role I play in your administration."

Hitler raised an eyebrow, then reached up and smoothed his hair. The smile returned to his face and he pointed his open palm toward the door. "Well put, Elise. Well put. I do believe there is a lot of truth in that statement."

Elise walked through the doorway and retrieved the gun from under her desk. For a moment, she believed Adolph was going to ask her to shoot Yakov. It was strange, but the implication that he may not be as loyal as one would think was definitely there, though unspoken. Her thoughts traveled back to the discussion about his lack of a mark and the doubts began to creep back into her mind. Had

Yakov lied to her? Was he really a traitor? Did Hitler have his suspicions? Why hadn't he gone on his mission yet?

Elise made a quick call to security who asked for ten minutes to bring the limousine to the front door. She stood waiting in the lobby of their Moscow office while Hitler talked on his cell. She didn't want to believe her doubts, for she was truly starting to care for Yakov. But how could she love a man who was a liar? She looked over at Hitler and wondered at his sudden interest in her security. Or was it just a sudden interest in her? This was a startling possibility, one that Elise decided she would have to ponder carefully in the days to come. She'd never considered that kind of a relationship with him, but then again, who cared for his personal needs more than she?

The limousine pulled up to the front curb and Yakov got out of the front seat to open the door for the two passengers. Elise had not realized he would be with them and she nervously glanced between the two men. Adolph confidently got into the vehicle, while Yakov threw her a confused look. He got back into the front seat and the driver spoke.

"I just want to make sure I've got this right. You want to go to the indoor gun range?"

"Correct. My dear Miss Orion is long overdue for a lesson in handling a gun."

Elise was almost certain she saw Yakov grimace as Hitler spoke the word "dear," but that could have been her imagination. This whole situation was uncomfortable and confusing. She had plans for dinner with Yakov, which she hoped he would not mention in front of Hitler. This was going to be an interesting night.

For goodness' sake, Elise. Everything was much easier before you kissed him. What were you thinking? You've worked so hard to get exactly to this place and you might blow it over feelings. Feelings! Of all things . . .

Elise turned her thoughts to the gun case on her lap. She shook her head and stared out the window. This day could not end soon enough.

twenty-three

May

It was the longest five weeks of Noah's life. Why women couldn't plan a wedding in a confined space with a week's notice didn't make any sense to him, but the date was set for the beginning of May and he'd just have to make the best of it. While Tara worked on her dress and paper decorations with the women and younger girls in the compound, Noah and Charlie prepared his new home in one of the empty rooms. They hung shelves, moved dressers, wired Noah's stereo system, and hung a few pictures. The room wasn't large, but Tara found two chairs and an area rug in the barn above that she wanted along with Noah's bedroom set and soon the room was ready. Dave spent time each week with the young couple, doing some practical marriage counseling and soon it was time to be married. Not soon enough, but the day finally arrived.

At three forty-five, Noah sat in his room with Charlie and waited for Dave to come get them. Noah had imagined this moment and when the door opened, Noah stood. But instead of a smiling friend as his imagination would have provided, Dave entered with a serious look on his face and this alarmed Noah. What could possibly be wrong?

"She doesn't want to go through with this." Noah made it a statement rather than a question. It was his best guess. Now things would get awkward when he saw her. Maybe he could talk to her. Or maybe he should just wait and let Dave tell him what's wrong.

Dave walked over and sat on the bed opposite Noah. Noah sat also and Charlie joined them.

"No, nothing like that. I don't know exactly what it means, but the cable feed in the eating area is out. Someone's checking on the wiring, but I suspect that the service was just cut off."

"Anything else unusual?" Noah didn't like what he heard.

"No, everything else is fine. I just thought you should know."

There was a knock at the door and Cal stuck his head in.

"Dave, can I see you a minute?"

"Come on in, Cal. You can talk in front of these guys."

"Fredo wanted me to tell you the gas stoves aren't working and though there are candles everywhere for the wedding, the lights in the kitchen and bathrooms went out. He went up and checked the meter and the gas has been shut off. A couple of us switched the generators from natural gas to reserve gas for heat and electricity, and we'll just have to use them sparingly."

Dave shook his head. "They've figured out that there are functional utilities at a vacant location and shut them down. This doesn't mean they know we're here, but they're getting closer."

Noah looked from Charlie to Dave. Both men were deep in thought. "What should we do? What can we do?"

"First, we're going to have a wedding, then we're having a prayer meeting." Dave stood and turned to leave. He looked back at Noah, checking his watch first. "You've got five minutes."

"We'll meet you out there in five."

Noah and Charlie also stood, and when Dave and Cal left the room, Charlie turned back to Noah. "Let's pray about this, Noah." He bowed his head and five minutes later the men headed to the living room area.

Noah saw that the main area had been cleared of tables and couches, and chairs from the eating area were lined in rows, with a center aisle down the middle. Candles lit the room and the compound's occupants were already seated. Josh Busch, a seminary graduate who was ordained, stood up front and Charlie and Noah joined him. Noah had chosen a white dress shirt, with black pants and a black tie. He didn't look near as good as he would have in a tuxedo, but it was the best he could do.

From the front, Noah could see the work the women had put into the decorations. There were no fresh flowers, but the room was covered with paper flowers the women and children had made from construction paper. They had placed two small end tables with pitchers, overflowing with multicolored paper flowers, up front for the bride and groom to stand between. It looked great, but Noah wasn't that interested in the paper flowers.

As Noah waited for Tara to enter his eyes met his mother's. She was already tearing up and blowing her nose, and he gave her his patent crooked smile. He walked over to her and kissed her on the forehead, then returned to his place in between Josh and Charlie. Someone must have pressed *play* on a boom box because the sound of violins softly filled the room. In the back of the room, Tara entered on Dave's arm. She was wearing a dress Noah had never seen before, a white strapless with soft pink trim. Her hair was pulled up on her head with a few curls falling. Small white paper flowers were tucked here and there.

Despite the troubling events at the compound, Noah's mind completely turned to his wife-to-be. He felt that his knees might give out at the sight of her. She only had eyes for him at that moment and never stopped looking at him as Dave led her down the aisle and to his side. When she reached the front, his sister, Tami, stood up beside her and the ceremony began. Dave gave her hand to Noah and sat down in the front row. Then Josh began the short charge.

Noah looked at her hand in his and then into her eyes. As Josh explained the unusual circumstances in which the Lord had chosen to bring them together, the words started to fade and all Noah could hear was the sound of his own voice in his head.

*Lord, there is a part of me that wishes I could have truly pro-
vided for this woman, that I could have had the freedom to be the
husband You have called me to be. But the circumstances being what
they are, I'm not going to question Your timing or mine. You are sovereign and though our marriage will be short-lived, I promise to love
her and put her needs before my own. Thank You so much for her,
for how she makes me feel, for bringing her safely here. I can hardly
believe—*

"Noah, do you need some time?"

Noah's attention snapped back to Josh, standing in front of him
with his Bible open.

"I'm sorry, what did you say?"

There were some stifled chuckles among the families and Tara
gave him a confused look.

"You just need to repeat after me."

"Oh, yeah, right. Let's start at the beginning, okay?" He gave her a
smile and raised his eyebrows apologetically. A few minutes later he
and Tara had completed their vows and Josh gave a final charge.

"Therefore, what God has joined together, let no man put asunder,
which I really doubt will happen before the rapture, so don't worry
about it. Go ahead and kiss her!"

Tara looked at Noah and laughed, as did the others in the room,
and Noah drew Tara into his arms and kissed her. The families
cheered and the new couple turned and faced the crowd. Then Josh
made the final announcement.

"It is truly an honor to present to you for the first time, Mr. and
Mrs. Noah Greer."

Noah took Tara's hand in his but as she started to walk to the back
of the room, Noah stopped her. She looked at him, as if she wondered
what he was doing, and as the people cheered again, he pulled her close
to him and whispered in her ear, "We've got to wait a minute." She
pulled away and nodded. When the group quieted down, Noah spoke.

"Before we have dinner, Dave wants to talk with you, so, Dave . . ." He looked to his friend who had stepped back to the front of the room. Noah and Tara sat down in the front row.

"I don't want to put a damper on the festivities, but I also need to be honest with you all. Some of you know, so it's only fair to keep communication open. Not only did the cable go out this morning, but we have also lost our electricity and gas this afternoon."

There was a collective moan and Tara looked at Noah with fear in her eyes. He put his arm around her and nodded for her to keep listening.

"I know this is disconcerting. There's good news and bad news. The good news is that we have gas storage units that are full and unused, which should run our generators for quite some time, however we're going to have to be efficient in our use of electricity and heat. We can't leave lights on in our bedrooms if we're not in there, nor in the bathrooms. We have thousands of candles, and will use those whenever we can. So, losing our utilities wasn't unexpected."

Noah exchanged looks with Dave and then Charlie. He shifted on his feet a bit and put his hands in his pockets. Noah waited for the other shoe to fall.

"The bad news is that we don't know if the authorities know we're down here or if they just shut off the utilities because the residence above ground is abandoned. But we can't panic. Christ told the disciples that when they saw the Antichrist desecrate the temple to go and hide. That's what we have done. Perhaps we've missed some details, but we've done our best to be faithful to His teaching. In Revelation, there are seven churches that are described. Six of the seven are struggling and in each case, they are told to overcome, despite their spiritual decay or the persecution outside the church. One church is faithful, and while being told to overcome, they are also told that because of their faithfulness, God will keep them from the hour of testing that was to come upon the world. It is our prayer that God will consider us faithful, in preparing a hiding place, in spreading the truth, in looking for the signs He spoke about in His Word. At this point, we can't stop what is happening up there"—he pointed to the ceiling—"but we can continue to call on God's protection and put our care in His hands."

Noah raised his hand and Dave pointed at him. Noah stood.

"The night Hitler revealed himself as the Antichrist, I had a visitor. We all did. He was the angel who warned about not taking the mark." Several of the people nodded. "My angel told me that the Lord knew of my plans and that they were good. He told me to be careful, but in the end he said one word. Overcome. I know the Lord knows about us. Look at how many of us got here—only by His sovereign hand! We have to trust and be overcomers. The angel told me to overcome. I'll never forget it."

Charlie was sitting at the far end of the front row and he stood. "My angel said that, too. He said the Lord was pleased with our plans and to overcome."

Another of the original seventeen-member fellowship stood. "Mine, too."

"And mine."

"Mine, too!"

One by one the members of the fellowship stood. Soon all seventeen but Dave had affirmed the message to overcome which had been given them. Finally, Dave spoke.

"I received the same message. So we cannot doubt and we cannot fear. We have to stay here and trust that the Lord will protect us. Before dinner, let's spend some time in prayer. Gather as families and let's take the next few minutes to ask for His help in our time of need."

Noah took Tara's hand to pray with his new bride, just as Dave walked up to them.

"Do you mind if I pray with you?"

"You gave me away, so you must be family!" Tara smiled and patted Dave on the back. Soon, Charlie and Thomas joined them.

As they sat together, Noah asked Thomas if he was all right, considering the concern on his face.

"I'm just worried about this."

"We all are," Charlie said, "but we have to trust Him. What good will worrying do?"

"But I wasn't faithful like the rest of you. Maybe they've tracked me here and everyone will pay for my ignorance."

"Hold on a minute," Tara interrupted. "You're not the only one who is benefiting from another's faithfulness. I shouldn't be here either, but for Noah and God's care of me. Plus you've been here for months. Something would have happened by now. Listen, you can't beat yourself up, Thomas."

"Why would God promise protection, and then bring you here to expose all of us?" Dave shook his head. "No. I don't know what will happen, but I do know the Lord will have a remnant to return to. If we are part of that remnant, then praise the Lord! If our lives are required of us, then so be it. We have faithfully obeyed the call to hide and from now on, it's in His hands."

After a time of prayer, the families moved into the eating area, which had been decked out like a reception hall. Paper flowers were in the center of every table, white Christmas lights hung across the ceiling and candles flickered everywhere. A dance floor had been cleared in one corner and Cal Moeller had volunteered to handle the music. Fredo served up a feast, creations from the pantry that Noah decided he would just eat and ask what they were later. Soon the group was dancing and eating, and after cake, Noah leaned over to Tara and whispered in her ear.

"If we slipped out now, I doubt anyone would notice."

He smiled at her, hoping she was willing to go. She put her hand on his cheek and gently kissed his lips. "I thought you would never ask."

The next morning, Noah realized his wish. He woke with Tara in his arms and reached for the light. When she opened her blue eyes, he wondered for a moment if he had died and gone to heaven. But that question was quickly answered by a tentative knock on his door. The newlyweds sat up and Noah called to the intruder.

"Yes?"

"Sorry, Noah. It's me, Charlie. We have a little problem and I thought you should know about it."

Noah looked at Tara and she shrugged her shoulders. He got out of bed and unlocked the door.

"What's up?"

By the look on Charlie's face Noah knew this wasn't going to be good.

"Thomas is gone. He took a van."

"Gone? When did he go?"

"I woke up this morning and his bed was empty. He must have left in the night sometime."

"Where do you think he went?"

Charlie shook his head. "I don't know. Maybe he went to see if Robin was still at the jail. He was losing his mind down here and he must have taken the keys from my dresser during the reception last night. Either way, I doubt we'll see him again."

"Thanks for letting us know." Noah closed the door and turned back to Tara. "I can't imagine what he's been going through his mind. I was going crazy when I didn't know where you were, and add to that two daughters. He just couldn't get over his guilt."

Tara stood and walked over to the chair in the corner of their room. She put her robe on and sat down. "What can we do about this? We all tried to help him, but if he's gone, there's nothing we can do anymore."

"He's not thinking straight. Maybe I could—"

"Stay here and take care of your wife." Tara gave him a stern look. "You can't go running after him, Noah. You don't even know where he is. You need to stay with me."

Noah looked at her and furrowed his eyebrows. She waited for his reply.

"I was going to say, maybe I could *pray* with you for him. Got a problem with that?"

Tara face lit up. She stood up and ran over to Noah by the door. She threw her arms around him and kissed him. "Was that our first fight as a family?"

"If it was, I think I won."

"Oh, this marriage thing is going to be so fun!" She kissed him again, and quickly Noah forgot about Thomas and turned his full attention to his wife. After all, "stay here and take care of your wife" was actually pretty good advice he was willing to embrace.

As he carried his new wife back to bed, a fleeting thought of Thomas crossed his mind.

I wonder where he went. Did he go back to his house? Or would he go to the training facility? He only has one tank of gas. Could he really go that far?

In reality, Thomas didn't get far.

The wedding was torture enough, but then the fellowship's claim that they had somehow warranted special protection from God pushed him over the limit. Obviously God wasn't protecting him, forcing him to suffer over the unknown status of his family. He could no longer take one more pat on the back, one more well-meaning hug, one more sober shaking of a head, as if they understood his predicament.

What did they expect him to do? Sit around for a couple of years and wait to be raptured? Great, so then he could spend eternity known as the man who ditched his wife and children for the safety of an underground bunker. How could he ever face his daughters in heaven, let alone Robin?

No, he would remedy this. And he would do it right away. He sat at the reception, watching the newly married couple dancing in each other's arms, completely lost in each other's eyes and it made him want to vomit. The candlelight, the music, the laughter—how could he join in as if he had something to celebrate? The only other person not dancing was Dave, but at least he knew where his wife was.

Thomas couldn't sleep. After hours of listening to Charlie and Cal's steady breathing, he had gotten up. He pulled on a pair of jeans and a sweatshirt he had left on the floor between his bed and the wall. He reached for a flashlight from his nightstand and quickly found his shoes. Once dressed, he made his way through the room to Charlie's dresser. He had seen him drop a set of car keys in his top drawer a few weeks back and hoped they were still there. If not, he would walk, but he couldn't stay and live with himself anymore.

He opened the drawer and felt around inside. Immediately he touched the cool metal of a set of keys and he wrapped his fingers around them, so they wouldn't make a sound that would wake the others. He shut the drawer, slid the keys into his front pocket, grabbed a jacket from the closet and left the room.

It was five thirty. No one would be in the kitchen yet, since the reception had gone so late the night before. He made his way to the back of the compound and through the kitchen. The door to the stairwell was locked, so he was careful to lock the door behind him when he left. Then he made his way above ground into the garage. It was empty, but he heard they had stored a couple vans in one of the barns on the property and he easily found them. The keys must fit one of the vans.

Thomas considered that after he found his family, he could go to Noah's house and grab the extra food. He would return with his family intact and food for the fellowship—he'd be a hero. But that thought quickly dissipated as he sat in the cold van.

Where should he go first? His house? The jail? The training camp? Or maybe even Robin's parents' house? No, he would go to the jail. He would have to find a safe place to observe and then maybe at night he could look in windows. He had to figure out if Robin was still being held there. Since her name hadn't shown up on the camp list, she had to be there. Maybe he could ask someone to help him.

Thomas tightly gripped the steering wheel and leaned his head back on the headrest. This was never going to work. How was he going to find his family? There was always Wayne. Things haven't been easy for Thomas and maybe he could obtain some mercy from his friend. There was a time that Wayne would have given his right arm to have Thomas work with him. If he could meet with him, alone, he might be able to convince him to help Thomas and Robin. After all, the guy has kids of his own. He could appeal on behalf of the kids.

Yeah, this might just work.

Thomas backed out of the barn, then got out of the van and shut the barn door behind him. He slowly made his way down the dirt road that led to the highway. Spring was in the air, and though it was dark, he could see new leaves were filling up the trees. Once on the highway heading into town, Thomas turned up the heat and turned on the radio, trying to find a news station to see what was going on in the world.

About five miles up the road, he saw taillights ahead. It was nearing six o'clock and the early birds in Creston were waking up. He continued on carefully, then noticed the taillights ahead of him braking. He realized that there were several cars lined up, stopped on the highway, police lights flashing in the distance. At first he thought there had been an accident, but as his car rolled up behind the others and came to a stop, he couldn't see anything out of the ordinary. He suddenly realized that he had forgotten a hat, and he pulled the hood of his sweatshirt over his head. Looking in the mirror, he thought he looked like a thug with his hood up, so he took it off and pulled his hair over his forehead to hide the fact he wasn't marked.

One by one, cars rolled through the police stop. He watched as an officer approached the car in front of him, spoke for a few minutes to the driver, and then let him pass. His heart started to pound and he silently said a prayer for protection. Then it was his turn. He pulled his car forward and stopped. The officer came to his window and he rolled it down.

"Good morning. Sorry about the stop. We're just . . . wait a minute—" The officer put his hand up to his ear, as if he was listening to an earpiece. He smiled at Thomas and held up one finger. "Just a second. I'll be right back."

Thomas watched him walk back to his cruiser and get in the driver's seat. For a brief moment Thomas prayed for the officer to actually pull away. But when he got back out of his car with a piece of paper in his hand, Thomas had the sudden urge to hit the gas and floor it. But then he'd have a chase on his hands and he'd never win in this van.

The officer came back to the window. Thomas smiled and waited for him to speak. The officer handed the piece of paper in his hand to Thomas.

"Are you Thomas Larson?"

Thomas took the paper and looked at it. It was his head shot, taken when he was first arrested. His heart continued to pound and he tightened his grip on the steering wheel for a second time that morning. He turned to the officer, not knowing what to say.

"We've been looking for you, sir. Could you please take your right hand off the wheel and turn your vehicle off?" The officer had drawn his gun and was pointing it at Thomas's head.

Thomas slowly reached and turned the key to off. Then he returned his hands to the wheel. He looked at the officer, who had been joined by a second patrolman.

"Could you please pull your hair from your forehead?"

Thomas pulled back his hair and the officer pointed a flashlight at his head. The light blinded him for a moment and he shut his eyes.

When he opened them again, the gun was once again pointed at his head. The officer didn't speak but just held the gun on him. Thomas sat still, wondering what would happen next.

Then, from a second squad car, a third officer shouted, "He said if you have verification, just get it over with."

Thomas heard the metal click of the trigger in the officer's hand and saw the flash from the gun. And in the blink of an eye, Thomas had the answers to all his questions.

Wayne Durbin sat on the edge of his bed and waited for the second call. One minute later, it rang. He picked up the phone and put it to his ear.

"We can mark Larson off our list." The caller went on, "The surveillance video shows his van turning from an old dirt road just south of town onto the highway. There is an abandoned farmhouse and some barns over there."

"Who owns the land?"

"Conover is the name. It's one of the farms that still had utilities but no owner record of marking up, so just yesterday we shut off the power."

Durbin rubbed his forehead. "Good work. I knew sooner or later we'd catch someone coming out of one of those abandoned properties."

"By the time you break for lunch today, we should have them all in custody, sir."

"Get them to the camp right away. Don't bring them here. I'm done with this game. The sooner they're disposed of, the sooner we can get on with our lives."

"Yes sir, I'll call you when it's over."

"I might see you over there."

Durbin hung up the phone. He was wide-awake now. His wife rolled over next to him and asked who was on the phone.

"Don't worry about it. It was good news. I think we just found the remaining unmarked citizens."

She leaned up on one elbow. "The ones that were hiding?"

"Yeah."

"That's great news. I'm so happy for you."

Durbin leaned over and kissed his wife on the forehead. "Go back to sleep. I'm going to make some coffee and read yesterday's paper."

He headed toward the kitchen, picking up his briefcase from the front hall closet. After starting the coffee, he sat down and opened his case. There, next to the paper was his picture of Hitler.

"So, you found them?"

"It looks like it. I'll know in a few hours."

"And where will they be taken?"

"Straight to the camp and killed." Durbin's callousness toward nonmarkers no longer surprised himself. He reached for his newspaper and unfolded it.

"What about the children?"

"From the compound?" His eyes looked up from the paper at the idol.

"From the compound and at the camp. How long do you think you can keep unmarked people a secret?"

Durbin shifted in his chair. He didn't realize that his idol knew about the children. "They're children. We can't get a mark to stick unless they ask for it."

"I don't care what they are, no mark means death. If you put a gun to their heads, they'll take the mark. Trust me."

Durbin thought a moment. He was really sick of this and he was worn down. When he signed on for public service, he had no idea it would lead to genocide. He was tired of fighting, stalling, and defending.

"Fine. I'll send the order to get rid of the Creston children as well as the adults. Then this nightmare will be over and we can all move on."

"Don't be frustrated, Wayne. You're so close and by the end of today, you'll have the restraints taken off your requests and then life will change quickly. Think of it—new facilities, more wells—before you know it, this town will double in size. You're on your way to realizing your dreams, Wayne. You just have one hard day left."

Wayne didn't need a cheerleader, but it had worked. He started to think about life after nonmarkers and he smiled. He was so glad it was about to be over. He was tempted to ask his idol if the Memorial Park nuisance would quiet down once this was over, but he thought he might be pushing his luck. It was going to be a glorious moment, one he had waited a long time for, when he would walk through the park and ask that idol for an updated count. When he said zero, the floodgates would open.

And the conversation was just hours away.

twenty-four

May

Adolph Hitler was busier than ever lately. Elise hardly ever saw him. His push for unity in the world had caused him to be on the road for days, even weeks at a time. He and Ferco Szabo were rarely apart, Hitler delivering astounding speeches and Szabo following them up with spectacular demonstrations of power. They were the hot ticket in Europe—every speaking engagement was packed, standing room only to hear the great Adolph Hitler pontificate on the perils of hell and his domination over death. He offered eternal life to all and promised physical sustenance to the world. Szabo had perfected turning water into blood and throwing fireballs from his fingertips. They were really quite a pair—the proverbial one-two punch.

Though he was gone a lot, he still kept close contact with Elise. He started to send her gifts of a more personal nature than his first one—perfume from Paris, flowers from Japan, jewelry from Thailand. At first she was a bit concerned about the gifts, but he assured her that he desired simply to show her his appreciation for her service. She accepted this explanation and the gifts as well. Besides arranging for her to continue shooting lessons, Hitler made sure she was pampered with only the best gifts magogs could buy.

As for Yakov, Hitler rarely traveled without him. This was the difficult part about being involved with her employer's head of security, for Elise missed her time with Yakov. However, there was a perk. As Hitler continued to shower her with gifts, Yakov was even more careful that his gifts were more valued and desired than his employer's. Elise was pretty sure that Adolph was unaware of the competition for her affection, but she was amused at the effort Yakov put in to top his boss. Every gift, no matter what the cost, always included a note of affection, which was the one thing Adolph had thankfully never done. There were times Elise worried she was playing with fire, but then she would laugh off her fears and enjoy the attention.

Hitler had arrived home two days earlier and still had one more day before he and his entourage hit the road again. He was rather moody and spent a lot of time in his office, alone. The scent of cinnamon was beginning to fill Elise's office, too, and now, she knew what that meant. Though she had never seen or heard him, she knew that Lucifer was still a main source of counsel for Adolph and she had no desire to find out any more about that relationship than necessary.

That particular morning, Adolph had actually beaten her to the office. This rarely happened and was always a cause for concern. But Elise didn't let it rattle her. She quickly got the coffee going and powered up her computer. By eight, Yakov had arrived and asked her if she wanted to get some lunch later. He said he would be back at noon and she readily agreed.

Adolph didn't come out of his office all morning and she knew better than to disturb him. He was preparing for several appearances, as well as an FWP leadership summit where updated numbers would be presented. Needless to say, he had high hopes.

Yakov showed up a little early and waited as she finished a few things Then they left. He fidgeted in the car, making small talk, and constantly checked his watch, so Elise was starting to become suspicious that he had bad news. He had made reservations at their favorite little restaurant in the shopping district of Moscow and after placing their order, she finally asked.

"You don't seem like yourself, Yakov. What is going on?"

He reached across the table and took her hands in his own. "I don't know, Elise, I am getting tired."

She straightened in her seat. "Of me?"

He smiled. "No, never of you. Of the road. It's tiring and I miss being with you, seeing your face every day."

She returned his smile, as the waiter brought them two glasses and a bottle of white wine. He removed the cork and poured half a glass for each of them. Though Elise politely declined a glass, Yakov insisted.

"I can't have this," she protested after the waiter left. "I still have work to do. Adolph would have my head if he smelled alcohol on my breath."

"It's only half a glass and by the time you're done eating, no one will be the wiser." Yakov raised his glass and held it for a toast. She reluctantly picked up her glass.

"To a lasting partnership."

She reached forward to touch his glass with hers and something caught her eye. Lying on the bottom of her glass was a ring. A diamond ring. And not a small one at that. Elise felt her hand start to quiver and she looked at Yakov. He wasn't smiling, but he wasn't frowning either. His eyes were glassy and for the first time in her life, she saw true emotion on his face.

"I love you, Elise. I want to be with you and I want you as my wife. When I am away from you, I can hardly focus on my job. All I can see is your face. Please agree to be my wife."

Elise set her glass down and cocked her head to one side. "I think I need to see the ring dry first." She plunged her fork into the glass and fished out the ring. She dried it with her napkin, taking her dear, sweet time. Out of the corner of her eye, she could see a bit of concern on Yakov's face and she experienced another first with him—she was in the driver's seat! She held the ring up, examining it in the candlelight. Then she looked back at Yakov. He had suffered long enough.

"It's lovely, but not as lovely as you. I love you, too, Yakov, and I would be honored to become your wife." She handed him back his ring and then held out her left hand for him to do the honors. Gently he slid the ring on her finger and stood. He leaned over the table and kissed her. Suddenly, the restaurant was filled with cheering and violins, and the staff marched over with some hired musicians to make the celebration complete. Elise felt her cheeks flush with joy. But the joy was short-lived.

"Does Adolph know about this?"

Yakov shook his head. "We've got a little problem there. I think it is time for my role to change. I sense some tension with him and I think it is because of you. You may not be able to stay in your position either."

Elise was flattered at his concern, but she had no intention of leaving her job. "He needs me, Yakov. I know him better than anyone and this is an unusual position. I can't just hand him over to a new assistant—it's too complicated for that. You know what I'm talking about." She raised her eyebrows and he conceded.

"Well, once his push for marking the world is over, things may calm down."

"Has he spoken with you about your undercover assignment?"

"No, he hasn't said anything lately."

"Well, we need to tell him about the engagement. It's better if he hears it from us."

Yakov looked at his plate and pushed the food around with his fork, deep in thought. Elise waited for a response.

"I'll figure this one out. Don't worry. But for now, let's wait to tell him."

"Why wait? I am excited and now I have to pretend I'm not!"

He reached across the table and took her hand again. He played with the ring on her finger and smiled. "It does look good on you. I just need some time. Wear it, but be careful. If you think he has an ear, then tell him. He's just been so distracted lately. Any idea why?"

The discussion turned to work and forty-five minutes later Elise was back at her desk, basking in the glow of her latest gift, though it rested in her pocket rather than on her finger. Yakov left to pick up dignitaries from the airport and she needed to set up the conference room for an afternoon meeting. She left her desk and took a stack of papers and pens to the conference room. Once alone, she took the ring out and put it on her hand. As she carefully laid the printed agendas in front of each chair, the door opened and Hitler entered.

"Do you need something?" She wondered why he would come in before the meeting time.

"Yes, Elise. I need to speak to you."

"Sir?"

"I have received some disturbing news today."

Elise stood with her hands clasped behind her back. For a moment she wondered if he was speaking of the engagement. Instinctively, she pulled the ring off her finger and carefully slid in into the back pocket of her pants.

"What would that be?"

"For months I have been warned that my life has been threatened from within. I have carefully investigated my closest team members and have found one wanting. Elise, are you able to think clearly and not let friendship cloud your emotions?"

"I don't understand."

Hitler walked closer to her and she feared another vision of hell, so she averted her eyes. "Life is full of choices, Elise. The day you marked your head, you chose me." He paused and she was unsure of his intentions. He took another step closer. "The Enemy has stood on a foundation of lies, proclaiming that God is love and wants a relationship with His creation. He has taught His followers to lie, and that is what sets us apart. I have never lied to you. But you have been lied to and today it ends."

Elise could feel his breath on her face and slowly she raised her eyes. He stood just inches away and his voice was low. "There is a group of people who have planned my death in a spectacular manner. They have infiltrated my cabinet in order to obtain vital information and I now have verification of when their plan will come to fruition. And you are at the center of it all."

Elise drew a quick breath, but didn't move from her position. "What do you mean? Do you think I am a traitor?"

"No, but Agent Vasiliev is. And he is using his friendship with you to gain the information he needs for my assassination."

"That is ridiculous, sir. Why would he need me? He is your security advisor, for heaven's sake. He knows more than me." Elise felt her pulse racing and struggled not to sound too defensive.

"You need to trust me, Elise. And when the dust settles, you will see how you have been manipulated. But I plan on turning the tables on them. And I will use you also."

"What do you mean?"

Hitler reached around Elise and she flinched a bit. He pulled out a chair from the table and told her to sit. Then he sat beside her.

"When I gave you the gun, it was for your protection. It was also so that you would be comfortable with it. I wanted Vasiliev to see it around and not be alarmed. But now, you must get the information I need from Vasiliev and then you must kill him. He must not be allowed to contact his organization so that they remain unaware that their plan has been revealed. I have watched your friendship grow even as I have known his intentions. Now you are close enough to extract the details of the assassination and then dispose of him."

Elise forced herself to sit in the chair. Her stomach churned and her temples pounded. "Why don't you trust Yakov? What evidence do you have that he is a traitor?"

Hitler leaned forward in his chair. "Did you know he is not marked?"

Elise didn't know how to answer this question. If she said yes, then she may be considered an accomplice to his plan. If she said no and he somehow knew she was lying, this could be disastrous, too.

"He said you asked him not to take the mark."

Hitler set his jaw and his eyes flashed. She saw true anger and it frightened her.

"He said you wanted him to infiltrate a rogue group of nonmarkers and that he needed a clean head to do it."

"I am hurt you would believe that lie."

Elise had no defense. She chose to believe it because she had allowed her emotions to think for her.

"Has he ever questioned me to you? Has he ever tried to plant seeds of doubt in your mind?" She sat thinking, remembering past conversations. "Has he ever asked you to leave me?" That one hit home, as well as the others.

"I am not doubting his feelings for you, but they are grounded in a need to use you and now you are faced with a choice. Use your relationship to save my life. Or be used to take it. Who do you believe, Elise? Him or me? Have I ever lied to you?" He picked up her shaking hand and held it to his heart. "I have cared for you and watched over you for years now. I know you trust me. I need you to do this for me."

Hitler stood and walked to the door, leaving Elise in her chair. "We will talk later, but he will arrive soon with my guests. I am sorry you are in the middle of this, Elise, but I know you are strong enough to do what is right. We don't have days to discuss this. My intel says we're down to the wire."

He closed the door and Elise sat perfectly still. Her mind was racing. She loved Yakov and had just promised her life to him. But somewhere in the back of her mind, she had stored a box full of doubts and that box had now spilled into her thoughts. Adolph's words fit the puzzle pieces together and she didn't like the picture they formed.

She pulled the ring from her pocket and wondered if it was even a real diamond. Her chest heaved and she stifled a tear. She would not let her emotions take over. She had work to do.

Elise Orion stood and finished prepping the room for the meeting. Then she went back to her desk and transcribed her notes from the past couple of days. She forced herself to complete the task at hand, but that box of doubts still needed to be picked up and disposed of properly.

And she knew there was only one way to do it.

Tara stood in the bathroom, toweling dry her hair. She and Noah had stayed in their room pretty late that morning and the bathrooms were empty. It was a nice change to have a hot shower and all the elbow room you need to yourself. She squeezed a small amount of gel into her hand, ever aware of the decreasing supply, and fingered it through her damp locks. One final toss and she was ready to find Noah. She gathered her toiletries and headed back toward their room.

There was some commotion at the end of the hall, a scream and Tara turned to see what was happening. Suddenly the quiet, empty hall was filled with people and they were running back toward the living area, pounding on bedroom doors as they ran. Someone grabbed Tara's arm and started to pull her along. She couldn't see Noah and she called out his name. People were pushing and it was getting out of hand. She pulled her arm away and forced her way against the flow to get back to their room. In the middle of the crowd, Tami, Noah's sister, called to her.

"What's happening?"

"We've got to get to the south tunnel! Someone is ramming the door in the kitchen from the stair well. They've found us! They're here!" She grabbed Tara's arm again and started to drag her along, but again Tara broke free. She finally got to the room and opened the door. Noah was gone. She looked back into the hall and she could see the last person turn the corner and disappear. Fear completely overwhelmed her and she froze. She slammed the door shut and looked around the room. Where could she hide? She shut the light off and felt her way along the wall to the bed. She climbed over the top of the bed and onto the floor on the far side of the room. She couldn't fit under the bed, but she pulled some of the bedding over her and waited.

It was quiet for a few moments and then she heard footsteps running down the hall. Lots of them. One by one they passed her room, calling out things like, "The south tunnel! Find the south tunnel!" Tara's heart ached and she started to cry. As the compound filled with officers, she heard doors down the hall being opened. One by one they were working their way toward her room. Occasionally she heard an officer call out, "All clear" and then another door would be opened. Soon they were at her room.

The door flew open and the light was flipped on. Tara didn't move a muscle, except to shut her eyes tightly and hold her breath. She heard someone enter the room. He walked to the closet and opened the door, then shut it again. Then for a brief moment he stood still in the room. She thought her lungs would burst, but she refused to breathe. Then, as quickly as he entered, he left, shutting the light off but leaving the door open. Tara exhaled and shifted her body so that she could see under the bed and across the room.

Men in black pants and black zippered jackets were running up and down the halls. They wore combat boots and had their guns drawn. Then came the cry that broke her heart.

"We've got them! Hey, everybody! We've got them!"

Tara found herself holding her breath again. In the distance she could hear children crying and parents hushing their children, but other than those few words an eerie lack of conversation. The hall was still empty but for a few officers who stood just outside her door in the hall. A dull ache in her leg forced her to shift her weight, but a few minutes later her shoulder was in pain. Her movements were agonizingly slow, so as not to draw any attention to her room. She listened as the men discussed their plans to take the residents of the compound by bus to the training camps.

The slight sound of footsteps increased and then they started to file past her door. Her compound family. Captured. She desperately tried to see Noah, but from where she was lying, she couldn't see any faces, only feet. She didn't see his shoes, but that didn't mean he wasn't there.

Thirty minutes later, Tara lay on the floor of her bedroom, still afraid to move. Minutes ticked by and then, without warning, the light in the hallway went out.

Complete darkness.

Complete silence.

Complete emptiness.

Life at the compound was finished. And her day-old marriage was over.

Tara was alone. She untangled herself from the bedding under which she'd hidden and stood. She felt her way around the room until she found Noah's dresser. On the top, she found a flashlight and turned it on. The door was still open and she walked toward it. Carefully she looked up and down the hallway, until she was sure it was empty. No lights, no sounds, just darkness. Then she made her way to the eating area. She just needed to sit and think. Where would she go? What could she do? Less than twenty-four hours ago Tara was doing her hair for her wedding and now she was alone. She could hardly process the chain of events.

When she entered the eating area, she guided her flashlight around the room. A few chairs were turned over, but as a whole, the room looked untouched. Then she pointed her light at the kitchen and saw the form of a man standing in the doorway. For a moment she thought it was Noah, and her memory of him in the doorway of the barn flooded her mind. She took a step in his direction but then she realized her mistake when the man raised his weapon.

She wasn't completely alone.

Black Cap had known they were coming. The minute Thomas Larson had pulled out of the barn, he knew he would be spotted. He had tried to warn Noah to be careful concerning who was brought into the compound, but this one really wasn't Noah's fault. He had originally thought it would be the girl who would be the death of Noah.

Earlier that morning Black Cap had received the information he had been waiting for. Now that his instructions were clear he knew exactly what he was allowed to do. He had been with Noah for so long, that nothing Noah did was even a surprise to him anymore. He knew exactly how Noah would react and he knew exactly where Noah would go next.

Black Cap would just wait for the right moment and then finish his assignment. It wouldn't be long now.

Noah wanted to be sure it wasn't a trick. He sat in the darkness, straining his ears for a sound. His legs were starting to cramp from crouching on top of the toilet seat. Finally he stood and stretched his legs. When the raid began, he had been in the shower and by the time he got his clothes on, the officers were in the compound. He'd run into a stall and climbed onto a toilet, leaving the door ajar. Twice officers had run through the bathroom; the first time they missed him and the second time he thought he had been discovered, but then the rest of the residents had been found and the officer in the bathroom had run out to help corral people. It was nothing short of a miracle that he'd been overlooked. But it wasn't the first time he'd become invisible, and he was starting to feel invincible.

Except for the fact that his wife was gone. That fact brought reality rushing back and Noah stepped down from the toilet. The lights had gone out about thirty minutes earlier, but he had seen a flashlight in the hall and knew officers were still in the compound. When he finally felt he had waited long enough, he exited the stall and in the darkness, felt his way out of the bathroom. It was so dark he couldn't see his hand in front of his face. In the hallway, he stood a moment to listen for movement or any sign of life.

Nothing. Perfectly still.

Confident it was safe, he felt his way along the hallway, trying to find his room. He had a flashlight on his dresser and wasn't going to get very far without it. Bedroom doors were left open and Noah counted openings as he went down the hall. His was the eighth door to the left and soon he was pretty confident he had made it to the right room. He entered the room and felt the light switch. Out of habit he flipped it, but nothing happened. He put his hands lower and entered the room, feeling for the bed. Once he reached it, he worked his way around to the other side of the bed and then put a hand on the wall. The dresser was to the right of the bed, on the opposite wall and he carefully found his way there, only tripping once on the bedding on the floor. He could picture in his mind's eye where the flashlight was but as he felt around the top of the dresser, he found nothing. Then he remembered the candle in the bottom drawer. He reached down, found it and the packet of matches, and lit the candle.

He made his way down to Dave's room. The door was open, and when he looked inside, it was undisturbed. Noah went to Dave's dresser and found a flashlight sitting on the top. He turned on the light and blew out the candle. Then he started opening drawers and looking through them.

They have to be in here somewhere.

But the keys to the remaining van were not in the dresser. Then he went to the nightstand and turned it inside out. Still no keys. Then on to the closet. He felt the pockets of the pants and jackets, and then saw a box sitting on the shelf above the hung clothes. He reached and took the box off the shelf and carried it over to the bed. He sat and opened the hinged lid of the wooden box. Lying in the corner were the keys. He grabbed them and shoved them in his pocket. But before he closed the lid, a picture caught his eye. He took it out and shined the flashlight on it.

It was a picture of Dave and a woman. His arm was around her and they were standing up to their waists in a river, both in rain gear, their hats dripping with water. She was struggling to hold up her salmon while he laughed, but both were clearly enjoying themselves. There were a few other pictures in the box. Another one of Dave and the same woman at a White Sox game. Noah smiled. He knew Dave was a closet Sox fan. A third picture was of the happy couple sitting at a dinner table. They were dressed to the nines, and it looked like they were on a cruise. Noah put the pictures back in the box.

Dave looked so happy with his wife. Noah's heart broke for Dave, Tara, and himself simultaneously. He could not even imagine what Dave was feeling at the moment, assuming he was still alive. All the planning and preparations for the compound and in one fell swoop it was all over. But seeing his happiness in the pictures brought an even more desperate truth to light. Noah's wife was with Dave and if he didn't do something, his day-old marriage was over.

"But what can I possibly do? I know I promised just yesterday to love her and put her needs before my own. I can't stay here. I can't let her die without a fight."

Noah stood, and headed toward the kitchen, leaving Dave's box on his bed. He stopped at his own room, grabbed a coat, and ran down the hallway. At the entrance of the eating area he stopped in his tracks.

We criticized Thomas for going after his wife and ignoring God's protection. What makes you think you can save her?

He dropped to his knees, his heart pounding and his temple throbbing. He shut off the flashlight and laid it on the floor next to him. He grasped his heart and cried out to the Lord.

"What should I do?"

His voice echoed through the room. He put his hands on the ground and lowered himself until he lay prostrate on the cool tile floor. He closed his eyes and held his breath. The stillness had a calming quality. He forced himself to stop speaking in his head and just listened to the silence. He was at a complete loss and the silence enveloped him.

Then he had a dream.

A dream that became his vision.

twenty-five

May

Elise was still confused, but she didn't have much time to think. Hitler had stressed the immediacy of the situation. His intelligence pinpointed an event on Hitler's next travel schedule as the assassination target. Why was she so vital to the information, since Yakov would receive greater security data than even she herself would? He would have the room layouts. He would know the guest list. He would personally place the security force into position before he ever arrived. What could she possibly reveal that would put Adolph's life in danger that Yakov didn't already know?

But Adolph said if he left the day after tomorrow without the proper information, he might not return alive. How could he put this kind of responsibility on her shoulders? She begged him to cancel his travel plans, but he refused. He said true leaders did not live in fear, but had to keep their engagements to keep the public confident in their leadership. And he said everything he needed to know was in Vasiliev's head. She just had to get it out.

Elise had called Yakov and invited him for an engagement celebration at her home. She would leave work early, buy groceries, and make him dinner. This was a rare occasion, for Elise had become more of a takeout kind of girl. But she told him she wanted to be alone with him. No street musicians, no waiters, no noise. Just the two of them.

He arrived two hours after she had gotten home. She had set the table for two and was finishing tossing a salad when he knocked at her door. When she opened it, Yakov was not visible, for a bouquet of fresh orchids hid his face. She reached for them, and pulled them and their deliverer through her door and kicked it shut with her heel. He lowered the flowers and bent over them to place a warm kiss on her lips. Her heart fluttered a bit and she hoped for the best.

"Something smells wonderful. And here I asked you to marry me without even knowing you could cook!"

"Come on in, I'm just about ready."

Yakov left the flowers in her hands, took off his coat, and laid it on the couch.

"Can I help?"

"Sure, you can open the wine and pour. I'll bring out dinner."

Elise had braised veal and vegetables together into a hearty stew, perfect for a hungry Russian man. Fresh bread and a tossed salad completed the meal. As they sat across from each other, Yakov seemed distracted. He glanced around the room several times, in between checking his watch. She was used to having complete control of his eyes, but not tonight.

"Thank you for the flowers." Elise struggled to pull him into the conversation.

"Aside from getting engaged, how was your day today?" He forced a smile.

"It's always hectic when Adolph is in town."

"But it will slow down after another day, then."

"Yes, I suppose it will." She tore a piece of warm bread from the loaf and reached for some butter.

"I worry about Adolph. Lately he has not seemed like himself."

"What do you mean?" Elise buttered her bread and set it aside.

"He is so angry all the time. Do you ever get tired of his moods?"

"Well, I know when to stay away. He's not that hard to read." Yakov picked at his stew and Elise frowned. "So, it doesn't taste good?"

He looked up at her, startled. "Oh, no. It's fine. It's just that . . . well, Elise, I need to speak to you about something. This is hard to say, but I think we have a problem."

Elise put down her spoon and wiped her mouth with her napkin. "What is the problem?"

"I think he knows about us."

"Why do you think that? I didn't say anything today. I mean, he knows we are seeing each other."

"Do you remember that undercover assignment?"

"Yes."

"He wants me to go. He talked to me this afternoon and said he would give me the file before he left. He wants me to stay behind and leave within the week."

"How can he travel without you?"

"He is replacing me with Raef."

"Replacing you? Permanently?"

"He said he didn't know how long I would be gone, and he needs someone to step into my place."

Elise put her hand over her mouth and thought for a moment.

"What does this have to do with us?"

Yakov leaned forward in his seat. "I don't think he likes our relationship. I think he is jealous and wants me gone. He hasn't mentioned this assignment in months, then on the day we get engaged, he tells me he's sending me away? Can that really be a coincidence?"

"What can we do about this?"

"I need to go on this trip with him, Elise. His meeting in Brussels is well publicized and it's a security nightmare. And Raef is not the man to handle this assignment."

"You're jumping to conclusions, Yakov. Sometimes things just happen this way."

"You can tell him to take me along. He listens to you. Tell him that you are worried about him and would feel better if I was there. Tell him Raef is not as good as I am and that you don't trust him. As a matter of fact, Raef should not even come. He's a security risk in my opinion."

"Have you shared this with Adolph?"

"He's just not thinking straight. I need to be on this trip. Let's get through it and then I will resign. But I'm not going undercover. I think it is unduly dangerous and I think he knows it, too. I think he's sending me away to keep me from you."

"I still don't understand why you feel that way about Raef. Just quit now. I'll put in my resignation notice too and we can leave together."

A beep was heard coming from the kitchen and Elise stood. "That's dessert. I have to take it out of the oven."

She walked into the kitchen and took a deep breath. She struggled to assess her predicament. Was Yakov using her relationship with Adolph so that he could make sure the assassination went as planned? If he would be willing to leave with her tomorrow, then perhaps he wasn't involved in a plot to kill Adolph. Why was this trip so unusual? Raef was a competent agent. She took the apple pie out of the oven and returned to Yakov.

"How about this: just let Raef handle this trip, and by the time Adolph gets back, I will have wrapped up what I need to and we'll be done. I'll tell him about us and that we can't work the hours he needs us to once we're married."

"Oh, that'll go over real well. I'm sure he'll understand." Yakov threw his hands up in frustration.

"You don't have to go on this trip, is all I'm saying,"

"Elise, there are things you know nothing about. Security is one of them. You can't just walk away from a big event like this. I am the only one who knows all the details. I have to be there. What if something would happen to him? How would I ever forgive myself for not being there?"

Elise decided to play her final card. It was her last chance.

"Maybe you want something to happen. Maybe that's why you don't want Raef there." Elise waited for his response.

"What are you talking about? That makes no sense."

"You were right, Yakov. He does know. But not about us. He knows about you."

Yakov sat upright in his chair. "What are you talking about, Elise?"

"He knows about your plan. And you don't have to go through with it, Yakov." She stood and walked over to where he was sitting. She kneeled at his feet, rested her hands on his arm, and lowered her voice. "I'll leave with you tonight. We'll disappear. I love you, Yakov. We can put all of this behind us."

"What are you talking about? Put what behind us?"

"The assassination. You don't have to do this. Just tell me your plan and this will all be over."

Yakov pulled away from her and gave her a quizzical look. "What assassination? You think I would . . . ?"

"He knows about it and he warned me."

"He said I was going to try to kill him? He told you that? Has he lost his mind?"

"He said you work for an organization that wants him dead. It was their plan for you to infiltrate his security from day one and that's why you don't have a mark."

"Elise, I told you why I don't have a mark. He told me not to take one!"

"He said the assassination was planned for this coming trip and that you were using me to get information."

"What information? What could you possibly tell me that I don't already know?"

"Well, you're asking me to talk him into letting you go and leaving Raef home? Is Raef a threat to your plan?"

Yakov put his head in his hands and squeezed his temples. Elise could see a vein in his neck pumping. She reached up and touched his arm.

"We can run away. If we tell him who you are working for, Adolph will help us hide. If you're in over your head, he can make us disappear. Whoever you are working for won't find us." Elise softened her voice. She loved Yakov and for a moment she honestly thought they could run away together.

"I work for Hitler. He can find anyone he pleases." He pulled his hands from his face and turned his eyes on Elise. "I can't believe you don't trust me."

"I'm just saying, you don't have to go through with this. Adolph has given you a way out by putting Raef in your place."

Yakov turned his chair so he was directly facing Elise on her knees. He leaned forward and grabbed her shoulders. "Listen to me, Elise. Hitler is not well. Everyday he becomes more and more paranoid. Do you remember when he had me test you? He does that with all his employees. He trusts no one. This is probably just an elaborate test to find out if either of us is truly loyal to him. I have a job to do and that is to protect this man. I'm not walking away from it because he's paranoid. This summit in Brussels is an important meeting and I have to be there."

"No. You don't." Elise was starting to show her frustration.

"Can't you see he wants you to doubt me?" He raised his hands in frustration. "He's been showering gifts on you and now he is sending me away. He wants you for himself."

"That's not true!"

"Elise, think about it. He's not been himself lately. He never sleeps. He's constantly behind locked doors. I'm the only one holding him together. He needs me at that meeting."

"You hold him together? You're his security agent! He gets his strength from Lucifer!"

"You don't know the half of it, Elise. He needs me. He's just testing you. He wants to see if you'll be loyal to him. We've got to put an end to these games." Yakov stood and walked over to the couch. He grabbed his coat and started to put it on. "I'm going over to talk to him right now. This can't go on."

He turned and the blood drained from his face. Elise was standing four feet from him, pointing her pistol at his chest.

"I can't let you leave, Yakov." She felt warm tears stream down the sides of her face.

"Put that down, Elise, before one of us gets hurt."

"I tried to give you an out. I offered to run away with you. But you just kept pushing."

"Elise, he's lying to you. There is no assassination plan. Now, I'm leaving."

Yakov turned toward the door.

"Stop, Yakov. I can't let you leave."

Yakov turned back. "So, what happens now?"

"I have just one more question. Please tell me the truth. Why don't you have a mark?"

"I told you, Elise. He asked me not to take it."

Elise had no choice. She had gone over all the options in her head. If she waited too long, he would overpower her. And she couldn't let him leave. Her future was at stake. Yakov stared at her but didn't move. His eyes looked sad, but not frightened. It was almost as if he knew he had lost.

"I love you, Yakov. We could have worked this out."

She squeezed the trigger of her pistol and then dropped it to the floor. Yakov immediately fell. She stood frozen at the sight of her dead fiancé. Down the hallway to her bedroom a door opened and a man entered the hall. He walked through the living room and stood beside Elise.

"Well done, Eva."

Elise stared at the dead body. Adolph's Freudian slip did not surprise her. She had heard him call her name on several occasions behind closed doors.

"When did you know he was telling the truth?"

"When I looked into his eyes."

"Why did you pull the trigger?"

"I made my choice when I took the mark."

No one said much in the buses to the camp. A thunderstorm was pouring rain down in buckets, providing enough background noise to cover the soft whimpering of the children. There were armed guards on each bus, so it wasn't like they could openly discuss their predicament. And what was there to discuss anyway? Charlie knew, as well as everyone else, exactly where they were going and what was going to happen. He just prayed it would be quick and painless. Not for his sake, but for the sake of the women and children.

The children. Charlie looked around his bus at the little ones on their mothers' laps. There weren't that many, but he had come to love their laughter and their little faces. He wondered if they were still separating children or if they were just disposing of them, too. He would soon find out.

When they arrived at the camp the people were quickly ushered out of the buses in single file into a large pole barn. There was nothing fancy about it. It was heated, and there were rows of benches that filled half of the main room. As they entered, they each gave their name and social security number to an officer sitting at a table in the entrance. Charlie was amazed that their master list was so thorough. They knew exactly who was marked in Creston and who wasn't. Everyone's name was on their master list.

Charlie had spotted Tara sitting on one of the benches and cautiously made his way over to her after giving his information. Several officers wandered through the room, weapons slung over their shoulders. The people sat mostly by families, comforting each other. Occasionally a crack of thunder would quiet the room, but then the people would resume their low conversation. The officers allowed it, but Charlie didn't know how long that would last.

"You okay?"

Tara lifted her eyes to him and nodded.

"Where's Noah?"

"I don't know. I was in the restroom when the raid started and I was able to hide in my room until it was over. But after they shut the electricity off, I thought they were gone, and I came out of my room with a flashlight, and they took me. They must have thought some were hiding."

"I saw you get on the other bus. But where could Noah be?"

"Well, he wasn't on my bus and he wasn't on yours, so he must still be at the compound."

"I'll stay with you as long as they let me." Charlie put his arm around the young bride's shoulder and gave her a squeeze. She looked down at the floor and spoke again.

"We're not going to get out of this, are we?"

"No."

"Any idea how they do it?"

"No. But the good news is, when it's over, we're with Jesus."

A smile came to her lips. The thought made him smile, too.

"Keep your eye on the prize, Tara. It's not going to be so bad. People have lost their lives for Christ throughout the ages and now we're going to be added to that list. It's a privilege, really."

Tara chuckled. "Noah loved your outlook on life. He said you always had a way of changing his perspective and placing it where it should be. You're a true encourager, Charlie. Thanks."

"I know God, Tara, and this is all in His plan. I had hoped that we would make it to see the rapture from the earth's point of view, but the heavenly view will be just as spectacular."

A few of the officers slowly passed by and Charlie sat quietly for a moment. He glanced to the back of the room and it looked like everyone had been signed in. Oddly enough, they were leaving the children with their parents and this troubled him. They also weren't separating genders, which most likely meant they weren't going to be there for long.

"If they take you off alone, they're going to try to give you one last chance to take the mark. No matter what they threaten, Tara, don't take it."

"Trust me, Charlie, I know. I saw what the mark did to my mother."

A man in a suit walked to the far end of the room, past all the benches, and stepped up to a microphone. Charlie recognized him immediately. It was Mayor Durbin. Charlie wondered why he would bother to come all the way out from Creston to the training facility. It couldn't be to get votes. Would he play the law enforcer or the politician?

"Is this thing on?" Durbin tapped the mike and his voice rumbled through the room. The residents of the Conover Compound, as they were labeled, quieted down and waited for their fate to be explained.

"Well, folks, it's finally over. My search and your hiding." He looked around the room and Charlie heard a few sniffles here and there. He reached over and took Tara's shaking hands and squeezed them. She looked at him and he mouthed, *It's okay.*

"I am sure by now you realize you are the final hurdle for Creston. The FWP has withheld much-needed funds from our city because of you. But today the game ends. Twenty-four hours from now you will either leave this building with a mark on your head or you'll leave this world altogether. It is not my desire to lose any of you. That's why I am here. I am clearing my schedule so that I can stay here and answer any of your questions and concerns. I want you to know, outside of this room there is a huge price on your head. But inside, I value your citizenship, and I want you to be able to go home, tuck your children in bed and continue on with your life as you knew it. No, as a matter of fact, things won't be the same. They'll be better. I promise you. But the clock is ticking."

The politician.

Tara and Charlie sat as Durbin continued to present a rosy picture of life with the Federation of World Powers. He thought it was interesting that Hitler's name never came from Durbin's mouth, almost as if he avoided it at any cost. He knew that name would stir the angst of this particular group. So he steered around it, explaining the peace that had supposedly come to the world since May fifteen. He assumed they had been completely out of touch with the world and he gave a one-sided perspective of progress and prosperity.

Charlie's mind wandered to Noah. He glanced over at Tara and said a quick prayer that the Lord would keep him from coming for her. Her fate was sealed. He would join her soon enough. He had given Noah, as well as Dave, the information from that man from Michigan and hopefully Noah would make his way to North Carolina, where the Michigan church was hiding. That was his best chance for survival.

But Noah was bullheaded, and didn't think clearly when it came to women. Now that he had a wife, there was no predicting what he would do.

Noah gripped the steering wheel of the van tightly as he sped toward the training camp. He wasn't exactly sure where it was, but had a good idea of its general whereabouts. His heart raced and he could feel the adrenaline flow through his veins. The Lord had blessed Him and now He had a job to do. He was confident in his calling, and if he completely misunderstood, then he would get to heaven a little earlier than scheduled. But God had given him a gift and he wasn't going to abandon it.

Through the rain, he saw the green highway sign he had been looking for. In large white letters it said:

Federation of World Powers

Training Facility

2 miles

Noah took a deep breath and continued to talk to the Lord. Two miles later he exited the highway and started down the long road to the camp. There was a barbed-wire fence enclosing the facility and a guardhouse at the entrance. Noah slowed down and an officer carrying an umbrella stepped out. He rolled down his window.

"May I help you?" the officer asked.

"I'm with the group that was just brought in this morning. Uh, apparently they forgot me. Could you tell me where I could find them?"

The guard drew his gun with his free hand and pointed it at Noah. Noah held his breath and raised his hands from the steering wheel.

"Step out of the vehicle, sir."

Noah put the car in park and obeyed. As he stood in the pouring rain, the officer pulled a radio from his belt and spoke into it.

"I need some help at the gate. I've got a nonmarker looking for the Conover Compound group."

"What?" squawked a voice at the other end. "There with you at the gate?"

"Yeah, he's standing right next to me. No mark on the forehead. He wants to join his friends."

"Does this guy have a death wish?"

"I guess so. Will you send someone over?"

Noah stood awkwardly with the guard while they waited for another officer to arrive. He was put in a jeep and driven to a large pole barn that had two buses parked outside.

Those must have been the buses that took the residents away. They must have really been packed in.

The officer who was driving looked at Noah, water dripping from his hair, as he pulled up alongside the buses and parked.

"You know we could have just shot you at the gate, no questions asked."

"I doubt that, but if you want to believe it, go ahead."

The guard didn't take well to his tone and he pulled his own gun out of its holster and pointed it at Noah's head. Noah didn't even flinch.

"You really doubt it? I could prove you wrong right here."

Noah wanted to say, *go ahead*, but he didn't want to tip his hand. So he said nothing. After a moment or two, the officer put his gun away and said, "Get out. You've made a mess already. I don't want to have to clean blood from the jeep, too."

He grabbed Noah's arm, pulled him from the Jeep, and led him into the pole barn. Officers were stationed around the perimeter of the room and at the doors. The people sat on benches on the far side of the room and were eating what looked like box lunches. He looked at his watch. It was after six. He was feeling a bit hungry himself. Noah was taken to a side room where he was given a towel to dry off, and asked his name and social security number. Then he asked to speak to a superior, claiming to have a message for him. They told him to sit in a chair and wait.

A few moments later, another door opened and Dave Conover walked in, followed by Mayor Durbin. Dave met eyes with Noah and his head jerked back in surprise.

"Don't tell Tara I'm here—I'll be out in a minute."

Dave looked confused but continued on through the outer office and back into the large gathering area. Durbin looked at Noah.

"You asked to speak with me?"

"Yeah, can we go in your office?"

"I have an officer in there with me, you are aware of that, aren't you?"

"That's fine."

Noah followed Durbin into a small office and shut the door behind him. Noah was surprised how small the man was in person. Durbin sat at a desk with an officer standing behind him, and Noah took the chair on the opposite side.

"Now . . . you just arrived? Is that right?"

"Yeah, I was left behind at the compound."

"How did you get here?"

"I drove a van we had in one of the barns."

"Well, I appreciate you turning yourself in, but I have to admit, it's a bit unusual, considering the situation."

"I can see how you would see it like that. But I have come with a message for you."

"A message from whom?"

"God."

Durbin leaned back in his chair and looked over his shoulder at the officer. Noah suppressed a smile, as the look on Durbin's face was rather amusing. He knew Durbin thought he was crazy.

"Okay." He leaned forward again. "And that message from God would be . . . ?"

"He has a plan and will preserve for Himself a people for His return. Unfortunately for you, this group is on His list."

"And He told you to tell me this."

"Well, technically, He wasn't like, 'Tell Durbin this, this, and this.' It was more like I had a vision and I thought you should know the plan, before you put too much effort into disposing of His church."

"Interesting. Well, I have a message for you."

"Yes?"

"Your God doesn't rule here, I do. And you have until noon tomorrow to get marked, or I am going to have you killed. There is no discussing or negotiating. I am tired of this song and dance, and I am ready to be done with it. By tomorrow afternoon, I am going to call the FWP headquarters in DC and let them know Creston is completely marked. As a matter of fact, I need to thank you."

Noah cocked his head to one side. "Why?"

"Because when we signed in your group, there was one missing resident. I can't get my funding until I have one hundred percent participation, which means I would have had to go look for you. But you did me a favor and turned yourself in."

Durbin sat smugly in his seat, but Noah didn't back down. He wasn't shaking. He wasn't even scared. He had the truth and he held it up like a beacon.

"Well, consider yourself warned. We're not going anywhere anytime soon, unless Jesus comes Himself to get us, so . . ."

"Get out of here." Durbin stood and pointed at the door. "What's your name?"

"Noah Greer."

Durbin turned to the guard. "Make sure he's in the first group."

Noah left the room and was taken out to the main area. Immediately he saw Dave standing with a group of men. Dave took a step toward him, but Noah held up his hand. He motioned with one finger, while he scanned the room for Tara. And then he found her. She was sitting on a bench, talking with Charlie. Before he realized what he was doing, he was running toward her. He heard a few people say his name as he passed them, but he didn't stop. He had one goal and he would not stop until he reached it.

"Noah?" Charlie stood and Tara shifted in her seat to look behind her.

"Hi, guys. Did you miss me?" He gave her his crooked smile and she jumped up and threw her arms around his neck.

"This is really starting to become a habit with us," he said as he squeezed her tightly.

"How did you get here? Did they find you?"

"No, actually, I drove here myself."

Tara pulled away and from the look in her eyes he could tell she wasn't happy. "No, Noah. You didn't do that! You didn't come here because of me?"

"You bet I did. You're my responsibility now and I wasn't going to leave you alone. Besides, where else would I go?"

"Noah, they're going to kill us. You drove to your death."

Noah reached up and cupped her face with his hands. "Everyone has to die sometime, and I'd rather die with you than live without you. Anyway, no one is dying any time soon."

Charlie jumped into the conversation. "Depends on your definition of soon. Noon tomorrow . . . is that soon enough?"

"Yeah, I know what they think will happen, but I'm working off a different set of plans. Good to see you, buddy, but I need a minute." He drew Tara back into his arms and kissed her.

She pulled away again. "Noah, good grief! We're serious here."

"So am I." He kissed her again.

Noah felt a tap on his shoulder and turned to see Dave. "How'd you get here?"

"I took the van. I was in the shower and hid in one of the stalls. An officer came in just as you all were found in the south tunnel, so he ran out before checking my stall. He never came back and before I knew it, I was alone."

"And so you drove here?"

"Yeah, it's a long story."

Dave sat on the bench opposite the one Charlie and Tara were sitting on. "Well, we've got the time."

They all sat and Noah took a deep breath. He looked at their eager yet confused faces and hoped he would do the vision justice.

twenty-six

May

Wayne Durbin drove back to his office at seven thirty that evening. It had been a long day and because of his generosity, he had prolonged the whole ordeal. It should have been over by now, but no, he thought he would be a nice guy and try to save those people's lives. Now they had a night to sleep on it and by tomorrow they had to make their decision. Wayne knew deep down that no one was going to take a mark. It was really just an exercise in futility. No matter, it would all be over tomorrow.

But that Noah Greer had really bothered him. Durbin didn't believe his vision, but his arrogance was annoying.

Are some people that blind that they don't even fear death?

He thought back to several conversations he had with Thomas about God. Thomas's view of God and Hitler's view were quite opposite. But Hitler had firsthand experience. He'd seen God and he'd been through hell, so that testimony weighed a lot more than Thomas's version of a loving God Who had a plan for his life.

Durbin knew his wife would be waiting for him, but he had to do one more thing before he could call it a day. He parked his car in the Mayor's parking space and reached for his umbrella on the passenger's seat. He buttoned up his raincoat to the top and looked out the window. The wind was picking up and the rain was still pretty heavy. He would have to make it quick. Whether out of obligation or habit, he needed to report the day's events to the idol.

He got out of his car and made his way through Memorial Park. Durbin struggled to walk and stay covered from the rain at the same time. After a few minutes, Durbin spotted the park idol. He made his way closer and could barely make out its face in the blowing rain and dimly lit sidewalk. The idol addressed him first.

"Kind of messy out tonight for a visit, wouldn't you say?"

"We found the group that was hiding underground."

"Nicely done. Have you disposed of them?"

"Tomorrow at noon."

"Hmmm . . . high noon. What is it with you humans? Everything is always a Hollywood moment. It will probably make a good headline."

"That's just the time we picked. We gave them twenty-four hours to mark up and then it will be over."

The demon's eyes glowed an eerie orange mist but tonight, Durbin could see them clearly. They were like small balls of fire.

"You gave them twenty-four hours? You gave them ten months! You really think another day is going to make a difference? Sometimes I wonder if you really understand the urgency of your situation."

The wind pushed him off balance and Durbin decided he didn't want to prolong this conversation any more than necessary. A flash of lightning and the roll of thunder made him even more anxious to leave.

"Listen, we've done what we were told and now we can get our funding."

"Funding. That's what motivates you, isn't it? Well, my dear, small-minded mayor, there is a much bigger battle going on here." The fire in the demon's eyes intensifed and beneath the surface of the statue's metal, Durbin could make out the impish head of the demon. With each phrase more body within the statue was revealed. "It's not just your destiny that is at stake here. It's mine and I have seen the wrath of God. It's not a pretty sight." By now his midsection was revealed. "There has been a war waging for thousands of years and the final battle is now. Unfortunately you ignorant humans are central to the battle and our hands are tied because of your inability to reason or think beyond your personal bank accounts."

Durbin's eyes scanned the hairless, gangly body of the demon, whose skeletal wings stretched out behind the statue. He had seen a demon only once, the one who'd killed Rabin, but never in person and it was terrifying. When the illumination reached the demon's full height the mercury lamps in the park popped and shattered, one by one.

"This has nothing to do with putting your town on the map."

Pop.

"This has nothing to do with lining your citizen's pocketbooks with magogs."

Pop.

"This has nothing to do with peace in the world."

Pop. Pop. Pop.

The demon thrust his hands through the bronze and reached for Durbin. They extended much longer than humanly possible, but Durbin couldn't move. Despite the wind and rain, he prepared himself to be burned by the touch of the demon, but his hands stopped just inches away from Durbin's throat. He could feel their heat.

"This has everything to do with rulership, and if you humans do not succeed, then you and I will spend eternity together and no earthly metal will limit my reach."

Pop. Pop.

Durbin tried to speak but he couldn't form the words. The demon withdrew his arms back into the figure of the statue.

"Kill the children, Wayne. You may think you've successfully hidden them, but I know you have a building full of them. Hundreds of them in your little boarding school. Kill them and be done with it."

The final lamp blew and the park was completely dark except for the glowing demon. "Tomorrow at noon I want this over." Then the glowing faded to black and Durbin was left in the dark alone.

He felt a tightening in his chest. He turned and began to run through the wind and rain back to his car. He slipped and fell to one knee, soaking his pant leg and the sleeve of one arm, but he got back up and continued to run. The sound of the rain was deafening but Durbin thought he heard the idol laugh when he fell. When he got to his car, he slammed the door and sat in silence for a moment.

Thomas was right about one thing. He had bought into a system that took the lives of his citizens rather than protecting them. This was much bigger than he had ever dreamed. Tomorrow, he would have to tell the marked families that he was putting down their unmarked children. This was an impossible task. There will be an explosion of emotion and someone will have to take responsibility for the decision.

And that would be him.

Durbin began to shake. Whether from fear or the cold, it didn't matter. His dream was over. This was a loaded locomotive careening through his town and he couldn't stop it. Perhaps he could get away with not telling the people for a while—put a prerecorded loop of the kids sitting in class and just play that over the *Internet*.

You know what, Wayne? It doesn't matter anymore. You have been raised up for a task and even if you feel bad now, you have to finish it.

Durbin put his key in the ignition and started up his car. He remembered when he'd first gotten the call about the burning outside Creston Bible Church. It had gotten out of hand and a family was murdered by the mob. It was this mob mentality that just might save him. Alexander Magorum had been his hero and now Adolph Hitler stood in his place. Did he ever make excuses for his actions? Did anyone ever question him?

You have given these families a year to comply. It's not your problem anymore. Don't hide your actions—a true leader makes no excuses.

Announce in the morning that at noon tomorrow that facility will be emptied of Creston residents, once and for all. Being one of the last towns in Indiana to finish this up, you're the only one with citizens left there anyway. The other mayors have pulled this off and survived, and so will you.

He cranked up the heat and put the car into reverse. He would go home and write a press statement that would be e-mailed to the newspapers by six the next morning. Durbin tried to suppress the guilt of his decision by looking at the actions of his peers. They were not better mayors than he was, and they weren't evil men. They just didn't fear the response of the people the way he did.

Durbin had no choice. The picture of that hairless creature reaching for his neck was permanently burned into his memory and he would do whatever it took to avoid eternity with that thing.

The gift sat on the counter and Noah reached for the silver foil paper and scissors. He had never been very good at wrapping gifts, but this was a special gift. He was so proud of the gift and loved it with all his heart. Just looking at it made him smile, so he wanted to wrap it as carefully as he possibly could. He knew it was the perfect gift and when he gave it away, the receiver would be impressed.

He cut the paper the perfect length, taped the sides down flat, and then put a beautiful shiny blue bow on top. It was done. It was beautiful.

The next thing he knew, he was running down a dark hall. There was a light he was running toward, but it wasn't a bright light. When he came to the end of the hall, he had the choice of either going right or left. It looked like he was in a theater foyer, with multiple openings down either side. The faint glow of light came from each rounded opening. He turned to his right and walked to the first opening. Four feet in front of him was a half wall. The room itself was large, like a stadium, round in shape with a balcony running all the way around the perimeter of the room. There were a few spotlights shining down on the center of the stage and he walked to the edge of the balcony and looked over.

The stage was completely empty except for one thing in the dead center. The lights were shining on it. He squinted to force his eyes to focus and then he realized what it was.

His gift.

The silver foil paper reflected the spotlights and made the package glow. But he recognized the blue ribbon and knew it was his gift. How it got down there, he didn't know, but he had to go get it so that he could give it to the intended receiver.

He looked around and didn't see a stairway or even a door. He figured he could hang over the side and let himself drop the fifteen feet or so to retrieve the package, but he wasn't sure how he would get out once he got down there. Then he heard a noise, kind of a scraping of something heavy and metallic across a stone floor. It was a door opening onto the stage from the far left side. One by one massively large lions walked through the door. He counted nine in all. Once they all cleared the door, it closed again and the lions circled the package. Occasionally they sniffed the package and one slapped at it with its oversized paw.

Noah felt his heart begin to race. This was his package and it had a very important purpose. He had to give that package to the receiver. And that was the only gift he had. He couldn't let it be destroyed by these lions. So, without really thinking, he climbed over the railing and dropped to the floor of the stage. The lions all turned and looked at him. They opened their huge mouths and roared, and the sound was deafening. He could feel his heart still racing, but all he could see was the gift. Slowly he started walking toward it. One of the lions stepped in his direction and he froze. Drool dripped from the corners of the lion's mouth and Noah caught his breath. In one swift movement this lion could end his life, but worse than that, he could destroy the gift. The lion walked toward Noah and rubbed against his leg. The sheer strength of the lion's body was terrifying, but Noah couldn't take his eyes off the gift. The lion bumped him again and Noah stopped and looked at the lion. Then the lion lay down.

He continued on to the gift and another lion brushed up against him, as if he was trying to stop him from reaching the gift. But as Noah kept moving, the lions, one after another, would bump him then lay down. Soon, all nine were on the floor and Noah had made it to the gift. He picked it up and examined it. It was unharmed and relief flooded over him. This gift was so important.

Then, directly across from where the lions' door had opened, another large metal door opened. It didn't slide but swung open onto the stage. There was a man standing there, in jeans, a black jacket, and a baseball cap. Noah recognized him immediately. It was the angel who had come to his home the day Hitler revealed himself. The angel walked toward him and when he reached Noah he spoke.

"It's time to bring your gift to the Lord. Are you ready?"

Noah felt a joy well up from within like he had never felt before. He wanted to holler at the top of his lungs, but he forced himself to simply nod in agreement. The excitement was intoxicating.

The angel touched his arm and pulled him toward the door. There was a light shining through the doorway that was brighter than anything he had ever seen. It hurt his eyes and yet he couldn't help but stare at it.

Then the angel spoke again. "Noah, you were chosen to overcome."

"You were with me every step, weren't you?"

The angel smiled and led him into the light.

Noah looked at his friends. Tara wiped the tears from her eyes, and Charlie and Dave had faraway looks on their faces.

"It was unlike anything I had ever dreamed before. I never remember my dreams and when I opened my eyes and realized I was lying, face down on the floor of the compound, I quickly stood to make sure I wasn't on the stage anymore. It was so real. What I felt was so vivid. I know it was a vision from God." He turned to Tara. "That gift is you, Tara. You are the greatest treasure in my life. I knew when I stood up that I had to come here. There's no way you're going to heaven without me at your side." Then he looked at the men. "The angel at my door told me to overcome. He told you that, too. But I don't think we can overcome without God's help and I think He is providing a protection for us. I may be wrong, but when I was with the lions, I had no fear. And coming here, I feel the same way."

Dave rubbed his chin. "So you think we're going to be spared the slaughter? I don't know that we've been promised that."

"This was a vision from God, Dave. I wish you had received it, too, because then you'd understand how I feel."

"Well, you're here now and we'll know tomorrow. This may be our last night here on earth and between you and me, I'm ready to go home."

Noah sat among his fellow overcomers on the benches. It didn't take more than a few moments for them to decide that they didn't feel like overcomers, but they liked the title.

That night, Noah curled up on the floor next to his precious gift and held her tightly in his arms all night. If this was his last night on the earth, he wasn't going to waste it sleeping. He was going to spend it in prayer preparing to see His Savior.

Black Cap noticed the wind picking up outside. The rain had stopped hours earlier but he knew the wind was no longer part of the weather system. He knew what he was up against and reinforcements were on their way. The stronger the gusts, the more demons arrived. Initially they gathered on the roof of the facility, all in a hairless bundle, picking at each other and slapping each other around. Black Cap was amazed at the physical decay the fall had on angelic beings. But he had no fear. They were a sorry lot, fueled by delusion and anger. They had strength, but not overpowering strength. Occasionally Black Cap would get a surge of sympathy for these dysfunctional, fallen angels, but then his anger at their disobedience and rebellion always returned with fervor.

He stopped at two hundred and four, and the number continued to rise. Black Cap wondered why so many would be released to this event, but by now, as the number of believers was quickly diminishing on the earth, there was a greater surge to finish the task. Black Cap wondered how much longer Yahweh would wait. Another large group arrived and Black Cap decided to just head back indoors and wait for the others to gather. Tomorrow would be a good day. He looked forward to stretching his wings a bit.

The public started to arrive around eight fifteen the next morning. It was on the six o'clock news that the final group was captured, and by noon they would be discarded.

"Discarded." That was his word. It sounded a lot more sanitary than "killed." Even "disposed of" sounded harsh, but "discarded" sounded like something of no value being put out of the way. And that was exactly what was happening.

He was told most of the crowd was there to celebrate the finality of the project, but there were some parents desperately seeking moments with their children. He told the officers to let parents visit their children, unless they looked like they might cause trouble. Any parent who refused to leave by eleven thirty could just die with their child for all he cared. He wanted this over more than anything he had ever wanted.

Wayne wrestled with whether or not he should drive out there to oversee the process. He never had done that before and though his conscience was becoming more and more calloused by the day, the thought of seeing piles of dead bodies burning was not one he wanted in his memory bank. Too vivid. Too real.

He didn't want television crews shooting either. This was not a newsworthy event. He just needed the public to know that the reason the funding hadn't arrived yet was because this subversive group had successfully hidden for the past year. But they were found by his hardworking law enforcement team, and now the battle had been won. At least in Creston. The rest of the world was not his problem.

Durbin had to expend great effort to put the thought of the children out of his head. He had called the director of the boarding school first thing that morning. Fifty-four more high schoolers and one hundred twenty-one middle schoolers had taken the mark and had been returned home. The numbers were falling steadily but time had run out. There were officially only just over two hundred children left, most from nonmarked families and they had no one to return to, so the loss should be minimal. So should the outcry. This is how Durbin justified their deaths in his head, but his heart was struggling to fall in line.

So, he made his decision. He would stay at his office and wait by the phone. Undoubtedly he would get several calls, but they were easier to stomach. And in a few hours, it would all be over.

Tara was surprised she actually slept. When she opened her eyes, she was lying with her head on Noah's chest, his arm supporting her.

His breathing was steady and she raised her head to see if he was asleep. He smiled at her.

"Good morning. I'm glad you slept so peacefully."

"Sounds like the rain stopped. Did you sleep at all?" Tara sat up and stretched her arms over her head.

"No, but I wasn't really trying to sleep. They brought in some breakfast about fifteen minutes ago. Do you want something?"

"I don't feel like eating."

"Well, I don't know how much food they'll bring in later so you'd better eat." He stood and stretched himself. Before she could protest, he was gone.

Tara rubbed her eyes to wake them up. She looked around the room. It was quiet, considering there were almost one hundred and forty of them in there, sleeping on a hard cement floor. And yet, many were still asleep. That was definitely a gift from God, because knowing what was coming today could have easily made last night unbearable. But they all slept. It was a blessing.

Tara took a deep breath and stood. She stretched and then tried to straighten her clothes a bit. And her hair. She walked over to where they had lined up a few port-a-johns and waited in a small line for her turn. Soon she was back on a bench next to Noah, a cup of coffee and an apple in her hand.

"So, what time is it, Noah?"

"It's almost ten."

"We really have learned to hibernate! It's amazing how everyone is sleeping."

There was a slam at the back of the room and Tara turned to see several officers working their way up to the microphone system. There was a growing sound coming from outside and Tara wondered if there were protestors. More likely, they were gawkers. Her heart started to pound and she grabbed Noah's hand. She knew what was going to happen today, but she didn't want to be separated from Noah. His confidence that they were going to survive the day and many more to come hadn't been embraced by her mind and she was resigned to die. Though ending her marriage so abruptly wasn't ideal, leaving the cares of this world behind was appealing and she was tired.

The officer at the mike spoke. "Good morning. If anyone would like to get the mark, this is your last opportunity. If you will follow Officer Marshall, he'll take you to the marking room."

The officer next to the one at the mike stepped forward and walked down the center aisle of the benches. He stopped half way and waited for the residents to rise and follow. But no one did.

One minute passed.

Then another.

Then a third.

No one stood. They just looked at the officer at the mike.

"Okay then. You know your fate. In an hour we will come and take the first group, and sixty minutes after that this will all be over. Maybe then you can ask your Maker why He put you through this."

The officers left and the overcomers were alone in the main part of the pole barn. Tara clung to Noah's hand. He just smiled as if he didn't have a care in the world. He nodded toward the front of the room and Tara looked back at where the officers had been standing. One of the high school girls walked up to the mike. It had apparently been left on and she cleared her voice.

"I was thinking I would sing a song I learned at my youth group. It has been on my mind this morning and it goes like this . . ." Then, with the sweetness of what Tara thought might be a voice straight from heaven, the little round-faced, blonde girl began to sing:

Mighty is Your love, O Lord, Holy are Your ways
Though our chains are freed, we're captivated by our need
To honor You, O God
So we lift up our hands to You, we stand in awe of You

We pour out our heart surrendering all to You
So with all that we have in this life, with everything we are
Lord we offer You, our surrendered hearts

When she stopped, the whole room was silent. Dave, who was sitting on the opposite side of the room from Tara and Noah, stood.

"Sing it again, Trisha."

The young girl closed her eyes and started over again, and this time, a few people stood and joined her. Then she sang it again and the simplicity of the words were easy to learn. Before she knew it, Tara had stood and joined the residents in lifting their song of praise to the Lord. Hands raised, eyes closed, tears falling, they lifted the name of Jesus for one final time here on earth.

The music echoed through the room. Tara was ready and hoped it would be fast. At exactly eleven o'clock, forty-five armed and masked officers entered the large holding room at the Training Facility. The residents had gathered together in the center of the room, hugging and saying their temporary good-byes, knowing they would be reunited in heaven. There wasn't fear, there was just resolve. Tara watched the men encircle the group. Their weapons were raised, as if they were just going to gun them all down at one time. But then she knew that would be foolish—to shoot into the middle of a circle, so that thought left and she pulled on Noah's hand.

He wrapped his arms around her and whispered in her ear, "Everything's going to be fine. You are my precious gift from God and I will be with you until we finally see Him." Tara shut her eyes, laid her head on his chest and waited for what would happen next.

The room was quiet again. The peace she felt was indescribable. She heard no movement, not even from the officers. After a moment or two, Noah whispered again in her ear, "Are you watching this?"

Tara opened her eyes and pulled back from Noah's chest, his arms still around her. She looked over his shoulder at the line of officers.

They were about twenty feet away. The automatic rifles they were holding were attached to a shoulder strap. When the men had entered, the guns were in their hands, pointing at the crowd. Now, one by one, the men were pointing their guns to the ground, letting them hang on the straps. She watched one as he reached up and took off his mask. He rubbed his eyes and shook his head. At first, she thought he had something in his eye, but then she realized it was more than that.

The officer reached behind him and put his hand on the wall. He leaned back and called to the man next to him. Tara soon realized that every officer was struggling at the same time and asking for help. Then she figured it out. They couldn't see.

They'd become instantly blind.

Confusion fell over the faces of the guards as they called out to each other and the room filled with the men's voices. Many of the men squatted and sat on the floor, frightened to move because of the darkness.

The overcomers watched in disbelief. Before their very eyes, God had struck the officers with blindness. Dave broke from the group and made his way to one of the officers. He reached out and gently touched him. The officer grabbed his gun, but Dave said something and the man let the gun fall again. Dave led the man to a bench and sat him down. More men broke from the group and aided the blinded officers. Within minutes they were all sitting and though panic was still on their faces, the yelling had stopped. Tara watched as Noah knelt in front of an officer and spoke with him. Then he stood and called to her.

"I'll be right back." Then he yelled to Dave. "I'm going to get them help."

Noah ran to the back of the room and opened the door to the outside. As he stood in the doorway, Tara could see that beyond him there was a large crowd gathered outside, as well as additional officers. Dave stood up on one of the benches and raised his voice.

"Just hold on a second, guys. Help is coming."

Soon, five officers from outside were running behind Noah as he led them to the handicapped officers. Immediately, they were on their radios, calling for backup. The residents took seats on the benches across the aisle from the men and some stood along the side wall. They just watched. Within minutes, another large group of officers arrived and the blinded ones were led away. As far as Tara could tell, the blindness hadn't subsided for any of them. It was an incredible miracle. Whether or not it saved their lives was yet to be seen.

It amused Tara that no one addressed the residents, but when the last officer exited the building, the noise level returned. The people cheered and laughed, hardly able to believe what had happened. Noah returned to Tara and said, "What did I tell you?" She cocked her head and said, "The day's not over." But she definitely felt a release in her heart. Maybe she wasn't going to die today.

twenty-seven

May

Wayne Durbin slammed down his phone. This was unacceptable. Supernatural, but still unacceptable. He got up from his desk, grabbed his coat, and headed outside. He ran across the parking lot and headed toward the park. He passed a few people on the sidewalk as he approached the idol, but didn't stop and greet them the way he usually did.

"Hello? Are you in there?"

The eyes opened and the idol spoke. "My job is done here. You have your quota. What do you want from me?"

"Listen, I can sit quietly while you lecture me on my inability to understand the urgency of our circumstance. However, when I act as you have instructed and I get shut down by the Enemy, you have to take some responsibility for that. I can only do what is humanly possible. You have to handle the supernatural."

"What are you blathering on about?"

"My officers were blinded today. They couldn't carry out the executions because their sight was taken from them. What do you say about that?"

The eyes throbbed with a yellow glow. "I've seen that before somewhere. It's an old trick. Perhaps you shouldn't have waited until today, but I assure you, you have more help there than you need."

"There was no help! That's what I am trying to tell you." Durbin felt his blood boil, and although the temperature was mild, he was starting to sweat.

"What do you think I am, omnipresent? I can only be one place at a time. But we are a well-organized army and I have no doubts you have help. So, go back to work and get your job done."

"Well, if you're so gifted, why don't you get out there yourself? You aren't doing any good here. I'm telling you, I'm going to try one more time and then it's your problem."

"That's where you're wrong, Durbin. This is your problem until it's over, and don't you forget it."

Wayne turned and stormed away. He felt in his pocket for his keys. He went to his car and headed out to the facility. He was going to personally make sure this albatross was off his back for good, even if he had to take matters into his own hands.

"Round two."

Noah watched as a new set of sighted officers entered the holding facility. This time, instead of circling around the residents, they hollered for them to stand against the side wall. The people stood and moved toward the wall, men standing in front of their families, Noah in front of Tara. She wrapped her arms around his waist and held on tight.

The officers lined up on the far side of the room, guns pointed at the group. Noah set his jaw and waited to see what would happen. He didn't hear any sniffles and even the children were paying attention. As he looked at the officers, his eyes started to blur. He reached up and rubbed them, trying to clear them, but they were still fuzzy for some reason. It was like looking at someone while under water. The room shifted and swayed a bit and it suddenly hit him. The officers were wearing masks again but this time there were breathing mechanisms attached. They must be gassing the residents.

He felt light-headed and he turned to Tara. She was rubbing her eyes.

"I think they're gassing us."

"What do you mean?"

"That's why our eyes aren't focusing."

Tara's eyes widened and then a smile filled the rest of her face. "Oh ye of little faith. It's your turn to be amazed."

Noah turned back around and the room was still blurry, but there were little bits of light falling from the ceiling, almost like sparks from a welder but not as thick. Gently floating specks of light, coming from the ceiling. Tara's grip tightened around his waist and she put her head against the outside of his arm.

Images were now appearing. They were larger than humans and floated a few feet above the floor. Wearing flowing white robes that shimmered with soft colors, there were large appendages on their backs that looked as soft as clouds but glowed like the moon.

Wings.

Angels.

Protection.

Noah pulled Tara in front of his body and gave her a better view. The angels were much clearer now and his light-headedness was fading. They filled the room in a wall between the officers and the residents. From floor to ceiling, they moved their wings to hold themselves steady and Noah was dying to run to the other side of the room to see their faces, but he couldn't have gotten through the wall. Yet somehow he could see through them. He could still see the officers, though the angels' presence was perfectly clear.

Once again there was a unified response from the officers. Facedown, on the ground, paralyzed with fear, but it wasn't over yet. A strong wind blew the front door open and Noah could feel the breeze hit his face, but it wasn't cold. It was warm, no—hot. The door slammed shut again and the breeze whipped around the room. Noah watched as the angelic army backed up and curved its outer ranks around the residents, like a shield. The wind could not penetrate the wall of angels and Noah breathed a prayer of thanksgiving.

Black Cap positioned himself in the middle of his battalion. He ordered the angels to cut off access to the overcomers by curving their formation back to the wall on either side of them. Flaming swords appeared in their hands and they waited for the wind to show itself. After a few moments of characteristic, uncontrolled scattering, the demons showed themselves and hovered in front of the angelic warriors.

"You have no authority here," one of the demons hissed at Black Cap.

Black Cap looked at the angel to his left and right and then answered its claim. "I believe you've got that backwards."

"This is our dominion and we still rule. I command you to leave."

Black Cap's eyes flared with a righteous anger. "You lost your right to command when you fell from heaven. I know you, and your dominion is a little farther south."

The demons hissed and shifted nervously in front of him.

"Then we'll have to escort you ourselves." The hissing demons cheered and twisted their hairless bodies into glowing spears.

Black Cap called out to his warriors, "Hold your ground. No one gets through."

And then the mayhem began.

Noah could hardly believe his eyes. The same hairless demons he had seen at Hitler's announcement were now visible in the room. The women gasped at the sight of them and many of the small children covered their eyes by turning to their mother's legs for shelter. Noah wanted to look at Tara but he couldn't tear his eyes from the scene.

The demons had transformed themselves into glowing stakes and were fiercely jabbing at the angels, trying to break through the wall that protected the believers. The officers continued to lay facedown on the ground and Noah was tempted to call to them to lift their heads. He wanted them to witness this display of power to the glory of God, but he couldn't get his voice to work. Instead he continued to watch.

The angels hardly moved. Their motion was more fluid. When one leaned to its right, it was as if the whole wall shifted. Poetry in motion. But all the angels were moving in different directions all at the same time, so there was an ebb and flow to the wall that was the most beautiful thing Noah had ever seen. In his mind, he could hear the *Hallelujah Chorus* and he knew it was just his heart soaring.

Not one angel was touched by the demons. They deftly warded off the blows with their mighty swords. They hardly broke a sweat. It was as if they had done this for millennia. The demons on the other hand were absolutely frantic. They jabbed and poked, screaming and hissing all the while. Occasionally one needed to rest and would reshape as a demon and stand to catch his breath. His eyes would flicker a bit, but when they glowed again, his strength would return.

Then, as if on cue, the demons all joined together and made one gigantic, fiery club. It pulled back, far to Noah's left and began to swing at the angels. But the minute it reached the wall of warriors, three of the angels blocked it with their swords and the demons separated and went flying.

Noah watched in amazement. The battle went on and on. Then suddenly, the demons stopped, reshaped, and stood in front of the angelic wall. After a few moments, one stepped forward.

"You can't stay here forever."

Black Cap answered. "We don't intend to."

"When you leave, we will finish our job."

"Oh, your job is done here. When we leave, you'll have a worse scenario than this to deal with. You'll have to face the wrath of Elohim."

At the name of Elohim, the demons recoiled. They covered their ears and wailed as if in pain.

"Oh, stop that," Black Cap scolded. "It's not like you were born yesterday. Now, if you want to continue to wear yourselves out, then have at it. But we have explicit instructions from Elohim that this group will not be harmed, and we plan to carry out our objective."

Again, pain-stricken howling at the name of Elohim. Black Cap rolled his eyes and then pounded his sword on the ground.

"We're not leaving and you know we never rest. You do what you want, but you won't touch these people, I can personally guarantee that."

"There's a way around you and I'll figure out what that is. Don't think you've won, because this battle has just begun."

Black Cap didn't bother to respond. The demon's words were empty and lifeless, and it was obvious to both sides. Black Cap decided his wards had seen enough.

Noah couldn't hear the conversation. With their backs to the group and the thick wall of protection surrounding them, the voices were muffled at best. After a short discussion between the central angel and one of the demons, the demons disappeared and the wind started to blow again. It swirled through the room, knocking over anything that wasn't nailed down. Benches fell over, paper plates went flying, a couple of garbage cans were carried high into the air and then dumped on the floor and even posters on the wall were torn off. Noah was amazed at the maelstrom.

Then the door opened and the wind blew out, slamming the door shut in its wake. Noah looked at the men on the floor. Maybe they were dead, because none of them had moved an inch. Then his eyes started to go out of focus again. The wall of angels was fading into a liquid landscape that returned the residents of the compound back to reality. Faint light sparkled down from the ceiling and then just before they were all gone, the center angel turned to the people.

"Now we're in a waiting game." He floated high above the group, wings thrusting behind him every couple of seconds to hold him in place. His face was smooth and white, and his voice was firm, yet comforting at the same time. "There is no explanation but Yahweh. You are now in His full care. You will be overcomers if you remain faithful to the end."

One last pump of his wings and he was gone. But Noah knew better than to think they were left alone. The angel was still there, they just couldn't see him. Noah turned and embraced his gift.

"The lions have been tamed and now we just have to wait until the Lord comes to get us."

There was a noise at the door and Noah, with the rest of the group turned to see Mayor Durbin and more officers standing in the entryway.

"What is the meaning of this?" he yelled.

At the sound of his voice the officers on the floor started to move. Slowly they sat up and some rubbed their heads.

"Shoot them! For goodness sake! What is the matter with you?"

The officers stood and reached for their weapons that were lying on the ground. Noah wondered what would happen next. They had been terrified at the sight of the angels, but now the angels were invisible. Would the men dare to shoot?

Slowly the men walked toward Durbin, keeping an eye on the residents as they walked. Once they reached the mayor, they laid their guns at his feet and continued out of the facility.

"What is wrong with you? Are your weapons broken?"

One of the men stopped and spoke to Durbin. "After what I just witnessed, you shoot them. I'm done with this job." He took off his badge and slapped it into Durbin's palm.

Durbin stormed out of the facility and the extra officers followed.

Noah sent out a loud whoop and the overcomers broke into cheers. He grabbed Tara and twirled her round and around. Eventually the people moved away from the wall and spread out around the inside of the facility. It was dark outside, as Noah could see out one of the side windows at the back of the large room. He looked at his watch and couldn't believe it was almost nine. Ten hours earlier the excitement began and from a spectator's perspective, the day had flown by. He felt his stomach growl and wondered if any one else was hungry. He hadn't eaten since breakfast.

One of the children wandered over to the stack of boxes that held their dinner remnants from last night. No one had bothered to take the trash away and somehow it had survived the windstorm. The boy opened the top box and then set it on the ground. Noah thought he might even be hungry enough to eat leftovers tonight. Then the boy picked up another box and set it on the ground. Then he pulled one from the middle of the stack, opened it and turned to his parents.

"They're all full! Every one of them!"

Several adults ran over to the boxes and shook them.

"He's right! They're full! Come on, everybody—dinner's on!"

Noah ran and got two boxes and everyone ate until their stomachs were filled. Noah thought his roast beef sandwich was the best he had ever eaten. He loved watching Tara laugh in wonder, as she unwrapped warm chocolate chip cookies.

"It's like the angels just made them for us!"

Noah shook his head. "Come on, did you see any wise old angels? Those cookies were made by some talented grandmas up in heaven and brought down to us!"

"It's just unbelievable, Noah. To see His hand and to know I should be dead. I know heaven is so much greater than this world, but He keeps sparing us the pain. I don't understand why."

"The time is fast upon the world when God will no longer withhold His response to their sin." Dave had joined them for dinner. "He said He would cut the Antichrist's rule short for the sake of His elect. If He is putting this much fire power here to protect us, it must be getting down to the wire."

"What do you think Durbin will do next?" asked Tara, cookie in her hand.

"We've got two groups trying to take us out right now—the demons and the humans. Who knows who will get their next shot in." Noah took another bite of his sandwich. "The humans can't get past first base, but they're not smart enough to give up. Now," he said still chewing, "if I were in charge, I think I'd put all the people outside, without coats and just let them freeze to death."

"Really?" Dave wiped a crumb from his shirt. "Interesting. But considering it's May, that might take a while. We'd probably starve before we'd freeze. I think I'd just drop a bomb on the facility from an airplane. Blow the place to smithereens."

Charlie had joined them and jumped into the conversation.

"Oh, I was just thinking about this. You know what I'd do? I'd open a gas line into the building and toss in a grenade. That would work, too."

Tara stood. "You guys are sick, you know that?" Noah looked up at her and decided she wasn't joking around. "How can you sit there and think of such disgusting things? What if they are recording us in here? You want them to try any of your creative methods?"

Noah reached for her hand and pulled her back down to the bench. "We're just goofing around, Tara. It's what guys do."

Suddenly the whole building rocked. It was as if a bomb had gone off but there was no impact point. The fluorescent overhead lights swayed violently and the bench Noah and Tara sat on overturned.

Before he could catch himself, Noah was lying on the ground, his wife wearing a surprised look next to him. He stood and then helped Tara to her feet, as the building continued to shift. They stumbled to keep their balance and Noah saw many people chose to simply sit.

"Maybe something happened outside," yelled Charlie, over the noise of the shifting building.

"If this is an earthquake, I didn't know they lasted so long!" Noah yelled back.

Noah heard the sound of stressed metal, as if it was being forced to bend. He quickly glanced around the room and saw that the roof had started to peel up from one corner. It lifted with each rock of the building and Noah feared the entire structure would collapse. A couple more large shakes and the electricity went off. Generator lights turned on, but more rocking of the building eventually knocked those lights out, too. The parents grabbed their children and everyone ran to the opposite side of the room from where the roof was lifting. Noah's eyes quickly adjusted to the darkness, and he grabbed Tara's hand and pulled her along, stepping over benches to get to the back of the room.

"Maybe it's a tornado!" He had to yell to her because of the noise.

In just a few seconds the roof had peeled back about halfway and the shaking stopped. The sudden end to the rocking caught Noah by surprise. A few final sounds of settling debris and then the room went quiet.

Then Noah saw it. He looked out the large opening in the roof. It was a perfectly clear night, no rain or clouds, just a sky full of stars. But the stars were falling, one after another, almost like fireworks on the fourth of July.

"The moon—it's red!" A voice from the corner hushed the crowd.

Noah lifted his head and saw the darkening moon. The sign of His return. This must be it. He looked at Tara's upturned face and put his arm around her waist.

"We're going home, Tara. It's time . . . it's His time."

The earthquake hit the facility at exactly 9:27. Wayne was meeting with a few of the officers at the mess hall, trying to figure out how to fix this nightmare. The building rocked and swayed. At first, he thought they had been hit with a bomb, but then he realized it was an earthquake.

In Indiana.

In May.

Nothing was making sense anymore. Shortly after the first rumble, the lights went out and a call came over the radio. One of the officers turned on his flashlight and grabbed his radio to respond.

"Yeah, Terry, we're here. What's wrong now?"

"Is the mayor with you?"

"Yeah."

"I need to talk to him.

Durbin took the radio. "What now? I'm hardly in the mood for this."

"They're gone, sir."

"Gone, who's gone?"

The voice cracked, as if in fear. "The children, sir. Every last one of them."

"What do you mean?" Durbin put a weary hand to his head.

"We came in to check on the children after the earthquake and they were all gone."

"Have they run out of the building? Are they outside?"

"We've looked everywhere and they're just not here. Even their beds are strange. The way their covers are on the beds, sir, it's like they just vaporized."

Wayne looked at the other men in the room. "We'd better get over to the other group. I don't like the sound of this. Maybe they took the kids."

Once again, Durbin was on the run. He grabbed his coat and ran out into the night. The holding facility was across campus, so he would ride in one of the Jeeps.

Outside, Durbin looked around to see if there was any damage from the quake. The electricity was out and for some reason the generators hadn't kicked in, and it was dark.

More than just dark.

It was black dark.

The officer with him shined the flashlight on one of the Jeeps parked outside of the mess hall and they made their way over to it. Durbin stopped before getting into the Jeep and looked up at the sky. There were no stars and for a brief moment, Durbin thought there must be a heavy cloud cover, but then he saw the moon. It was a deep red, much darker than any atmospheric anomaly he had ever seen. It was so dark that it was barely visible. But it wasn't black, it was blood red.

Just above the moon was a small star. Durbin could feel his chest start to tremble.

"This can't be good," he said aloud, but the officer didn't respond. He was too busy staring at the Star.

As the Star drew closer, Wayne saw another light. No, there were many lights. They were being shot from the ground, like bottle rockets way high into the sky. He looked to see where they were being launched from and his heart lurched within him. The lights were coming from out of the top of the holding facility.

And they weren't lights.

They were his prisoners and it was as if they were glowing.

The Star in the sky was closer now, but Wayne could no longer look at it. His shame had overwhelmed him, and he fell to his knees and covered his face. He would answer to that Star for all the atrocities he had committed, all the sins he had excused away, all the wrongs he had ignored. That Star was his judge and there was no place to hide.

He put his hands over his face, unable to watch as the Star continued his descent to earth.

Elise Orion watched as Adolph Hitler stood out on the balcony of his Jerusalem penthouse apartment. His body was shaking, though the earthquake was long over. She saw him lean over the balcony and vomit. He raised his head again, stared off into the distance, then turned to come back inside. His face was white, as if he had seen a ghost, and his eyes were black. He walked toward her and stopped just in front of her.

"He's come back for me, Eva. All my work, and I failed."

She forced herself to reach up and gently touch his cheek. It was an attempt at comfort. "You don't know that, Adolph. I believe in you."

He did nothing to hide the panic in his voice. "I can't stop him. It's too late for me." Hitler grabbed Elise by her arms and she winced at his grip. "I did my best. I tried as hard as I could. I just didn't have enough time."

Elise stared into his frightened eyes and tried to calm him down. She had seen him upset before, but never scared.

"It's not over, Adolph. Most of the world will fight with you. You are a man of strength and power like the world has never seen and they will follow you. I knew you were meant for greatness the first time I heard you speak in Moscow. You said you would change the world and you have. You have to continue on in this battle. You are a born leader. That's why I chose to follow you."

Adolph loosened his grip and his hands dropped to his side. His eyes softened and the panic drained away. He straightened his back and stared directly into Elise's eyes. Without an expression on his face, he spoke.

"Then you chose poorly."

He turned and walked back to his bedroom.

Elise stood still for a moment and watched him walk away. Then she went out to the balcony. Beyond the temple was a hillside. It was there that she saw Him, sitting on His white horse. He was so far away, yet it was as if He was on the balcony with her. His eyes weren't cold or soft. They were angry with an emotion so strong it sent chills down her spine. Her body began to tremble.

Elise had been thorough in her research on the two witnesses. It had led her to the prophetic book at the end of His writings, and she knew what it said about this Man. From the balcony, Elise could see where the earth had separated in the quake and she had seen the stars fall from the sky. She could tell the city below her was in chaos, from the sounds of voices and alarms going off. And now He was here. So far, everything was happening just as the book said it would.

The book said that after the moon turned to blood, His wrath would come and it would be directed at the rebellious world. It was going to be horrible, and supernatural, and unbearable. They could not survive His wrath. The ancient writings explained that clearly.

Her mind drifted to Yakov. At the mention of his name, the dull ache that had taken residence in her heart since he died intensified. She wondered if he would have led the revolt against this Man on the horse. He probably wouldn't have believed the ancient writings, but now he was gone. She had spared him from the wrath to come. He wouldn't have to experience the terror that awaited the world. Perhaps his murder truly was an act of love.

Elise came back inside from the balcony and walked to her purse that was lying on the couch. Her gift from Adolph was inside. She took the pistol in her hand. The pain of her broken heart now spread to the rest of her body, completely saturating her mind. She knew what she had to do. She pushed the button on the handle, removing the safety. She had used this pistol once before to take a life, and now she would take another.

Elise looked up and saw her reflection in the mirror above the couch. She tucked her long, blonde bangs behind her ear with her left hand, holding the pistol in her right. Her cheeks were flushed a bit and the rose in her cheeks made her smile. It was a strange sight, her holding a gun in the middle of the beautiful penthouse. She glanced around the room that she had personally decorated and sighed. She had fooled herself into thinking he would be her savior, but now she knew the truth. She was not willing to partner with weakness. She took a deep breath and prepared herself for what she had to do, and then a thought occurred to her.

It's strange how history has a way of repeating itself.

Without even knowing it the people started to walk out of the corner and into the center of the room. All heads were raised to view the signs in the sky. Noah watched as the tail of shimmering light behind each falling star burned out and left the sky as black as coal. One by one they fell until the sky was completely dark. Blackness enveloped the room and no one spoke.

Then a small pinpoint of light appeared, just above the right side of the reddened moon. Noah squinted his eyes to try to focus on the light and his heart skipped a beat.

"It's Him, Tara."

Noah felt Charlie come along his other side and he pointed at the light. It was quickly approaching and was nothing like the stars. It was white and it was clear at the same time.

"There He is, Charlie. This is it." Noah could hardly contain his emotions, yet he was inexplicably calm. He longed to see the look on Charlie's and Tara's faces, so he tore his eyes from his deliverance for just a moment. Tara's eyes were upturned and her mouth was open, as if she wanted to say something but the words wouldn't come. Noah looked to his other side and was startled to see it wasn't Charlie beside him, but the angel with the black cap he had met at his front door almost a year earlier. He instantly remembered the angel's deep blue eyes that lit up and glowed. They were glowing again, but this time it was a warm, dancing glow. Noah heard a loud voice call, "Come home, Noah" but it wasn't from the angel's mouth. It startled him to hear His voice so clearly, and then the angel spoke.

"Get your wife. It's time to go."

Noah grabbed Tara's hand and she looked over at the angel. Tears were streaming down her face and she whispered to the angel, "Thank you."

The angel shed his human clothing and suddenly his wings appeared. "No need to thank the messenger." He stepped in between Noah and Tara and wrapped his large arms around their waists, and they were off.

Noah looked at the ground and it was quickly disappearing. He raised his head and watched as his angel increased the speed. Each thrust of his wings sent them farther, faster into the presence of their Savior. Noah couldn't look at Tara. He couldn't tear his eyes from the light. The gap between them was quickly closing, and then suddenly he was there and the light completely enveloped him. It was everywhere. Not only could he see it, but he could feel the light. It wrapped itself around his body and Noah took a deep breath. It was air he had never breathed before, clean, fresh, pure, holy. The angel no longer held him but his feet were on something firm. He fell to his knees, for in his anticipation, he had completely lost all strength.

He lifted his face and put his hand up above his eyes to try to see where he was. Then he saw Him. His face glowed like the sun, but Noah could see Him perfectly. And He was perfection. He was love, He was compassion, and He was grace. Mercy flowed from His eyes and He reached out His hand to Noah. Noah placed his hand into the nail-scarred one and stood. He smiled at Noah, nodded His head and said one word. Noah's heart soared and he entered into eternity with his Lord and Savior leading the way, the echo of his earned title ringing in his ears.

Overcomer.

gd Book
Fiction